Starfall

A Starstruck Novel

BRENDA HIATT

Dolphin Star Press

Dolphin Star Press

ISBN: 1-940618-11-8
ISBN-13: 978-1-940618-11-1

DEDICATION

For everyone who loves a happy ending

I

Sovereign Emileia

1

Automatic shutdown

"WE ARE COMING."

The message resonated through my mind as I gripped the alien communication device. But what did it mean?

I'd thought my main job was done when I finally interfaced with the Grentl device and averted Nuath's destruction in the nick of time…all of twenty minutes ago. But then the device had activated again, to send this frightening, baffling message.

I tried to focus my thoughts, to get more information. *Coming here, to Mars? When?* I thought frantically to them. *And why??*

But instead of answering, they again pulled images, experiences, directly from my brain. Before, it had been like reliving all of my sixteen years in the space of a few minutes, but this time I re-experienced only the most emotionally intense moments of my life.

Not surprisingly, most had occurred over the past year—the last eight months, really—beginning with the first day of my sophomore year at Jewel High. The day I met Rigel.

With breathtaking rapidity, I again felt the astonishing jolt of our very first touch, the one that created our bond, followed by the successive gut punches of learning not only that Rigel was a Martian, but I was, too. Not just Martian, but their long-lost Princess!

I re-experienced the wonder of my first kiss, panic at learning the usurper Faxon's forces wanted to kill me, grim determination when I decided to face them rather than flee. Tension, then triumph, when Rigel and I used our combined ability to create an electrical force to disable our attackers' deadly weapon. A blissful pause, then the shock of learning Sean O'Gara, not Rigel, was my intended Consort, or life mate.

Exhilaration at running away with Rigel to keep the *Echtrans* from separating us forever gave way to crushing disappointment at our capture, then terror that they'd either wipe Rigel's memory or kill him to solve the "problem" of our bond. Relief when the *Echtran* Council agreed to let Rigel return to Jewel unharmed if I pretended to date Sean for their political ends.

Now more recent emotions flooded me: the crushing weight of learning only I could save Nuath from the Grentl; the dizzying rush to get me to Mars in time; anger and despair when Rigel's grandmother snatched him away because of the scandal we'd created with a stolen kiss; relief again when I was Acclaimed Sovereign after a hard-fought campaign, one step closer to saving Nuath…and happy anticipation that I'd finally get Rigel back.

Then, before I could brace myself, I was brutally shattered by reliving Rigel's final message: he'd voluntarily had all memory of me erased and left for Earth without me. As the enormity crashed over me once more, I desperately wrenched my mind free of the communication device, releasing it with a cry of anguish to collapse on the floor beside it.

"No, no, no, no, no." My arms around my knees, I rocked back and forth, back and forth, willing it to not be true, until a firm hand on my shoulder stilled my motion.

"M! M, snap out of it! Please."

"Sean?" Completely disoriented, I blinked at him, crouched beside me. How did he get into my bedroom?

"Yes, M, it's me. Are you hurt? What just happened?"

"Rigel," I whispered. "He…he *left* me. He—"

Sean gave my shoulder a little shake. "I know. You told me already, remember? You let me watch his message. But what happened just now, with the Grentl? Can you tell me?" His voice was gentle but insistent.

Gradually, I became aware of my surroundings. I wasn't in my luxurious Palace bedroom after all. I was huddled on a cold stone floor in a closet-sized room—the secret room containing the Grentl device. Shivering, I struggled to focus, to push my freshly-experienced pain away so I could remember. So I could answer.

"I…It worked, didn't it? They didn't cut the power?"

He nodded. "It worked. You saved us all. Saved Nuath. You were a champ. But then—"

"Eric died," I blurted out, suddenly remembering. "I could never have done it without his help. Or yours." I lifted my head to look Sean in the face. "Thank you."

"You're welcome." He gave me the ghost of a smile, but the concern didn't leave his blue eyes.

I looked around the small room, empty except for the two of us. "Where's your dad? And Eric?"

"Dad took Eric back to his room since people from the hospital would come looking for him once their monitors showed he'd died. Dad didn't know how long you'd be, um, connected to the communication thing this time and was afraid to wait."

I nodded slowly, trying to remember. To care. "How…how long was I—?" I glanced at the device.

"About half an hour this time. Not nearly as long as the first time. But it seemed to mess you up more." There was a question in his expression, but answering it would shove me back into that yawning abyss of despair.

"How about I take you upstairs?" Sean suggested when I didn't respond. "Dad will want to hear about whatever you learned."

When I made a feeble move to stand, Sean effortlessly lifted me to my feet, keeping hold of my hand to lead me toward the door. It didn't occur to me to pull away. All my attention was focused on putting one foot in front of the other so I wouldn't have to remember, wouldn't have to think about the bleak future stretching in front of me.

A future without Rigel.

When Sean half-carried me from the secret elevator into my Royal apartment's sumptuous living room a few minutes later, Mr. O'Gara leaped to his feet and Sean's sister Molly rushed forward to hug me.

"You did it, M, you're a hero! You saved Nuath!"

Her gushing forced a tiny smile from me. "With lots of help." I glanced at Mr. O, then at Sean again.

Cormac, my normally impassive Bodyguard, bowed from his position near the doorway. "I would like to express my gratitude as well, Excellency. Thank you."

Mr. O regarded me closely. "Are you all right? Nels Murdoch and Devyn Kane will be here in an hour, expecting the full report I promised them. What happened after I left? Why did the device reactivate?"

"No, Dad, she's not all right." Sean lowered me onto one of the couches, his arm still around me. "That second session took even more out of her than the first. You can question her later."

Though he was clearly not happy at the delay, Mr. O gave a terse nod. "Very well. I suppose we can all learn the details at the same time."

I sent Sean a grateful glance before turning apologetically to his father. "I…I'm not sure I'd make much sense now anyway. It's all still a jumble." In fact, the only thing I recalled clearly was that final, devastating memory. Grief swept over me again and I shuddered.

Sean squeezed my shoulders gently, sympathy flowing from his touch. "C'mon, let's get some food into you. It's way past lunchtime."

What I really wanted was to be alone with my misery, but I didn't argue when Molly started laying out an extensive meal on the long dining table. I even managed a few bites, mechanically chewing and swallowing.

"C'mon, M, have a bit more," Sean urged. "You've barely eaten anything since breakfast yesterday."

Breakfast yesterday—right before the bottom dropped out of my world.

I looked from Sean to his father and back. "Did…did you tell him? About—?"

"Yes, Sean told me yesterday. Though I'm sorry for the loss you must be feeling, it was a noble, selfless thing that Rigel chose to do."

The sound of Rigel's name was like rubbing alcohol on an open wound. It was all I could do not to gasp at the pain. Sean put a comforting hand over mine, where it lay on the table.

"Hey, it'll be okay, M. It will, you'll see. Just…give it some time. For now, try not to think about it."

"Good advice." Mr. O's heartiness made me wince again. "Your schedule will be full enough to keep your mind occupied for some time, as things have stacked up during this delay."

He started listing upcoming items on my agenda, but I'd already withdrawn into my thoughts again. While *he* could dismiss Rigel's desertion as yesterday's news, to *me* it felt like it had only happened an hour ago. I took an automatic bite of broccoli to avoid talking, then flinched, remembering broccoli was Rigel's least favorite food.

At my shaky sigh, Mr. O regarded me narrowly. "You do look tired, and no wonder. You'll be able to rest once this meeting is over. Would you prefer to have it here, or in one of the conference rooms?"

"A conference room." A place without any painful memories might help me focus.

"I'll message them. Molly, why don't you pick her out something to wear?"

Molly nodded eagerly. She loved this part of her job as my Handmaid. "I know just the thing."

As always, she did. When we left the apartment ten minutes later, I was arrayed in an emerald green tunic over a shimmery gold split skirt. Like everything in my closet here, it was both flattering and elegant—and light years nicer than anything I'd ever owned back in Jewel, Indiana. Not that it mattered now.

"Conference Room Six," Mr. O said aloud.

As we followed the holographic blue line to our destination, I strove to recall details from my two recent sessions with the Grentl device.

Nels Murdoch and Devyn Kane stood when I entered the conference room, then bowed, right fists over hearts.

Devyn straightened first. "Excellency, you have performed a great service today. All of Nuath has cause to be extremely grateful to you."

"Indeed," Nels echoed. "It is a debt that can never be repaid. If the people knew what you'd done for them, you would be lauded as the greatest heroine of our time."

I just smiled stiffly and took the chair Mr. O indicated, at the head of the oval table.

Once we were seated, Devyn cleared his throat and glanced at Mr. O'Gara. "We, ah, were promised a report?"

"Unfortunately, the experience was extremely draining for the Sovereign. Excellency, do you feel up to sharing with us whatever you learned?" Though Mr. O's expression was sympathetic, I sensed lingering irritation that I hadn't filled him in first.

"I'll do my best." I began with Eric Eagan's insistence on coming to the Palace to help me find and use the device, even though he was at death's door. I was determined that these few, at least, know and remember the heroic final act of his three-hundred-plus year existence. When I paused, Devyn nodded respectfully.

Nels, however, shifted impatiently. "But did the Grentl agree not to cause any more power outages?"

"Not…exactly. At first, the device bombarded me with images, memories, of others who'd used the device. My great-grandmother,

Sovereign Aerleas, my grandfather Leontine, even Faxon. Then it went the other way, with them pulling out *my* memories. Replaying my whole life."

"This all happened in the space of two hours?" Mr. O looked slightly dazed.

I nodded. "But I only got bits and pieces, everything flashed past so quickly."

"Amazing," Mr. O marveled. "What an interesting way to communicate. And what happened the second time the device activated?"

"Second time?" Nels exclaimed, clearly startled.

"Yes, just a few minutes after the power failure, er, didn't happen. That time they did send a message." I took a deep breath, bracing myself for their reactions. "They said…'We are coming.'"

Everyone in the room paled visibly. Mr. O found his voice first. "Coming. Here? To Nuath? When? To do what?"

"I don't know. They just stuck that single thought into my head: 'We are coming.' No where, when, why, nothing."

"But what does it mean? *Why* would they be coming?" Nels's fear was palpable. "Can't you stop them, talk them out of it? Should we evacuate the colony?"

Mr. O made a calming gesture. "You didn't ask for more details?"

"I tried to, but they just…pulled more out of my head." Now I guiltily realized I'd let go of the device in mid-recall when hit by that final, devastating memory—something Eric had cautioned me not to do. I hadn't tried touching it again after that. Should I have? I shivered at the thought but Sean put a supporting arm around my shoulders.

"Without more answers, it's difficult to know how to prepare, or if we even should." Devyn sounded more thoughtful than scared. "Perhaps they merely wish to assess our status firsthand."

"We also have no idea of a time frame," Mr. O pointed out. "I know very little about the Grentl, but apparently they are exceedingly long-lived?" he glanced at me and I nodded. "It could possibly be decades, even centuries, before they arrive."

"Or hours," Nels interjected, still on the verge of panic.

"In which case I doubt there is anything we can do. If their intentions are hostile, even decades of preparation might not be enough to stop them."

I wasn't sure what Mr. O was suggesting. "But…shouldn't we at least get Scientists working on it? You said yourself that Eric should have told a few others."

"Eventually, perhaps. First we'd need to determine who can safely be trusted with the information. If the mere fact of the Grentl's existence is likely to panic the populace, imagine what news of their one communication would do."

"I didn't mean we should tell the media. Besides, Gordon Nolan already knows, at least about the Grentl and the device. And Rigel's grandmother, and all the Healers who were there when—"

I broke off abruptly, jerked back to excruciating awareness of the gaping hole in my heart. That memory extraction was the very last time I'd seen Rigel. Was it really only three days ago? It seemed like another lifetime. One that still had hope in it.

Mr. O seemed not to notice my sudden distress. "That was unavoidable. In any event, they have all sworn complete secrecy."

"You need to go back to the device," Nels insisted, his eyes still wide with fear. "Now. Find out when they're coming and what they mean to do when they get here."

Sean tightened his grip on my shoulders, speaking for the first time. "What she needs to do is rest. She's told you everything she knows so far. If you want to keep arguing or planning or whatever, you can do it without her."

Though Mr. O seemed as startled as I was by Sean's forceful tone, he didn't protest. "Sean is right. We appear to be safe enough for the moment, thanks to the Sovereign. Perhaps after some well-earned rest she will be able to enter into further discussions of our options. Gentlemen." He rose, pointedly adjourning the meeting.

With obvious reluctance, Nels and Devyn bowed and departed. The moment the door closed behind them, I sagged where I sat, my last bit of energy gone.

"Let's get you to bed." As he had in the Grentl room, Sean gently helped me to my feet, then supported most of my weight as we returned to my apartment. After helping Molly get me into bed he hesitated, regarding me searchingly. "You sure you'll be okay? I can stay if—"

"No, go on. I'll see you later. Probably tomorrow." I kept my voice steady by sheer force of will.

Sean watched me for several more heartbeats, then gave a little shrug. "Okay. Call if…if you need anything?"

I nodded, not quite meeting his concerned gaze, and he finally followed his father from the apartment.

Molly lingered, her brow still furrowed with sympathy. "Can I do anything else for you, M?"

"No. But thanks." She was the only one in her family who'd ever been at all sympathetic to Rigel and me as a couple, but right now I desperately wanted to be alone with my heartbreak.

Once she was gone and my bedroom door shut, I dragged myself to a sitting position against my pillows and switched on the vidscreen, the volume low enough it wouldn't be heard from the other room. Even knowing what it would do to me, I felt a compulsion to replay that awful final message from Rigel. Maybe I'd missed some loophole, some shred of hope…

"I've decided to go back to Earth immediately," he told me again in that terrible, emotionless voice. "You need to be with Sean now, for the good of Nuath. But because it will hurt too much to see you two together from now on, I've asked to have the last year of my memory erased before I go. I know I'm taking the coward's way out, and I'm sorry for that, M, and sorry I can't tell you a proper goodbye. I hope in time you'll be able to get over me and be happy with Sean. He's not a bad guy, you know, even if I haven't always been his biggest fan.

"By the time you get this message, the procedure will already be done, and I'll already be on board the *Luminosity*. I'm bringing along a letter for my parents explaining what I've done and suggesting we move away from Jewel, so please don't try to come after me. Your focus right now needs to be on keeping Nuath safe, both from this immediate threat and into the future. Please do your best to stay safe and to be happy. Goodbye, M."

Destroyed all over again, I curled myself into a tight ball of misery and let the tears come.

2

Reserve capacity

My crying jag eventually exhausted me enough to fall into a fitful sleep filled with nightmares—but every time I jerked awake, it was to a reality even worse than the awful dream that woke me. Then I'd swing wildly between desperate determination to ignore Rigel's request and go after him, *make* him remember, and such despair that I again cried myself to sleep. When I finally dragged myself into the shower hours after daybreak, I felt like I'd been run over by a truck.

Sean came for breakfast, again cajoling more food into me than I really wanted, then he and Molly spent the next few hours trying to draw me out of myself, inch by painful inch. While I appreciated that they cared, their very sympathy, which I sensed all too clearly, was a constant reminder of my loss.

By the time their father joined us for lunch, I'd reached a fragile equilibrium between dissolving into tears and a detached numbness where nothing mattered at all. Even so, Mr O'Gara's smile when he greeted me was jarring.

"You'll be pleased to know I've spoken again at length with both Nels Murdoch and Devyn Kane and we've agreed that until we know more, we should proceed normally."

I hadn't progressed far enough to smile back. "So Nels isn't still calling for the colony's immediate evacuation?"

"Devyn and I were able to calm him somewhat. We also pointed out the logistical impossibility of such a thing, which he was forced to acknowledge."

Molly paused in the act of setting out food from my recombinator. "Why is it impossible?"

"Simple mathematics," her father replied. "Think. We have but four ships, all built along the same lines as the *Quintessence.* Even by cramming passengers in to the point of discomfort, each has a capacity of perhaps two hundred. An average round trip between Mars and Earth is ten days, allowing for repairs, refueling and restocking of supplies, which allows a maximum of twelve round trips per ship in a typical four-month launch window. Only three months remain in the current one."

Grasping at the distraction, I did some quick mental calculations. "So we can only get ten thousand people from here to Earth during a full launch window? At that rate, it would take more than fifty years to get everyone off Mars. Shouldn't we have already started, Grentl or not? According to Shim, our power will only last another century or so."

"Indeed." Mr. O waited for me to sit, then took his own seat at the table. "Unfortunately, that project was still in the planning stages when Faxon seized power. So many were in denial, even in the Legislature, that more resources were devoted to research on extending the colony's power supply than to implementing a measured emigration."

"So how did Faxon plan to invade Earth with only four ships?" Sean asked.

"He conscripted Engineers, Metalworkers and Mining resources to build more ships. None are yet complete but it's possible his efforts may allow us to speed up emigration in a decade or so. Meanwhile, we must look to the *current* welfare of Nuath and its people by putting a proper government in place. It's what I'd originally hoped to do upon my return here."

Before he'd known about the Grentl, in other words. A matter he now seemed eager to dismiss. Between bites, Mr. O read aloud from his omni screen, listing the dinners, meetings and audiences he'd lined up for me over the next week or two. It was every bit as packed a schedule as when he'd managed my campaign to be Acclaimed Sovereign. Just listening to it made me tired.

"Of course, once you designate a Regent, much of this sort of thing can be delegated to him. Or her. We can't have our new Sovereign working herself into poor health—though perhaps just now it's good you'll have so much to occupy you."

The implication made my heart hurt.

After lunch, Mr. O switched on the big vidscreen to see the latest news. The top stories were still mainly about my recent Acclamation and Installation—nothing to hold my interest. I was starting to retreat into misery again when a news story came on about potential Regents. They displayed a long list, nearly a hundred names, each with a favorability rating. Some I recognized from my studies or my campaign for Acclamation, but many were unknown to me.

The names of the four Royals on the *Echtran* Council were listed, and those who'd been on the *Quintessence* with us—including Quinn O'Gara, with a favorability rating of 76, second only to Devyn Kane's.

"Hey, good showing, Dad," Sean exclaimed, grinning.

I turned to Mr. O in surprise. "You're in the running for Regent? I didn't know that."

"Technically no one is *running*. It will be your prerogative to name any qualified person you choose—that is, any Royal of the requisite age and experience who has lived on Mars. In other words, anyone from this list."

"You're a really popular choice, Dad." Molly sounded impressed and proud, but Mr. O shrugged.

"Perhaps, but I would never presume on my acquaintance with the Sovereign to put myself forward when she's met so few of the other candidates. Many will be attending tonight's reception and dinner, including those who arrived last week aboard the *Luminosity*."

I flinched at the name of the ship Rigel had taken back to Earth. Without me.

Mr. O didn't seem to notice. "More will be returning over the next month or two, though many are sending video presentations ahead for your consideration. I recommend you begin reviewing those as soon as possible."

I supposed he was right. The sooner I named a Regent, the sooner I could go back to Earth. "Would you *want* to be Regent?" I asked curiously. That would make my choice pretty easy.

He shrugged again but I sensed he wasn't nearly as indifferent as he pretended. "I'm flattered you would ask. Of course, there would be a fair number of details to work out."

"Like Mum." Sean was clearly startled that his dad would even consider such a thing. "She's stuck on Earth as part of that *Echtran* Council isn't she?"

"Oh, I hadn't thought of that," I admitted. "I guess my Regent will have to stay on Mars, especially since we all need to get back to Earth before anybody realizes we aren't still in Ireland." My heart lifted slightly. Maybe I couldn't hunt Rigel down and make him remember me, but at least on Earth we'd both be seeing the same stars. And someday maybe, just maybe…

Mr. O raised an eyebrow, almost like he guessed my thought. "Surely you realize, Excellency, that there will be strong resistance to you leaving Nuath, even with a Regent in place?"

"*What?*"

Sean and Molly gaped at their father, too, but he took no notice.

"Did the Council not talk to you about that?"

"About me never coming back? No! I even asked them about it point-blank and Malcolm admitted it would raise lots of questions on Earth if I didn't return. If they'd even *hinted* I'd have to *stay* on Mars, I never would have come at all. Especially—"

Especially without Rigel. Even if I never saw him again, I positively recoiled at the idea of us being stuck on different planets—permanently.

"You must realize how important it is, during this sensitive rebuilding time, that Nuath's Sovereign remain available to shepherd the necessary changes through to completion." Mr. O'Gara spoke calmly, persuasively. "Not to mention the situation with the Grentl."

I shook my head vigorously. "No. I *have* to go back! What if my aunt and uncle demand a search for me? A bunch of stuff could come out about Bailerealta and *Echtrans* and, well, everything!"

"They won't demand a search if they have reason to believe there's no point to such a thing."

I stared at him, a whole new horror creeping in. "You mean if they think I'm…dead?"

His apologetic expression was answer enough.

"Really? You'd do that to my aunt and uncle? To my friends?" I *wanted* to believe Aunt Theresa and Uncle Louie would be upset if they thought I'd died. Bri and Deb would, for sure. The thought of never seeing *any* of them again was beyond awful, totally apart from being so far away from Rigel.

"Wow, that's pretty harsh, Dad." Sean exchanged a worried glance with Molly, who nodded.

"No harsher than the situation warrants. I've discussed the matter with Devyn and Nels, as well as the *Echtran* Council. We feel that the risk to Nuath of your leaving is great enough to outweigh all other concerns. Matters on Earth can be handled so as to minimize the risk of discovery. *Echtrans*, of course, would be informed via MARSTAR that the story of your death is false, to forestall any panic there."

"But…wouldn't that mean I can't *ever* go back?"

"Not as Marsha Truitt. But that was never your true identity, Sovereign Emileia."

I groped for another argument, one that might sway him. "Wouldn't Sean have to stay here, too? And Molly, since she's my Handmaid? I can't believe Mrs. O'Gara is okay with that, when she has to be on Earth because of the Council."

"Lili and I have messaged back and forth a good deal over the past day or two. She agrees that, particularly if I accept any office of importance under your Sovereignty, it would make the most sense for her to step down from the Council and join us here. In fact, she has already looked into booking passage once she arranges to pack up our belongings in Jewel and tell everyone there that we've decided to move back to Ireland."

I felt slightly dazed. Apparently they'd worked out every single detail—without even consulting me!

"You can't do this! I'm the *Sovereign*." Tears of frustration threatened, making my voice quiver. "If I decide to go back to Earth, who's going to stop me?"

"It would not be hard to convince any ship captain that transporting you away from Nuath right now would amount to an act of treason. You'd be asking someone like Captain Liam to choose between a direct order from you and the good of his people."

My threatening tears spilled over as I realized, appalled, that he was probably right.

His voice became gentle again. "Tell me, were you really so happy in Jewel? I had the impression you'd been eager to escape it most of your life."

I immediately opened my mouth to deny that, then closed it again. Because it was true—or had been until Rigel arrived. Apart from my friendship with Bri and Deb, my life in Jewel before Rigel had been pretty dismal: barely tolerated by my aunt, picked on by half the school, ignored by the rest. I *had* wanted to escape, had worked hard in my classes in hopes of winning a scholarship that would take me far away from Jewel and Indiana.

"That's different," I finally said. "That would have been *my* choice. This isn't." Especially since staying on Mars for good—or even for the next few decades—meant I'd never have *any* chance of seeing Rigel again, even from a distance.

"I truly am sorry, Excellency." Mr. O'Gara managed to sound like he meant it. "It was never my wish to deceive you in any way. I'd hoped by now that you cared enough about Nuath's people and their future to put them ahead of mere personal concerns." He rose. "I suggest you get some more rest. When you've had time to think things through, I'm confident you will agree this way is best."

Refusing to soften, I glared after him as he left, then immediately rounded on Sean and Molly. "Did you know, either of you? That they planned for me to never go back?"

"Of course not." Sean was emphatic.

Molly shook her head as well. "Mum and Dad told us exactly what they told you. We assumed we'd all go back during this same launch window."

"Do you think they're right, though? That it would be some kind of disaster for me to leave?"

I could sense Sean's sudden conflict. "Well…there *is* the Grentl thing. What if they call again or need to be convinced not to attack or something? You're the only one who can talk to them. Plus there's all that government stuff Dad talked about." His expression was apologetic. "They totally should have told you all this upfront, though."

Though Molly voiced her agreement with that last bit, it was obvious neither of them were nearly as upset as I was by the thought of staying on Mars. Which made sense, as they'd always thought of Nuath as their home. But it wasn't mine. Even if I *had* wanted to escape from Jewel most of my life, I could never regard this fake underground habitat as "home."

Sure, I'd agreed to come here and be Acclaimed Sovereign to save Nuath from being destroyed, but the only part I'd looked *forward* to was using my authority so I could be with Rigel for good. Now… Now I had *nothing* to look forward to.

Still, much as I hated to admit it, Mr. O was right. I couldn't just turn my back on Nuath and its people. Like it or not, I was Sovereign now, and the responsibilities that went with that were here, not back in Jewel. Responsibilities like figuring out what the Grentl's message really meant, and choosing a Regent, and doing what I could to get the Nuathan government up and running.

Things that might, possibly, keep me from dwelling on the fact that by tomorrow Rigel would be back on Earth, with no memory of me or all we'd been to each other. It was too late to change that. But maybe a new sense of purpose would help me to hold myself together until my pain faded…even if it took years.

As Molly dressed me in yet another gorgeous gown that evening, this one of flowing amethyst studded with actual amethysts, I tried to block out her depressingly obvious sympathy by thinking about the evening ahead.

"There!" Molly stepped back. "What do you think?"

I faced the mirror, prepared to gush so I wouldn't hurt her feelings, but the sight of myself so amazingly decked out startled me to silence. This shade of purple was perfect with my coloring, somehow enhancing the dark green of my eyes. And the amethyst tiara set off my golden-brown hair beautifully, brightening the highlights I hadn't had a year ago.

Highlights I had now because of my bond with Rigel.

"Molly, you're a magician." I put as much enthusiasm into my voice as my suddenly-constricted throat allowed.

"Your wardrobe makes it pretty easy. I'd better change, too." Molly had her own beautiful *Chomseireach* (Handmaid) wardrobe, and soon she was arrayed in an embroidered pale blue tunic with darker blue leggings. Not nearly as ornate as my getup but every bit as pretty—and a lot more practical.

Sean and his father arrived a moment later, both resplendent in shimmery tunics, shorter than Molly's, over form-fitting leggings. Sean looked handsomer than I'd ever seen him, the deep blue of his tunic the same color as his eyes. I tried—hard—not to remember how incredible Rigel had looked in his Bodyguard uniform during his too-brief stint in that role.

"Already there has been media speculation about the fact you haven't been seen for more than two days, so tonight you *must* do your best to appear as, ah, normal and competent as possible," Mr. O said as we left my apartments.

Normal? I wasn't sure what normal was, without Rigel. This empty, dead feeling? "I'll do my best." It was all I could promise.

Mr. O regarded me narrowly for a moment. "Please do. Perhaps we should brush up on a few policy issues in case they arise in conversation."

He began drilling me on the same questions we'd practiced before my Acclamation and was clearly relieved when I was still able to reel off the answers. I, however, was painfully aware of the ones he *didn't* ask—because my relationship with Rigel was a moot point now.

When we reached the main state dining room, I was irresistibly reminded of the last time I'd eaten there, my very first day at the Palace. I'd been excited, distracted, looking forward to Rigel's imminent arrival…which had never happened. Swallowing, I squared my shoulders. I'd promised Mr. O I'd do my best, and I would. Even if it killed me.

For the first hour, drinks and appetizers were served by Palace staffers as the guests milled around, schmoozing about politics. I did my best to be pleasant and regal, matching faces and names as I evaluated each one as a possible Regent. None of them impressed me much. By the time the bell rang for dinner, Mr. O'Gara still seemed my most viable option—which made me realize (duh!) that must be the "office of importance" he'd meant earlier. No wonder Mrs. O was willing to resign from the Council and relocate to Mars.

The guests now moved to the long, black stone table. I sat first, spreading my amethyst skirts around me, then the others took their seats, by order of rank, each bowing formally as they did so. Sean lifted my orchid-adorned finger bowl and I did the ceremonial three dips of my fingers and dried them on the tiny linen cloth Molly handed me. Sean then held the bowl for Cormac to use, who then held it for Molly, who handed it back to Sean. Finally, Sean dipped his fingers into his own bowl, the signal that everybody else was free to dip their own fingers and start eating.

The whole ceremony was an excruciating reminder of our practice dinner at Rigel's house a month ago, after his Bodyguard test—a test he'd passed with flying colors. I remembered how proud of him I'd been…and how Sean had needled him into jealousy with snide remarks while Rigel stood where Cormac stood now, behind me.

Though the food Molly spooned onto my plate looked and smelled amazing, I was so overcome by that memory I couldn't enjoy any of it. Still, conscious of so many observers, I forced myself to take bite after mechanical bite. As the second course went around—Cormac duly tasting my food and Molly serving it to me—snippets of prior conversations with Rigel, spoken and silent, popped into my head.

How many times had he told me he'd love me forever? Sworn I could never alienate him, that he'd always be my strength? Broken promises, every one.

Desperate for distraction, afraid I might crumble right there at the table, I made myself relive yesterday's events, especially Eric Eagan's heroic final hours, when he'd taken me down to the secret room with the Grentl device and shown me how to use it.

With a quick, indrawn breath, I suddenly sat up straighter.

Sean, on my left, noticed at once. "What? What's wrong?" He spoke softly enough that only his father, on his other side, heard him.

"I've just remembered something important." I looked past Sean to give Mr. O a significant look. "I'll tell you as soon as this thing's over."

3

Private key encryption

IT was another two hours before I could diplomatically excuse myself, long after dessert was served. Yawning, I accompanied the O'Garas back to my apartment, hoping not every State dinner would be this tedious.

"You had something to tell me?" Mr. O asked the moment my outer door closed, shielding us from potential prying eyes and ears. "About the Grentl?"

Apparently he hadn't dismissed them quite as thoroughly as I'd thought.

"That Archive stone Eric showed me, right before he helped me use the Grentl device. He said it might be helpful afterward but I only just remembered it tonight. I'm sorry, I should have—"

Mr. O stared at me with an arrested expression. "No, I'd forgotten as well, and with far less excuse. You're right, it could be vitally important. Can you retrieve it now, tonight?"

When I nodded, Sean put a hand on my shoulder. "I'll come, too."

"And I, Excellency." Cormac bowed to me, then Mr. O'Gara. "With your permission?"

Molly and her father remained behind while Sean, Cormac and I hurried to the secret elevator concealed in my office. I thought to glance down at a certain star-shaped crystal Eric had said would turn blue whenever the Grentl device activated. It had been blue yesterday morning, before I'd responded to them, but now it was reassuringly clear. Or *was* that reassuring, under the circumstances?

I palmed open the lift, which took us to the sub-basement where the Grentl room was hidden. Retracing yesterday's path down the dimly-lit hallway and maze-like storage cavern with its towering stacks of containers, we reached the secret room without incident. I palmed that open, too.

Sean and I went in but Cormac hesitated, staring at the foot-square cube that was the Grentl device. Then, getting a grip on himself, he followed us inside.

I went straight to the little panel in the wall next to the inert device and covered it with my hand. It opened to a little recess containing a purplish, crystalline stone maybe an inch thick and two inches across, like a flattened sphere. It felt warmer than it had yesterday when I picked it up, with that same *mine*-ness I'd felt from the Scepter and the Grentl device itself. Interesting.

When we rejoined the others in the living room a few minutes later, Mr. O's eyebrows rose. "You have it?"

In answer, I held up the Archive crystal.

"Excellent. How does it work?"

I blinked. "I, um, thought maybe you'd know?"

He held out a tentative hand. "May I?"

Though I felt an odd reluctance, I placed the flat, round crystal on Mr. O's outstretched palm.

The instant it touched him, he gave a sharp gasp of pain and dropped it onto the thick carpet between us. "I…I can't. It appears only you can safely handle it." He seemed visibly shaken.

"I'm sorry!" I stooped to pick it back up. "I had no idea it would —"

"Not your fault." He examined the hand the archive stone had touched. "No damage seems to have been done, but this will make it difficult for anyone but you to figure out how it works. That should be your priority, whenever your other duties do not interfere."

I nodded. A new challenge, one both interesting and important, would be a welcome distraction from the constant ache in my heart. "Any suggestions where I should start?"

"None. Unless you've found anything here?" He glanced around the apartment. "Perhaps a journal or log left by prior Sovereigns?"

"I haven't exactly looked yet. But I will."

"Yes, do. Though perhaps not tonight. We have that breakfast meeting at eight, then petitions in the Royal Audience Hall followed by a luncheon and a meeting with the Healers. After that, I'll do my best to rearrange a few things to give you time to devote to this new project. I, ah, recommend against mentioning it to Nels just yet."

I managed a wry smile. "Yeah, I'd rather not have him nagging at me while I'm trying to figure it out."

Mr. O's smile looked more genuine than mine felt. "I'm glad we are in accord. Good night, Excellency."

He headed for the door but Sean hung back. "I'll catch up in a minute, Dad, okay?"

Though his father raised an eyebrow, he nodded, bowed to me and left.

Sean turned to me, his bright blue eyes as sympathetic as they were interested. "It's great you remembered that Archive thing. Wish *I'd* thought of it yesterday. Figuring it out will probably do a better job than all this political stuff to—"

"To distract me?" I finished, making him grimace. "I'm sorry, Sean, that's not fair." Especially since I'd had that identical thought just now. "You haven't gloated once about Rigel leaving, even though you have every reason to be glad."

"Hey, give me a little credit. It's true I was never a fan of you two as a couple, but I didn't want you hurt. Ever." He held my gaze, willing me to believe him.

"I know. And I really am grateful. You've been right there for me ever since we got to Nuath." I paused, then added in a bitter rush, "Unlike Rigel, who deserted me right when I needed him most."

Sean made a small motion of denial but I plunged on.

"No, it's true, you know it is." A totally unexpected surge of anger —at *Rigel*—swept through me. "He said himself he was taking the coward's way out and he was right. Nothing can *ever* excuse what he did to me."

Sean shook his head again. "I thought the same thing at first M, but—"

"But what?" My sudden anger threatened to spill over onto Sean. "You agree with your dad that what he did was all noble? That it was 'the right thing to do'?"

Sean hesitated for a long moment, then shrugged, not quite meeting my eye. "No. Hurting you definitely wasn't right. But…you should still cut him a little slack. These past few months were pretty rough on him, and I…well, I made it worse, lots of times."

Surprise at his unexpected defense of Rigel undercut my new anger —but I refused to let go of it. It felt so much better than despair. Empowering, even. "You're a good guy, Sean, you know that? Maybe if—"

"Look, I…I gotta go." Still not making eye contact, he turned toward the door. "We'll talk tomorrow, okay? And, uh, good luck with that Archive thing."

I frowned after him, wondering what could have sparked his sudden change in attitude, then shrugged. I already had enough puzzles to solve. That one would have to wait.

A few minutes later, as Molly was finally helping me out of my fancy gown, I let my gaze wander around my bedchamber. Surely, if prior Sovereigns *had* left any sort of record or clue for their descendants, it would be somewhere in this apartment?

The Royal chambers, I'd learned, contained a variety of compartments and amenities accessible only by someone with Sovereign blood—like the secret elevator. A non-Sovereign couldn't even use the hot water shower (something less than 1% of households in Nuath boasted, water on Mars was so precious). If not a journal, maybe there was some kind of crystal reader hidden in a genetically coded hidey-hole I hadn't found yet.

As soon as Molly left, I put a robe on over my nightgown and channeled the welcome energy of my newly-discovered anger at Rigel to begin a systematic search.

"So, did you, um, find anything last night?" Sean whispered as we all headed to my breakfast meeting the next morning.

His wariness reminded me of how strangely he'd reacted when I'd suddenly gotten pissed at Rigel last night—and reminded me I needed to *stay* pissed if I didn't want to return to that awful pit of misery I'd lived in since getting his message. The hole that used to be my heart was still a long way from healed—if that was even possible—but anger dulled the pain, at least temporarily.

"Not yet," I told him, "but I'll keep looking."

Mr. O heard and nodded approvingly. "That's the spirit. I knew you'd be able to put that, ah, disappointment behind you."

I stiffened. *Disappointment?* It was such a massive understatement, it had the opposite effect he clearly intended, pointing up the enormity of my loss. As despair crept over me again, my anger started slipping away. Desperately, I snatched it back. I needed that anger and the strength I drew from it to be the leader Nuath required right now.

Sure enough, the breakfast meeting was so boring, I had to consciously re-stoke my new anger at Rigel to keep me focused. While Palace staff discreetly served breakfast and cleared empty plates, a dozen or so acting ministers presented reports on their various areas of Nuathan welfare.

It could have been interesting if they'd been sharing actual data. Instead, they mostly spouted pompous nothings about "rebuilding Nuath to its former glory," etc, etc. I was sure these ministers all had decades more experience than I did, but it didn't seem like any of them knew as much about their supposed areas of expertise as they should, given their positions.

When the talk turned to elections, I finally spoke up. "I understand the heads of certain *fines* are now serving as some of the acting ministers?" I couldn't help noticing none of those non-Royal ministers had been invited to this particular meeting.

Deirdra, the acting Elections Minister, nodded. "We didn't have quite enough, ah, capable Royals remaining after Faxon's overthrow to head all twenty-seven ministries, Excellency, so we were forced to draw six acting ministers from other *fines.* Now, however, enough Royals are available to replace them."

"Wouldn't it make more sense for me to confirm all the acting ministers until every *fine* is able to nominate enough candidates to stand for a proper election," I suggested.

"*Every* fine?" She seemed taken aback. "During your grandfather's tenure—"

"The Sciences and the Royals made up the whole legislature. I know. But given current circumstances—"

Mr. O'Gara cleared his throat noisily. "Ah, perhaps these details can be discussed later, Excellency? It wouldn't do to make any hasty decisions, I'm sure you agree."

"But—" I glanced over to see him giving me a disapproving, even alarmed look and realized I should have talked to him before making such an apparently radical suggestion in front of all these ministers who might or might not fully support me.

"I, uh, suppose I should speak with my advisors before we make any sweeping changes."

Deirdra's worried expression cleared. "Of course, Excellency. Very wise."

As the conversation moved on, I tried to use my new emotion-sensing ability to sort out which reports, requests and people I could trust…which stirred a sudden memory of Rigel urging me to "read" the Royals on the ship, during our trip to Mars.

I swallowed. Would I ever reach a point where *everything* didn't remind me of Rigel?

The moment the meeting ended, Mr. O glanced at his omni. "This ran a bit late. You barely have time to change before the first petitioners are due in the Audience Hall."

Molly and I hurried back to my apartment, where she hastily decked me out in one of the formal, gem-encrusted gowns appropriate for Royal audiences. But when we rejoined Mr. O and Sean on our way to the Audience Hall, Mr. O frowned.

"Where is your Scepter? You'll be expected to have it for this."

Oops. It was true that all the pictures I'd seen of prior Sovereigns in the Royal Audience Hall had shown them holding the Scepter—which I hadn't touched since the day I was Installed, it was so ostentatious. "Back in my bedroom. Should I—?"

"I can get it," Molly volunteered. "It's in that cabinet in your closet, next to the jewelry one." She'd shown me how to give her handprint access to most of the wardrobe cabinets, so I wouldn't have to open them for her every time she dressed me.

"Thanks, Molly."

She must have run—way easier in her outfit than mine—because she managed to return with my Scepter just as we reached the imposing gold-figured double doors of the Royal Audience Hall.

"Got it," she panted, handing it to me a half-second before the doors were flung open by two bowing Palace staffers.

I took the Scepter from her, again experiencing that curious *mine* feeling.

"Ah, good." Mr. O surveyed the still-empty Hall. "Let's get you situated before the petitioners arrive, shall we?"

Somewhat hampered by my heavy gown, I crossed the enormous room, mounted the dais at the opposite end and seated myself on the ornate golden *cathoir*, or throne. A half-minute later the doors opened again to admit the mayor of Newlyn, my first appointment.

"Sovereign Emileia." A member of the Agricultural rather than the Royal *fine,* Mayor Balfour folded himself practically in half, his bow was so deep. "I come to request your intervention in our dispute with Bailecuinn over water resources. Our hydroponics have been shorted of late, resulting in lowered production of the leafy greens Newlyn is so deservedly known for. Bailecuinn, on the other hand, has yet to see any drop-off in their grain production. Therefore, our immediate need is clearly greater than theirs."

He went on to spout data on Newlyn's water reclamation plant and how that water had been apportioned over the past few years. When he finished his rapid-fire analysis, I forced a smile.

"If you'll send all pertinent figures to Mr. O'Gara, we'll review both your claims and theirs. Mayor Cheara is scheduled to make a similar appeal on behalf of Bailecuinn later this morning."

Though I could sense he wanted to argue his point further, Mayor Balfour bowed and retreated, since each petitioner was only allotted a five minute audience.

Absently playing with my Scepter during the brief break between appointments, I noticed that the translucent pink stone embedded near the top happened to be the *exact* same shape and size as the purple Archive stone. Could that possibly mean—?

My next petitioner was announced before I could check whether the pink stone might be removable, forcing me to turn my attention to her, instead.

After two hours listening to litany after boring litany involving Nuathan minutiae (Mayor Balfour's case on water resources turned out to be one of the more riveting ones) I decided Nels, Devyn and the others must have been crazy to have actually *wanted* this job. No wonder you had to be born to it.

My very last appointment turned out to be Nels Murdoch himself, though not with a petition. Instead, he pulled up a holo-screen from his omni, oriented so I could see it.

"As you requested, Excellency, I have collected a few names for your consideration as possible members of your Advisory Council." Not surprisingly, Devyn was at the top of the short list, which also included Mr. O'Gara, Phelan Monroe, whom I'd met on the *Quintessence*, and four others I'd met in passing last night and at my post-Installation Royal Reception.

"Thank you, Nels. I'll consider each of these carefully." I'd need to conduct in-person interviews to figure out which ones I could trust.

Nels nodded, then glanced at Mr. O. "I don't suppose you have any more details yet about that, ah, problem we discussed two days ago?"

"We're working on it." Mr. O smiled reassuringly at him. "The Sovereign has discovered something that may be of assistance."

I nodded, since Nels clearly needed reassuring. "We think previous Sovereigns may have left information that will tell us how to proceed without, er, aggravating the situation."

Seeming way more relieved than my vague reassurance justified, Nels bowed his way out.

As we left the Audience Hall, Mr. O informed me I had forty-five whole minutes before my luncheon. I headed back to my apartment as quickly as my stupid formal gown would allow, eager to experiment with the Scepter before mentioning my new theory and possibly giving anyone false hopes.

Molly helped me change from my court dress into a simpler outfit in shades of green for the luncheon, then I asked her to give me a few minutes alone. Retrieving the purple Archive stone from the secure cubby where I'd stashed it, I held it up to the Scepter's pink stone. Except for color, they were identical. Did that mean they were *both* Archives?

I wouldn't know until I could figure out how the darned things worked. Setting down the purple stone, I covered the pink one on the scepter with my hand, since that seemed to open all the genetically coded locks. Nothing happened.

Keeping my hand on the stone, I experimentally said, "Activate?"

Nothing.

"Open?"

Nothing.

"Access Archive."

Nothing. Hm.

Plucking my electronic scroll-book off my nightstand, I flipped it flat and called up my English-Nuathan dictionary. Picking up the Scepter again, I tried various combinations of Nuathan words while touching the pink stone.

"*Gnomhachtaigh!*"

Nothing.

"*Farsaing! Farsaing chartlann!*"

Nothing. Maybe it wasn't even a verbal command at all?

"*Chartlann rochtana?*" I tried without much hope and suddenly the whole Scepter vibrated. Then, emanating from the pink crystal orb at the top, a hologram of a man appeared in front of me—a man I recognized from textbook pictures as Sovereign Leontine. My grandfather.

4

Random access memory

"OH!" I breathed, gazing wide-eyed at the perfectly lifelike image now standing before me.

At my faint sound, the incredibly real-seeming Leontine turned toward me, like he was actually *looking* at me. "New Sovereign?"

"Yes?" I had no clue what the protocol was for something like this.

"You are alone?"

"Yes."

"Name and lineage please, for integration purposes."

"Um, Emileia. Daughter of Mikal and Galena."

There was a brief pause, then the image of my grandfather smiled. "Emileia. My granddaughter. All grown up now?"

"Uh, sort of. I'm sixteen."

He frowned at me. "My son, Mikal. I find no record of him in the Archive. Why is that?"

"I'm sorry, sir. I was told he never became Sovereign. He and my mother escaped to Earth—with me—when Faxon took power, but they were both killed there. Murdered by Faxon's people. I was only Acclaimed a few days ago."

"I see. You came to Mars from Earth?"

"Yes, just three weeks ago. And I just this minute figured out how to access this Archive. The pink stone in the Scepter *is* an Archive, right?"

He nodded gravely. "It is. Normally you would have been shown how to access it by your predecessor. But as that predecessor seems to have been me, it appears I never had that opportunity. The first thing I would have told you is to guard the contents of this Archive carefully. Its very existence is known only to Sovereigns, their Consorts, and occasionally one or two of their most trusted advisors. The Sovereigns have felt it wisest for that to remain the case."

"Oh. Okay. I'll, uh, keep it as secret as I can." Good thing I hadn't shared my theory about the Scepter with anyone yet.

Leontine's expression was kindly but serious. "How old were you when your parents were killed, Emileia?"

"Less than two years old. Earth years, that is." Though Nuath now used the Earth calendar and had its clocks synched with Ireland's, I didn't know if it had always been that way.

"I am sorry." He actually sounded—and looked—it. But how could that be, if he was a recording?

Rather than wonder, I asked. "How…does this work, exactly? I mean, no offense, but you've been dead for more than fifteen years. How can I be talking to you now?"

"This Archive holds the stored images and recorded experiences of all previous Sovereigns from the time of its creation by Arturo, son of Tiernan, to the present. During my grandfather, Sovereign Nuallen's, time, we developed the technology to store personality profiles as well, allowing a more authentic interaction with any more recent Sovereigns you may choose to access for information or advice. When integrated with the Scepter, the Archive is capable of virtual intelligence. Learning, if you will."

"You mean I can just ask questions? And you—or other, older Sovereigns—will just…answer me?"

He smiled again. "Precisely. It can be an extremely valuable resource."

No kidding! I'd been wondering who I could trust enough to put on my Advisory Council, when I had the best Advisory Council possible right here in my hand! For the first time since getting Rigel's terrible message, real excitement bubbled up inside me.

"You will be expected to store your own experiences in the Archive for your eventual successors as well," my grandfather continued. "It is how we have ensured continuity of purpose and knowledge down the centuries."

Okay, *that* creeped me out a little, thinking of storing my*self* in this thing for any kids or grandkids I might have way in the future. But that was the least of my worries right now, when I'd been given this incredible gift.

"I understand. I think. I mean, I assume there are instructions or something for that?"

"You need only ask. Meanwhile, as you were clearly not trained at the Palace during your youth and lost your father at such an early age, there must be much you need to know."

I nodded eagerly. "*So* much! Like, pretty much everything! I don't even know where to start. No, wait, yes I do," I corrected myself. "Please, sir, I need to know everything you can tell me about the Grentl."

For the first time, Sovereign Leontine frowned at me. "All information on that topic has been stored separately, for security reasons. I'm afraid you will not be able to access it via this Archive."

"Oh, that's okay. I have the other one here." I held up the purple stone. "Do I open it the same way I did this one, with the Scepter?"

His frown relaxed. "I see we have a very resourceful new Sovereign. No doubt you already have experiences that will be valuable additions to the Archives. Yes, it is accessed the same way. To exchange the stones, simply press down on this one with your hand and rotate it to the left to remove it from the Scepter. Replace it with the other by pressing down and rotating to the right."

"Should I, um, turn this one off or something first? I can put this Archive back the same way, right?" I felt suddenly panicky at the thought of *not* being able to see my grandfather again when there were so many things I needed to ask him.

"Yes, you can exchange the stones whenever necessary, though the other Archive should be kept in its secure location when not in use and its existence guarded even more closely than this one. The command *chartlann fionragh* will discontinue transmission until reactivated. I look forward to continuing our conversation, Emileia."

"Can you?" I was genuinely curious. "Look forward to it, I mean. You're not…in some kind of limbo in there when I'm not using the Archive, are you?" That sounded awful.

To my relief, he shook his head. "A figure of speech, based on how I would have spoken—or felt—when alive. My true consciousness went to its reward at my passing."

I wasn't sure what to say to that. "Um, okay, until later, then. And…thanks. *Chartlann fionragh.*"

Even though I'd expected it, I felt a pang when my grandfather abruptly disappeared. Reassuring myself that I'd be talking with him again soon—probably in the Grentl Archive—I put my palm over the pink stone. Before I could twist it to the left, a tap came on my bedroom door.

"M, er, Excellency? That luncheon starts in five minutes."

"Shoot." I'd forgotten all about that stupid luncheon. Important as it was, unlocking the Grentl Archive would have to wait. Quickly, I replaced the purple stone in its cubby and the Scepter in its special cupboard in my closet.

"Coming!" I called to Molly.

Even without finger bowls to remind me of Rigel, the luncheon was painful to endure. Several Royal guests I'd met previously still had memory problems, thanks to Faxon, and introduced themselves like they were meeting me for the first time. It served as a brutal reminder that even if I saw Rigel again someday, even if he got some of his memories back, he'd never again be the Rigel I remembered. That Rigel—*my* Rigel—was gone forever.

My meeting afterward with Adara, the Head Mind Healer, was even worse. She'd been the one to oversee the extraction and display of Rigel's memories, where the truth about the Grentl had come out. The very last time I'd seen Rigel. Maybe if I'd insisted on staying long enough to talk with him afterward…

I forced my attention away from that excruciating what-if to focus on Adara's report on the progress of some of the very Royals I'd just seen at lunch.

"Unfortunately, most recoveries are progressing more slowly than we'd hoped, but we are developing new therapies constantly, some of which show great promise," she was saying. "We are hopeful others will soon be able to return to their families, if not—immediately—to their duties."

"What sorts of therapies are you using? Have *any* of those who had memories wiped recovered completely?" I tried not to sound as desperate for reassurance as I felt, but her expression was sympathetic.

"Two people so far have made what appear to be nearly full recoveries, but they had suffered the least tampering, before Faxon became powerful enough to compel full cooperation from our staff. I regret to say that the memory erasures performed by those of us with more training have been much harder to treat."

Along with the sympathy I sensed from Adara, I also detected anxiety…and guilt. I had a suspicion why. "Tell me, Healer Adara, did you have a hand in Rigel Stuart's memory erasure?"

Though she nodded calmly enough, her emotions spiked sky-high.

"I did, Excellency. Because of my qualifications and expertise, I was asked—" She darted a quick glance at Mr. O'Gara. "That is, he and his grandmother requested I supervise the procedure."

"So you were there for the whole thing, before and after? Did he —"

Mr. O cleared his throat. "Excellency, we have only a few more minutes and if you don't mind terribly, I'd very much like to ask about the status of my daughter Elana."

With an effort, I bit back the questions I was itching to ask—like whether Rigel had had second thoughts or any last words for me. Did I *really* want to know?

"Oh. Of…of course. How is she doing?"

Visibly relieved, Adara immediately began talking about the O'Garas' oldest daughter, who was still in the Mind Healing facility in Pryderi, and who had made notable progress.

Mr. O smiled broadly at hearing Elana was now recovered enough to receive visitors. "Thank you. Sean and Molly will be delighted to hear the good news about their sister. And now, I really must get the Sovereign to her next appointment."

Because he seemed so eager to hurry me away from Adara before I could ask any more questions, I tried to probe his feelings as we headed to my next meeting. But all I picked up was a determined sense of purpose. Surely, if he was hiding anything, I'd be able to sense it?

Sean and Molly had headed out of the Palace to visit friends in Glenamuir immediately after the luncheon, so they got to escape all my boring afternoon and evening meetings. When Molly got back to my apartment, just in time to help me change for bed, she was eager to tell me all about her afternoon.

Though I knew I was being a bad friend, I faked a huge yawn. "Sorry, I'm just so sleepy. You can tell me the rest tomorrow, okay?"

Immediately contrite, Molly laid out my nightgown and left. The second the door snicked shut, I raced to the closet and carried my Scepter and the Grentl Archive to the ottoman at the foot of my bed.

I twisted the pink stone to the left, like Leontine had told me, and it popped right out into my hand. Setting it next to me, I inserted the purple stone in its place, twisting it to the right.

"*Chartlann rochtana.*" This time the staff projected an image of a woman in flowing robes of beautiful peacock blue.

"*Aethne?*" she asked. Keeping hold of the Scepter, I snatched up my Nuathan dictionary to look up the word she'd used. Ah! It meant "identity."

"I'm Sovereign Emileia, just Acclaimed," I said, hoping this Archive wasn't completely in Nuathan. That would slow things down enormously.

To my relief, she responded in English. "Sovereign Emileia. Noted. Genetic imprint verified. This is the Archive documenting initial and continuing contact with the Grentl, commencing in the third year of my reign. I am Sovereign Aerleas."

I'd figured she must be, but seeing this young-looking image of my great-grandmother, a woman who'd been dead for over a hundred years, still boggled me. "I'm, uh, glad to meet you."

She nodded, but her expression didn't change.

"I need all the information you can give me about the Grentl and how to use their device. They sent a, uh, message, but I don't know how to respond. When I tried, they just pulled more memories out of me."

"Yes. This is how the Grentl access information. When they request a report, the Sovereign must absorb the necessary data about the colony's current status, then interface with the device to transfer that data to the Grentl."

Aerleas sounded mechanical, not like a real person at all. Surely she hadn't actually talked like that, since she'd been one of the most popular Sovereigns ever. Maybe this Archive wasn't as sophisticated as the other one, with personalities and all?

"They didn't exactly request a report. The device activated and I got to it as soon as I could, since they were messing with Nuath's power. They didn't ask me anything, though, just pulled my life history out of me—and stopped the power glitches."

"No report was sent?"

"I guess not? I hadn't 'absorbed data' or anything. But then the device activated again, just a few minutes later, and they said, 'We are coming.' I tried to ask *when*. And *why*. But they just pulled more stuff out of my head."

"Did you allow the Grentl to terminate the connection?"

"Er, no. I think I might have let go early." I saw no point in explaining why, to this non-personality version of Aerleas. I hoped the one in the other Archive would be easier to warm up to.

"It is possible they would have said more. You have only recently imprinted on the device?"

"The day before yesterday. Yes."

"It took me many years to establish sufficient rapport with the Grentl to safely initiate contact. Even then, they often declined to respond. I recommend you allow the Grentl to initiate all contact at this time."

That was *so* not helpful! "Can you maybe give me an overview of *all* communications with the Grentl?"

"Earliest communication was with two extra-solar researchers, five years before my Acclamation. They discovered little beyond the fact that the Grentl are from a distant part of the galaxy. Repeated attempts to question the Grentl resulted in the device disabling one of the researchers. Six years later, a small team of Communications Engineers made another attempt at contact. They also had limited success, with a similar conclusion. At the Grentl's request, I was next to interface with the device, at which time I imprinted upon it. The Grentl then cautioned that only I was to use it from that point forward.

"In subsequent sessions, all but three initiated by the Grentl, I was able to learn more about them. By no means humanoid, the Grentl are a hybrid organic and energy-based life form that reproduces by fission. Their keen interest in the development of the colony of Nuath led me to believe they originally founded it for experimental purposes. The Grentl do not measure time as we do, sometimes treating a span of many years as though only days have passed since the previous communication. Also, they are wary of revealing too much about themselves to lower life forms, as they consider us."

"Wow. How did you learn all that, if they don't like questions?"

"Over time, my interactions with the device became reciprocal, allowing me to receive impressions from the Grentl much as they received impressions from me. I was never able to ascertain whether this was deliberate on their part or not. I felt it wisest not to ask."

So they wouldn't block her from finding out more, I assumed.

"As with you, at first they were able to access the whole of my conscious memory. Over time I learned to limit the scope of what they received."

Ah! "Can you tell me how you did all that? I don't want to piss them off or anything, but I really do need to get more information about what they plan to do. I'm not sure I can afford to wait until they contact us again. They might just…show up or something. We need to be prepared."

She paused for a long moment before answering. Maybe searching through the Archive?

"There is no precedent for the sort of message you received. Given the potential urgency of your situation, I will attempt to assist but it is possible you will be unable to achieve the same reciprocal communication I did. My son Leontine was never able to do so, nor to limit what the Grentl took from his mind. Therefore he relied primarily on data chips to transmit his reports."

"I understand. But I have to at least try."

Aerleas nodded gravely. "I concur. Keep in mind, however, that direct questioning of the Grentl is likely to end badly."

"Got it. So…what do I do? Just grab onto the device again and wait for them to, uh, pick up?"

"Essentially." Still not a trace of a smile. "On the few occasions I initiated contact, that is what I did. On three occasions, they responded. On four others, they did not, though I waited for over an hour each time. When they did respond, it was within twelve minutes."

I'd give it at least half an hour, then. "If they do answer, how do I get information from them without asking questions?"

"Listen. Reach out with your mind. I grew better at this with practice."

I wondered if it would be anything like when I used to "listen" for Rigel's thoughts. Pain lanced through me at a memory so precious, so…gone. Quickly, I asked another question.

"When you did achieve that two-way kind of communication, what kinds of things did you, um, talk about?"

"Their primary interest was the status of this colony: population, air quality, food and power reserves. At irregular intervals, they have specifically requested updates on these things. I initially shared that data directly, after absorbing it myself but later a data port was installed per the Grentl's request and instructions to allow for more efficient transmission of numerical data. Consult one of the Grentl-cleared Engineers for further instruction on use of the data port should it be needed."

Not that there *were* any Grentl-cleared Engineers now that Eric was dead. It wasn't something I needed to know right now, anyway. Unless the Grentl *did* want a report?

"When was the last report sent?"

Aerleas abruptly dissolved, to be replaced by my grandfather, Leontine. "Most recent contact with the Grentl occurred in the seventy-second year of Sovereign Leontine's reign." He sounded just as mechanical as Aerleas had, showing no sign he recognized me. Which made sense, since this was a totally separate Archive. Still, it fleetingly made me think of how Rigel would act if I ever saw him again. I quickly forced my mind back to the matter at hand.

"The seventy-second… Um, how long ago was that? In Earth years?"

"Forty-six Earth years."

"And what was communicated then?"

"The Grentl requested an update on the colony's status, which I provided as a data file. Displaying now. For security reasons, no text may be transferred from this Archive to any other storage medium."

A large rectangular screen replaced Leontine's image, black print on a white background, filled with statistics on the colony's status at the time. At the end a narrative summary briefly outlined changes since the prior report, thirty-four years earlier.

Power reserves had declined, which had been compensated for by consolidating three villages and putting two others on reduced energy—now voluntarily inhabited by technophobes, I knew. Government structure was mentioned in just a sentence or two, noting a slight shift in *fine* representation in the opposite direction from how I hoped to move things. No mention whatsoever of Earth or the *Echtrans* there. Odd, since I knew they'd been involved in the first Moon landings, which would have happened fairly recently when this last report was written.

Curious, I inquired about that omission.

Leontine's image reappeared. "Sovereign Aerleas cautioned me against mentioning any contact with Earth. She believed, based on years of communication with the Grentl, that such information might provoke them to take measures against either Earth or Nuath to prevent further interaction."

Yikes. They'd definitely learned about it from me, and from Faxon, too. "Um, why?"

"She intentionally never told me what specific risks she perceived, as I was never able to learn her method of shielding my own thoughts from the Grentl. It is why I sent my reports via the data port rather than directly, as she had. As contact with Earth continued to increase over the course of my reign, filtered reports seemed safest, given Aerleas's concerns."

Good to know about that option…if it wasn't already too late.

"How often do the Grentl ask for reports?"

"The time between requests varies. On average, every thirty-nine Earth years."

Past time for another one, then, which was probably why they activated the device to begin with. If I sent their overdue report, maybe they wouldn't come here in person after all? It was definitely worth a try!

"Where can I find all the data I'll need for a new report?"

"All data is available at any Sovereign's request. Method of retrieval is addressed in the main Archive."

Wow, this Archive really *was* limited strictly to the Grentl!

"Thanks," I said, even though it wouldn't matter to this stripped-down version of my grandfather. "*Chartlann fionragh.*"

5

Intrinsic error

ACCORDING to the clock on my bedroom vidscreen, it was past one in the morning—and I had to be at another stupid breakfast meeting at eight. Even so, I went ahead and popped the Grentl Archive out of the Scepter, replaced it with the main Archive and activated it, smiling as the more lifelike version of my grandfather appeared in front of me.

"Emileia." He smiled, too. "You now have the information you require?"

"Some of it," I told him. "I need to know how to call up all the colony data so I can put together a report for the…you know."

"Certainly. Have you set up your secure channel yet?"

There was *so* much I didn't know! Stuff that only prior Sovereigns could tell me. From all I'd read, I was the first Sovereign ever who hadn't been mentored by a Sovereign parent or grandparent for at least a few years before being Acclaimed. "Um, no. How do I do that?"

At his direction, I activated a sub-menu on my vidscreen, created a password (*not* "cornfield") and secured it genetically with a touch on the control pad. Next, he showed me how to access every database on the planet, pointing out which ones I'd need to compile my report—though without ever mentioning the Grentl by name. We kept at it until after two, by which time I was too tired to think straight.

Finally, regretfully, I said goodnight to my grandfather and deactivated the Archive, vowing to continue as soon as possible.

Unfortunately, the next day was frustratingly like the one before. As I hurried from appointment to appointment, I started to wonder if Mr. O was *trying* to bore me to death, just so I'd hurry up and appoint him Regent. The fact that Sean and Molly had been excused again today—this time to go sightseeing—lent weight to my cynical theory.

If that really was his plan, it just might work. Rather than painstakingly evaluate all the eligible candidates, I was increasingly tempted to simply give the job to Mr. O so I could hand off all this dull, day-to-day stuff and devote my time to more important things—like preparing that report for the Grentl.

"I thought you were going to schedule me enough free time to figure out that Archive?" I finally whispered on the way from one stupid meeting to the next.

He looked sharply at me. "Have you made any progress?"

"I, um, haven't really had a chance," I fudged, since Leontine had more or less sworn me to secrecy. "That's kind of my point."

Mr. O nodded thoughtfully and pulled out his omni. "While I think it's likely we needn't worry any time soon, it would be best to verify that. I'll free up tomorrow morning for you to work on the problem."

"That would be great. Thanks."

Molly was bubbling with excitement when she and Sean joined us in my living room late that afternoon. "M, you have *got* to see the Central Pillar! It's so cool, how far up it goes—like a whole mile! And there are these murals all over the sides that look really old."

"Not that we could get very close, what with that protest going on." Sean sent a worried look at his father.

"Protest?" Already Mr. O was reaching for the remote to turn on my main vidscreen.

Sure enough, the top story was about a Populist rally at the Central Pillar, led by Crevan Erc, head of Nuath's anti-Royal movement. Nearly three hundred people had attended, though about that many had also gathered to voice their opposition to his platform and their support for me as Sovereign.

"Hm. No real cause for concern, I'd say, based on their dwindling numbers." Mr. O sounded relieved. "Still, I suppose they may bear watching."

He was about to switch off the vidscreen when I suddenly glimpsed a familiar name among the various headlines in the sidebar. "Morag Teague releases statement."

"Why is Rigel's grandmother in the news?" I exclaimed, pointing.

Mr. O hesitated for a moment, then clicked on the story. The new screen showed a smiling Morag Teague (which was nearly as weird as seeing my Aunt Theresa smiling) giving what seemed to be a prepared speech.

"Fellow Nuathans, I am pleased to report that my grandson, Rigel

Stuart, has unequivocally proven that he values Nuath's welfare above his own desires. Rather than risk undermining Sovereign Emileia's transition to her new role, or her relationship with her intended Consort, Rigel has elected to have all memory of his association with her erased. In addition, he has left Nuath permanently, returning to his parents on Earth. Needless to say, I am very proud of my grandson for making such a selfless decision. He has shown himself a credit to both our family name and to his race. I hope all Nuath will forgive and forget Rigel's prior poor judgments, as I have done. Thank you."

My stomach began to churn. How dared she? Wasn't it bad enough that Rigel had abandoned me when I needed him so badly? Now, with Morag's smug public statement, all Nuath knew I'd been ditched. When the video started over again, I grabbed the remote myself and switched it off.

"That awful, awful woman! I wouldn't be surprised if she somehow brainwashed Rigel into doing what he did."

Mr. O frowned. "It's conceivable Morag helped to persuade him to such a sensible course, Excellency, but 'brainwash' is rather a strong term."

"Is it? She had those Mind Healers messing with him—"

I broke off. None of them knew about the one private omni conversation Rigel and I had managed after his grandmother snatched him away.

She and Mr. O had only convinced Rigel to go with her by insisting it would be the best thing for *me*. Had his grandmother and her Mind Healer buddies taken that a step further, insisting a memory wipe would also be to my advantage?

During our very last conversation, though, Rigel had *sworn* he'd never let them undo our bond, no matter what. Another broken promise…

Mr. O was talking about my schedule again but I barely heard him. My mind was too busy vacillating between fury at Morag Teague and renewed pain at Rigel's betrayal.

"…since no one else is authorized to attend those meetings in your stead. Unless you've given more thought to the matter of naming a Regent?"

With an effort, I shook free of my agonized thoughts to focus on his words. "With the schedule I've had the past two days? I've barely had time to breathe."

Though he hid it well, I sensed his disappointment. He really did want me to appoint him. But then Mrs. O would come to Mars and I'd be even less likely to ever return to Earth and see Rigel again. If there was even the slightest chance he hadn't made that choice completely of his own free will…

Still, I couldn't imagine getting to know any of the other Regent candidates as well as I already knew Mr. O. And anyone else qualified would probably feel as strongly as he did about me staying in Nuath. Why was I even hesitating?

"I'll try to make a decision soon," I promised. "I'll review those videos and go over all the names right after I work on the, uh, Grentl thing."

That evening I left the Palace for the very first time since getting Acclaimed, to attend a gala reception being thrown by half a dozen Royals who were celebrating their recent return to Nuath after several years of "exile" on Earth—at least, that's how they worded it on the invitation Mr. O'Gara forwarded to me.

"This evening should be a bit livelier than what you've had to endure so far," he assured me, seeming more relaxed than I'd seen him since leaving Indiana. "The O'Derrys used to be famous for their parties and I can guarantee there'll be music."

He was right. The venue turned out to be a glittering ballroom on the second floor of the Culture Ministry building, decorated by displays of Nuathan art representing the past two thousand-plus years. I examined the paintings on the walls and the sculptures on pedestals with interest, since the earliest ones, in particular, were dramatically different from any classical or even ancient art I'd seen in books on Earth.

And, as Mr. O had promised, there was music. Much of it sounded distinctly Irish—upbeat tunes with fiddles and flutes—but some pieces reminded me more of African or maybe Arabian stuff. I didn't have enough musical background to guess any better than that but I enjoyed it—or would have, if I hadn't kept remembering Morag Teague's nasty public statement and imagining all the other guests pitying me.

At one point, when Mr. O wasn't watching, Sean managed to slip me a glass of *spakriga,* Nuath's answer to champagne.

"Just don't tell my dad," he cautioned, his bright blue eyes twinkling mischievously. "I figured after the past couple of days you could stand to relax and loosen up a little, eh?"

No kidding! Undeterred by Cormac's frown, I downed it quickly, before Mr. O could see me and confiscate it. Bubbly and slightly sweet, it only made me sputter a little.

"Mm, it's really good," I exaggerated, since Sean was clearly waiting for my reaction. Not that I'd ever had anything else alcoholic to compare it to.

The *spakriga* did relax me, I realized a short time later. Mr. O'Gara was back at my elbow, guiding me toward or away from certain people, depending on whether he thought they were ones I needed to talk to or avoid. I found myself smiling a bit more easily and answering a bit more freely than usual—probably no bad thing.

Near the end of the evening, though, the music started to seem too loud and my responses to people grew shorter and more stilted. As my artificially high spirits soured, I became angrier than ever at Rigel for what he'd done to me, and at his grandmother for talking him into it, then telling the world.

I was especially pissed at Gordon Nolan. He was more at fault than anyone, since without his interference there never would have been a scandal in the first place and Rigel would still be my Bodyguard. Now that I was Sovereign, maybe I could somehow make Gordon pay—and I was in just the mood to do it. Not that I'd seen him since the day I was Installed.

"Guess Gordon didn't have the guts to come tonight," I snarked to Mr. O and Sean, glancing around the big room. My head was starting to ache slightly, probably from that stupid glass of *spakriga.*

Nola O'Derry, our hostess, overheard me and laughed. "Ah, Excellency, I did hear you and Gordon Nolan had a bit of a falling out. Not that I blame you. Unpleasant man. Shifty eyes. But you needn't worry he'll cross your path again anytime soon. He left this morning for Earth aboard the *Luminosity.* No doubt he thought his prospects better there than here, now you've assumed your rightful role."

She wandered away, still chuckling—clearly she'd had a *lot* more *spakriga* than I had—but I stared after her, my mouth hanging open.

"This morning?" I rounded on Mr. O. "The *Luminosity* left this *morning?*"

"I, ah, haven't been following the launch schedules, but apparently so." I sensed way more discomfort from him than showed outwardly. "But even had I known—"

"You wouldn't have told me? Why?" But even before he answered, I knew.

"What would have been the point, Excellency?" He kept his voice low. "It would only have upset you again, to no purpose. Rigel made his choice, and it was a wise one. The sooner you can resign yourself to that, the better."

"Easy for you to say," I whispered fiercely, belatedly realizing people were starting to stare. "*You're* not the one who has to—"

He made an urgent motion to quiet me, then signaled to Cormac to summon our limo. "This is not the place for such a discussion, Excellency. We should make our goodbyes."

By the time we were all in the hover-limo for the short trip back to the Palace, my first shock had faded somewhat, though my anger remained.

"Okay, maybe now you can tell me why you never mentioned Rigel was still here in Nuath as recently as *this morning* when his last message to me said he was already gone. And don't tell me you didn't know." It had been totally obvious he was lying about that, even if I didn't quite have Mrs. O's lie-detector ability.

Mr. O inclined his head. "Very well. Yes, I knew. But surely, had Rigel wanted *you* to know, he would have told you himself? No doubt he said what he did so that you wouldn't try to stop him when he knew he was making the right choice."

"But—" I stopped, my gut twisting painfully as the truth of his words sank in. When Rigel recorded that awful goodbye message, he *must* have known he wouldn't be leaving until days after I received it. He also must have realized that if I knew, I'd go straight to the hospital in Pryderi to demand he stay in Nuath and have his memory restored. And he didn't want that. Didn't want *me*.

I sank back in my seat, tears of hurt and fury prickling my eyes, but I refused to let them escape. I was Sovereign now and I was *not* going to cry in front of anyone, not even the O'Garas. Molly and Sean both looked sympathetic, but were they, really? Not until we were pulling into the garage beneath the Palace did I have enough control of my own feelings to probe anyone else's.

Mr. O's were what I expected—still that grim sense of purpose. Molly was as sorry for me as she looked. But Sean…Sean was broadcasting even more inexplicable guilt than he had a couple of nights ago, when he'd defended Rigel against my first surge of anger. He'd told me he felt bad he'd been so hard on Rigel, but now I thought I knew the real reason.

"You knew too, didn't you?" I asked him as we made our way through mostly-deserted passageways to the Royal wing of the Palace. "That Rigel hadn't really left yet?"

"What? No! I swear I didn't. *I* would have told you if I'd known." Sean frowned at his father.

"I'm sure Sean had no idea," Mr O affirmed smoothly. "In any event, the point is now moot."

Because Rigel was finally gone beyond recall. No wonder his grandmother's statement hadn't been broadcast until today. It also explained why Mr. O had seemed so much more relaxed tonight.

Before turning down the hallway leading to his and Sean's quarters, Mr. O paused. "Excellency, as I may be spending less time at your side over the next day or two, it occurs to me that I should have your omni security code, in order to forward any urgent messages."

I blinked. I'd all but forgotten about my omni this past week, I'd been so busy. Of course, with Eric Eagan dead and Rigel gone, no one could have called me on it anyway. They were the only ones I'd ever given my secret code to.

"You did set up a security code, didn't you?" Mr. O prompted.

"Yes. It's…cornfield." Just saying it made my heart hurt, remembering the special times Rigel and I had spent in our hidden clearing there. Special times that were also gone forever.

Mr. O tapped the code into his omni. "If you'll synch your omni with mine, any updates I make to your schedule will instantly be available to you."

"Um…"

"I can show you how," Sean volunteered with another disgruntled look at his father. "I'll be there in a few, okay, Dad?"

Mr. O sent a searching look at Sean and then at me before nodding. "Very well, but don't be too long. Even with her lighter schedule, the Sovereign should get an early start on that, ah, matter we discussed earlier."

Sean, Molly, Cormac and I continued to my apartments without a word. I was still trying to get my hurt and anger under control so I wouldn't lash out at any of them, since they hadn't done anything to deserve that.

As soon as we were inside with the door shut, Sean turned to me apologetically. "M, I'm really sorry. I didn't know about the *Luminosity* not leaving till today, but I—"

I cut him off. "Come on. I'll get my omni so you can show me how to synch it." Tears were threatening again and I didn't think I could hold them back much longer. I wanted to get this over with as quickly as possible, so I could be alone.

Leaving the others to follow me or not, I went into my bedroom and yanked open the drawer of my nightstand. The omni was near the back, behind my lip moisturizer and a packet of tissues, where it had been since the morning after I was Installed. The morning I'd received Rigel's final message.

I'd change that stupid password tomorrow, I decided. It was time to face up to the fact that the past was the past and couldn't be changed. Time to move forward. Maybe I'd use a Nuathan word this time, something with no connection to my old life on Earth at all…

Glancing down at the omni in my hand, I noticed the message indicator blinking.

"That's weird. I have a message, and it's from some name I don't even recognize. How did they get my code?"

"Play it," Molly suggested. "See what it is."

Shrugging, I punched up the message. And nearly dropped the omni when Rigel—*Rigel*—started talking.

"M, I really hope this gets to you." His voice was low, urgent. "I've been hoping for a chance to contact you, because I don't know what they've told you or are planning to tell you. Whatever it is, don't believe them. I'm sending this from an omni I swiped off a desk at this hospital place. I've been here for days now, ever since they brought me here for that memory extraction they made you agree to.

"They've apparently decided I'm some huge security risk because I know about the Grentl but they won't tell me what they plan to do about it. Maybe wipe my memory or even kill me, like they nearly did in Montana, I don't know.

"Since they won't want to piss you off, especially now that you're Sovereign, they might try to tell you this was all my idea or something like that, but it's not true! I love you, M, and would never, *ever* let them erase that from my life! I'm just worried they'll— Oh, crap, someone's coming. Gotta go. I'll try to—"

His voice cut off like he'd been interrupted—or caught.

Mouth open, I stared at the omni, my mind seething with questions…and sudden hope.

6

Total harmonic distortion

I whirled to face the others. "Did you hear that? How—? They must have *forced* him to record that horrible video message, must have drugged him or something."

"Then maybe he didn't really—" Molly began excitedly, when Sean interrupted her.

"Oh, crap. M, I'm really, really sorry. I've been thinking all along I should tell you, and I was *just* about to, I swear. You have to believe me!"

"Tell me what? That you really did know Rigel was still in Nuath, and that they were still doing awful things to him?"

"No! I wasn't lying about that. I had no idea he was still on Mars. But I did suspect something might be…off. I didn't say anything sooner because I wasn't sure, but now…"

"What, Sean? What did you suspect?"

He swallowed visibly. "That video message Rigel sent. Did you…I mean, do you still have it? It might be easier to show you than explain."

Though I'd kept meaning to erase it so I wouldn't be tempted to watch it again, I hadn't yet been able to bring myself to do it. "I still have it. But what—?"

"Play it." His voice was gruff, almost harsh.

Torn between hope and fear, remembering what that video had done to me the two times I'd already seen it, I called it up and hit play.

Rigel's face appeared and I sucked in another quick breath. No, even with the hope that unexpected omni message had given me, I really hadn't been ready for this.

"Hey, M." Rigel's face, his voice, were almost expressionless, just like I remembered. "You might want to sit down to listen to this."

I quickly looked up at Sean, to ask why he was making me do this, but his eyes were intent on the screen.

"I've had time to do a lot of thinking," Rigel continued woodenly, "and I've come to a decision. You're not going to like it, but I think it's the right thing to do. What we had together was wonderful, but I think we both knew it couldn't be forever. You hold a position now that requires you to make sacrifices and I need to be one of those sacrifices."

"There!" Sean exclaimed, pointing. "Did you notice that?"

Confused, I paused the video. "See what?"

"Back it up a little and play that last bit again." I did, and now Sean leaned in until he was nearly touching the screen. "There. Look when he says the word 'sacrifices' here, and here. It's *exactly* the same—inflection, expression, everything. And his mouth was just slightly out of synch with the words right before that, where he says 'position now that requires,' and then it's fixed again. Now keep watching.

I did, wincing to again hear Rigel tell me goodbye, that he was intentionally having all memory of me erased from his life. But a moment later, Sean told me to pause it again.

"This bit, too. Look, you can see a tiny jump in the image, from here—yeah—to there. I had to watch it three times that first day and I'm still not a hundred percent positive. Transmission glitches could have caused some of this stuff. But…I think this whole thing might be fake."

"Fake?" I swung around to stare at Rigel's paused image, my heart now pounding in hard, slow strokes. "How could—" I stopped, flashing back to my last day of school before leaving for Ireland, the answer suddenly, blindingly, obvious.

Trina had faked a picture on her phone that looked so much like I was having sex with some faceless guy, Rigel had been convinced it was Sean and Sean convinced it was Rigel. They'd been ready to kill each other and I'd nearly gotten expelled when I confronted Trina and she ended up with a broken nose. If Trina could do that with Photoshop, how much more convincing a fake could somebody like Gordon create using Nuathan technology? How could I have been so blind??

Looking at the omni I still held, I suddenly noticed the time stamp on the new message and gasped. "Rigel just sent this the day before yesterday—*after* that video was sent, so it *had* to be fake! No wonder Rigel didn't sound anything like himself in it. I figured it was because he felt so awful about what he was about to do, but if they cobbled it together from a bunch of clips, that would totally explain it. And you suspected from the very start?"

Glumly, Sean nodded.

Abruptly, I was furious again. "Why didn't you say something right away?" I practically shouted. "I would have had time to stop them! I was the freaking *Sovereign*. I could have *made* them do what I said!"

Sean stared at the floor, his face scarlet with well-deserved shame. "I almost did tell you, but time was so tight—you only had twenty-four hours to find the Grentl device and stop them from imploding all of Nuath. I was afraid if I said anything, you'd forget all about saving Nuath, you'd be so frantic to get to Rigel. I couldn't risk the whole colony on a hunch. And if I was wrong, well, it would have been awful to give you false hope when you were already so destroyed." He looked up, his blue eyes pleading for forgiveness.

Sean obviously thought those were good excuses, but to me they sounded lame. "You *knew* you weren't wrong. And now…it's too late. Rigel's really, truly gone. As of *this morning*. Why didn't you at least tell me once I'd stopped the power failure?"

At Sean's suddenly closed-off expression, I leaped to a guess. "Your dad? Did he have something to do with this? Would he really do that to Rigel? To me?"

"No way!" Molly protested, looking wildly from me to Sean. "I can totally believe that Gordon guy would do it. Maybe even Rigel's grandmother. But not Dad!"

Sean shrugged, still looking totally miserable. "I don't know. He definitely hasn't said anything to me about it. Maybe…maybe everything in that video was a lie? The memory wipe, the leaving, all of it? We can't *know*—"

"Not yet." Ruthlessly stifling the temptation to hope for that much, I channeled my fury at Sean into cold purpose. "But we will. Tomorrow I'm going to find out *exactly* what happened. And when. And who was involved. Bet on it."

When Mr. O and Sean showed up at my apartment for breakfast the next morning, I implemented the part of my plan I'd shared with Sean and Molly last night, and which they'd more or less agreed to.

As soon as we sat down, before Mr. O could say anything that might piss me off all over again, I said, "Since I have a few hours free, why don't we all go visit your daughter Elana? Sean and Molly were saying last night how much they want to see her and have me meet her."

Though he seemed startled by my suggestion, I didn't detect any suspicion. "Ah, I'd rather assumed… But I don't imagine an hour's delay will make much difference. I'd very much like to see her myself, and you'd no doubt appreciate a break from your duties."

"Thanks. And you're right, I would." Not that I intended this to be a break, since my main *duty* right now was to ferret out the truth about Rigel. The Grentl could wait.

As soon as we finished breakfast, we headed for Pryderi and the Mind Healing facility there. Even more than my recent meeting with Healer Adara, the squarish crystalline building with its deceptively soothing blue corridors reminded me forcefully of the last time I'd been here, the last time I'd seen Rigel, though he hadn't seen me…

Which also reminded me of the guilt and anxiety I'd sensed from Adara when I'd mentioned Rigel. If anyone knew the truth it was likely to be her—and I fully intended to get it out of her.

"Will Elana recognize us?" Molly asked worriedly as we approached her sister's room.

"I believe so," replied the Healer who'd been overseeing Elana's treatment, and who'd met us in the spacious lobby. "She's made excellent progress these past two weeks and is remembering more and more of her past life. It's her short-term memory that is the main issue now, as with so many of our patients who underwent similar abuses at Faxon's command."

A moment later he showed us into a nicely furnished and decorated room—the living room of what seemed to be a small apartment. A young redheaded woman I recognized from the O'Garas' pictures fairly flew out of a chair near a window to greet us, arms outstretched.

"Dad!" she exclaimed, wrapping Mr. O in a fierce hug that nearly brought tears to my eyes. "Nobody told me you were coming today. And Sean? Molly? How…? I never quite believed them when they said it's been over two years, but just look at you!" She released her father to hug each of them in turn.

"Oh, Elana, it's so wonderful to see you," Molly cried, hugging her sister back just as tightly. "I missed you so much! We just heard yesterday you were finally well enough for us to visit and we came as soon as we could."

"You're so grown up," Elana marveled, holding Molly at arm's length to take a good look at her. "And Sean, you've grown at least a foot! You're practically a giant! But where's Mum?"

Healer Bowyn spoke from the doorway. "Still on Earth, Elana, remember? She's on the *Echtran* Council there now, a very important job."

"She is? Oh, yes, you did tell me that, didn't you? Or did I see it on the feeds? I'm never quite—" Just then, Elana spotted me hovering in the hallway behind the Healer. "And who— Oh! Apologies, Excellency! I recognize you from the feeds, of course. Forgive me, do. I was so excited—"

"No, no, it's fine," I quickly assured her, feeling like an awkward intruder at such an emotional family reunion—which I now realized played right into my plan. "Um, why don't I let you all catch up privately? You must have tons you want to say to each other. Healer Bowyn can show me to the waiting area and I can watch the news or read or something."

All four O'Garas protested—Sean and Molly halfheartedly, since they knew this was part of my plan—but I insisted. Mr. O was so eager to spend time with his long-lost daughter, he finally agreed, too. I stepped back into the hallway where Cormac waited impassively and Healer Bowyn quietly closed Elana's door behind us.

"That was very thoughtful, Excellency. If you'll come this way?"

"Actually, I'd like you to take me to Head Mind Healer Adara. I need to speak with her about a matter of great urgency."

The Healer raised his eyebrows. "But you indicated—"

"I know. It was necessary. If we can please hurry?"

Though clearly confused, he didn't dare disobey what amounted to an order from his Sovereign. "Of course, Excellency. This way."

A few moments later, he rang the chime outside Healer Adara's office, though the door stood open. She looked up from her desk on the opposite side of the room, saw me…and blanched.

"Excellency!" She scrambled to her feet and bowed deeply. "This… this is a surprise. How may I help you?"

I turned to Healer Bowyn. "Thank you. I'll find my way back to Elana's room when I'm through. Cormac, please wait for me out here." Figuring I'd get more out of Adara if we were alone, I stepped into her office and closed the door.

"I have some questions I believe you may be able to answer."

Her anxiety was palpable even from across the room. "Questions, Excellency?"

"About Rigel Stuart. You already admitted having a hand in his memory erasure. I'd like to know every detail you can give me about what led up to that erasure—and exactly who was involved."

"I was…ah…"

"Sworn to secrecy?" I guessed. She nodded unhappily. "By whom? Maybe whoever forced you to be part of this plot had that authority then, but I'm pretty sure I outrank them now."

After hesitating for another long, tense moment, she let out a gusty sigh. "You're right, Excellency, of course. I have been exceedingly uncomfortable with the entire proceeding from the start, and it will be a relief to finally unburden myself about it."

"Please proceed." I seated myself regally across from her, more than a little amazed at my outward command given how my stomach was roiling with worry. Would the truth be even worse than what they'd made me believe?

Adara gave a decisive nod, though I noticed she didn't quite meet my gaze. "It began the day we all witnessed the memory extracted from Rigel Stuart revealing the existence of aliens with the potential to destroy us. When you left, the others remained—Nels Murdoch, Quinn O'Gara, Devyn Kane, Gordon Nolan and Morag Teague. For over an hour they debated what should be done and finally agreed upon the course we followed from that point until the present. I did argue against it, Excellency, on both medical and ethical grounds, but Quinn insisted he was empowered to act on your behalf. Eventually he and the others persuaded me that the possible risks to Nuath—and to your eventual rule—were great enough to outweigh my concerns."

"And exactly what *was* the course they agreed on?" I felt like leaping over the desk to shake the rest of the story out of her, though I was also terrified of what her next words might be.

"They…we…decided the safest thing would be to erase all knowledge of the aliens—and all memory of his association with you—from Rigel Stuart's mind. His grandmother was particularly emphatic about the latter." Now she did glance at me, her expression sympathetic.

"So his memory really was wiped." I twisted my hands together in my lap. "Just the last year, or…all of it?"

"Oh, just the last year, of course. Certainly he'd done nothing to justify the *tabula rasa.* But even a year, especially at his age…" She shook her head regretfully. "Before that was done, Quinn, Devyn and Gordon had us extract additional memories from him, in order to learn as much as possible and so that a few memories might be given…special treatment. Nels Murdoch and Rigel's grandmother had left by then, so were not part of that discussion, though it's possible they were later told."

No worse than I'd thought, but no better either. "And he left aboard the *Luminosity* yesterday? With Gordon?"

Adara nodded sadly. "Yes. Gordon was to oversee things at the other end. Though he may well have left for other reasons of his own, as well."

Like escaping my wrath once I learned the truth? At least the other traitors were still here in Nuath, where I could deal with them.

"So how was all this explained to Rigel? What was he told, once his memory was erased?"

"Nothing, at least at this end. It was thought best that he be unconscious for the journey to Earth, so he was put into a medically-induced coma immediately after the erasure. His overall health should not be at risk," she added quickly, at my horrified gasp.

"A coma?" I echoed faintly. "Are you sure—?"

"Even *Echtran* Healers should have no difficulty reviving him on his arrival, Excellency, and one of our own accompanied him on the ship."

Along with Gordon, who I didn't trust an inch. "What about that fake message they created to deceive me? Whose idea was that?" That had been the lowest blow of all, making me believe Rigel did all this willingly.

Adara looked genuinely confused. "Message? I was told nothing about a message, Excellency, though I did see Morag Teague's public statement, claiming that Rigel acted of his own accord. Quinn stressed it was important you believe that, and Devyn and Gordon spent a fair amount of time alone with Rigel the first two days he was here, but I was never told what they talked to him about."

That must be when they'd obtained the footage to put together that video I'd been sent. But why had they sent it so soon, risking me finding out the *Luminosity* hadn't even left yet?

Because I'd demanded Rigel be brought to the Palace, I realized. Mr. O discovered I'd done that the evening I was Installed and I'd received that message the very next morning. Almost certainly *not* a coincidence!

Again I cursed myself for not being more suspicious from the start. But I didn't have time now to beat myself up—not when there was so much I still needed to know. "What's the plan for when Rigel gets to Earth? Did they say?"

She shook her head. "Not to me, other than a mention of you never encountering him again. I'd guess they intend him to live somewhere far removed from any place you might visit, should you ever return to Earth for any reason."

Oh, I was going to return, all right! On the very next ship, if I could.

"The other day, you reported a lot of progress in restoring erased memories. I've seen some of the evidence myself." I tried not to think about how messed up some of those people still were. "Can you send me all the details on how you've managed that?"

Now her expression was so pitying it scared me. "Excellency, I'm sure you'd like to think Rigel's memory can be put back just as it was, but that is extremely unlikely. Certainly, it's not as simple as informing him of everything he's forgotten. In fact, we've found that method to be rather dangerous to a patient's mental state, occasionally leading to a psychotic break, as their perceived reality is so at odds with what they're being told. This is even more likely in Rigel's case, as actual blocks were put in place to prevent him remembering particular events."

"Blocks?"

"Yes. It's a procedure we occasionally use when a person has undergone extreme trauma and wishes to have a particular memory permanently removed. The odds of accessing a memory that has been blocked in such a way are extremely remote, I'm afraid."

"What kind of blocks? What did you do?"

"Normally, the traumatic memory is overlaid by a different, innocuous one, created for that purpose. There was not time in Rigel's case to create completely new memories, so actual prior memories were used instead. Memories that were deemed not to be, ah, sensitive in any way."

Obviously, anything to do with the Grentl would be considered "sensitive." But did that also mean memories about the special relationship Rigel and I had, like our *graell* bond? Probably. At least they hadn't stuck in fake memories of him hating me or something. One tiny thing I could be grateful for.

"I'd still like you to send me whatever information you have on possible treatments, no matter how unlikely you think they are to work." Maybe, if Rigel and I re-bonded…

"Of course. I can send you my files on what has worked best in typical cases, though I'm afraid much of it may not apply to Rigel's situation—even if you should find a Healer on Earth able or willing to attempt it."

"Thank you." I stood. "You've been very helpful, Healer Adara. I'll make certain you suffer no repercussions from those who would have preferred you to keep the truth from me."

She stood as well, then bowed deeply. "I am ever at your service, Excellency, and apologize again for the part I played in this deception. Please believe that my allegiance is wholeheartedly yours."

I thanked her again and left, my mind working furiously—in both senses of the word—to figure out what my next step should be.

7

Protection relay

THOUGH my first instinct was to march straight back to Elana's room to ream Mr. O for his duplicity, I realized in time how awful that would be for the others. Better to go to the waiting room, like he thought I had. I'd wait for him there…and plan my attack.

Back outside the office, I frowned uncertainly at Cormac. Healer Bowyn was gone, and without him I didn't know where to go. Maybe this building had a directional system like the Royal Palace's?

"Visitor waiting area," I said clearly. Sure enough, a blue line immediately appeared on the floor, which soon led me to a soothing blue room with cushy chairs. I'd barely sat down when Sean appeared in the doorway.

"Um, Excellency?" He glanced warily at the handful of other people scattered around the room. "Do you want to come meet Elana properly now? She'd like to, so Dad sent me to get you."

I nodded and got up. Planning would have to wait.

"So? Did you find out what happened?" he whispered as soon as we were alone.

"Yep, and you and Molly aren't going to like it. Neither will your dad, when I get through with him."

Sean glanced down at me in alarm. "You're not going to accuse him in front of Elana, are you?"

"No, though waiting won't be easy." I didn't respond further to his questioning look, just worked, hard, to rein in the fury still seething inside me.

Molly and Mr. O'Gara were sitting on either side of Elana when we reached her room. Though they were both smiling, I sensed sadness, too, that Elana was still clearly far from her normal self. No, I wouldn't unleash my anger on Mr. O just yet. Soon, though…

"I'm glad to finally meet you, Elana." I pasted a smile on my face. "Sean and Molly have told me so much about you."

Elana immediately jumped to her feet and bowed. "Excellency! I'm very happy to meet you, too. Molly has been telling me what good friends you two have become, and I know Sean always—that is—"

She glanced uncertainly at Sean. "I mean, it's wonderful those rumors we believed all those years turned out not to be true."

My smile came closer to being real. "Thank you. I look forward to becoming friends with you, too." Not that I planned to stay on Mars long enough for that to happen anytime soon.

With a regretful look at his oldest daughter, Mr. O stood. "We really must be going, Elana. The Sovereign has duties to attend to. But I'm sure we'll be back to see you soon, and Healer Bowyn says you may be able to join us at the Palace in a month or so, at the rate you're improving."

"The Palace?" Elana looked blank for a moment, then smiled. "Oh, are you living at the Palace now? That must be lovely!"

Molly's strained expression implied they'd already told her that—maybe more than once—but she quickly hid her distress with a smile. "You'll love it there, Elana, just wait! And we'll come back soon, okay?"

They all hugged again, then we joined Cormac in the hall to head back to the Palace. Now? Should I say something to Mr. O now? But there were Healers and aides within earshot and I had a feeling once I started, things might escalate into a major scene. Better to wait for someplace a little more private.

The moment we were all in the hover-limo, I took a deep breath and turned to face Mr. O.

But before I could say anything, Molly let out a sob. "Oh, poor Elana! Did you see how thin she is? And how she kept spacing out? I mean, they told us to expect that, but still…"

Sean shot me a warning glance as he put an arm around her shoulders. "Hey, they said she's getting better all the time. But yeah, it's hard to see her like this. I can't even imagine what she must have been like at first."

Mr. O nodded sadly. "It's possible she may never be what she was before. But she was clearly happy to see us, so we'll try to spend as much time with her as our schedules—and her Healers—will allow." If it weren't for what he'd done to Rigel—and me—I might almost have felt sorry for him.

Impatient as I was to lambast Mr. O for his perfidy, I couldn't quite bring myself to do it while they were all still so emotional about Elana and her condition. Staring out the window as Cormac drove us back to Thiaraway, I went over everything Healer Adara had told me, fitting together more pieces of the puzzle and getting madder and madder. By the time we reached the Palace, I was ready to explode.

Sean must have sensed that, because he put a hand on my arm as we were getting out of the limo. "Not yet," he murmured so softly the others couldn't hear. "I need to talk to you first."

I sent him an angry glance, ready to argue, but the urgency in his blue eyes made me hesitate. "Better be soon, then," I muttered. Not trusting myself to even look at Mr. O, I headed straight for the Royal wing, walking so quickly Molly had to trot to keep up.

"Are you okay?" she asked as I palmed open the ornate double doors of my apartment.

"No." I glanced over my shoulder and saw Sean and Cormac, but not Mr. O.

As soon as we were inside, Sean confirmed that was his doing. "I told Dad that Molly and I needed a little more time. So? What did you find out? You're obviously pretty pissed at Dad."

I gave a humorless laugh. "You might say that. Turns out the whole thing was his idea."

Molly's gray eyes went wide and horrified. "What? Are you sure? What did Dad do?"

"Conspired with Devyn, Nels, Gordon and Morag Teague to have Rigel's memory wiped and to pretend it was all Rigel's idea. This was before I was even Acclaimed, right after that memory extraction. Then he bullied Healer Adara into going along with it and swore her to secrecy. Rigel is on his way to Earth in a *coma* right now! And when he wakes up he won't remember me, or Jewel or anything. They even put *extra* blocks on his memories of me so they can't be restored." A tear escaped from the corner of my eye to trickle down the side of my face.

Though Molly looked stricken, still not wanting to believe, Sean's expression hardened. "I was afraid that was it. The way Dad acted after I told him about that video… But why take the risk of you figuring out the truth by sending it so soon, when Rigel wasn't even off-planet yet?"

"Because I ordered Rigel's grandmother to bring him to the Palace. Remember? Your dad saw Morag Teague's message promising she'd have him here by noon the next day, and he definitely wasn't happy.

And the very next morning I got that fake video. He must have called Devyn or Gordon and told them to send it right away. Maybe if they'd had more time, they'd have been able to make it even *more* realistic, who knows?"

Sean's mouth compressed into a grim line. "No wonder Dad's been keeping you so crazy busy these past few days. He was probably afraid you'd find out the *Luminosity* hadn't left yet or pick up on other clues if you had time to think it through and go digging."

"Yeah, he claimed it was to keep my mind off of Rigel." I snorted. "Which was true, just not the way I thought." Bile rose into my throat again at the depth of Mr. O's duplicity. "He might have kept me from finding out the truth until it was too late to stop them, but I can still make them pay for what they did. And then I'm going after Rigel, no matter what they say!" I headed for the vidscreen, to summon Mr. O to face my wrath.

"Wait, M." Sean spoke urgently. "Think. What's the most important thing?"

"Getting back to Earth. Getting to Rigel. Doing whatever I can to…to fix what they did to him!"

"Is it really? What about the Grentl coming? What do you think Dad and the others will do if you announce you're leaving, while that's still hanging over everyone's heads?"

I glared at him, my hand on the vid control. "They won't be in any position to do anything! I'm the Sovereign. I can have them all locked up for…for treason or something."

"Without a trial or anything? Think who you're dealing with—Nels Murdoch, who was Interim Governor until last week, Devyn, who was your main rival for leadership of Nuath, and my dad, who's generally regarded as a hero, who's always been known for putting the good of Nuath ahead of everything else."

"Do you really think *this* was for the good of Nuath? Why should I even listen to you?" I flared, my rage at Mr. O—and myself—spilling over onto Sean now. "You had a chance to stop this, remember? You *knew* that video was fake and never said a word!"

"And I'm really sorry, okay? *Super* sorry." His blue eyes blazed into mine. "I swear I'm not making excuses for my dad, because there aren't any. He screwed up big time. I saw what that video did to you. If you hadn't been able to pull yourself together to contact the

Grentl, a quarter of a million people would be dead now and it would be his fault."

"Then why—?"

"Stop and think for a minute, M! If you're not careful, you could make things even worse for Rigel and maybe for you, too. What's to keep them from sending word ahead so Rigel never wakes up from that coma, huh? Or banding together to have you declared incompetent or unbalanced or something. You haven't named a Regent yet, so it wouldn't be hard for them to convince the people one of them should take over, at least until the Healers can 'evaluate' you."

I stared at him, breathing hard, as his urgency finally penetrated my anger. "But..." I looked over at Molly, who now had tears running down her cheeks. "What do you think I should do? I can't just let them...let them..."

"No, you can't. You won't. *We* won't. But we need a plan."

He was right, much as I didn't want to admit it. My first priority had to be protecting Rigel until I could get to him. "In that fake video, Rigel said he was bringing along a letter asking his parents to move away from Jewel, but who knows what it really says? Maybe orders for them to go into hiding or worse. I need to send a message right away, before Rigel gets to Earth. And I know just who to send it to!"

There was only one person on Earth I could think of who was both influential enough and trustworthy enough to help me. Turning back to the vidscreen, I opened the secure channel Leontine had shown me how to create. "Message to Shim Stuart, Earth, highest security setting."

Once I'd sent my message to Shim explaining everything that had happened and begging him to keep Rigel safe in Jewel until I could get there, I felt a little better. If anyone could protect Rigel, Shim could.

For good measure, I also sent a secure message to Rigel's parents, telling them that no matter what that letter or anyone else said, under no circumstances were they or Rigel to move away from Jewel before I got there, adding that Shim could give them the details.

When I was done, I faced Sean again. "Now, how do I get to Earth myself? Your dad probably *can* convince all the ship captains not to take me, just like he said. Maybe if I play up the Grentl threat, convince them all that we need to get as many people off Mars as possible during this launch window—including me? It's not like we know what the Grentl are planning yet."

"Dad will say that's all the more reason for you to stay in Nuath, so you can deal with them. Since nobody else can," Sean pointed out.

"Yeah, well, it's not like I've had a *chance* to 'deal with them' yet, your dad has been keeping me so busy. Maybe he hasn't only been afraid of what I'd learn about Rigel? Doesn't it strike you as weird he's been so focused on all this government stuff, considering the possible threat from the Grentl hanging over us?"

Sean grimaced. "Dad's been all about getting Faxon out and rebuilding Nuath's government for as long as I can remember. It's what kept him going all those years we had to pretend to be Ags, taking all the crap Faxon's supporters dished out, watching our Royal friends get dragged off. Now he's finally in a position to do what he's always wanted to."

"Maybe if I have him arrested before he can get word out—"

Molly gasped and I turned to look at her. "I'm sorry, Molly. But I need to know, right now, if you're with me or against me. Are you going to warn your dad about this?"

Though her lower lip quivered, she shook her head. "No. I still can't believe he'd do something like this, but… Even if he thought he was acting for the best, it wasn't right. Doing that to Rigel, then lying to you about it? No. I'm on your side, M. I promise. But…I really don't want you to hurt my dad."

Rather than make a promise I wasn't necessarily willing to keep, I just said, "Thanks, Molly. I know this is really hard for you, and I'm sorry. You never deserved to be put in this kind of position."

She managed a tremulous smile. "Neither did you. What are you going to do next?"

Unfortunately, I wasn't sure what my best, safest course would be —for Rigel *or* for me. I desperately needed advice, but the person I'd relied on most was Mr. O—the *last* one I could trust now. And while Sean *might* have my best interests at heart, Mr. O was his father. Besides, Sean didn't have enough experience to—

Of course! The answer was so obvious, I nearly slapped myself in the forehead.

"I need some time alone to think. Sean, tell your dad I'm doing, um, Grentl stuff. It's probably better if I don't see him again for a little while, know what I mean?"

"Yeah. It won't be easy for me to act normal around him, either, but maybe I can find out more without tipping him off." With one last, searching look that broadcast both worry for me and anger at his dad, Sean left.

"I'll be in my room," I told Molly. "Why don't you…I don't know, watch a movie or something? Get your mind off things for a while."

Her smile was halfhearted, but she nodded. "I'll try."

Shutting myself in my room, I quickly retrieved my Scepter. "*Chartlann rochtana.*"

A second later, my grandfather, Leontine, stood before me. "Emileia. You have more questions?"

"I do—but they're kind of tricky ones. There are people, um, close to me that I can no longer trust. But they're pretty powerful in Nuath. Together, they probably have more influence than I do, and they definitely have lots more experience. Before I found out how they betrayed me, they were the people I was mainly relying on for advice. Now…I need yours."

"Of course." His holographic brow creased in apparent concern. "Do you believe yourself to be in danger from them?"

I bit my lip, considering. "Maybe not physical danger, but I'm worried if I confront them, expose what they've done, they might—I don't know, stage a coup or have me declared unfit or incompetent or something. And there *is* someone else they might hurt if I'm not careful."

"I see. Are you aware of the various Palace security measures available to the Sovereign? All can be accessed from here, without anyone else the wiser. Only twice in Nuathan history have they been necessary, but they were put in place for just such an eventuality, should allies become enemies."

"Then…why didn't they work against Faxon?" I couldn't help asking.

Leontine looked thoughtful, which I'd realized by now meant he was searching the Archive. "It appears I did not have enough warning to put the measures into place. I have no record of what happened after my final Archive entry, but based on the tenor of Nuathan politics at the time, I would guess that I was either assassinated in some public place, outside the Palace, or by a Palace insider I'd had no reason to suspect and therefore guard myself against."

Hearing him mention his own murder so calmly weirded me out, but his theory made sense. I at least had the advantage of *knowing* who my enemies were. "Okay, what do I do? How can I keep them from sending word to Earth to hurt my…my friend, or from somehow rendering me powerless?"

"The simplest and most logical solution is to confine them all to the Palace itself and restrict their communications. That should limit their ability to act against you in any significant way. In addition, I recommend you enable your personal fail-safe security system, should it transpire that you are physically threatened after all."

"What's that?"

"It was put in place during Sovereign Tiernan's time, when an ambitious member of his Advisory Council turned against him and sought power of his own. When the system is active, a trigger word spoken anywhere inside the Palace proper will immediately create a stasis field within a twenty foot radius of your person."

He proceeded to show me how to activate that system, then walked me through setting up my trigger word, which would only work with my own voice imprint. Since it needed to be a word I wouldn't use accidentally, I went with "arboretum," a place with even more happy Rigel memories than the cornfield.

Once that was done, Leontine explained how, once I had all my traitors here in the Palace, I could keep them from sending messages to Earth or even elsewhere in Nuath. After another half-hour's conversation with my grandfather, I felt satisfied I'd covered every base I could think of.

"Thank you. I can't tell you how awesome it is to have you right here for advice like this when I need it."

Leontine's smile was fatherly—or, I guess, grandfatherly. "It is my pleasure, Emileia, and indeed my very purpose. Should you ever need advice of a more personal nature, I hope you will not hesitate to seek it from my mother, Aerleas. She was justly revered for her great wisdom in matters of both state and of the heart."

Even though I knew he was a recorded hologram, I felt myself blushing. Apparently Leontine had figured out more from me than I'd realized. "That's, um, really good to know. I'll remember that. Talk to you soon, okay?"

At his nod, I deactivated the Archive. Shaking off the pang I always felt when my grandfather's image vanished, I stowed the Scepter back in its cubby, already planning my next move.

8

Reactive power

I emerged from my bedroom to find Molly watching some gardening show on the main vidscreen.

"Molly, do you mind pausing that? I have a call to make."

Though she was clearly curious, she immediately complied. I didn't take time to explain, not wanting to lose the tiniest bit of my resolve. Instead, I brought up the call function and punched up the contacts for Mr. O, Devyn and Nels. I considered including Morag Teague but decided against it. Not only wasn't she a particular threat, but she'd already ensured her own punishment by irrevocably alienating her only family.

"I'd like you all to meet me at the Palace in Conference Room Three at one o'clock. It's extremely important. Thank you." I hit "send," then turned to Molly. "That gives us half an hour to grab some lunch."

She opened and closed her mouth a couple of times, her eyes wide with worry. "But…what was that about? What are you going to do?"

"You said you were with me, right? I'm not planning to hurt your dad, if that's what you're worried about, but I'm also not going to let him or the others hurt Rigel any more than they already have. Or me, either. Just trust me, okay?"

Swallowing, she nodded. "Of course. Forgive me. I should never have questioned—"

"No, Molly, it's fine. Don't go all formal on me. I'll explain everything later, to you and to Sean. So, lunch? Just a sandwich for me. And some tea."

Looking only slightly relieved, she hurried to the recombinator and a moment later I was scarfing down a turkey and swiss sandwich while I continued to compose a script in my head for the coming confrontation.

The vidscreen pinged three times while we ate, each one a confirmation from the three men I'd summoned. None asked for details, which was good, since I had no intention of sharing any ahead of time.

At three minutes till one, I left for the conference room, telling Molly she could finish watching her show. Cormac, of course, came with me. "I doubt it will be necessary, but I'd like you to, um, stay alert during this meeting," I told him as we walked. "Just in case."

"Always, Excellency." His voice was impersonally professional, but I could sense his curiosity, nearly equal to Molly's earlier.

All three men were already waiting in Conference Room Three when I arrived. They rose and bowed to me in unison, their expressions eager. Mr. O spoke first.

"Well? Have you learned more about the Grentl and their intentions? Sean told me—"

"Sean told you what I asked him to tell you. But that's not why I've summoned you all here." With a glance at Cormac, who had his back to the only door, I said clearly, "Security setting alpha."

Nels and Devyn exchanged a startled glance and Mr. O'Gara frowned. "How did you—? I mean, why did you feel that was necessary?"

"Just a precaution." I smiled, but it probably wasn't a very reassuring smile. "I know what you three—and Gordon and Morag Teague—did to Rigel, and that the message he supposedly sent me was fake. Since you've all demonstrated your willingness to ignore Nuathan law and ethics, as well as your loyalty to me, in pursuit of your own ends, I'm not taking any chances."

"What?" Nels exclaimed. "Who—? I had nothing to do with any false messages, Excellency, I assure you."

I pinned him with a glare. "But did you agree that Rigel's memory should be erased and that I should be told he did it voluntarily?"

He shifted uneasily from foot to foot. "I was, er, persuaded that course would be best—safest—for Nuath. But beyond that one discussion, I wasn't involved in any of the particulars."

"What we did *was* for the good of Nuath," Devyn declared, standing shoulder to shoulder with Mr. O now. "Quinn pointed out that it was by far the safest thing to do, for all concerned, and I—all of us—concurred. Once you told young Stuart about the Grentl, it was the only possible course open to us."

"Yes, Excellency, do try to look at this rationally." Mr. O'Gara put on the fatherly expression he'd used so often with me—and which I'd always believed sincere. "I know you must be terribly upset, but we had the welfare of all Nuathans to consider."

"Don't talk to me about 'welfare' or 'best courses,'" I snapped. "You stole a year of an innocent boy's life and then *lied* to me about it! I don't believe you even considered any other course before deciding this one was 'best.' It may have been the most *convenient*, especially for you, but no way was it *best*. After watching that memory extraction, you had to know full well Rigel wasn't going to tell anyone about the Grentl. This was about getting him away from *me*, permanently. Wasn't it?" I directed that question at Mr. O but he refused to flinch.

"I won't deny that was a consideration, Excellency. Your maintaining any sort of relationship with Rigel Stuart had the potential to undermine your authority as Sovereign, just as it interfered with your Acclamation. The people of Nuath—"

"Oh, spare me your lofty speeches! You were scared. Scared of what the Grentl would do if I didn't stop them, scared that Rigel might somehow distract me from that, scared that if he and I were together it would mess with all your sacred Royal traditions that say I'm supposed to be with Sean. Scared that once I was Sovereign you wouldn't be *able* to keep us apart anymore. Why else would you erase every memory he ever had of *me*, not just of the Grentl? And why else would you have had Devyn and Gordon create that awful video to convince me it was all Rigel's idea, then go on about how noble it was?"

Devyn made a gesture of protest. "I believed and still believe that what Quinn proposed was indeed noble. It allowed you to do what was necessary to prevent the destruction of Nuath while at the same time removing a potentially serious security risk."

"It wasn't *noble*." I spat the word. "It was *evil*. Rigel is a sixteen-year-old boy who'd committed no crime, yet you wiped his memory and exiled him to Earth without any kind of trial, without even telling him—or me—what you planned to do! Even violent criminals have more rights than that under Nuathan law. What you did to Rigel," I said directly to Mr. O, "was exactly what Faxon did to your daughter Elana. He probably insisted he was acting for the good of Nuath, too."

Mr. O'Gara opened his mouth, no doubt to issue a denial, then closed it again, the color slowly draining from his face. For the first time, I sensed uncertainty from him, perhaps even a tinge of horror, as he absorbed the parallel—one he'd apparently missed until this moment.

The others seemed not to notice.

"What…what do you plan to do?" Nels's voice shook noticeably, while Devyn still appeared completely unapologetic.

Standing a little straighter, I lifted my chin and looked each of them directly in the eye. "None of you will leave the Palace until such time as I see fit to allow it. You can arrange to have personal items brought here for your comfort, but no unscreened messages will be sent to anyone in Nuath or on Earth. And you will assist me in getting to Earth myself, on the very next ship, if possible."

"This is absurd, Excellency," Devyn immediately protested. "You can't possibly mean to keep us all prisoner here. And how will a proper government be restored if you abandon Nuath with no alternate leadership in place?"

"Not to mention the issue of the Grentl," Nels added, looking positively scared now. "Remember, they said they're coming and we still don't know when, or what they plan to do when they get here, or…or anything. And you're the only one who can find that out or maybe stop them, like you did before. Please! You can't just—"

"Calm down, Nels," Devyn advised him. "Of course she can't. Excellency, I find it hard to believe that you would abandon your own people to possible anarchy and the threat of annihilation by the Grentl, simply to rejoin your boyfriend. Surely the Sovereign line is made of sterner stuff than that?"

Oh, he was good, all right! No wonder he'd come so close to being elected leader of Nuath. And, unfortunately, he made a valid point. One I'd managed to ignore in my desperation to get to Rigel at all costs.

"The Sovereign line does not ignore its obligations, nor does it practice deceit. While I made a promise to Rigel that I intend to keep, I am also fully aware of my duty to the people of Nuath. I will of course do what I can to deal with the Grentl before I leave, though I can't guarantee I'll be able to deter them. I will also appoint a Regent, though obviously it won't be any of you. My Regent needs to be someone I can trust."

At that, both Devyn and Mr. O winced. About time.

"Excellency, not even the Sovereign has the authority to imprison anyone without due process." Mr. O was clearly striving for a reasonable tone, but I could hear the strain in his voice. "I understand that you're upset right now, but—"

"Due process?" I echoed. "Like the due process you gave Rigel?"

He swallowed visibly.

"Sure, I could follow Nuathan law to the letter for a situation like this." Luckily, I'd memorized every single statute last year. "That would mean a public trial for all three of you, to include media representatives. Do you really want to explain what you did, and why, to everyone on Mars? I thought the whole point was to keep them from finding out about the Grentl."

Their expressions showed they hadn't had time to think of that particular ramification. I smiled—a real smile this time.

"Consider yourselves my guests. No one will think it strange that the Sovereign wants her most important advisors close by during this 'difficult time of rebuilding our government, our infrastructure, and our very society.'" I quoted the same words Devyn had used at the beginning of his campaign against me. "Nels, Devyn, someone from the Palace housekeeping staff will be here shortly to show you to your new quarters. Now, gentlemen, if you will excuse me?"

I inclined my head regally and swept out of the room.

Not until I was in the thankfully deserted hallway did I let out a sigh of relief. While that confrontation had been immensely rewarding, it had also gotten dicey there at the end, forcing me to make promises I didn't want to make. As the tension seeped out of me, I felt wrung out.

"What do you think, Cormac?" I asked my Bodyguard as we headed back to the Royal wing. Behind me, I heard raised voices as the three men argued among themselves, probably pointing fingers. "Did I go too far?"

"On the contrary, Excellency." I was startled by the deep respect in Cormac's voice. "For several moments there, I could have sworn it was Sovereign Leontine himself in that room instead of his granddaughter. You handled them just as a ruler should. Though they may not say so, I guarantee they all respect you far more than they did before, and deservedly so."

Gratified and incredibly touched, I glanced back at him with a misty smile. "Thank you Cormac. That means more to me than you know, given your long association with my father and grandfather. Please don't think the reason I want Rigel back is because I'm not happy having you as my Bodyguard."

"I quite understand that, Excellency." His words were accompanied by a rare smile of his own.

Back in my apartment, I headed straight for my bedroom, again assuring Molly I'd explain later. The sooner I fulfilled the two promises I'd made to those three traitors, the sooner I could join Rigel on Earth. Retrieving my Scepter from the closet, I activated the Grentl Archive.

Using the colony databases my grandfather Leontine had shown me from the main Archive, and with this version's help, I put together a detailed report for the Grentl. He again advised against including any mention of Earth, though I was pretty sure that cat was already out of the bag. Surely, that was more Faxon's fault than mine? I hoped. It would be beyond awful if almost the first thing I'd done as Sovereign was precipitate a Grentl attack.

"Power reserves have fallen dramatically since my last report," Leontine commented, displaying the two figures side by side. "Far more than between that report and the previous one, thirty-four years earlier."

He was right. I pulled up that number for all the previous reports and saw that while power had slowly but steadily declined over time, maybe since the very start of the colony, the drop was far greater over the past forty-six years.

Curious, I searched a few other databases and discovered that the precipitous drain had occurred during Faxon's tenure. Not only had he or his people introduced inefficiencies into all sorts of systems, from transportation to agriculture, but whatever secret military stuff he was doing—those particular files were missing—had also used an enormous amount of power.

To my inexperienced eye, it looked like Nuath's century or so of continued existence might now have been cut to barely half that. Assuming, of course, that the Grentl didn't plan to wipe us out even sooner.

Finalizing the report took nearly two hours. It would have gone faster if I hadn't had to keep switching out the Archives. The version of Leontine in the main Archive was the most helpful by far, but he had to keep censoring himself to avoid any direct mention of the Grentl.

"I guess I understand the security reasons behind this," I said when it happened for the fourth time, "but it seems kind of silly. I mean, nobody but a Sovereign can access either Archive, right?"

"Not as far as we know," he agreed. "But there is always a risk of… hacking, I believe is the modern English word? It seemed a sensible precaution when my mother set up the system."

"I suppose," I said, thinking of Faxon. "Anyway, can you show me how to store my report on a data chip? And how to make it work once I, um, get where I need to go?" I didn't use the G word, since it made this version of Leontine clam up.

"There should be empty data chips in the small drawer to the right of your vidscreen." There were. "This process is quite simple. As for the other, can you not ask one of the Engineers to accompany you?"

I shook my head. "There aren't any. Eric Eagan was the last, and he died right after showing me…how to do what I needed to do."

"Eric? In my time, he was by far the oldest of those with that knowledge. I did not expect him to outlive me—though apparently my demise was no more natural than that of your parents." He was *so* much more like a real person than his image in the other Archive.

His comment reminded me that at some point I'd need to sit down and add my own short history to the Archive. Not only would it be useful for later Sovereigns—still a weird thought—but it might help my grandfather, or any other Sovereigns I might consult, to advise me better going forward. I didn't have time now, though.

"So, the data chip?" I held one up.

"Yes, of course. There is a slot halfway down the Scepter, between the two green stones. Insert it there and give the command to copy the most recent report. I'm sure I need not caution you not to leave the chip lying around. I recommend you erase it after you are finished."

Swapping out the stones again, I did as he told me, then swapped them back, my report now in digital form, in my pocket. "Oh, how do I use the data chip…downstairs?" I asked my grandfather.

"With no Engineer to show you, all I can say is that it works much the same way, in reverse. Look to the lower left for the slot."

That was more detail than I'd expected him to give me, given his reticence about the Grentl. I hoped it would be enough.

"Thank you…Grandfather."

He smiled down at me with an incredible illusion of genuine fondness. "You are most welcome, my dear. Good luck. Until we speak again."

I nodded, a lump in my throat, and deactivated the Archive.

9

Termination discharge

RETURNING to the living room, I messaged Sean to join us so I could bring him and Molly up to speed at the same time. Less than a minute later he arrived, slightly breathless, while Molly was nearly bouncing with impatience to hear what I had to say.

"Did you confront my dad after all?" Sean was clearly anxious. "Even after what I said? I heard your message telling him to meet you. He hasn't been back to our apartment since."

"I did—and Devyn and Nels, too—but don't worry. I took some precautions first that I hope will keep them from retaliating against Rigel or me."

His eyebrows went up. "Precautions?"

"Turns out the Palace is equipped with some pretty cool security features only the Sovereign can use—which I did. Now none of them can leave or call out. Unfortunately, that probably means I'll be seeing more of them until I can arrange to get myself on a ship to Earth."

"They'll let you do that?" Molly looked totally boggled. "Did they say so?"

"No, but they can't really stop me. I did promise to name a Regent first, and to try and deal with the Grentl. Which I'd planned to do today anyway."

Determined to get that task out of the way as soon as possible, I headed toward my office and the secret elevator that would take me down to the room with their communication device.

"What? Right now?" Clearly alarmed, Sean stepped in front of me. "Remember what that thing did to you last time?"

As if I could forget. "It's the only way to find out what their intentions really are—assuming they'll tell me, which they might not."

"Can I come this time?" Molly surprised me by asking. "I haven't seen it yet."

"Sure, we can all go." Why now? But no matter what I learned from the Grentl this time, even if it was nothing at all, I'd find a way to spin it so I could get back to Earth—and Rigel—as soon as possible.

I palmed open the hidden elevator and we all squeezed inside for the brief trip to the sub-basement. Molly, Sean and Cormac followed me through the warehouse-maze, where I used my palm again to make the wall disappear so we could go inside the secret room.

"Whoa. Is that…it?" Molly asked, pointing at the Grentl device on the far side.

I was heartened to see some of the sparkle back in her eyes as she took in her surroundings. Even if the Grentl didn't answer, it was worth bringing her down here for the distraction it was giving her from her distress over her sister's condition and her father's perfidy.

The communication device was still inert—as I'd expected, since the signal crystal in my office hadn't turned blue. Now that I knew to look for it, I easily found the slot Leontine had described on the lower left-hand side of the cube.

"You guys stay back, okay? Just in case." I was thinking of what the device had done to Faxon and those early Linguists, back in Aerleas's time. No point risking the others getting caught in any backlash if they decided to zap me for my effrontery.

Figuring I should "wake up" the device before sending my report, I positioned myself in front of it and stretched out my hands, one over each of the two projections. Steeling myself, I took one breath, two breaths, then on three I grasped the prongs simultaneously, as Eric had shown me just two hours before he'd died.

For maybe a dozen heartbeats, nothing happened. Then, slowly, the projections warmed in my hands. Once I was sure I was feeling more than just the heat of my own sweating palms, I reached out with my mind. Not with words, like I'd done last time, but more like the way I used to try to pick up Rigel's thoughts when he was right at the limit of our telepathic ability. Searching. Listening, like Aerleas had said.

At first all I received were vague impressions of space, with formless shapes moving around me. Then I caught snippets of incredibly complex thoughts flitting through that space. Suddenly the prongs sent a tingling series of impulses through me and I sensed a definite presence—like they'd suddenly noticed me trying to eavesdrop.

I sharpened my focus, "listening" harder, trying to keep the information flowing my way so I could learn enough to make a guess at their intentions. But they were stronger than I was. Before I could even attempt to block them, they started sucking memories out of me again, picking up where they'd left off four days ago, when I'd suddenly let go of the device.

Again I experienced Rigel's terrible video message but this time, knowing it was fake, it didn't have nearly the same impact on me. Instead of letting go, I hung on tighter as they replayed my shock at hearing I wasn't expected to leave Mars, my excitement at "meeting" two of my ancestors, my learning the stunning truth about Rigel and, finally, today's confrontation with Mr. O and the others.

My turn, I decided, when the brief flood of images and emotions ceased. Reaching out with my mind again, just like I would with Rigel, I silently sent, *You said you are coming. Here?*

"*YES.*"

I sucked in a quick breath. An answer! *Why? What are you coming to do?*

"*TERMINATE EXPERIMENT.*"

My stomach clenched. Even though I didn't know exactly what they meant, it didn't sound good at all. Letting go of the left-hand prong, hoping that wouldn't interrupt the connection, I fished the data chip out of my pocket, fumblingly inserted it into the slot, then grabbed the projection again. *Did that come through? Is it what you wanted?*

Another agonizing wait, then: "*REPORT RECEIVED.*"

I let out the breath I'd been holding, but I didn't dare relax. *Are you still coming? You won't…terminate Nuath, will you?*

There was an even longer silence, during which I sensed several minds in conflict with each other, like they were arguing. By focusing harder, I was gradually able to discern actual thoughts, or, rather, images, though one overlapped another so quickly none of them made much sense. A weird ovoid object hovering in space. Hundreds of small, sparkling clouds moving together in a cluster. A collection of brightly colored marbles scattered across a swath of black velvet.

Then, finally: "*NOT NECESSARY.*"

I was almost afraid to believe it. *So…you're not coming here after all?*

Instead of an answer, the projections abruptly cooled in my hands, the signal that the Grentl had hung up. I tried again to stretch out with my mind, but now there was nothing to touch. It was like when the walls of my quarters on the *Quintessence* had blocked Rigel's thoughts from me. Even so, I hung on for another few minutes.

While I waited, I tried to decipher the jumble of images I'd received from the Grentl before their last reply. Again I saw that ovoid shape in space. A ship, maybe? I wasn't sure. And those bright marbles…

As I concentrated, the memory grew clearer. The black velvet I'd seen was the blackness of space, dotted with distant stars. And those marbles resolved into what were unmistakably planets. But which planets? Though my eyes were fixed unseeingly on the device I still grasped, in my mind I still saw those wheeling orbs of various sizes and colors. A blue one swam into focus and it was all I could do not to exclaim aloud.

Surely, that marble in the center was Earth? Which would make that reddish one off to the left Mars, the brilliant white one on the other side Venus. I could even see—yes!—a tiny white sphere next to the larger blue one. Earth's moon. But…I had no clue what it all meant.

Finally I let go of the device, stepping away with a cautious sigh of relief. Whatever those images had been about, they'd definitely told me they weren't planning to come here and destroy Nuath. Which meant I'd now done everything I could to keep the colony safe and could move on to what mattered most to *me*: getting back to Rigel.

"Well?" Molly asked breathlessly when I turned. "What did they say? They must have said *something*, you looked so intense. Are they… really coming?"

"No. After I sent my report on that data chip, they said it wasn't necessary."

Sean let out a whoop, making me jump. "You did it! Again!" He was grinning ear to ear.

Now Molly was grinning, too. "Dad and the others *have* to let you go back to Earth now. As soon as you name a Regent, anyway."

At that, Sean's smile dimmed noticeably. "Right. What Molly said." The sudden shift in his emotions from jubilant to jealous was impossible to ignore.

"I'm sorry, Sean, but you know I have to try to fix what they did to Rigel."

"I know. And I'll help any way I can, just like I promised. I owe you both that. It's just… Never mind. C'mon, let's get back upstairs and tell Dad and the others the good news."

* * *

When we all got back upstairs I sent a quick message summoning Mr. O and the other two traitors back to Conference Room Three. I invited Sean and Molly to come along this time, so they could hear the whole story, too.

All three men looked wary when they arrived.

"May I ask what is this about, Excellency?" Devyn sounded far more respectful than before, just as Cormac predicted. Good. "Surely you don't have news about the Grentl already?"

"Actually, I do." Though I was still royally pissed, I allowed myself a small smile. "I've just communicated with them again and it appears they don't intend any harm to Nuath after all."

"Oh?" A skeptical eyebrow went up, though Devyn's tone remained respectful. "On what do you base this, ah, encouraging news?"

I sat down and gestured for the others to do the same. "In going through some secure entries in the Sovereigns' private files, I discovered that the Grentl have been requesting reports every forty years or so. Since it had been longer than that since the last one, I hoped sending a new one might change their minds about coming here—and it seems to have worked."

"But…what exactly happened? Did you actually speak with them?" Mr. O asked eagerly. Along with curiosity, I sensed distress—distress I'd noticed the moment he arrived. Was it possible he was finally sorry now for what he'd done?

Now wasn't the time to ask. "After I'd put my report together, I went back to the device. It took the Grentl a minute to answer, then they pulled a little more out of me, bringing them up to the present. Finally, I was able to ask a question or two."

"And what did you ask?" Devyn demanded. "What did they say?" The respect wasn't nearly as pronounced now. I shot him an irritated glance and had the satisfaction of seeing him straighten slightly.

"I asked if they're really coming here. They said yes. So I asked why—what they were coming to do. They said… 'Terminate experiment.'"

I heard Molly gasp from behind me and suddenly fear dominated all three men's emotions.

"Terminate… But you just said they weren't going to— What

experiment? Nuath?" Nels's voice shook.

"I assumed so. Anyway, that's when I sent my report. After a couple of minutes, they said they'd received it, so I asked if they were still planning to come here, if they still planned to terminate us. And they said it was no longer necessary."

Devyn frowned. "Then Nuath is safe now? That report was all they wanted?"

"I think so. I did ask, just to be sure, but they…" I hesitated, that jumble of impressions I'd sensed, or thought I sensed, teasing me again. "They, um, hung up," I concluded. Until I figured out what all those images meant, better to stick to the facts.

All three men sat back in obvious relief, any earlier skepticism gone.

"This is excellent news," Mr. O'Gara said. "We have cause to be grateful to you yet again, Excellency."

"Yeah, well, try not to show it the way you did before," I couldn't resist saying.

Now there was no mistaking the guilt in both his expression and emotions. "Please believe I never intended to cause you so much distress, Excellency. Perhaps, had I realized—"

"You realized. Or would have, if you'd been willing to."

He bowed his head, not even attempting a denial now.

"It's obviously too late now." I was in no mood yet to be forgiving. "Anyway, while Nuath may be safe from the Grentl, it turns out we have another problem."

"Oh?" Mr. O's head came up and new tension suddenly radiated from everyone in the room.

"While I was putting that report together, I called up the history of energy use and power reserve levels, among other things, and discovered that Faxon used a crap-ton of power over the fifteen years he was in charge. Why our so-called acting Minister of Energy never noticed, I don't know." I flicked a glance at Nels, since he should have caught that, too, during his time as Interim Governor. "It looks like Nuath is going to run out of power a lot sooner than anyone thought."

Devyn leaned forward again, clearly concerned. "If that's true… Can you perhaps send us the figures you're talking about, Excellency? We should go over them, see if anything has been missed, brainstorm ideas."

"I can direct you to the pertinent databases. Most of them are accessible to anyone who bothers to look."

The more I thought about it, the more outrageous it seemed that no one else had noticed the problem long before this. While as Sovereign I had the advantage of pulling all of the colony databases together quickly and easily, surely Nuath's various acting ministers should have checked the ones dealing with their own areas of influence?

Mr. O'Gara was frowning thoughtfully. "Even without a Grentl threat, this news about the power reserves will likely make accelerated emigration advisable. Given that, it might be useful to speak with the acting Minister of Space Travel, so we'll have his most current figures and projections to hand. I'll arrange for a meeting first thing tomorrow. Ah, if that meets with your approval, Excellency?"

"Yes, I think that would be very useful. Please message me with the time and place, once a meeting is set. I'll let you know when I've resolved the matter of a Regent."

I rose and the others, caught off guard, had to scramble to their feet to bow before I left them again.

Sean returned to my apartment for dinner, claiming that eating with his father would kill his appetite, he was still so upset at him. While I had a hard time believing much of anything could put a dent in Sean's enormous appetite, I didn't object. Once dinner was over, though, I didn't encourage him to hang around.

"No, it's not because I'm mad at you," I said when he asked. "Though I still think you should have told me about that video a lot sooner. But now that I've kept my promise about the Grentl, I need to figure out who to name as Regent."

"Oh. Yeah. Guess I can't be much help with that—though once you have some names, maybe I'll know things about some of them and can help you narrow it down?" A question still lurked in his eyes, but I wasn't ready to *completely* forgive him yet.

"Sure, that would be great. Thanks. And if you really don't want to go back to your dad's apartment, you and Molly can always go do something else. I'll just be watching a bunch of vids and taking notes until bedtime."

After a moment's discussion, they decided to check out the Palace's gym—something I ought to do myself, it had been so long since I'd gotten any real exercise. But I had every intention of being back on Earth practicing taekwondo again before I got *too* much more out of shape.

Molly went to change and I headed to my office to start plowing through the three or four dozen videos sent to me by hopeful Regents.

10

Transfer capacity

BY the time I got too sleepy to continue, I hadn't even made it through a quarter of the Regent applications. Only three had been from people I'd actually met—two members of the *Echtran* Council, still on Earth, and Phelan Monroe, who'd been on the *Quintessence* with us.

Some of the videos lasted twenty minutes or more, with long, boring lists of accomplishments and lofty plans for Nuath. But even the more interesting ones only showed that the applicant was a decent speaker, not whether he or she was trustworthy. For all I knew, half of those impressive claims weren't even true. This past week had severely eroded my confidence in the honesty—or competence—of Royals in general.

Finally, after reading back over the very short list I'd made of those who might be marginally acceptable, I gave up and went to bed. Though I was tempted to chat with my Archived ancestors for a bit first, I resisted, since Mr. O had messaged that our meeting with the acting Minister of Space Travel was scheduled for nine a.m. I'd get back to my interminable queue of videos after that.

Ambrose, the acting Minister of Space Travel, turned out to be one of the few *non*-Royal acting ministers—an Engineer who also headed up the Space Transportation facility in Arregaith.

As he went over his report, two things became obvious: first, that he was far better prepared than any of the Royal acting ministers I'd met with. Second, that Mr. O had intentionally put off this particular meeting until after the *Luminosity* left Mars.

"Please note, Excellency, that while we prefer to wait until a ship is booked to at least eighty percent capacity, occasionally one will launch with fewer aboard." He pointed to a detailed holographic chart showing the manifests and schedules of all four ships for the rest of the current launch window.

Sure enough, there was the *Luminosity*, due to arrive in Bailerealta, Ireland shortly before dawn tomorrow morning. The *Horizon*, currently en route to Mars from Dun Cloch, Montana, would land here the next day. Now that we were near the middle of the launch window, trips each way only took three days instead of the four our *Quintessence* journey had taken last month.

"There seem to be more people traveling in this direction than to Earth," I commented with a glance at Mr. O. "Shouldn't it be the other way around? We've known for a while now that Nuath's power is starting to run out."

Acting Minister Ambrose's eyebrows rose. "In fact, that is something I've suggested myself, Excellency. However, the interim legislature has so far been unwilling to mandate such a thing."

"Hm. If we do manage to persuade the legislature—and the people—to go along with an accelerated emigration plan, just how quickly *could* we transport Nuathans to Earth?"

He immediately pulled up a different set of holographic charts but unfortunately his figures were even more discouraging than Mr. O's estimate had been.

"As you can see, though a ship can theoretically complete a round trip journey in ten days during the middle month of a launch window, in practice our ships have waited at least a week at each end before returning. This is to allow for thorough systems checks, any necessary recalibrations and occasional reconfigurations."

"Reconfigurations?"

"Of living and common areas, to better accommodate specific bookings, such as when you traveled here aboard the *Quintessence*. To refit all four ships for *maximum* capacity would require much more extensive changes and would likely take a month or more."

After raising his eyebrows at me in an "I told you so" way, Mr. O brought up Faxon's preparations and asked if they might help at all.

The minister frowned. "During Nels Murdoch's tenure, most of those additional resources were redirected to general colony maintenance, as so much of our infrastructure was allowed to deteriorate under Faxon. I'm afraid the ships Faxon commissioned were never completed."

"Maybe you should have a few Engineers take a look at the ones that were started. See if they can be tweaked for transport instead of attack," I suggested. "Anything that might speed up the process would be a good thing, unless there's some kind of breakthrough on extending Nuath's power supply."

Earlier this week, the acting Minister of Energy—an obviously incompetent Royal—assured me that they'd resumed research on that nearly as soon as Faxon was out. But though that was the solution the vast majority of Nuathans still hoped for, he'd admitted there'd been no real progress beyond additional conservation measures.

"Of course, Excellency. I'll also look into ways to shorten the turnaround time for our existing ships. The more quickly we can reduce Nuath's population, the longer our remaining power will last."

As soon as we left the conference room, Mr. O'Gara turned to me. "I feared this would be the case, but perhaps if those ships of Faxon's can be put to good use, we may still be able to do what's necessary in the decades ahead. Of course, there is also the chance our Scientists will discover either a new power source or a way of extending what we have."

Since Nuath's power was nearly all derived from a series of fuel cells developed and left here by the Grentl, using at least two elements not found on Earth *or* Mars, that seemed pretty unlikely to me.

"The trick will be convincing enough Nuathans to emigrate," I said. "We need to get as many people as possible on the ships still heading to Earth during this launch window, and as few as possible on the ones coming here."

Mr. O nodded, his expression grim. "I called up those databases last night and…I'm afraid you're right. We can't afford to gamble Nuath's continued existence on a breakthrough that is still, at this point, theoretical. If you would allow me, and perhaps Devyn, to pay a visit to the legislative building to speak on your behalf—"

"Like you did with Healer Adara? Thanks, but I'd rather speak on my own behalf."

He stopped walking and turned to face me fully. "Excellency, I… I've had time now to think about what you said yesterday. You were right. I had no right to ignore both Nuathan law and the basic principles of justice and decency, no matter my motives. By doing so, I did indeed lower myself to Faxon's level. I want you to know that I am sincerely sorry for what I did—what I convinced others to do—and for the pain my actions caused you."

"And for possibly ruining Rigel's life?"

"That, too. In any case, you have my word I will never again attempt to undermine your leadership in any way. Nor your relationship with young Stuart, should it ever become possible for you to resume it, unlikely as that seems now."

I pinned him with my gaze for a long moment, probing his emotions. He *seemed* completely sincere—right now, anyway. Finally, I nodded.

"I appreciate that. And with any luck, I'll get to hold you to the second half of that promise sooner than you expect."

Leaving him to frown after me, I headed back to my apartment to return to the arduous task of finding a Regent—something I *had* to do if I didn't want to leave Nuath's fate in the hands of the very men who'd betrayed me.

Except for one longish meeting with the acting Ministers of Energy, Technological Development, and Planetary Resources—which only reinforced my belief that most of the Royals plugged into those roles were incompetent—I spent the next two days wrestling with the Regent dilemma. I'd thought the hardest of my two promises would be dealing with the Grentl but this one was turning out way worse.

After finally winnowing my list of "marginally acceptables" to twenty, I invited input from Sean, Molly and Cormac—the only people in Nuath I really trusted now.

"Maybe not Hogan Kelly or Tara McBride," Sean commented, scanning down my short list. "Back on Earth, Mum mentioned both of them as Royals who'd tried to stir up sentiment against you."

"And Phelan," Molly added. "She was the one on the ship, right? I heard her saying stuff about Rigel, after, you know, what Gordon did, that you definitely wouldn't have liked."

I scratched those three off my list. "What about you, Cormac? Any thoughts?"

My Bodyguard was frowning. "I did encounter nearly all of these people during my tenures with your father and grandfather. I hate to say so, Excellency, but I'm not certain any of them are either influential or strong-willed enough to resist manipulation by Quinn O'Gara or Devyn Kane, should they attempt such a thing."

Which they totally would. Neither would be content to sit passively on the sidelines for long, no matter how sorry Mr. O might be right now. In fact all three men had already tried several times to get around the security protocols I'd set up, according to private alerts I'd received. The last thing I wanted was a Regent who'd end up as their puppet.

"Gah. Will I have to personally interview every single candidate on the planet and evaluate them face to face? That will take ages and I want to get back to Earth *now!*" I huffed out a frustrated breath. "Sorry. And thanks, you guys. I really do appreciate your help, even if I don't sound like it."

A few minutes later, Molly and Sean went off to have dinner with some friends who'd just arrived that day aboard the *Horizon* and Cormac returned to whatever he'd been reading before I'd asked for his input.

Temporarily setting the irritating Regent matter aside, I started scanning my other messages. Since I was no longer having them routed through Mr. O, I had to deal with them myself, at least until I found a proper secretary. Or a Regent…

Among the mountain of requests for audiences and invitations to events all over Nuath, I discovered the files Healer Adara had promised me on memory restoration. Eagerly, I downloaded them and started reading, only to find them hopelessly technical, using all sorts of jargon—much of it in Nuathan. What little I did understand was pretty discouraging.

I was highlighting the few things that looked like they might be remotely useful in Rigel's case when my vidscreen pinged to show an incoming call. Glancing up, I was startled to see Shim Stuart's name displayed on the screen. I'd been checking the channel for interplanetary messages frequently, hoping for a reply from Rigel's grandfather. But…this *wasn't* an interplanetary call. It was from right here in Nuath!

Fumbling a little, I opened the connection. "Shim?"

Sure enough, Shim's wise, familiar face appeared on the screen. "Excellency. I am delighted to see you in good health. Let me extend my congratulations on your Acclamation, in addition to those already sent on behalf of the *Echtran* Council. From which I have resigned, by the way. Is it at all possible for us to meet sometime in the next day or two? There are a few matters I would very much like to discuss with you personally."

"Of course! Are you here in Thiaraway? Can you come to the

Palace right now? Have you had dinner yet?"

His smile let me know I was babbling. "To answer your questions in order, Excellency, yes, yes, and no. May I consider that an invitation?"

"Yes! If…if you don't mind, sir?" Becoming Sovereign hadn't changed my instinctive deference to Shim. I trusted and respected him more than anyone I could think of. "I would be very, very pleased if you would join me for dinner in my apartment as soon as you can conveniently get here."

"Thank you, Excellency. I will be there shortly."

I quickly let Palace security know that Shim was to be shown directly to my quarters, then went to the food recombinator to order up a dinner worthy of such a distinguished guest. Not until I was selecting the chocolate mousse for dessert did it hit me that if Shim was in Nuath now, he couldn't possibly have been on Earth when I'd sent him my message about Rigel.

Just then, the door chime sounded and Cormac showed Shim into the apartment.

"Excellency." He swept me a deep bow and it was all I could do to just incline my head instead of bowing back. Shim was as imposing as ever with his thick shock of white hair and lined, aristocratic face. When he straightened, his clear gray eyes glinted down at me with the same almost superhuman intelligence I remembered.

"I'm so glad you're here! But…I guess you didn't get my message? About Rigel?" He looked tired, so I motioned to one of the plush chairs and we both sat down.

"I did, Excellency, but not until arriving in Nuath this afternoon, when it was forwarded to me from Earth. I had no idea they meant to send Rigel back so soon."

"You mean…you already knew what they planned to do to him? Before you left Earth? Before my message?"

Shim nodded gravely. "Indeed. It is why I resigned from the Council. Quinn messaged his wife, who shared it with the rest of us. Most of the others felt the course he proposed was necessary, no matter how unorthodox and, may I say, unethical it was. I did not agree and moved that the Council insist Quinn do nothing so extreme until other options had been thoroughly explored. Unfortunately, I was outvoted."

"So the whole *Echtran* Council was in on this?" My instincts had clearly been right to cross those Royals off my Regent list, even if I knew them—*thought* I knew them—better than any of the others.

"Nearly. Nara also resigned in protest. Unfortunately, that leaves Kyna the only non-Royal currently on the Council, which I fear may lead to further unwise decisions—or, at least, decisions informed far more by politics than by science."

And make the Council even less likely to listen to me. "What made you decide to come to Mars? Don't you still have your research job in D.C.?"

Shim shook his head. "I tendered my resignation there, as well. My intention in coming was to do whatever was necessary to forestall Quinn's plans for Rigel and, of course, to support you in any way I can. After we received word of Eric Eagan's demise, as well as that of his colleagues in the know, I realized I was perhaps the only Scientist left who might be able to help you with the Grentl device, should you need to deal further with it. Weighing all factors, I felt I could serve the Nuathan people, and yourself, more effectively here than on Earth. I only regret I was unable to arrive sooner."

"I wish you *could* have gotten here in time to stop what they did to Rigel, but that's not your fault. Mostly…it's mine. If I'd kept my promise to you and never told him about the Grentl, none of this would have happened." My insides squirmed with guilt. "Then they'd have had no reason to erase his memory or send him away or…or anything. In fact, I probably would have been Acclaimed the very day we got to Mars."

"I seriously doubt that, Excellency. From the news that filtered back to Earth, your, ah, indiscretion during your first hours aboard the *Quintessence* would have been enough to delay your Acclamation. And I strongly suspect Quinn—and the Council—would have found another pretext to separate you permanently from Rigel, had you not provided them with one. As for your promise, I forgive you. Given your bond with my grandson, it was an unreasonable thing to ask, however much the Council insisted upon it."

Shim's understanding smile comforted me even more than his words, bringing tears to my eyes. "Thanks. That makes me feel a *little* better. But there's so, so much I need to tell you! I know Mr. O'Gara sent reports, and I sent a couple myself, but—"

"Perhaps over dinner?" Shim's eyes twinkled slightly with something that might have been amusement. "I find that the older I get, the more I appreciate my creature comforts."

I jumped up. "Of course! Cormac, since Molly is out, would you mind setting out our food? Everything's already programmed into the recombinator."

Cormac bowed and within moments had the table set and our first course arranged on plates. When he went to stand behind me, I waved him to a chair, as usual.

"Ah, I'd prefer to eat later instead, if you don't mind, Excellency?"

Since he was clearly uncomfortable sitting at the table in front of Shim, I suggested he eat in his room rather than wait, since I had a feeling this might be a really long meal.

"There are things you wish to tell me?" Shim prompted, picking up his salad fork.

That was all the invitation I needed. Practically ignoring the gourmet feast I'd arranged, I talked almost nonstop, pouring out everything that had happened since leaving for Mars a month ago. Since Cormac was out of earshot, I even told him about my Scepter and the two Archives, realizing when I mentioned Leontine that Shim reminded me of him a little. I also described in detail my three interactions with the Grentl device. The only thing I left out were the confusing images I'd received when I'd tried to "eavesdrop," since by now I wasn't positive I hadn't imagined them.

Shim himself retrieved our entrees and desserts from the recombinator, refusing to let me do it, though I countered by asking him to please call me "M" instead of "Excellency" in private.

"Anyway, since you didn't get my message before leaving, I'm extra glad I also sent one to Rigel's parents," I said, finally winding down after nearly two hours. "But will they be able to keep him safe without you there?"

He looked thoughtful. "Given the security protocols you were foresighted enough to put in place, he should be well enough for the time being, as it is doubtful anyone on Earth yet knows that the deception practiced upon you was discovered. However, I will send a few discreet messages of my own to ensure further safeguards for my grandson, at least until—"

"Until I can get there myself," I said eagerly. "You'll help me do that, won't you?" I was suddenly seized by an idea so obvious, I couldn't believe it hadn't occurred to me an hour ago.

"That, my dear, is a separate discussion, and one that should probably wait for tomorrow, when I will doubtless feel rather sharper than I do right now. Though I hate to say so, I don't adjust to time changes as quickly as I used to in my younger days."

"I'm sorry! I totally forgot you'd be jet-lagged, coming from Montana. Of course we can wait till tomorrow to talk more. Will you stay here at the Palace tonight? That way you'll get to bed sooner and it will be that much easier to meet in the morning."

"That is very gracious of you, Ex— er, M. I accept your kind offer and thank you also for the most enjoyable meal I've had in some time."

I messaged the housekeeping staff to have a room ready for him as quickly as possible, then turned back to Shim, nervously clasping my hands in front of me.

"Sir, I know it's not what you came to Nuath for and I don't know how long you'd planned to stay but...would you consider becoming my Regent? I can't imagine *anyone* else who'd be even a fraction as good at it."

He blinked at me in obvious surprise—the only time I could remember *ever* seeing Shim surprised. "I'm exceedingly flattered, of course, but you must realize how unprecedented such an appointment would be? There has not been a non-Royal Regent in—"

"More than eight hundred years. I know. Not that there've been that many Regents in Nuathan history anyway. It's perfectly legal, though. I remember reading it last fall, when I was researching all the Nuathan law I could because of Rigel and, well, you know."

In fact, I'd read that particular bit while Rigel was driving our stolen car, when we'd run away from Jewel to keep the Council from separating us. That memory made me realize Shim was right that even if I hadn't told Rigel about the Grentl, they'd have found some other way to keep us apart.

With a faint smile of understanding, Shim inclined his head. "Very well. If you are certain you are prepared to deal with the inevitable repercussions of such an unorthodox appointment, it would be my great honor to serve as Regent to Sovereign Emileia—long may she reign."

11

Power exchange

SHIM hadn't been gone ten minutes when Molly and Sean returned from their evening out, both of them in such high spirits I wondered if *spakriga* or something similar had been served at their dinner.

"M, you'll have to meet Oriana and Kerry," Molly told me. "Oriana was my very best friend in Bailerealta, and Kerry and Sean both played basketball there—and here, too, when they were like nine or ten. They moved from Bailrealta to America just a month after we did, but now they're here in Nuath, to stay!"

I didn't want to spoil Molly's mood by pointing out that *nobody* could really be here "to stay," since we needed to start getting people off-planet instead of having more come here from Earth. Because it would be so controversial, I also didn't feel like getting into the whole thing about Shim being my Regent tonight, so I faked a yawn.

"That's great. I'm glad you guys had such a good time."

Molly was immediately apologetic. "Oh, wow, I didn't realize it's so late! You'd better go, Sean, so I can help M get ready for bed. Can you at least sleep in tomorrow?"

I shook my head. "Another important meeting first thing in the morning, so I really should get to bed. G'night, Sean."

Sean was clearly disappointed to be dismissed so quickly, but he didn't argue. As soon as Molly had turned down my bed and laid out my nightgown, I said goodnight to her, too, so I could jot down some notes for my meeting with Shim tomorrow—and for the speech I planned to make to the legislature afterward.

After some thought, I decided to make my Regent announcement without giving any advance notice to Mr. O and the others. That way they'd have no chance to try to talk me out of it or undermine me in any way. Sure, they'd be shocked and upset to find out along with everybody else, but I considered that a bonus, since it totally served them right.

Sean had only just joined Molly and me for breakfast when Shim showed up as arranged, at eight o'clock. I'd planned it this way, so I could fill them both in at once.

Not surprisingly, they were both stunned. Molly only stammered slightly as she greeted him, but Sean was less polite. "How did—? What are you—? But you're supposed to be on Earth, making sure…"

Which reminded me. "Did you send those messages you mentioned last night? To make sure Rigel stays safe till I can get to Earth?"

Shim nodded. "Nearly the moment I was shown into that most lovely room you provided for me, Excellency. I assumed you would not wish me to delay, so I did not. My friends and colleagues should be able to ensure no harm comes to him, especially since I took the liberty of invoking your name with my requests."

"Thank you so much!" The tension between my shoulder blades dissolved and I turned to Sean and Molly. "Remember how frustrated I was going over that list when you guys left yesterday? Well, meet my new Regent."

Molly let out a little squeak but Sean frowned. "Um… No offense, sir, but doesn't a Regent have to be Royal? Everyone else on that list —"

"I know," I said. "But no. Just another one of those things that's tradition but not law." I'd reread the statute before going to bed last night. "Lucky for me, huh?"

Over breakfast, Shim and I discussed the best way to break my news to the acting legislature and to the population at large. He suggested doing both simultaneously.

"Since you are determined on this course, it makes sense to garner support for it as quickly as possible. While the Royal-heavy legislature may protest, the rest of Nuath is overwhelmingly composed of other *fines*. Given what I've been reading about this new Populist party and the influence it gained while your Acclamation was delayed, this will likely be a popular move with their sympathizers, as well as many others concerned about their status now Royal rule has been reestablished."

Once we finished eating I messaged Mr. O'Gara, asking him to notify both the legislature and the media that I would be holding a press conference in the Legislative Hall at noon—and that he, Devyn and Nels were welcome to attend. I also hinted that their behavior there might determine whether their "house arrest" resumed afterwards.

Though he had to be dying to ask questions, Mr. O just replied, "Understood. Notifications sent."

I couldn't quite control the quiver in my midsection when I stepped up to the podium of the Legislative Hall at thirty seconds past twelve to face the entire acting legislature. The Royal House, or *Riogain*, only had forty-two Royals in it right now, rather than the sixty required by the Nuathan constitution. And while the *Eodain*, or People's House, did have a full sixty acting members, almost none of them were Royal. Pre-Faxon, more than half of them had been, despite that House being popularly elected from across Nuath.

Every one of the media's two-dozen-plus networks had sent at least one reporter, which meant everyone in Nuath, with the possible exception of a few technophobes, would be watching.

No pressure.

Ranged behind me were Cormac, Sean, Molly, Mr. O'Gara, Devyn, Nels and Shim. Though the others had clearly been surprised to see Shim, they'd greeted him with all the respect due his status as longtime leader of the *Echtran* Council. Still, I could sense nervousness, bordering on fear, from all three. Maybe they were worried I was about to publicly accuse them after all.

Touching the tiny microphone button on my collar, I cleared my throat, then waited while the ornate, high-ceilinged room fell obediently silent.

"Thank you all for gathering on such short notice. I know many of you have been concerned, both before and since my Acclamation, that my youth and relative inexperience might adversely impact my ability to lead Nuath. A reasonable concern as, traditionally, underage Sovereigns have had Regents appointed prior to their Installation."

I could hear my voice shaking slightly, even if no one else could, so I took a steadying breath before continuing.

"However, the circumstances leading to my Sovereignty were unprecedented in Nuath's history and therefore required some things be done differently than in the past. By the time Faxon's fall allowed for my return and Acclamation, neither my father Mikal nor his father, Sovereign Leontine, were alive to recommend a Regent.

Therefore, that choice fell entirely on me.

"Many, many capable and well-respected people have submitted their names for consideration, and I wish to extend my thanks to each and every one of them for their willingness to serve. However, given the unique circumstances in which Nuath finds itself, and in order to ensure the most efficient and effective rebuilding of our government and infrastructure, I have selected a Regent who did not actively seek that office.

"He will already be familiar to many of you, both from the time he spent working with Palace Engineers and Informatics researchers in the past, and for his exemplary leadership of the *Echtran* Council for the past seventy-two years. Shim was instrumental in helping me survive a deadly attack by Faxon's forces last year and it is largely due to his efforts that I was able to return to Nuath and take my place as your Sovereign.

"Therefore, it is with great pleasure that I present your new Regent and acting leader of Nuath until I attain my majority. I give you Shim Stuart!"

I stepped back and motioned Shim to the podium. As he stepped forward, I got a definite thrill of satisfaction at the stunned expressions on the faces of Mr. O, Devyn and Nels (whose mouth actually fell open, though he quickly closed it).

Touching the microphone button on his own tunic, Shim turned to face the legislature with his customary dignity and confidence. Most appeared nearly as stunned as the three traitors behind me, but I also heard a few cheers from the *Eodain* side, and from a handful of reporters.

"Thank you, Sovereign Emileia. May I say that it warms my heart to see how you have already grown into your new role. It is clear to me that the future of Nuath will be in exceedingly capable hands once you are of age to resume the full reins of power. To the rest of you, I ask for your patience and support, despite the Sovereign's seeming departure from long tradition by appointing me. Though I am not of the Royal *fine*, I have worked closely with Royals for most of my life. I hope to bring a different and necessary perspective to Nuath as we work together to rebuild it into the safe, prosperous and happy society it was intended to be.

"It is my intention to meet with some of you as early as this afternoon, with a view to scheduling the series of elections necessary to put our sadly disrupted government back on its feet as quickly as possible. Then we can move on to the business of restoring and even improving upon the infrastructure and quality of life we once enjoyed. Again, I thank you."

To the sound of now-enthusiastic applause from the assemblage, Shim bowed—my cue to again step up to his side.

"Shim and I will now be happy to answer questions, if you have them. Yes?" I nodded to the first reporter to get a hand in the air.

As we'd agreed, we took questions for a full hour, with me allowing Shim to answer more and more of them as time passed. Not surprisingly, by the end of the hour he'd thoroughly impressed nearly every person present—and probably the vast majority of those watching on the feeds—with his intelligence, experience and ideas.

Once the microphones were off, even Mr. O'Gara grudgingly admitted I'd made a good choice, though I could tell he wasn't really *happy* about it. As soon as the legislators and press began filtering out, I turned eagerly to Shim.

"Now, let's get back to the Palace and arrange my return to Earth. I'd like to be on the very next ship, even if it means taking a bunk in Steerage!"

"No way. No *way!*" Half an hour later, back at the Palace, I stared, aghast, at the four men facing me. "You agreed that once I stopped the Grentl from attacking Nuath and appointed a Regent, I could leave for Earth!"

"We agreed to no such thing, Excellency," Mr. O reminded me. "You yourself promised to do those things before leaving, but didn't ask for or receive any assurances from us in return."

"Quite true," Devyn said. "While we are all grateful that you indeed seem to have convinced the Grentl to leave Nuath alone, and that you were able to so, ah, expeditiously appoint a Regent, those two actions alone do not absolve you of all responsibility to your people."

"I'm afraid they are right, my dear." Shim spoke gently, but firmly. "Understandably anxious as you are to help my grandson, certain matters do require your attention before you can, in conscience, join him. If the only reason the Grentl feel no need to 'terminate' this colony is that it will cease to exist in fifty or sixty years due to lack of power, that gives us—gives you—a crisis of another sort to deal with. Have you any idea how quickly emigration can be effected, given our current resources?"

Because I was still too upset to reply, Mr. O answered. "We discussed exactly that with the acting Minister of Space Travel two days ago. At most, we might get a few thousand from Mars to Earth during the current launch window—assuming, of course, that people can be convinced to leave. *That* is the task to which I believe our Sovereign should now direct her energies."

"Again, I tend to agree." I sensed sympathy from Shim as well as confidence—in me. "Not only have you already won the hearts of the people, Excellency, but due to your upbringing on Earth, you are uniquely suited to the task of allaying their fears about relocating to the planet of our race's origin."

If it were just Mr. O saying this, I'd have assumed it was to keep me away from Rigel as long as possible. But I'd always trusted Shim, even when he told me things I didn't want to hear. And I *so* didn't want to hear this right now!

Anger and frustration tightened my voice as I fought back tears. "And how long do you think that will take? Months? *Years?*" Every *second* away from Rigel's side was a second too long!

Shim's expression told me he understood what I was feeling. "If we move quickly, as I think we must, I should think we can get you to Earth during the current launch window. Much will depend upon your persuasive abilities—but I rather imagine you will be strongly motivated to be as convincing as possible."

"Fine," I snapped, pissed even at Shim right now. "I'll record some videos that you can broadcast all over Nuath. If you don't think they're persuasive enough, I'll re-do them. But let's get started!"

"That may do for a start, but I also suggest a series of in-person appearances throughout Nuath in addition to your media appeals. Even in our advanced technological age, people do tend to appreciate a personal touch."

"I can help with the arrangements," Nels offered. "If I'm allowed to make outside calls?"

Though my stomach was positively churning at the idea of delaying my return to Earth, to Rigel, by as much as three whole *months*, I managed to keep my voice level as I asked Shim, "Are we sure Rigel really is safe now?"

At his nod, I turned to Nels. "Then I guess I can lift the blocks and you and Devyn can go home."

Nels seemed relieved, but Devyn said, "Actually, I'd like to remain at the Palace if you have no objection, Excellency. I had not yet arranged for permanent lodgings in Nuath and I can better assist Quinn and your Regent from here."

I shrugged, not much caring where Devyn stayed, as long as it was mostly out of my sight. I'd definitely keep my personal protection protocol in place, though.

"Whatever, as long as we get this emigration campaign started *now*. Because, no matter what, I'm getting back to Earth this summer!"

As always, Shim turned out to be right. Using the recent power glitches as our excuse, we had the acting Energy Minister order a complete systems analysis—something the idiot Royal had never bothered to do since being appointed. Of course, it confirmed what I already knew—that Nuath had maybe fifty years of power left at current consumption levels.

Once that information was made public, it became a whole lot easier to convince everyone, including the legislature, that emigration to Earth was necessary. Even so, while 87% agreed (according to the networks' incessant polls) that most Nuathans needed to emigrate, fewer than 25% expressed willingness to do so themselves. Which was where I came in.

Over the next twelve weeks I crisscrossed Nuath, visiting every town and village, some more than once, to add my in-person pleas to the ones I was making regularly through the *grechain*. I extolled the benefits of life on Earth (not that I'd seen much of it, beyond Jewel) and the expanded opportunities they and their children would have there, where *fine* no longer mattered and where, as *Echtrans*, they would enjoy natural advantages over the average *Duchas* due to their superior intelligence, adaptability, and other qualities.

Little by little, I won enough people over to fill the rest of the ships heading to Earth during the remaining weeks of the launch window. My own berth—which I insisted be far smaller than the one I'd had coming here—was finally booked as well…on the very *last* ship of the summer.

Not only was it the last, but because we'd extended the launch window past its usual cut-off to get more people out, my voyage would take six days instead of the four I'd spent getting to Mars.

Worse, even *after* I got to Earth, Shim insisted I'd need to make additional in-person visits to Bailerealta and Dun Cloch in Montana, as well as a few other, smaller *Echtran* settlements, to reassure the new immigrants. I'd also be involved in setting up a more extensive *Echtran* government, since the current Council—still two members short—wouldn't be able to handle everything themselves.

All of this meant I'd barely get back to Jewel in time for the first day of school—which meant coming up with a plausible excuse for my aunt and uncle to explain the delay.

Thanks, ironically, to Mr. O's nastily ingenious plotting, that turned out to be easier than expected. Following their original plan, the *Echtran* Council had already started a rumor in Jewel that both Rigel and I had been in a terrible accident in Ireland and were presumed dead. So it was just a matter of amending that rumor with the "news" that we'd miraculously survived—but would need all summer to recuperate before flying back to the States.

I couldn't help wondering how Aunt Theresa had taken both pieces of news, though I supposed I'd get some idea when I finally returned to Jewel. But whether she'd be overjoyed to see me again or pissed that I'd worried her for nothing, didn't really matter. The important thing was that I *would* be going back…and so would Rigel.

And once he and I were in Jewel again, everything would work out for both of us. I'd make sure of that.

Somehow.

II

Rigel

12

Resonance frequency

STANDING on the sidewalk in front of Jewel High, I nod automatically when a couple guys slap me on the back and say something about the coming year's football season. I don't really hear them, though. I'm too busy thinking how this is going to be the weirdest first day of school ever.

I've been the new kid at school more years than not, but this year is different. Because this year I'm not really a new kid, I just feel like one. Most everybody will know me but I won't know them. So not only weird, but awkward to the max.

My mom's Healer friends say some of my memories might come back eventually. Might. But as of this moment I don't remember a single thing between last summer, when my family was about to move from Indianapolis to Jewel, and this summer, when I woke up in a hospital in Ireland. A whole year of my life, gone. Poof.

"Hey, Rigel, how are you doing?" A pretty blonde girl puts a hand on my arm and looks me in the face, all concerned. "We heard about your accident and all, and I want you to know I'm here to help you with anything you need—anything at all."

"Uh, thanks, er…"

"Trina. Trina Squires. We were *super* close friends last year, but I guess you don't remember, huh?" Her big blue eyes are wide with sympathy. "Come on. I'll show you where Homeroom is. We're in the same one."

She holds out her hand to me. I frown at it for a second, then take it, not wanting to hurt her feelings. Other than Coach and the guys at football practice this past week, she's the first person at Jewel High I've met. Re-met. Something in the way she smiles and tightens her grip on my fingers makes me wonder if Trina and I were more than friends last year.

Not too shabby, if so. Judging by most of the other girls I see as we walk through the halls, she's one of the prettiest in school.

"Here we are," she says brightly, leading me into a classroom. "It's alphabetical, so you're right behind me." Her smile is positively dazzling. I smile back.

"Thanks, Trina. So…does everyone know by now? I mean, about me not, y'know, remembering anything?"

She shrugs and sort of shimmies into her seat. "Maybe not absolutely *everybody*, since it's the very first day of school, but the coaches told the football team and they told the cheerleaders, so word's been getting around. I'm head cheerleader this year, by the way! Isn't that awesome?"

"Oh. Yeah. Awesome. Congratulations."

"Hey, Rigel, great to have you back!" A boy my age slides into a desk across the aisle. "Sorry about what happened to you in Ireland, though. Total bummer. Still, Matt Mullins says you were looking pretty good in practice last week."

"Thanks." I wish I knew the guy's name. Guess I'll be wishing that a lot today—maybe all year.

Trina gives the guy a scolding sort of look. "Pete, you need to introduce yourself, remember? About the—" She taps the side of her head.

"Oh, yeah, sorry! Pete Warner. Must be weird, not remembering stuff, huh?"

"You got that right." I smile. It probably does seem funny to people. Just not to me.

A few other people within earshot start telling me their names and I try to link each name with something about the person to help me remember. So I can start refilling the big empty spot in my brain.

Donna Smith, in front of Trina, has spiky black hair. Black, blacksmith, Smith. Nate Villiers, in front of Pete Warner, looks a little like a guy I met in Bailerealta before coming back to the States. Bailerealta, villagers, Villiers.

The homeroom teacher tells us to quiet down and look at our schedules, so we mostly do. I glance over mine. They talked about having me repeat all my classes from last year but decided to let me stick to my original schedule on a trial basis. I hope that wasn't a bad idea.

"Remember to get an office slip from me if you need to make changes to your schedule," the teacher is saying when a girl rushes into the room, late.

This girl is almost as pretty as Trina, even with her face flushed with embarrassment—which somehow makes her cuter. Wavy, golden-brown hair sweeps across her shoulders as she apologizes to the teacher, then hurries to her seat. The seat right behind mine.

She's just passing Donna Smith when I feel it—the *brath*. This girl is Martian! Why didn't anybody—?

I break off my thought when she suddenly locks gazes with me. She has the greenest eyes I've ever seen. Beautiful eyes. Definitely need to find out *her* name. But before I can ask, she turns even redder and looks away. Looks upset. Then slips into the desk behind me, where her *brath* is so strong it makes my whole body tingle.

Weird. Nobody's *brath* in Bailerealta did that to me. Even though it was all Martians—*Echtrans*—there.

A minute later the bell rings. Trina jumps up and grabs my hand again.

"C'mon, Rigel, I'll show you where your first class is. I'm not in that one, but it looks like we have at least three others together." She's talking a little louder than before.

"Just a sec." Even though Trina's tugging me in the opposite direction, I turn to the Martian girl behind me. "Hi. We, um, probably met last year, but… Maybe you heard about—?"

"Yeah. I…I heard." Her voice is soft, but it goes through me like a lightning bolt, or a shot of adrenaline. Bizarre. "I'm M. Er, Marsha Truitt. It's…good to see you again, Rigel." She seems to be holding some strong emotion barely under control. I wonder what *that's* about.

Then her name suddenly registers.

"Marsha Truitt? Wait. That means you're—" Her green eyes go way wide and I immediately shut up, remembering almost too late I can't blurt out who she really is in front of everybody.

"Rigel, you're going to make me late to my class," Trina says, again too loudly, pulling harder on my hand. "Come *on*."

Embarrassed, realizing I'm still staring, I mumble, "Um, sorry," and let Trina lead me away.

Trina obviously thinks I was apologizing to her, but I wasn't. I was apologizing for nearly blowing the cover of Sovereign Emileia, supreme ruler of our people, both on Earth and on Mars. Glancing back over my shoulder I see her watching me with that same suppressed emotion in her green eyes.

And wonder why the hell my parents didn't tell me the freaking

Sovereign was going to be attending Jewel High this year.

"Here you go," Trina says at the door to my first class, Pre-Calculus. "Let me know if you need help, since you probably don't remember any of last year's Geometry or Algebra stuff. We were in the same class, so I can give you my notes and everything." Her smile implies we might do more than study if I take her up on her offer.

I smile back and nearly ask outright if we were dating last year. But don't. "Thanks. I really appreciate that. You'd better hurry now, or you'll be late."

"It would be for a worthy cause." She tosses her reddish blonde curls and winks at me, then walks off, giving me a good view of her swaying hips from behind.

I watch for a second, then go into the classroom, bracing myself for another round of introductions from people I should already know.

Apparently word has spread way beyond the football team and cheerleaders by now, because a bunch of kids come up to say hi and tell me their names, most adding what I knew them from last year. Wish Trina'd given me these kinds of details about us. Her. Us?

Two guys are running over the highlights of last year's football season for me when I again sense Martian *brath* nearby. I look around, expecting to see the Sovereign again, but it's a different girl. Also pretty, but with darker brown hair and gray eyes. How many *Echtrans* are there at this school? And why didn't Mom and Dad mention *any* of them?

"Rigel?" this new Martian girl says tentatively. "You…don't remember me, I guess?"

I shake my head. "Sorry. It's nothing personal. I don't remember anybody."

"No, no, I know." There's a tiny bit of relief in her voice, like she was hoping I'd say no. I wonder why. "I'm Molly. Molly O'Gara. We were friends last year. We, um, hung out a lot with M and Sean. My brother."

So Sean O'Gara's in Jewel too? Since the Sovereign's here, I guess that makes sense. I heard in Ireland he's her Consort. Or future Consort. I'm not exactly clear on all the political stuff, but I guess they're like engaged or something. "Nice to meet you again, Molly."

"Yeah. I…we…were worried. It's great that you're here and that you're okay. I mean, except for the memory thing."

I have to grin at her embarrassment. "Thanks. Maybe we can talk later?" She might be a good person to fill in some of the blanks Trina can't.

Even as I ask, I feel it again—that super-strong *brath* that can only be the Sovereign's. Even though I don't turn my head, I'm completely focused on where she is, coming up from behind my left shoulder. Passing me without a glance.

"Definitely! Later." Molly nods vigorously and goes to sit near the Sovereign, two rows away. M? Is that what people call her at school? I still feel her *brath*, way stronger than Molly's, even from ten feet away. Must be a Royal thing.

I'm still watching her when a cute, short blonde girl runs across the classroom and practically launches herself at the Sovereign, hugging her and squealing. "M! You *are* here! When you weren't on the bus this morning, Bri and I worried those rumors about you not coming back this year were true. I'm *so* glad they're not!"

The Sovereign answers more quietly, but with my extra-acute Martian hearing I have no trouble eavesdropping from halfway across the room. "Thanks, Deb. Yeah, it was touch and go for a while there. I didn't get home till last night, so Aunt Theresa drove me here early this morning so she could get me registered and everything."

"So—" Deb looks her over. "No cast or bandages or anything? You're all healed up from that accident? You can't *imagine* how I felt when I heard that rumor you were killed! It was awful! I cried and cried. But then, just a couple days later, we all found out it wasn't true. Bri and I—"

Class starts then, so the little blonde, Deb, shuts up. I'm still processing everything I just overheard. The Sovereign was in an accident, too? The same one I was in? If nobody knew for sure she'd be back, that at least explains why my folks didn't mention her.

I spend most of the period distracted by my thoughts and by the Sovereign's super-strong vibes. Even so, by the end of class I'm pretty sure I won't need Trina's help with math. Any healthy guy ought to feel disappointed by that. So why aren't I? Just because Trina's a *Duchas*? Am I prejudiced?

For the first time, I wonder if I'll learn things about this past year

—about myself—that I won't like.

In Spanish class, Trina motions me to the desk next to hers. "So, how was Pre-Cal? I can help you with Spanish, too. We had almost *all* our classes together last year. Maybe we should plan some evening tutoring dates this week?" She leans toward me and flutters impossibly long eyelashes.

"Yeah, maybe. So, um, what else can you tell me about last year? Not just schoolwork. Who I was friends with, what I did besides football, that kind of thing. It's weird not to know." I'll also ask the guys on the team some of this stuff after practice today. Last week we were all so focused on catching me up on the plays and all that I never even thought about it.

Shooting a quick glance at the teacher, Trina puts a hand on my arm and leans in closer. "I can only *imagine* what you're going through, Rigel, and I'll help *any* way I can! You and I were friends. Obviously." She slants a flirty look up at me. "And you hung out with most of the guys from the team, of course."

"Do you mean… Were we…" Jeez this is awkward! "Were you and I a…a couple last year?" There. I asked.

"A couple?" She trills a little laugh. "Duh! We were on Homecoming Court together!"

The way she says it makes me wonder, though. "So…did we date the whole year? Or did I, um, go out with anybody else?" She frowns and I quickly say, "It's just I wouldn't want to hurt anybody's feelings, y'know?"

She gives a little huff and I realize, too late, what a stupid question that was to ask Trina, no matter how much I need to know.

Before I can apologize, a girl with long, dark, curly hair on Trina's other side leans forward to look past her at me. "Hey, Rigel, I'm Bri Morrison. I heard what happened, so I know you don't remember me, but we used to hang in the same crowd last year. Right, Trina?"

Trina doesn't answer, just ignores her, and then the teacher starts class.

When the bell rings at the end of the period, Trina waits until Bri moves away, then finally says, "Okay, fine. You might have gone out with other girls, but nothing serious. You *definitely* weren't dating anyone else when you left for Ireland."

I'm not dumb enough to ask which other girls. Way safer to ask my teammates later. We're heading down the hall to our next class when a guy with bright, copper-colored hair makes a point of stopping to introduce himself. This guy is seriously tall, at least six and a half feet. He's also Martian.

"Hey, Rigel. You won't remember, but I'm Sean, Sean O'Gara. Just wanted to say how sorry I am this happened to you and that if there's any way I can help, I absolutely will."

"Thanks." I shake his extended hand. "I met your sister first period. She says we all hung out some last year?"

"Kind of a lot, yeah. We even went to, um, Ireland together. Seriously, anything I can do, just let me know." He smiles, claps me on the shoulder and continues on down the hall.

Trina glances over her shoulder at him. "Sean's our basketball phenom, kind of like you were—are—with football. And Molly, his sister, is on the cheer squad with me. She's really good."

Huh. So Trina *is* capable of saying something nice about another girl. Must mean Molly and I never dated.

I file that tidbit away as we enter the Chemistry classroom to find Molly and the Sovereign already there, sharing a lab table. Again, the Sovereign's special vibe is oddly compelling. Almost magnetic. Remembering how it distracted me in Pre-Cal, I don't argue when Trina drags me to a lab table on the exact opposite side of the room.

Even so, I find myself trying to listen in on whatever Molly and the Sovereign are saying.

"I'm sorry, M. This has to be really hard for you."

"Even more than I thought it would be." Like before, the Sovereign's voice sort of thrums through me. I swallow, hard. "But I'm still planning to do everything I can to—"

"Everyone, please pick up the syllabus sheets on your tables and look through them," the teacher says, so the Sovereign breaks off. For a second I'm ticked at the teacher for making her stop, she has such an amazing voice.

"This will be a fairly hands-on class, with one or two labs a week," the teacher continues, and it's not till then I realize *he's* a Martian, too.

Sheesh. This school is positively infested with us! Because Jewel is where the Sovereign grew up and all? I could swear they said in Ireland she'd gone off to Mars to be Sovereign there, but apparently not. I'll have to get Sean and Molly O'Gara to fill me in. They'll not only know what the other kids remember from last year, but the Martian side of things, too.

On the way to our next class, Trina and I end up walking right behind Molly and the Sovereign but Trina's chattering so much I don't get a chance to eavesdrop. I want to tell her to shut up but don't feel like I can afford to piss her off.

"Anyway, maybe some afternoons after football and cheerleading practice, you can come over to my house. It'll be fun, plus I can tell you more about all the stuff you don't remember, maybe jog your memory?"

In front of me, I see the Sovereign's head twitch like she's about to turn around. She doesn't, but she can obviously hear Trina's flirty prattle, what with Martian senses and all. From what Molly said, the Sovereign and I were actually friends last year, though my parents never mentioned it. I wonder if we were *close* friends or—

"Rigel, are you listening to me?" The edge in Trina's voice snaps me back to the present. Which is all I have now anyway.

"Sorry. I keep, um, spacing out."

Immediately Trina's all apologetic. "Poor baby. I keep forgetting how overwhelming this must be for you."

She keeps talking until we reach the classroom—which the Sovereign turns into right ahead of us, though Molly keeps walking. Man, I am never going to catch up in my classes if she's in practically every one! I know it's a tiny school and all, less than a quarter the size of Center North, where I was a freshman, but still.

This time I end up sitting the next row over from her, which means her *brath* affects me more than ever. Like my skin is too tight or something. Maybe I'll try to talk to her again after. If we really were friends, that shouldn't be too out of line.

I hope.

13

Reaction moderator

AT lunch, when Trina finally goes to talk to some of the other cheerleaders, I use the opportunity to get a few questions answered without pissing her off.

"Hey, Matt, can you tell me what the deal was with Trina and me last year? Or me and anybody else, for that matter?"

Matt, one of our receivers, glances after her and frowns. "You and Trina went out for a couple weeks last fall, got voted onto Homecoming Court together, but other than that you didn't really hang much with her last year. Not for lack of her trying, though. If you're still not interested, feel free to pitch her my way. Bitchy or not, she's pretty hot."

I force a laugh. "I may do that. So…did I go out with anybody else? Have any special friends or enemies? I can't tell you how weird it is not to remember anything—or anybody. I'm always worried I'll say the wrong thing."

"Yeah, that's gotta be tough. Let's see. There was the thing you and M—Marsha Truitt, I mean—had going at the start of the year, then you two were kind of off and on for a while after that. Until Sean O'Gara got here, anyway. Sorry, man, but she…kinda dumped you for him." He grimaces again, but in sympathy this time.

"Huh. Ouch. Maybe just as well I don't remember." I barely know what I'm saying, I'm so boggled to hear I once had a *thing* with the Sovereign.

Michael Best, on my other side, chimes in. "You were still mostly friends after, so it couldn't have been too bad a breakup. You even stayed friends with Sean, mostly, though sometimes you and he sorta went at it."

Whoa! "Like, getting into fights?"

"Nah. Not that I heard about, anyway. Just digs and stuff. Mostly over M. She probably loved it."

"Hey, that's not fair," says Jimmy Franklin from across the table. He's new on the Varsity squad, though he was JV last year. "M never tried to play you guys off against each other that I saw. Not like—"

He nods in Trina's direction. "She was always trying to rile both of you up. I heard her doing it more than once."

"Yeah, well, Trina and M go way back," Michael says. "In middle school and even before, Marsha was Trina's favorite punching bag. She always hated it if M got anything she wanted. Like you. And then Sean."

Matt starts laughing. "M sure got her back, though! You all saw that video Amber got on her phone, right? The day before you guys left for Ireland," he tells me. "I don't know exactly what Trina did, but I guess M finally got fed up and went after her. It was actually pretty funny, even though Trina ended up with a broken nose—which was totally her own fault."

"So don't go believing everything Trina tells you," Jimmy cautions me. "That one's *always* got an agenda. Or two."

"Still…" Matt's eyes stray to Trina, where she's apparently demonstrating a cheer to one of the other girls, her backside wiggling. "I wouldn't say no if she, y'know, offered."

The warning bell for next period sounds. As we all grab our trays I glance thoughtfully at Trina myself. Could she be coming on to me to make M—the Sovereign—*jealous*? Seems unlikely. Even if M and I did date briefly, which I still can't believe, we apparently broke up the moment Sean, her Consort, got to Jewel. Which makes total sense, though none of the guys would know that.

In U.S. Government, after lunch, I get my first chance to see the Sovereign and her Consort-fiancé-whatever together. The two of them and Molly all say hi to me, so I sit on the same side of the room with them. It helps that Trina's not in this class.

"Hey, Rigel," says the Sovereign's little blonde friend from Pre-Cal—incidentally *not* a Martian. "I didn't get a chance to reintroduce myself earlier, but I'm Deb Andrews. We were friends last year." She doesn't say it like Trina did—like we were something *more* than friends. Which is a relief since I don't need any more complications right now.

"Hi, Deb. Nice to meet you. Again."

Bri, the dark-haired girl from Spanish class, is here, too. The Sovereign is talking with her, apparently continuing some conversation they started at lunch about who went out with who over the summer. I don't pay attention to their words, just to the

Sovereign's voice, which still seems to affect me way more than anybody else. Or maybe they're all just used to it? Probably I was, too, before I lost my memory. Gonna have to develop my immunity all over again, I guess.

Even though they're sitting next to each other, I don't notice anything special about the way M and Sean talk to each other, or the looks they exchange or anything. Not like you'd expect between boyfriend and girlfriend, much less two people who are practically engaged. Huh.

Sean and I both have Weight Training right after Government, so I finally talk with him while we take turns spotting each other on the bench press.

"This has to be super strange for you." He says it quietly enough that even the guys on the next weight bench probably can't hear him. "It's kind of weird for all of us, too. I keep forgetting how much you, um, don't know. Especially since I'm not even sure exactly how much that is. What did they tell you after you, er, woke up?"

I give the barbell another couple of lifts, trying not to make it look too easy in case any of the other guys are watching. One drawback of Martian strength—trying to be inconspicuous about it.

"Not a lot. The doctors—Healers—think it could somehow mess me up to be told too much too fast, though I don't get why. Seems stupid to me. But my mom and dad are buying into it—my mom's a Healer, too—so it's been hard to get much out of them. You ready for a turn?" I ask in a normal voice.

We switch off, sneaking another ten pounds onto the bar in the process. "Actually," I continue quietly, "I'm hoping you can fill me in on some stuff most of the others here wouldn't know about. Like, why was I in Ireland in the first place? I'm guessing it wasn't really some scholarship thing?"

Sean grimaces like he's struggling with the weights, which I can tell he's totally not, any more than I was. "Nobody mentioned going to… um, anyplace other than Ireland?"

"Should they have? I mean, I know…M? Is it okay to call her that?"

"Yeah, everyone does here at school."

"Anyway, I heard she went, uh, off-planet. And just got back. Like, yesterday?" I remember what she told Deb in Pre-Cal.

Sean gives an exaggerated grunt. "Back in Jewel, yeah, but we all got back from… y'know…a while ago. She had all kinds of stuff to take care of—speeches and meetings and such—before she could finally come here. Otherwise I *know*—"

"Hey, you guys gonna use this other thirty-five?" Pete Villiers asks from behind me, pointing at one of the weights on the rack next to us.

"Nah, go ahead." I wait till he moves off, then, "When you say 'we all,' who do you mean?"

Sean puts the bar back on the rest. "Here, your turn again. Gotta make it look good. M, Molly, me and our dad. And a bunch of other people you wouldn't know—or remember, anyway, sorry."

I'm more disappointed than relieved. "Okay, so not me."

"No, you'd been back a couple months by then."

I nearly let go of the heavy barbell—which would have hurt a lot. "What?" Out of the corner of my eye I see somebody's head turn toward us, so I work to keep my voice super low. "You mean I *did* go? To…to Mars??"

Sean gives a tiny nod. "Just for a few weeks, but…yeah. Figured they'd at least told you that much."

"So I finally… and I can't even remember it!" It's the most grossly unfair thing yet about my stupid accident. "Wait. Is that where I really got hurt? Not Ireland? Is that why I came back early?"

Now Sean looks uncomfortable. "Look, if the Healers— I'm not sure how much I ought to be telling you. If they're right, and it could somehow screw up your recovery—"

"C'mon, I *need* to know this stuff!" But I can tell from Sean's expression he's worried he's already said too much.

I do a few more reps before he finally says, "Maybe if I knew exactly what they did tell you? Then I could, I dunno, fill in a *few* blanks?"

"Okay, yeah." Anything to get more details like that last bombshell. "Let's see. Last thing I remember, we were getting ready to move to Jewel, hoping to find the Princess. Mom and Dad told me we did, and that we all helped keep Faxon's people from killing her. But hardly anything about the school year except that I had a great football season and got that scholarship to study in Ireland. Nothing about M going to Ireland, or about you or your sister. Not that I'd have known to ask. Okay, I'm done."

I mean both my turn on the bench and the lame amount of info I was given. Sean and I swap again for his last set with the weights.

"Wow, all that time in the, uh, hospital, and you never found out more than that?" The way he says it makes me feel lame for not demanding more answers.

"Yeah, well, every time I asked questions, I got told it would probably come back to me eventually, that just *telling* me could keep my real memories from returning. Which I'm starting to think might have been a pile of crap to shut me up—or to keep my folks from saying too much?" Now I wonder how much *they* really know. I'll try to find out tonight. "Trust me, I did ask. A lot. Though the first month or so I was pretty out of it."

Sean's frowning again. Maybe from the weights, but I doubt it. "Let me, um, check with some people. If they say it's all right, I'll fill you in some more, okay?"

I wonder what people he means, but figure if he was willing to tell me he'd have said. "Okay. What about stuff, er, closer to home, then? School stuff? Molly said you and I and the—M, I mean, all hung out after your family got here last year?"

He looks relieved I've changed the subject. "Yeah, we did. All four of us, especially after…um, after the holidays."

"So I wasn't pissed about you and M being together, like some of the guys thought?"

He looks less relieved now. "Well, it was kind of— Sorry, I'm not sure if—"

I think I know what he's worried about. "No, it's cool. I know about the whole political thing with you two. They did bring me up to speed on the big news items, like Faxon being out and all. Anyway, I'm sure when it was all explained to me at the time I was totally fine with it, even if she and I hung out some before you got here."

His expression clears. "Yeah, okay. Glad I don't have to go into all that. Anyway, she and I…we're not exactly dating anymore, so it's all kind of moot now." He clunks the bar back on the rest. "Enough of this, don't you think?"

I'm not sure if he means bench pressing or this conversation. I want to ask what the deal is that he and the Sovereign aren't dating when they both know they have to end up together, but it seems like kind of a personal question. Maybe later, once I get to know Sean a little better.

Not till I'm changing for my last class of the day do I wonder why I even care.

My last class is Student Publications, which means being on staff for the school yearbook and website. Apparently I applied last semester…not that I remember, or have any clue why. Before I even get there, I sense the Sovereign's *brath* from halfway down the hallway. Which shouldn't even be possible.

I'm last to arrive, between changing after Weight Training and finding the room, tucked away in a corner of the school. Of the seven other students, the Sovereign is the only one I've already met. As far as I know.

Once I'm in the room, Ms. Raymond, who's also our English Lit teacher, shuts the door and turns to us with a big smile. "Welcome! We have an exciting year ahead of us, learning how to create and publish a quality website and online newspaper, and put together a first-class yearbook. Last year the Jaguar Journal was named third best in Indiana for high school blogs and this year we're aiming for number one!"

Two girls and the only other boy give little cheers. The rest of us just smile back.

"We'll spend today introducing ourselves and filling all the staff positions. Abigail, why don't you go first?"

Abigail, a tall, skinny black girl, starts listing all the stuff she did last year and finishes by volunteering to be editor-in-chief for the online newspaper. She's followed by the other girl that cheered, Becky, then the boy, Jeremy—a short, nerdy-looking kid in glasses. They were all on the staff last year, and the only ones excited to be here. The rest of us just say our names. The words "I'm Marsha Truitt" make all the hairs on my arms prickle.

Ms. Raymond asks for volunteers for a bunch of different jobs, from scheduling to layout to graphics. The three journalism geeks keep putting up their hands, willing to do several jobs apiece. The teacher tells the rest of us we can do proofreading and stuff until we learn the ropes, unless any of us have special skills we'd like to contribute.

"Rigel's really good with computers," the Sovereign suddenly says. "And I'm pretty decent at online research and stuff."

I stare at her, wondering where the heck *that* came from. How does she know I'm good with computers? If I even still am. It's not like I've had a chance to play with this year's models—though the two I see in the room look pretty old.

"Thank you, Marsha. In that case, why don't the two of you handle fact-checking?" She makes a note in her notebook.

The Sovereign shoots me a glance, then quickly looks away, like she's embarrassed or nervous. Neither of which make sense if we really were friends last year. If I supposedly went to *Mars* with her. Which I'm still not sure I believe, no matter what Sean said.

I spend the rest of the period sneaking peeks at her while Ms. Raymond drones on, explaining everything about the yearbook and advertising and journalism ethics and stuff. But I don't catch her looking back again.

At football practice, I do way better than last week. Not only do I remember all the plays—not from last year, just from last week—but my arm feels stronger, too. Guess I'm finally getting some muscle tone back after lying around in the hospital all summer. I can tell from Coach's enthusiastic recap he's nearly as relieved as I am. My performance last week must have worried him, though he didn't say so.

My dad picks me up after, but I wait till we're home to start asking questions because sometimes the way he and Mom look at each other tells me more than what they actually say. I know now there's a whole lot they haven't told me. What I don't know is why.

Mom's already home from the hospital where she works as an OB/Gyn. She greets me with a smile and a couple sandwiches to tide me over till dinner.

"How was your first day? As uncomfortable as you were afraid it might be?" Her hazel eyes, the exact same color as mine, are sympathetic—and a little worried.

"It was…enlightening," I answer, watching both her and Dad closely. Sure enough, they exchange one of their looks.

"What do you mean, Son?" Dad asks, taking half a sandwich himself and sitting down at the kitchen table. Mom sits beside him, definitely worried now.

I take a big bite of my sandwich—I'm starving—and swallow before answering, planning out my words. "I mean I learned more about my missing year in one day than you guys told me all summer. Seems like you left out a few important details. Like how I used to hang out with the *Sovereign*—who's back in school, by the way—*and* with her Consort and his sister, who're also back. Oh, and that I went to freaking *Mars* before my accident. You know, little stuff like that."

Now they exchange a much longer look, the kind that means they're using that special telepathy they have. Which I really, really hate.

"Hey, how about you talk to *me,* huh? I specifically asked about my friends at school and all you mentioned were the guys on the football team." I know my tone's accusing, even rude, but I don't care.

Dad frowns. "Rigel, I know it must seem like we deliberately kept things from you but please trust us, we had good reasons."

"Reasons like making me look like a complete idiot on my first day of school? I practically lost it when the Sovereign suddenly walked into my Homeroom. Not to mention two other *Echtran* kids and at least one *Echtran* teacher. You didn't tell me there'd be *any* others here."

Mom reaches across to put her hand on mine with that Healer calming thing she does but I pull away. "We didn't know, Rigel. Honestly. No one told us for certain that the Sovereign and the O'Garas were coming back to Jewel. The last we heard, it sounded unlikely. So there seemed little point in mentioning them when you had so many other things to adjust to and re-learn."

"And Mars? Are you going to claim you didn't know about that, either?" I put down my half-eaten second sandwich, my appetite gone.

"Yes, we knew," Dad says. "But the Healers felt it was best—"

"Yeah, I've heard that line all summer. And I believe it less every time I hear it. Why am I *really* being kept in the dark about so much stuff? How is telling me about things I did and the people I did them with going to screw up getting my memory back? Seems to me it would do the exact opposite. *Help* me remember."

Now Mom looks stern, which she doesn't very often. "Rigel, you simply have to trust that we have your best interests at heart. We've consulted with the most skilled Mind Healers available on both Earth and Mars and are following their recommended course."

But something in her expression tells me she's still holding back.

"Fine. I guess I'll just have to find out what I need to know from other people. Like Sean O'Gara. Or maybe from the Sovereign herself."

I slam out of the kitchen and head upstairs to my room, afraid if I say any more I'll regret it later.

14

Impedance

I hurl myself onto my bed and stare at the ceiling, trying harder than ever to *remember.* Sure, when my brain fog cleared around the end of June the Healers told me not to, that I should just let things come back on their own. But I tried anyway—and after today, it feels way more important. Because there's definitely stuff my folks, and maybe other people, are trying to keep from me. Stuff I'd *know*, if only I could remember.

Stuff about Mars?

I look up at all the model space ships hanging from my bedroom ceiling, models I built myself back in sixth and seventh grade. It wasn't till I was ten that my parents finally told me about *Echtrans* and the colony on Mars where they were born and everything. After I got over being totally freaked, I became obsessed with science fiction—movies, books, comics, games…and especially space ships.

There, by the window, are my three different versions of the Starship Enterprise facing off against a Klingon Bird of Prey. The Millennium Falcon is over the door, positioned like it's escaping from the Imperial Cruiser behind it. Above the dresser hangs the Battlestar Galactica. And right over my bed is…a flat, oval crystal, etched with the constellation Orion.

I sit up and frown at the unfamiliar crystal. It's suspended on a nylon filament, the same as my models. Looking closer, I notice Orion's left foot, the star Rigel, is blue. Where did *this* come from? It doesn't seem like the kind of thing I'd buy for myself. Maybe Mom gave it to me? For some reason, I don't think so.

Standing on the bed, I reach up and take it off its little hook so I can hold it, look more closely at it. And, for the first time since waking up in that Irish/Martian hospital, a ghost of memory niggles at the edge of my brain—then disappears. There's *something* important about this crystal.

Shoving my irritation at my parents aside, I head downstairs, the crystal in my hand. Mom's in the kitchen, making dinner. I walk up to her and hold out the crystal.

"Where did I get this? And when?"

She turns and looks, and I swear her face goes a shade paler. I definitely don't imagine the flash of fear in her eyes. Fear? But she covers it quickly.

"That? It…I believe it was a birthday present, from one of your school friends. For your sixteenth birthday, I mean. You had a party, here at the house, with nearly all of your friends. That must be where it came from."

Before she can go back to browning meat, I ask, "Which friend? Who gave it to me?"

Mom hesitates just a hair too long before saying, "I'm afraid I really don't remember, Rigel. Possibly one of the girls. Most of the cheerleaders came to your party, as I recall, as well as the football team. Nearly all of them brought gifts."

But this was the only one I hung right over my bed. That must mean it was important to me—then, anyway.

"You're sure you don't remember?" I press, mostly to see if she'll lie again. But she turns back to the stove so I can't watch her face.

"I'll think about it. Maybe it will come to me."

"Or I could ask around at school."

Her shoulders twitch, but she doesn't look at me again. "Yes, I suppose you could. Someone there may remember who brought it."

Irked all over again, I go back upstairs, still carrying the crystal. Might as well get started reading *The Crucible* for English Lit. But the whole time I'm reading, my eyes keep straying to the crystal on my desk—a dreamcatcher? Is that what they call these things?—and wondering.

Next day I take the bus, since it seems lame to have Dad drive me again. Supposedly I took Drivers Ed last year, but never actually got my license. So the bus it is.

When I get to school, I'm surprised to see the Sovereign getting off the bus ahead of mine, along with her friends Bri and Deb, and Molly O'Gara. I figured the Sovereign would be driven, maybe in a limo or something, but now realize that's dumb. No one at school—except the other *Echtrans*—know who she really is. Still, the bus?

Bri sees me and waves, then the others do too. The Sovereign smiles and looks like she might come over to me, but then she turns away and goes into the school with the other girls. Half a second later, Trina comes up behind me, from the direction of the parking lot, and grabs my arm.

"Silly, why didn't you say you needed a ride to school? I totally can drive you, you know."

I shrug. Even if she wasn't really my girlfriend last year, I don't need to make enemies. Especially when she's trying so hard to be helpful. "I don't mind the bus. I figure doing things the way I did last year might help me, you know, remember stuff."

She pouts a little, but more in a sexy than pissed-off way. "I guess that makes sense. I'd just like to spend a little time alone with you, Rigel."

"Yeah, we'll, um, have to do that sometime." I stick to the safer topic of schoolwork until I head to Pre-Cal and she heads to whatever her first class is.

Remembering that weird tingly thing I got from the Sovereign's *brath* yesterday, I wonder if it'll be less noticeable, now I know to expect it. But even as I think that, I feel it. I glance behind me, but don't see her. The tingling keeps getting stronger and when I walk into the classroom she's already there, watching the door.

For me?

She takes a couple steps in my direction and I tense up, determined to play it way cooler than yesterday. Her friend Deb says something to her and she stops to answer, then turns back my way and smiles…at Molly, who just walked in the door behind me. That's who she was watching for. Duh.

"How was your first day, yesterday?" Molly stops to ask me. "Did it get easier once you started re-learning names and everything?"

I appreciate how not-awkward she acts about the whole memory thing when most other people seem weirded out by it. "A little easier, yeah. It's going to take a while before people who were friends before *feel* like friends, though. Y'know?"

"Of course. We all must seem like strangers right now. If Sean or I can help, let us know, okay? Or M. She wants to help, too."

She glances over at the Sovereign and I look too, just in time to see her look away. Like she doesn't really want anything to do with me, much less "help" me. And why should she? Even if we were friends or…whatever…at the very start of last year, she's got way more important things to deal with now. Sovereign things.

Which suddenly makes me wonder why she's even *going* to high school, considering all the responsibilities she must have. Kind of strange, now I think about it. If I work up my nerve to talk to her again, maybe I'll ask.

My second day at Jewel High—that I can remember, anyway—is a lot like the first. I'm definitely no less attuned to the Sovereign's vibe. Maybe more. In our classes together I sometimes think she's sneaking glances at me, but I'm never quite sure.

Trina, on the other hand, is clingier than ever. Like she's trying hard to convince me we have all this history that the guys pretty much told me we don't. At lunch, I finally tell her—gently—to back off.

"Look, you've been great, helping me adjust and all, Trina. And I really want to stay friends. But until I start remembering, at least a little, I can't see trying to be in any kind of actual relationship. With anybody. If that's okay?"

Her blue eyes narrow between those long black lashes, and for a second I think she's going to tell me off. But then her glance flicks to the others at the table—football players and a few cheerleaders—and she flashes a smile.

"Oh, Rigel, of *course* I understand! No matter how much I'd like us to get back to how we used to be with each other, I'd *never* push you faster than you're comfortable with. I definitely don't want to make things even *more* confusing for you than they already are. If ever I do or say *anything* that makes you the least bit uncomfortable, you just tell me. Okay?"

"Okay," I say, even though I know—and she must, too—how awkward that would be, which means I probably never will. "Thanks for understanding, Trina."

She wraps both hands around my upper arm and dimples up at me. "I totally, totally do, Rigel. Don't you worry."

Stifling a sigh, I just smile stiffly back and turn to talk football with the guys.

In Weight Training, I pair up with Sean again, this time for squats, since I've thought of a bunch more questions to ask him.

"So," I mutter, once we're separate from the other guys, "did you check with whoever you needed to check with? Can you tell me more…stuff now?"

"I, uh…" He turns away from me to pull a weight off the rack. "There's stuff I probably shouldn't, but if you've got questions, I'll try to answer them."

Fair enough, though there are probably a million questions I don't even *know* to ask.

"Okay. You said yesterday I only went to Mars for a few weeks. Is that where I got hurt?"

Sean takes a while to clip the weights onto the bar before answering. "You, uh, actually went as M's Bodyguard—got special training and everything. And yeah, that's where you lost your memory."

"So I got injured protecting her?" That sounds *way* cooler than a car accident. "Did I, like, throw myself in front of a projectile or something?"

He positions the bar across his shoulders and squats. "Not… exactly. But a lot of people do consider you a hero."

I think about that as he does a few reps. "Can't you just tell me everything that happened? In order?"

Standing up again, he gives his head a little shake. "Even if I could, it'd take way too long."

"But—"

David Jaworski, one of the receivers on the football team, pauses on his way to the medicine balls. "It's so weird to see you guys acting like buddies without M or Molly running interference. Guess you worked everything out in Ireland, huh?"

Like I'd remember? I shrug and wait for him to move off before saying, "So Matt was right? We really didn't get along? Why?"

Again with the grimace I can tell isn't from the weights. "What you said yesterday. M. But it was more my fault than yours." He finishes his set and we switch places before he continues. "When I first got here, I was kind of…possessive. She didn't like it. And you didn't like it. Especially since neither of you knew about the whole Consort thing yet."

"But once that was all explained? I still wasn't cool with it?" For years, my dad drummed into me how important it was to get Faxon out and the Sovereign back in. To get everything on Mars back to normal. It was the whole reason we were looking for the lost Princess.

I should have been totally onboard with anything that would help.

"Well, it was kind of a shock, I guess, especially for M, since she was raised here, never knowing about, well, anything. Took a while for her to come around to the idea. She met you first, so you were... better friends with her than I was. And I kind of, well, took it out on you. More than I should have. Sorry, man."

I shrug, then start my squats. "Not like I remember, anyway. But she finally came around, right? The guys said you two were definitely a thing last spring. So why'd you break up?" I add in a rush.

"Yeah, she finally realized how important it was politically, and all. But she's...not really ready for that kind of commitment yet, I guess."

"She is just sixteen. Considering how long our, uh, people live, maybe she figures there'll be plenty of time later?"

Though I mean that to be comforting, Sean winces a little. "Yeah. Hope so. So, any other school-type stuff you had questions about?"

He obviously wants to drop the subject of him and the Sovereign so I start asking about last year's basketball season.

When I get to last period, Ms. Raymond assigns one of the new girls to work with Abigail on story planning and layout, another with Becky for reporting and editing, and the other with Jeremy on photography.

Then she hands me the log-in info for the newspaper website and sends me to the computer in the corner along with the Sovereign. Who I've *got* to start thinking of as M, disrespectful as it seems. Otherwise I'll screw up and call her "Excellency" or something, like I almost did when I first met her, which would be totally uncool.

She sits down next to me at the monitor. "So, um, how are you managing so far?" If it wasn't so crazy, I'd think she's almost as nervous to talk to me as I am to her.

"Okay, I guess. It'll probably get easier as the year goes on. Maybe I'll even start remembering stuff."

She presses her lips together for a second—I totally should *not* be looking at her lips!—before saying, "I hope so. How far back did they...I mean, what's the last thing you do remember? From before?"

I type in the URL for the school blog so it'll at least look like we're working—and also to give me time to think. Which is surprisingly hard with her extra-strong *brath* right next to me, making all my nerves jangle. Does she know what an unsettling effect she has on people?

"Last summer. We were getting ready to move from Indianapolis to Jewel."

"Do you remember…why?" She's staring at the computer, though her cheeks are pinker than before.

I quickly look at the computer myself. "Um, yeah. We were hoping to find…you." I say it super quietly, knowing she'll have no trouble hearing me.

She lets out a little breath. "Which you obviously did."

"Yeah. Is it true you had no clue who you were before that?"

"I didn't even know people like us existed, so how could I?"

I shake my head. "That had to be pretty weird for you, huh? The whole thing must have sounded totally insane. Who finally told you?"

Now she looks at me, those incredibly green eyes boring right into mine, making my heart race. "You did, Rigel."

"Oh." I don't know what else to say. There's something in her expression that makes me jumpy. Gives me an inkling why Sean was jealous last year. "You probably thought I was nuts, huh?"

She snorts a tiny laugh. "Well, let's just say I took some convincing, but between you and your parents, you managed it."

"So after that we were…friends? That's what Molly said." I'm not sure why I don't mention Sean, too.

"We were. Close friends." Again with that intense, questioning look in her eyes.

Swallowing, I glance away. "Um, that's good to know. So, I guess we should get to work cleaning up this website, huh?"

To my relief, she takes the cue and turns back to the computer, making occasional suggestions which I quickly implement. For the rest of the period we don't discuss anything personal and as much as I need to find stuff out, I'm glad.

Because I'm way too attracted to this girl and she's *absolutely* off limits. For all kinds of reasons. Totally apart from everything to do with her being the Sovereign, she's also Sean's ex and he's clearly not over her.

And even if he was, the two of them still have this whole Sovereign-Consort thing looming in their future, a joint destiny I can never be a part of. No matter how much else I might have forgotten,

I can't afford to forget that.

15

Touch potential

THAT evening, I try to get more out of my parents, especially about M and Sean. And M and me.

"Of course you were friends, Rigel," Mom finally admits at dinner. "You were the very first *Echtran* she ever met, and she was the first *Echtran* girl your own age that you'd ever met. It was natural you would spend time with each other."

"Even when we'd positively identified her, no one was quite sure yet what that would mean," Dad points out. "Faxon was still in power at the time."

"Exactly," Mom says. "Of course we hoped the news of her survival would revitalize the Resistance against Faxon, but for all anyone knew, Princess Emileia would never be more than a symbol, a rallying point for Nuathans and *Echtrans*."

In other words, back then there'd been no particular reason we *couldn't* date—not that they were admitting we had. "So how does that whole Consort thing work? Is it like an arranged marriage?"

Dad sets down his fork. "Essentially. It's traditional for the Sovereign to pair with a descendant of a previous Sovereign. Such pairings are believed to strengthen the qualities we look for in a leader, keeping the Royal line robust."

"So she and Sean are cousins?" Yuck.

"*Distant* cousins," Mom emphasizes. "But both from the Royal House, yes."

"And neither of them get any say about this? I thought Nuathan society was supposed to be all forward-thinking?" No wonder M wasn't a fan of the idea when she first found out. Was Sean?

Mom and Dad exchange one of their speaking glances before Dad answers. "The Sovereign and her Consort understand that observing tradition will be a stabilizing influence after everything Faxon did. That's far more important than whatever their personal preferences might initially have been. According to recent reports, they both seem comfortable with the prospect."

"But when we first told M—the Sovereign—who she was and

everything, we didn't tell her that part?"

Mom sighs. "Everyone assumed all traditional Consort candidates were killed long before we learned the Princess herself had survived. You may remember hearing how Faxon massacred hundreds of Royals, while others managed to flee to Earth?"

"But if the O'Garas escaped and were on Earth all this time, why —?"

"No, they stayed." Dad's now using his "politics" voice. "They went into hiding in a Nuathan farming community, concealing their identities while spearheading the Resistance against Faxon's rule, at great personal risk. Quinn and Lili O'Gara are among Nuath's greatest heroes and I'm sure they raised their children in the same spirit. Not until they were betrayed, late in Faxon's reign, did they leave Nuath, smuggled aboard an Earthbound ship."

Wow. Sean never bothered to mention he and his whole family are heroes, which is pretty cool.

"So, did Sean and the Princess find out about the Consort thing at the same time? And when did you—we—find out?" I don't know why I'm harping on that particular point so much. Maybe because Sean's the best friend I have so far, so I want to understand him better?

"Nearly everyone believed the Princess was killed at the age of two, which made the idea of a Consort moot," Dad reminds me. "Even after the O'Garas arrived in Jewel, we had no idea Sean was of that particular lineage, only that they'd been Royals in exile, and heroes. It was Sean's uncle Allister who revealed the truth, to us and to the Princess."

"Far too abruptly, in my opinion." Mom's face prims up with obvious distaste. "A diplomat, Allister was not."

"When was that?" I ask.

"Not until November, well after the events we told you about."

I assume she means the battle here in Jewel, where my family helped keep Faxon's forces from killing the Princess and invading Earth. Which I now realize must be why they made me her Bodyguard, and also why she summoned Grandfather to Mars and named him her Regent.

"What I don't get is why the Sovereign—and Sean—are back in Jewel at all. Shouldn't they be on Mars, doing whatever it is Sovereigns and their Consorts do?"

"Do you remember what I told you in Ireland about the need for accelerated emigration from Nuath to Earth?" Dad says.

I think for a second, since that was when I was still kind of fuzzy. "Because the power's running out sooner than expected?"

"Yes, due to Faxon's excesses. Since her Acclamation, the Sovereign has been working hard to persuade people to relocate from Mars to Earth. The news reports say that she returned to Jewel, and to high school, in order to lead by example, to demonstrate that it is indeed possible to discreetly and peacefully fit into *Duchas* society."

Huh. If I was supreme ruler of Nuath, especially after living my whole life in a podunk town like Jewel, I'd want to enjoy it for more than a few months. Guess that means I'm not exactly Sovereign material.

Finally, I ask the question that bothers me most. "So, if Sean and the Sovereign are both on board with that Consort thing, why aren't they a couple now? Sean says they're not, though they're obviously friends. Isn't that a little strange?"

Another long look between my parents. And when Mom answers, she doesn't quite meet my eyes. "Whatever their reasons, I imagine it's personal, Rigel, and something they'll need to work out between themselves. I'd, ah, recommend against getting involved."

Dad nods. "The last thing you'd want to do is interfere with a pairing that will go so far to restore confidence among our people, both here and back on Mars."

In other words, if they do know what's going on with M and Sean, they're not telling. Maybe they're right that it's none of my business. But I still want to know.

Though my memories of the last year are as stubbornly elusive as ever, over the next few days at school I do my best to fill in more blanks. The guys on the team help by answering some questions about what happened at school and Sean gives me a little more info about non-school stuff when we manage to pair up in Weight Training.

Friday I have to go light on the weights since tonight's our first game. Not till class is half over do I get a chance to talk privately with Sean. "Hey, tell me about when you and your family were in hiding and stuff. Must have been scary?"

He does another incline press. "Only the last week or so, when we had to bug out in a hurry. Before that, we just lived like Ags—farmers —in a little village. Mum and Dad snuck out to secret Resistance meetings, and a few times we even had them in our house, but they never let me or Molly sit in on them. Then a meeting got raided. Our older sister was captured and the rest barely escaped. They seized a lot of records, so it wasn't safe to stay after that. We were lucky a ship captain was willing to smuggle us out."

I guess that part was exciting enough. "What, um, happened to your sister?"

His mouth twists, making me sorry I asked. "She's…mostly okay now. Still back home—in Nuath, I mean. They're still treating her for mem— uh, for what Faxon's people did to her."

"What, did they torture her?"

"Yeah. Pretty much." He'd obviously been about to say something else, though, and stopped himself. Something else I'm not supposed to know about?

No, I'm being paranoid. Probably just something he'd rather not talk about, which is totally fair.

"My folks consider your whole family heroes," I tell him, hoping to lighten his mood. "Sounds like all our people do."

"Nah. Here, help me with this." I guide the weights back onto the rack, even though he doesn't really need my help. "You're more a hero than I've ever been, what with that big battle last fall and everything after. Like on Mars."

I snort. "Yeah, well, I'll take your word for it, but—"

"Doesn't seem quite real? I guess it wouldn't. But the news stories then said you and your family helped fight off a whole bunch of Faxon's people, that you risked your life to protect the Princess. That much is common knowledge, even if I can't say much about the other."

Meaning whatever happened on Mars *isn't* common knowledge? So maybe they don't *want* me remembering it? "Thanks, man. My folks have barely even let me read news stories. Something else the Healers warned against even though it seems like it would help. Might jog something loose, you know?"

Now Sean looks uncomfortable, like maybe he said too much

again. "Yeah, you'd think. But maybe they have their reasons."

"Right." Now my mood is souring. Not knowing stuff is getting really old. Which reminds me to ask about all those other *Echtrans* at school—our Chemistry teacher and the new vice principal, who sometimes patrols the cafeteria at lunchtime.

"Oh, yeah. There was another one last year, too, a Ms. Harrigan, but I think she's gone. Not sure about Mr. Abbot. I think M said he's a friend of your grandfather's? But Mr. Cormac—Cormac's actually his first name, by the way—is M's official Bodyguard. Came here from Mars with us. Guess they decided putting him in charge of school discipline would make it easy for him to do his job without raising suspicions. You've got to admit, he looks the part. Way more than Mr. Pedersen did—the guy everybody used to call 'The Warden.'"

"What happened to him?"

"Retired, I think. Anyway, pretty sure that's all of us. At the moment, anyway."

I want to ask Sean more questions but class is nearly over. Besides, what I most want to ask—what the deal is between him and M these days—is basically off-limits. When I hinted about it to Molly yesterday, she just said she "hopes everything will work out." But the way she said it made it even more obvious Sean still has it kind of bad for M.

On my way to last period, it occurs to me one way I can repay Sean for telling me so much stuff might be to help get the two of them back together. M's been acting a lot more friendly in general in the classes we have together, though we haven't really talked much since that once at the computer. If I get a chance, maybe I'll mention Sean to her, kind of nudge her his way.

The past couple afternoons Ms. Raymond had us all working separately, on different stuff. A good thing, since I still get kind of jumpy and tongue-tied around M. But today we're both at the same computer as before, fact-checking stories for our first online newspaper of the year. Which means I can start my campaign to help Sean right away.

I skim the print-out of the first article and read the highlighted bits out loud to M, who starts typing search terms into Google. When one of the pages takes a while to load, I plunge in.

"So. Sean O'Gara. Great guy, huh?" I try to keep my voice super casual but realize as the words come out how stupid I sound.

And, yeah, the look she gives me is startled and a little suspicious. "What?"

"Sean. You know. Molly's brother?"

"Yes. I know who Sean is. What about him?" Definitely suspicious now.

"Um, just that he's been helping a lot, filling me in on some stuff my parents didn't bother to tell me. He seems like a really nice guy."

M tilts her head back to look me straight in the eyes—which makes her *look* like a Sovereign. I try not to squirm under that direct gaze.

"Did Sean tell you to say that?"

"What? No! Of course not. He'd never— I mean, I know you guys used to date. But aren't now. And I know about that whole, um, Consort thing…"

"Sean *must* have mentioned that part."

I quickly shake my head. "I already knew. Found out back in Ireland. My parents talked about it some, too. Sean, not so much. But he's… You should probably talk to him. Work things out. Or something. Don't you think?" Jeez, I sound lame!

M tenses up and frowns. Then she narrows those incredible eyes, like she's trying to bore right into my brain. But after a long, nervous moment she relaxes and even smiles.

"So Sean's been nice to you, helping you? I'm glad. Because I actually, um, asked him to do that. I always hoped you two would become real friends, but—"

"But I never liked the Consort thing? No, Sean didn't tell me that," I add quickly when her perfect eyebrows go up. "But I figured, from a couple things he did say—"

She holds up a hand and I immediately shut up. I mean, she *is* the Sovereign. "Rigel." Her voice is softer now. Gentler. "I really hoped once we were in the same room together, especially once we had a chance to talk, you might start to understand. But I guess it's going to take, well… Don't freak out, okay?"

"Freak out?" Even though I have no idea what she's going to tell me, my heart starts to slam against my chest. No matter what it is, it's *got* to be something I need to know. "Okay. I won't."

"Good."

I wait, bracing myself for whatever it is she's about to say. But instead of revealing something shocking, like I expect, she just reaches over with her hand and touches my forearm.

16

Spark test

A jolt, like some combo of electricity and adrenaline, shoots up my arm and through my whole body until I swear the hair on my head must be standing straight up. I scramble backward so fast I nearly fall off my chair.

"What was that?" I whisper wildly. "What did you just do?"

I'm shocked to my core by what just happened—whatever the hell it was. But she just looks…expectant. Like she's waiting for something important to happen.

Funny thing is, I do feel like I might be on the verge of some kind of breakthrough. Or maybe a breakdown. I hold my breath, also waiting, though I have no clue for what. But the seconds lengthen and her expression slowly changes from eager anticipation to uncertainty and finally disappointment.

"You don't… You're not…?" She doesn't look or sound regal now. More like helpless and confused. I feel a weird urge to comfort her.

"What did you do?" I repeat instead, needing *some* kind of explanation. Surely her mere touch doesn't affect everybody like that, every single time? Or is that how the Sovereigns keep people in line? Except it didn't hurt, exactly. More like it…energized every cell in my body or something. I feel more awake than I can ever remember being.

Pressing her lips together like she's trying not to cry, she swallows, hard, and looks away. "I, um…I seem to have fried another computer."

Sure enough, the screen is black. I try tapping the space bar, in case it just went to sleep, but no. "Did you say *another* computer?"

She nods. "I'm kind of a disaster around electronics. Always have been. It's a, uh, static thing." Her voice is slightly shaky. Again I get that bizarre urge to comfort her, even though I have no idea why she's so upset.

"Yeah, I think it's an *Echtran* thing. I sometimes do that, too." I try to convince myself that's all that freaky adrenaline zap was, though I know better. Despite my own static issues, I've never felt anything remotely like that before.

Still unnerved, I reach for the computer. "Here, let me see what I can do." I unplug it and plug it back in, try turning it back on. Nothing. Finally I go to Ms. Raymond and tell her the computer conked out.

She comes over, does all the same stuff I just did, then frowns at M. "Mr. Morrison did warn me about you, Marsha—your propensity to short out computers, I mean. Apparently he was right."

"If you let me take it home, I can probably fix it over the weekend," I volunteer. "I really am good with computers. So's my dad. His job is troubleshooting computers and software."

Ms. Raymond's worried expression clears. "I'd very much appreciate that, Rigel, if you really think you can. The publications budget has been cut so much, a new computer or even an expensive repair would put a serious dent in it."

M and I spend the last ten minutes of class packing up the computer, a clunky old desktop. I'm careful not to brush against her in the process.

Just before the final bell rings, I whisper, "Seriously, what was that…thing you did, where you touched my arm? What did you think would happen, when you told me not to freak out?" Which I totally did anyway, I realize.

"It doesn't matter, since it didn't work. Have a great game tonight, Rigel. I'll come cheer, if my aunt lets me."

With a sad sort of smile, she picks up her backpack and walks out of the room.

By halftime, there's no doubt about it—I'm playing the best game of my life. Or, at least, that I can remember. My arm has never felt so good and it's like I know exactly where my receivers will be before they're even there. I'm faster, stronger, more agile than I've ever been in practice. It's like I can do no wrong.

Once or twice, while the defense is on the field, I wonder if my exponential improvement could possibly have anything to do with that bizarre zap I got from the Sovereign this afternoon. She obviously expected it to do *something.* I kind of doubt giving me rad football skills was what she had in mind, but who knows? Maybe she's a really rabid fan or something.

In the locker room, Coach Glazier is ecstatic. "I didn't want to mess with your head earlier, Stuart, but now I can admit that last week you had me worried. Especially after the town pitched in to help us double the size of our stands. But seeing what you did this half, I don't think we'll have any trouble filling those new bleachers. Looks like you're back a hundred and ten percent. Keep up the great work, son, and we'll be looking at an undefeated season!"

The other guys hoot and holler their agreement, then Coach launches into his halftime talk, mostly about getting the defense up to the same level as our offense. When we head back to the field for the second half, I look up at the supposedly new stands. Hard to believe they were even smaller last year. My gaze drifts over to where M was sitting earlier, on the fifty yard line.

Her friends Bri and Deb are still there, but she's gone. Squashing down a stupid prick of disappointment, I look a few rows higher to wave at my parents—and there's M, talking to them. Arguing with them? My mom shakes her head and says something and Dad nods agreement with whatever Mom is saying. M leans in like she's arguing again, then heads back to her friends, frowning. My folks watch her go. They both look worried. What the—?

Before I can even start to come up with a theory, the whistle blows. I shove my helmet back on and run onto the field. Another mystery that'll have to wait. Time to get my head back in the game.

At the final whistle, it's Jewel 41, Frankton 13 and the crowd explodes. Fans stream onto the field to congratulate the team—to congratulate me. I catch a glimpse of M through the crowd, just behind her friends, heading my way. Then I get a flash—*deja vu*?—of exactly this scene, excited fans coming toward me after a big win. And M. M is…

Suddenly another flash crowds out the first, this one even clearer. A memory of Trina running up to me in her skimpy cheer outfit, just like she's doing now. Of Trina and me…kissing.

The relief of *finally* remembering something adds to my high from winning the game. So when Trina reaches me, I return her hug and swing her around. "I remember this!" I tell her exultantly. "My first memory!"

"Oh, Rigel!" she squeals and plasters her mouth on mine. I let her. We must have kissed last year, since I remember it. But it still feels…

off, somehow. So when she lets go of me, I turn half away to talk to other people—like my parents, who've just reached me.

"Great game, son, just great," Dad says. He and mom are smiling now, not looking worried at all. Then, over Mom's shoulder, I see Molly O'Gara, who's also on the cheer squad, staring at me.

Molly looks upset, almost outraged. About Trina? Crap, I never went out with Molly, did I? Like in Ireland or something? I scan the crowd for M but now I don't see her, even when her friend Bri runs up. She hugs me like Trina did. I'm glad she doesn't try to kiss me.

"What an incredible game, Rigel! Even better than last year's opener!" She goes on gushing, while other people move in to slap me on the back and offer more congratulations.

I nod but I'm not listening because I've finally spotted M. She's not heading my way anymore. Before I can figure out her expression from here, she spins around and walks quickly away. Huh. The guys did tell me she and Trina don't like each other…

Another memory is starting to niggle when I'm suddenly hit by a second clear one—M and Jimmy Franklin, dancing together, a slow dance. And me dancing with Trina. Homecoming, maybe? I turn to Trina, who's still hovering by my shoulder.

"Did…did we go to a dance together last year?"

She dimples up at me and nods. "I told you we were on the Homecoming Court together. Oh, Rigel, you *do* remember!"

Bri frowns across me at Trina. "But—"

"Can't you see other people want to talk to Rigel, Bri? Give them a chance," Trina snaps.

Bri glares at her, but moves off. I wonder what she was going to say, but then my attention is claimed by a bunch of people still wanting to congratulate me before I head to the showers.

In the car on the way home, I tell my parents about those two flashes of memory, my first since waking up in Ireland. "So I guess Trina was telling the truth about us dating last year, at least first semester. From what some of the guys said, I figured she was exaggerating."

"Oh, yes, you and Trina were fairly close for a while," Mom says lightly. "Though it never became terribly serious, of course."

"Of course?" I echo.

"Well, she *is Duchas*. It's not as though you could ever tell her about, well, us."

"Oh. Right. Yeah." I guess keeping such a big secret would make a relationship kind of hard. Which reminds me. "How about Molly O'Gara? Did I ever go out with her?"

Mom glances back at me in surprise. "I don't believe so. Oh, you did take her to the Winter Formal, but I had the impression you just went as friends."

Because Sean took M? Wasn't that what the guys told me? But if Molly and I were just friends, why did she look so upset when Trina kissed me? Then I remember the other thing I wanted to ask about.

"So what were you guys and the Sovereign talking about at halftime?"

My parents exchange one of their looks, then Mom smiles at me over her shoulder. It looks forced. "She just wanted to know how you're doing. How you're adjusting."

"Nothing else? You're sure?"

"She did mention the emigration effort," Dad adds. A little too quickly. "Wanted suggestions on ways to help the newcomers make a smoother transition. I must say, it's good to see her taking such a personal interest rather than simply delegating everything."

Mom nods, still smiling. "By all accounts, by the time Sovereign Emileia is of age, she will be a very effective leader. It's really quite flattering that she wanted our advice."

Apparently they consider some things as important to keep secret from me as from any *Duchas*. I just wish I knew why.

Later that night, I stare up at the crystal dreamcatcher hanging over my bed, trying to force more memories to surface. Like who gave me that thing. Should I ask Trina on Monday if it was her? Somehow, I don't think it was. If I ask, and it was another girl, it'll probably piss her off.

Frustrated, I try to make myself to remember something as simple as my sixteenth birthday party. For a second I almost catch a flash of something—Sean O'Gara's face?—but then it's gone. I probably imagined it.

I think about the two clear flashes I did get, of Trina. Then about everything else that happened today, including my awesome game tonight. But as I drift off to sleep, I'm mostly reliving that inexplicable jolt I got when M touched me.

When the early-morning sun wakes me, bits of a dream still linger. I lie still, trying to hang onto the details, hoping for more clues about things I've forgotten. I was at school, in a classroom, and M was definitely there. As I concentrate, more comes back.

M and me, sitting near each other. A teacher talking. M was talking, too…except her lips weren't moving. Instead, it's like I could hear her voice inside my head, saying something about meeting after school. And then I thought back to her, agreeing. Wacky. Obviously not a real memory. More like wishful thinking based on what my parents sometimes do. But why with the Sovereign?

Disappointed and a little disturbed, I shake off the weird dream, glance up at the dreamcatcher, glinting in a sunbeam, and climb out of bed.

It takes Dad and me maybe an hour to fix the computer I brought from school—just a matter of finding the burned-out connection in the motherboard and re-soldering it. It's fiddly work and we don't talk much while we're doing it. That stupid dream I woke up to keeps niggling at me. I'd rather remember real stuff, like I did last night after the game.

"There. That should do it." Dad sets down the solder gun. "You want to put the case back on?"

I fit the housing over the components and pick up our tiny allen wrench. "Thanks, Dad. Ms. Raymond will be happy." The bolts secured, I glance over at him. "I wish you and Mom would tell me at least part of what's really going on. Like the real reason the Sovereign was talking to you at the game last night."

"I'm sorry, son. You caught us off-guard and we weren't sure what to say, which I guess was obvious. But there are issues—political issues—that we don't feel free to discuss with you just yet."

"Because of what the Healers said could happen?" I'm really not buying that anymore.

He sighs and looks away from me. "Not entirely. Sean O'Gara told you that you went to Mars with them last spring?"

"Yeah." I hold my breath, hoping he's finally going to give me some real information.

"While there you apparently heard things, saw things, that you, ah, shouldn't have. At least, that's what we've been told."

"Things? What things?"

Dad lifts a shoulder. "We don't know. They won't tell us. Something highly classified. Something that could put you, perhaps all of us, at risk, should you remember."

"You mean…you don't *want* me to get my memory back? Because it might be dangerous?" I *thought* all that crap about damaging my mind or health was bogus. But I never expected this!

"We were told it might be safest if you don't." He sighs. "I realize this is terribly frustrating, Rigel, and perhaps your memory will spontaneously return at some point. I hope so. But if it does, if you start to remember things that seem as though they could be risky for you to know…"

"I should keep my mouth shut?"

He nods, his eyes sympathetic. "That would be safest, yes."

In other words, I shouldn't even tell Mom and Dad. I wonder if it's something Sean knows? M—the Sovereign—must. But apparently there's no point asking.

"Thanks, Dad. And tell Mom not to worry, okay? I won't do anything to put you guys in danger, no matter how much I want to know everything that happened last year."

I don't promise to stop trying to find out, though.

17

Switching impulse

TRINA calls twice over the weekend, mostly to ask if I've remembered anything else. I can tell by the way she asks, she means about *her.* But I haven't. Not about her or anybody else, unless you count that ridiculous dream about M. Which I'm not stupid enough to mention to Trina.

She also insists on giving me a ride to school Monday. I know we weren't dating when I left Jewel last spring. Now I think of it, the fact she's only called our land line, not my cell, probably means she doesn't even have that number. But since it'll be easier to bring the computer back in her car than on the bus, I say that'll be fine.

I'm carrying the computer from her little yellow sports car to the school when I see M and Molly getting off their bus just ahead of us. I half expect Trina to avoid them, but instead she wraps her hands around my arm and sort of steers me their way.

"Hey," she calls out in a kind of singsong voice, "did you hear the good news? Rigel is starting to get his memory back!"

M and Molly both stare at me. Molly looks surprised and curious, but M looks almost shocked.

"Really?" Her green eyes go wide and now she sounds happy, eager. "What have you—"

"He's remembered *me,* mostly," Trina tells her with a smirk. "I suppose it makes sense that his most *important* memories would come back first. Right, Rigel?" She slants a simpering glance up at me.

"Uh, I guess? Just a couple of flashes so far, but I definitely—" I break off at the look on M's face, hurt and almost betrayed.

"Nothing about… I mean…" she begins.

Trina titters loudly. "Sorry, Marsha, guess you're just not all that *memorable.* C'mon, Rigel." With a last smirk over her shoulder, Trina drags me toward the school.

"That wasn't very nice." I glance back to where M is still standing on the sidewalk looking stunned. "I know you and M don't get along, but—"

"Not nice?" Trina bites out the words. "Maybe nobody's told you yet, but Marsha *broke my nose* last spring. That's a lot more *not nice* than anything I just said, don't you think?"

I just shrug. Because the look I saw on M's face just now bothers me almost as much as that crazy dream I had about her over the weekend.

M is the last person to arrive in first period. She doesn't even glance at me as she goes past. Is she mad at *me* because of what Trina said? There's no telling with girls.

Several times during class I catch myself watching her across the room. I feel even more weirdly drawn to her today than all last week. Something I've got to fight, for about a dozen different reasons.

Near the end of class I notice she and Molly are whispering together. No non-Martian, including the teacher, can probably tell, but their lips take turns quivering, a sure sign. Then M turns her head slightly, like something Molly said surprised her. After a second, she nods. And starts to look my way, so I immediately focus on my book. Wonder what Molly told her? Whatever it was, M looks less upset than when she came in.

When the bell rings, she gets up and heads straight for me. Startled, I just stand there.

"Rigel, I'm sorry I let Trina get to me earlier. It's not your fault she acted like that, even if it's true all you've remembered so far is…her."

I shrug. "Like I said, just a quick flash or two, after the game Friday. But it's *something*. Hoping more will start coming back to me now."

"I hope so, too. Maybe something a little more…pleasant than Trina." She doesn't sound nearly as snarky as Trina did. More like a joke aimed at herself. "Did you and your dad manage to fix the computer? I was going to ask when I saw you carrying it, before—"

Before Trina got all bitchy. "Yeah, we did. Fried connection in the motherboard. All better now." I have to stop myself from leaning in closer. It's like she's magnetic or something. Weird.

"That's great. Not that I doubted for a second you could." She smiles up at me, a warm smile that makes my stomach do a flip. "Well, I'll…see you in Chemistry. Bye, Rigel."

Giving me something that might almost be a wink, she heads down the hall. I stare after her for a long moment, appreciating her figure, which is every bit as good as Trina's. Then I give myself a shake.

This is the *Sovereign* I'm feeling all warm and fuzzy about! Not okay. Even if we did date briefly a year ago. That was then, this is now. Whole different ballgame. I need to remember that.

Trina is still clingy in Spanish but I've about had enough of her, after the stuff she said to M this morning. Looks like the guys were right about Trina, that she's basically a shallow, vindictive brat, no matter how sweet she sometimes acts. Toward me, anyway.

"I was thinking," she whispers, "maybe after football practice today, when I drive you, we don't have to go straight to your house. You know?" There's no mistaking what she has in mind, the way she flutters those lashes at me.

"Yeah, well, thanks, but…I'm taking the bus. Sorry."

Her eyes go wide, like she must have heard me wrong. "But Friday night you said… We…"

"I know. I remembered us being together last fall. Doesn't mean we automatically have to be now. I already told you I'm not ready for anything like that while so much is still blank."

I can tell she wants to argue more but the teacher looks our way so she doesn't. In Chemistry, though, she takes advantage of the fact we're lab partners to start back up.

"I'm sorry, Rigel, I said I wouldn't push and I totally have. I'll give you whatever space you need, okay?"

"Thanks. I'd appreciate that."

From the way her lips tighten, that's not what she was hoping I'd say but she lets it drop. For now.

In Lit class, M makes a point of talking to me again. Not about anything important, just the reading assignment. Trina glares at her the whole time but M only looks at me. Which makes my nerves tingle to where I can barely hear what she's saying. Even after class starts, her seat's close enough I have that skin-too-tight feeling all period.

I kind of like it, no matter how much I know I shouldn't.

Then, at lunch, M somehow ends up next to me in line, so close I'm positively jumpy. When we're almost to the cashier, I reach for a chocolate milk at the same time she's reaching for skim and her hand accidentally brushes mine.

"Sorry," she whispers when I flinch at a jolt nearly as strong as that one Friday. But she has that expectant look again, which tells me her touch wasn't an accident at all.

"Why do—? I mean, what's the deal with that…electrical thing? Do you always do that to people, like you do to computers?" I whisper super-quietly.

"Not exactly. It's—"

"Come *on*, Marsha, you're holding up the line," Trina says from behind me, even though I'm the one who made M stop.

M gives a little shrug and hands her card to the cashier to be swiped. Without finishing whatever it was she was about to say. As she walks away, I realize that the second she brushed my hand and gave me that jolt, my jumpiness went away. Instead, I again have that extra-wide-awake feeling again. Huh.

I'm half tempted to follow M to her table, demand more answers. But I can't, not in front of other people, most of them *Duchas*. So I go to my regular table with the guys from the team. Trina sits there, too, with a few other cheerleaders, but at least she's not all over me now. Guess what I said to her in Spanish bought me at least a temporary reprieve.

I think back to my only bits of memory so far, both involving Trina. Who, the more I'm around her, I don't even like very much. Why did I ever go out with her? Just because she's pretty? Was I as shallow as Trina last year?

Molly O'Gara walks past on her way to M's table and Trina calls out to her. "Hey, Molly, you know about the cheerleading cookout this Saturday, right? Your needy neighbor isn't coming for *another* sleepover, is she?"

"M isn't *needy* Trina. We're friends. I'll let you know about the cookout by Friday." Molly obviously doesn't like Trina much either, even if they're on the cheer squad together.

On the way to Government, I run into Sean. When we walk in, M and Molly are whispering together again.

"So, M and Molly had a sleepover at your house this weekend?" I don't manage to sound quite as casual as I meant to.

Sean frowns slightly. "Yeah. Otherwise her aunt wouldn't have let her stay late enough for—" Bri and Deb smile at us as they walk past and he breaks off. "Anyway, they're really good friends, especially since…Ireland."

Late enough for *what*, I wonder? Obviously more was going on than a girls' sleepover, probably something to do with M being Sovereign. Which her aunt and uncle know nothing about, according to Sean. They don't even know she's Martian, just took over raising her when her *Duchas* adoptive parents were killed when she was little. It must be weird—and hard—keeping the truth hidden from them all the time.

Kind of like my parents are doing to me?

Partway through class, the teacher reminds us to pair up for a project on the Constitution that will be due by the end of the quarter. M immediately turns to me with a smile.

"Rigel? Will you be my partner?"

"I, uh—" Sean, behind her, looks as startled as I am. And a lot less thrilled, though he quickly tries to hide that. "Um, Sean and I sort of agreed to be partners already, didn't we, Sean?"

Now he's trying to hide a look of relief. "Sort of. But if you'd rather—"

"No, it's fine," M says quickly, with a glance at Sean. "Molly?"

"Sure, M." Molly sounds enthusiastic, but her expression is wary as she looks back and forth between us. I get why.

And she's right. I absolutely don't need to complicate things between Sean and M more than they already are. Friendly as she's acting today, being her partner would probably do just that.

We're back to bench presses in Weight Training today. I half expect Sean to work with someone else so I can't pester him with questions, but he doesn't. In fact, he broaches the exact topic I was hoping to bring up.

"Hey, man, it would have been fine if you'd paired up with M in Government," he tells me as we're setting up our bench. "Sorry if I made you back off. Just took me off-guard is all."

I shake my head. "Nah, I'm no poacher. Even if you two are sort of on the outs right now." I leave that hanging, hoping he'll pick up on it, elaborate.

He doesn't, just shrugs. "Thanks but…seriously, don't worry about it." I can tell it costs him something to say that, though.

Feeling suddenly awkward, because I really *am* way more attracted to M than I should be, I change the subject. Slightly. "So, that so-called sleepover at your house. I got the impression it was something her aunt and uncle shouldn't know about?"

"Yeah. Now she's actually Sovereign, with duties and stuff, it's harder to keep them from getting suspicious. We live right around the corner and her aunt likes and trusts my mum, so most of the, um, official stuff happens at our house."

I finish clipping the weights onto the bar. "What kind of official stuff?"

"This weekend was a meeting with the *Echtran* Council. Or what's left of it. They're down two members, needed to talk about appointing replacements. Among other things." He seems relieved to be talking about less personal stuff.

"Oh, right, guess my grandfather had to resign his spot when he left to become Regent. Somebody else left, too?" I don't actually know much about the Council except that Grandfather was on it. I've never even met any of the other members. That I can remember.

Sean lies down on the bench and hefts the bar. "Yeah, one of the other Scientists. They suggested my dad or Devyn Kane fill one of the spots, but of course M was totally against it. Oh, not 'of course' to you, I guess. Sorry."

"Because of stuff that happened…earlier?"

He nods. "Besides, they're both Royal, which would throw off the balance even more. M insists they have to appoint two more Scientists, said she'd ask your grandfather for suggestions. They weren't happy."

"But…they have to do what she says, don't they? I mean—"

"In theory, but because she's still underage, they want her to at least take their advice, like she used to before she got Acclaimed."

"And she won't?" That seems kind of dumb. I'd think she'd want all the advice she can get, being just sixteen and new to the whole idea of being Sovereign and Martian and everything.

Sean does two more reps and sits up. "Not so much. I don't think she trusts them after— I mean, they never completely saw eye to eye on some things, but now that's even more true. Which can get awkward, since Mum's on the Council."

I wonder if that's one of the things that led to M breaking up with Sean, but can't think how to ask. I get on the bench and start lifting, then glance at the weights on the bar. Huh. Ten more pounds than

Thursday, but it feels like half as much. Weird. I wish I could put on more weight, test my limits, without attracting attention. Too risky, though.

Shrugging off the idea, I remember something else I wanted to ask Sean. "My dad finally admitted over the weekend there are things he and my mom don't want me to remember. Like…classified stuff. Do you know what he's talking about?"

When he doesn't answer right away, I look up to see him frowning down at me. "Look. M made me promise not to lie to you, so I won't. But I'm not sure that means I should tell you everything, you know? I mean, even your folks don't know about that, um, classified stuff. Hardly anybody does, outside of the Council and M."

"But you do?"

"Well…yeah. It was kind of unavoidable. Molly knows, too, but only a handful of others."

I do a few reps, thinking hard. Finally, I ask the question that's nagged at me ever since my conversation with Dad over the weekend.

"Is it *because* I learned about stuff I shouldn't have that I lost my memory? Did someone…erase it on purpose? When I was on Mars?"

Sean takes a deep breath, then nods. "Yeah. Yeah, they did. Sorry."

18

Contact resistance

I totally stop lifting to stare up at Sean. Even though I half-suspected it, I can't quite believe what he just told me. After a minute, a couple other guys come over and ask to use the bench, since I'm just lying there.

"Oh, um, sure. We're done, I guess." I'm too rattled to lift now anyway.

Sean and I move on to other equipment for the rest of the period, and other guys are too close for me to ask any more Mars-related questions.

When I get to last period, M's already in front of the newly-fixed computer. She gives me another of her irresistible, a-little-too-friendly smiles when I join her. Trying not to be obvious about it, I move my chair an extra inch or two away. Far enough that she can't "accidentally" touch me again.

"You're not afraid you'll short it out again?" I ask, nodding at the computer.

She makes a face. "I remembered to ground myself on the table leg this time. Usually I do that out of habit, but—" She shrugs.

But I distracted her Friday. By not reacting to that jolt the way she expected? "Can you tell me now what the deal is with that touch thing you do? You started to, at lunch."

After glancing around to make sure no one's close enough to hear, she looks me right in the eye. I can't look away. "It's not so much something *I* do. It's something *we* do."

"Huh?"

"You asked if I have that effect on everyone. I don't. Only on you. I'm guessing you're also way more sensitive to my *brath* than you are to anyone else's?"

I nod slowly. "I, um, figured it had something to do with, you know, who you are."

"It does. But not because I'm the Sovereign, or Royal, or anything like that. It's because I'm *me.* And you're *you.*"

If that's an explanation, it doesn't help much. "So let me get this straight. That…jolt thing only works on me?"

"And vice versa. I feel it too, every bit as much as you do." Her green eyes are wide, almost pleading. But I don't know what she's asking me for.

"Look, I'm not sure—"

"So, how is the research coming?" Ms. Raymond calls from across the room. "We have a newspaper to put together, you know."

We both jump a little and turn to face the computer. It's easier to think without her looking at me like that, though her nearness is still distracting. I pick up the printout from Friday and read the next item out loud. M types in a search string and we both scan down the results.

For ten minutes that's all we do. Ms. Raymond cruises by to check on us, nods, then moves to the other side of the room to talk to Angela about the lead story.

"So," I whisper, "are you saying that we—you and I—have some special…connection that nobody else has?"

She nods. "Did you feel…different at all, after I touched you on Friday?"

"Um." I remember how incredibly well I played at the game. "Yeah. I guess I did. Were you— Did you think it would make my memory come back or something?"

"I hoped it would."

I glance over my shoulder at the teacher and read the next item from the printout and wait till M types in the search term. "I did remember that little bit about Trina."

Now M turns away from the computer to look right at me again. "Exactly what *did* you remember about Trina? What would *possibly* make you—?" She breaks off, her cheeks going pink. I know what she's referring to.

"That's…what I remembered. Kissing her at a football game. So when she ran up a second later, I just…went with it." I shrug. "Probably won't do it again, though. Now that I've spent enough time with her to—"

"To realize what a you-know-what she is?" M arches an eyebrow at me. It makes me squirm a little.

"Yeah. I mean, she can be nice enough when she wants to."

M laughs. "Not to me. As you might have noticed."

I nod. "What she said to you this morning, by the buses, was totally out of line. Especially when you're so…"

"So…what?" Her expression is open, eager. Hopeful.

Memorable, I want to say. *Special.* Maybe even *perfect.* Luckily, I realize in time I can't say any of those things to her. "Uh, nice?"

She keeps looking at me and for a second I think another memory is about to surface, something about M. And me. Instead, I get that exact same flash of Trina and me dancing while M dances with Jimmy Franklin. Does that mean it happened more than once?

When I don't say anything else, she gives a cute little snort and turns back to the computer. "Thanks. I think." She starts clicking on search results.

I watch her, thinking about what Sean told me last period—that my memory was erased on purpose, for security reasons. I remember Dad telling me once that memory erasure is the highest form of punishment they use on Mars. What could I have done to deserve that? And wouldn't M, as Sovereign, be the only one who could authorize it?

So why is she acting like she wants me to get my memory *back*? I'd ask, but can't think of a way to do it that won't sound like an accusation. Plus it might get Sean in trouble, if he wasn't supposed to tell me.

I spend the rest of the period helping with the fact-checking for the newspaper blog. And thinking. A lot.

For the rest of the week, I'm careful not to let M touch me again, even though she comes close a few times. Until I know exactly what those touches are doing to me—and know more about what the deal is between her and Sean—I don't dare let whatever weird connection we have get any stronger.

Even without touching, when she sits right next to me in Lit, more bits of memory start surfacing. Not of the two of us, though. Mostly, I get flashes of M and Sean holding hands in the hallways at school. And once, M and Sean kissing in the school gym. In a crowd, with Sean wearing a basketball jersey, like it's right after a game.

I don't much like the stuff I'm remembering, but it's way better than nothing at all. Weirdly, though, none of these memories have any emotions attached to them, good or bad. They're just…images. Like, I can't tell if I was happy or upset about M and Sean kissing. Or even about me and Trina kissing.

Meanwhile, my dreams are the exact opposite.

Monday night I wake up in a cold sweat from a dream where M and I were in the back seat of a runaway car. I grabbed her hand and lunged over the the front seat and this huge spark arced toward the steering wheel, just as a stone wall loomed up in front of us. It was so incredibly vivid, my heart pounds like crazy until my lingering terror fades.

Then early Wednesday morning I have another bizarre car dream, only this time *I'm* the one driving. It's snowing, and M is in the front seat next to me. Snuggling against me. She feels so good that when I wake up, I want to get right back to sleep, continue that dream…and those feelings.

Much as I'd like to believe it could be based on a real memory, I know it's not. I don't have a driver's license, for one thing, and definitely didn't last winter. Not to mention how unlikely it is that M ever would have been snuggled against me…

Not till I'm up for real a couple hours later does it fully hit me how wrong it is to want M that way—even in a dream. After that, I'm even more careful to keep my distance from her.

Thursday, I bring my own laptop to school so I can work on that for the newspaper instead of sharing the old school computer with M, since that's the hardest place to avoid her. She looks a little hurt when I set up at a different table, but doesn't come right out and say anything. Still, just seeing that look on her face makes me feel like a jerk. Which I totally shouldn't. I'm doing the right thing.

At practice, Coach Glazier pulls me aside.

"You feeling okay, Stuart? You're looking sluggish out there, and you sure aren't throwing like you did Friday night. Let's see you do a forty."

He gets out his stopwatch and clocks my sprint. I can tell I'm slow, even before he shakes his head. "Yep, you're off by more than a whole second from Monday's practice. Whatever it is, son, try to shake it off before tomorrow night."

"I know, Coach. I'll do better. Sorry."

He claps me on the shoulder and goes off to yell at two defenders who are horsing around instead of doing their tackle drills. I square my shoulders and go back to firing the ball through the hoop on the sidelines, determined to buck up. Because Coach is right. I've been off for a couple days now. Not sick, exactly, but I'm not quite operating on all thrusters.

The next morning I eat an extra big breakfast with lots of protein —eggs, bacon and sausage—even though I'm really not hungry. Got to get my energy up for tonight's game in Alexandria.

If it really was M's touch that made me play so well last Friday—and lift so well Monday—the effect was temporary. I'm more than half tempted to let her touch me again, or even brush her hand myself. But I resist. Because I know tonight's game isn't the only reason I want to.

That afternoon in Publications she comes over to sit next to me where I'm alone at the big table with my laptop.

"Rigel, I know you're not feeling great," she whispers. "And I know why. Because I'm not feeling so hot myself. If you'd just let me—" She reaches for my hand but I snatch it away from her.

"No. Whatever this…this thing is we have, it's not right. And it's not fair to Sean, when he— I mean, when the two of you have to—"

Her green eyes narrow at me. "I don't *have* to do anything. Don't you start, too! I'm not letting my whole life be dictated by stupid Nuathan customs. The fact that you and I have this connection *proves* how stupid that one is!"

"But my folks said—"

"They're only repeating what they've been told. But even they know a lot more than they're telling you."

I shake my head. "Even if that's true, I can't afford to get… addicted to whatever it is you do to me. Stupid custom or not, I somehow don't see us ending up together. Do you? Really?" Now I'm the one holding *her* gaze, making it so she can't look away.

For a second I think she's going to bite my head off, but then her lower lip trembles. It makes my gut twist.

"I guess not. Not if you don't… I'm sorry, Rigel. I can't force you to remember. And I can't force you to…to like me." She gets up and goes over to the other computer.

Leaving me feeling like total crap, both physically and emotionally.

* * *

Midway through the third quarter, I'm wishing I'd gone ahead and let M touch me that afternoon. We're down nineteen points and I'm in no shape to turn things around. Two sacks, twelve missed passes…I totally suck tonight. Coach hasn't replaced me or even yelled at me, but he sure wasn't happy at halftime. Neither is the rest of the team.

The Alexandria fans, though, are ecstatic.

"Is this the guy we were so worried about?" I can hear from the home stands. "My grandmother throws better than that!" Sometimes Martian hearing isn't exactly a benefit.

I've mostly switched to handing the ball off instead of passing, but it's not enough to salvage this series of downs. Our running backs just aren't that good. Fourth and four on our own thirty-five and the punt team comes in.

Heading back to the bench—again—I tug off my helmet and chug some water, telling myself this thing is all in my head, that I still have it in me to turn this game around. I don't believe me.

Then, from behind me, I feel that super-strong *brath* that can only be M's. I turn around and see her right down on the sidelines next to Molly. Who's pushing her in my direction.

"Go on, M, I don't care what he said," I can hear her whispering from ten yards away. "If you don't want to do it for your own sake, do it for his. Or at least the team's!"

So Molly knows about that special touch thing? From what M said Monday, I thought it was some big secret between just the two of us. Guess not.

Weirdly, that makes me even more determined not to let her touch me—even if five minutes ago I was wishing she would. I stand up to face her, shaking my head, ready to tell her to get back in the stands.

But then something just behind Molly catches my attention—a big guy with a mean look on his face, barreling right at M's back, both hands out like he's going to grab her or something. He pushes past Molly, moving fast. Farther back, at least another twenty yards or so, I see Mr. Cormac, our vice principal—M's Bodyguard—running at the guy flat out. There's no way he'll get there in time.

I act without thinking, vaulting over the bench, then the three-foot-high orange netting stretched between the track and the field. M's eyes go wide. The big guy's right behind her now but she still has no clue he's even there. His hands are inches from the back of her neck when

I grab her by the shoulders and whip her around behind me.

"Back off, buddy," I snarl, sudden strength surging through me. From touching M.

He lunges to my left, still trying to reach her. "Have to—"

I draw back my right arm and whack him hard in the chest with the heel of my hand, shoving him backwards. "No. You don't."

"Only way to—" He bulls forward again, his expression almost berserked. The guy is obviously nuts. And Martian.

When he tries to lunge around me on the other side, I don't hold back but punch him as hard as I can, right in the face. He goes down like a ton of bricks. Mr. Cormac rushes up and I notice a glint of silver in his right hand.

"That was quick thinking, kid. Thanks," he says, bending over the dude on the ground.

I immediately turn to M. "Are you okay?"

She looks a little shaky, but she smiles. "I'm fine. Thanks to you. Again."

I figure she's referring to those times Sean told me about, last fall and on Mars, when I helped protect her. "No problem."

"You didn't hurt your throwing hand, did you?" She reaches out and takes my right hand in hers, examining it. Her touch sends shock waves through me—but in a good way.

"Nah. It stings a little but it'll be fine. I'm just glad that guy didn't —"

"Son, you should probably get back on the field," Mr. Cormac says, hefting the inert guy up, the tiny silver thing held firmly against his side. "I'll take care of things from here."

I glance around and sure enough, everyone nearby is staring. A little behind the vice principal I see Sean, who's come down from the bleachers to stand next to Molly. They both look shocked and worried. "Uh, yeah. I guess I should."

Mr. Cormac looks past me at M. "Ex— er, Miss Truitt? Perhaps you should come with me."

But she shakes her head. "No, I want to see the rest of the game. But thank you…sir."

He blinks—probably at the "sir." "Very well, if you insist." His nod is jerky, like he started to bow but stopped himself in time. With a frowning backward glance at us, he frog-marches her would-be attacker away.

"Thank you," M says, her hand still on mine.

Reluctantly, I pull away. It's way harder than it should be. "No problem," I repeat. "But why did that guy—?"

"I…I don't know. Cormac will figure it out, though." She speaks softly, quickly, as Coach and a couple of my teammates approach. "Do you know where the arboretum is? On Diamond, near the edge of downtown?"

"No, but I can find out."

"If you can, meet me there around one tomorrow afternoon." Before I can ask why, she shoots a quick smile at Coach, who's right next to me now, and hurries back to the bleachers.

"What was that about, Stuart? Who was that guy?" Coach demands.

I shrug. "No idea, but it looked like he was about to hurt the…that girl, so I, uh, stopped him."

Coach grunts. "Normally I'd chew you out for leaving the bench like that, but I guess it was for a good cause. Just…don't do it again."

"No, sir. I won't." I can't imagine ever needing to. I hope.

"Good. In case you didn't notice, defense managed to hold them at the forty. I had to burn a time out because of your heroics. Don't make me burn another one."

Nodding, I grab my helmet off the bench and run onto the field.

19

Alternating current

THERE'S barely a minute left in the third quarter when our offense takes the field, but with that boost I got from M's touch, I put the time to good use. In just three plays, we get our first touchdown of the game. So when the fourth quarter starts, we're back within twelve points, less than two touchdowns from winning.

Which turns out to be no problem at all. At the final whistle, the score is Jewel 27, Alexandria 22.

"Well, son, guess playing the hero was exactly what you needed to turn this game around," Coach Glazier says, slapping me on the back as the rest of the team converges to celebrate our win. "Great job!"

A minute later our cheerleaders, then our fans storm the field to join the celebration. A squealing Trina is obviously angling for another kiss but I don't cooperate this time. I'm too busy scanning the crowd for M so I can ask why she wants me to meet her tomorrow. Finally I see her—with Sean, who sat next to her the whole last quarter. Looking protective. Which makes sense after what happened.

"Excellent finish, son." Dad reaches me, Mom right behind him. "We were starting to worry about you out there, but you sure pulled it together for the fourth quarter." Mom nods, smiling, but I can see the concern in her eyes. About me, or about what happened with M?

I don't get a chance to ask until I'm off the team bus back at Jewel and in their car.

"That was some quick thinking, getting between that man and the Sovereign," Dad says. "It was obvious he intended her harm."

"No kidding. You didn't see his face. The guy was totally crazed. And *Echtran*, by the way."

Mom turns around in her seat to stare at me. "*Echtran*? Really? What did he say?"

"Not much. I didn't give him a chance. Then Mr. Cormac took over. Did you know our vice principal is the Sovereign's Bodyguard? Sean told me. Worked out well tonight."

"It would have worked out better if he'd been close enough to stop her attacker before you had to intervene." Dad sounds pissed.

"Yeah, well, he can't exactly stay glued to her side without looking like a perv. But hey, looks like some of my Bodyguard training stuck, even if I don't remember getting it. Did *I* stay glued to the Sovereign's side after they made me Bodyguard? If so, no wonder Sean was jealous."

Mom shoots a glance at Dad. She looks worried again. "Did Sean tell you he was jealous?"

"He told me he was last year, at least at first. He hasn't had any reason since I got back." Only because he doesn't know how I'm starting to feel about M. Which I don't plan to tell him, since it can't go anywhere anyway. "How long *was* I her Bodyguard, anyway?"

"The Council made the appointment official just before you left for Ireland. However, her current Bodyguard replaced you as soon as you reached Nuath. So less than two weeks, I suppose."

Not really long enough to make Sean jealous—unless I was unofficial before that? "Why was I replaced?"

But at that, Mom stiffens. "I don't think we should tell you that, Rigel. It's the sort of information the Mind Healers warned against. Sean shouldn't have told you about being her Bodyguard at all."

"Or about me going to Mars. I know." Yeah, I'm still bitter. I'm guessing I was replaced because of that classified stuff I'm not *allowed* to know. I doubt the Mind Healers have anything to do with why my parents are afraid to tell me.

I'd nearly talked myself out of meeting M at that arboretum she mentioned. Because of Sean. Now I abruptly decide to go after all. Not only do I really want to know what that attack was about, it's also time to man up and ask her once and for all if she's the one who had my memory erased. And why.

"I think I'll go for a bike ride this afternoon, start re-learning my way around," I say as I finish lunch the next day. "Especially downtown Jewel. When the guys talk about the places they go, I want to know where they mean."

Both my parents seem to think that's a reasonable idea. Mom even digs a little map out of one of the kitchen drawers and hands it to me. Even though I already Googled the arboretum, I take it.

"We have maps of Indianapolis and all of Indiana, too, if you want to study them later," she says.

"Thanks," I reply, though I feel more like saying, *Gee, you mean that's allowed?*

Downtown Jewel—what there is of it—is about five miles from our house, which is out in the boonies, surrounded by farmland. Easy enough on a bike. The arboretum is right where M said, on Diamond, Jewel's main street, a few blocks past the post office.

It's not quite one when I get there. The arboretum turns out to be a sort of walled garden, maybe two acres, with all different colored roses straggling over the walls and on trellises. And…it seems vaguely familiar.

Huh. First time I've had that reaction to a place. Or anything, really. I stand near the entrance, taking in the gravel paths winding between flower gardens and trees. The people walking dogs and pushing strollers. Then I feel M's *brath* behind me, like last night at the game, and turn around.

"You came!" She gives me a big smile. I notice she's a little sweaty —on her it smells disturbingly good—and is carrying some kind of duffel.

"So did you. What's that about?" I nod at the bag she's holding.

"Oh." She glances down at it. "Taekwondo class. After five months away, I have a lot of catching up to do. So…do you want to sit down, so we can talk? I forgot it would be crowded this time of year, sorry."

I follow her to a metal bench by the opposite wall and sit next to her. Not too close. "It's cool you do taekwondo."

She smiles again. "You said almost the exact same thing the first time I mentioned it, last fall."

"Yeah?" I wonder if I've been repeating myself a lot. "So, what was the deal with that guy who attacked you last night?"

"He claims to be a hard-core anti-Royalist who's been watching for a chance to get rid of me once and for all. But Cormac and the others think he was really sent by someone else, though they couldn't get him to admit it."

"Others?"

"The O'Garas and a couple members of the *Echtran* Council. Cormac took the guy back to Jewel, to the O'Garas' house, so they could decide what to do with him."

I'm curious about logistics, given how everything has to be kept secret from the *Duchas.* "Mr. Cormac's your Bodyguard, right? How does that work, if your folks—aunt and uncle?—don't know about Martians or who you are or anything?"

"He's staying across the street from me. Mrs. Crabtree rents out the room over her garage."

Convenient. Too convenient to be chance—someone must have arranged it somehow. "But he doesn't drive you to school or anything? I know you take the bus."

"It would look pretty strange if the vice principal drove me to school. He's got a bunch of Nuathan surveillance gadgets, though, to monitor my house and the perimeter of the school. And when I go out, like to the O'Garas' for meetings, he usually follows at a discreet distance.

"Even so, he gets frustrated that he can't stick close enough to protect me the way he's been trained to, without blowing my cover. Like at the game last night. Thanks again, by the way. You probably saved my life. Cormac thinks the guy was planning to break my neck."

That crazy dude was big enough to have done it, too. I shudder. "Just glad I saw him in time to stop him. So, did the Council decide what to do with him?"

"They're shipping him off to Montana, to the *Echtran* compound there, Dun Cloch. Supposedly there are Healers there who can, um, get more information out of him whether he's willing to talk or not." She looks suddenly uncomfortable. I think I might know why.

"You mean they'll pull stuff out of his brain? Then what? Wipe his memory?"

She flinches.

"Not saying he doesn't deserve it," I add quickly, because he totally does. Then, in a rush, "Will you tell me what *I* did to deserve that?"

Her eyes go wide. "You… How did you know—?"

"Dad mentioned it might be dangerous for me to remember some stuff, which got me thinking. When I asked Sean point-blank, he admitted my memory had been erased and it was no accident. Don't get pissed at him for telling me, okay?"

"I won't. I'm the one who told him not to lie to you. There've been way too many lies already and you deserve to know the truth."

"Which is?"

She holds my gaze, a crease forming between her eyebrows. "Your memory wasn't erased because of anything *you* did wrong, Rigel. It was because of something *I* did."

An ice cold stone drops into my belly. "You mean…you really did order them to wipe out the whole last year of my life?"

"No!" She forgets to whisper and a few heads turn our way. Her face has gone several shades paler. "Of course I didn't order it! Did Sean tell you I did?"

I shake my head. "I just figured, since you're, y'know, Sovereign, nobody else would have the authority—"

"No, they *didn't* have the authority, but that didn't stop them. Your memory was erased because I told you about…about something I'd promised not to, something nobody's supposed to know about. At least, that's the excuse they used. I didn't even know they'd done it until, well…it's all kind of complicated."

She's so upset, I have to believe her. Even if I don't understand. "Can't you just tell me everything? Except that big classified secret?"

For like five seconds she just looks at me, like she's trying to decide. Then she sighs. "I want to, Rigel, but there's so much. It would take hours and hours. Plus…I'm not sure if I should. The Healers—"

"Yeah, my mom has gone on and on about how the Healers say it could somehow screw with my recovery if they tell me stuff, but I'm pretty sure that's just to keep me from asking too many questions. Isn't it?" I'm being borderline rude—to the Sovereign—but I'm more frustrated than ever.

"That's probably part of the reason, but not all. After I found out…what they did to you, I made the Mind Healers give me all their research on restoring erased memories. They have kind of a lot, because Faxon erased memories from most of the Royals he captured on Mars. They discovered—the hard way—that giving too much information too quickly, just *telling* people what they've forgotten, can have side effects. Like messed up short-term memory."

"And you believe them?"

She nods sadly. "I met enough so-called 'cured' Royals to see it firsthand. I'm not sure any of them will ever be completely normal again. I…I don't want you to end up like that, Rigel."

I suddenly remember something else Sean said. "Is that what happened to Sean's other sister?"

"He told you about Elana? Yes. They say she's slowly improving, but…"

"Yeah, Sean didn't really want to talk about it." Now I get why. Also why everyone's so reluctant to tell me even everyday, non-secret stuff. Which totally sucks.

Trying to swallow my disappointment before it chokes me, I turn away from M and look out across the arboretum. And again get that sense of *déjà vu.* "It's weird, but…I almost feel like I remember this place."

"You and I used to come here a lot." M's voice is soft. Cautious. "It was one of our, um, special places."

I turn back to her, frowning. "So we really did spend a lot of time together last fall?"

She nods, her green eyes searching mine. Something niggles, then I get another of those flashes—image without emotion—of her with Sean, his arm draped over her shoulders.

"What?" She looks concerned and I realize my face must have given it away.

"I just got another of those memory flashes—I've been getting more and more of them lately."

"What kinds of things are you remembering? Besides that one with Trina, I mean. Can you tell me?"

I lift a shoulder, try to smile, but it feels crooked. "I've had others with her—me dancing with her. And you dancing…with Jimmy Franklin. And with Sean. Holding hands with Sean. Mostly stuff like that." I don't mention the one of her and Sean kissing. Even if the memory didn't come with emotions attached, thinking about it now bothers me. More than it should.

"Nothing about…you and me? Together?"

I shake my head. "Nothing." Except for my dreams, but they're way too crazy to be real. "You say we spent all this time together, had this special…thing together. If that's true, shouldn't most of my memories be about you? Us?"

Her eyes narrow and her lips press into a thin line, like she's pissed. At me? "Not necessarily. Not if they specifically blocked them. I knew they'd done that with the ones about the…the big secret, but they must also have blocked your memories about *us*. Our bond. I'd hoped maybe they didn't have time, but…"

"What do you mean, blocked? Blocked how?"

"I don't completely understand the process, but apparently they can…can bury certain memories deeper than others, overlay them with other memories, even fake ones. In your case, they chose memories they considered safe, then stuck those on top of the ones they especially *didn't* want you to get back."

My head is starting to spin. "Wait. So you mean these…these flashes I keep getting are things they *put* there? So I *would* remember them? Why? And who the heck are "they," anyway? Who did this to me?"

"People who claimed—maybe even believed—they were acting for the good of Nuath. Only one is in Jewel now, and I'm not sure I…" M bites her lip. I try to ignore the effect that has on me, stay focused on her words instead.

"Someone here in Jewel? Who? Someone I know?"

"Sort of." I can see she's really struggling over whether to tell me. Because of who it is? Or because of what she thinks it could do to my brain or something?

"Look," I say, "if there's somebody right here in Jewel who's got it in for me, shouldn't I know who?"

She gives a little sigh. Which I tell myself is *not* sexy at all. "Okay. Sean's father."

"Whoa. Seriously?" And all this time I thought Sean was my friend! "So Sean—?"

"Sean didn't have anything to do with it."

"But he knows? That it was his dad?"

M nods. "He and Molly were really upset when I told them. Even though he's their dad, they both thought what he did was terrible. Mr. O'Gara realizes it now, too, and has apologized like a hundred times. Of course, that was after I found out and went ballistic on him and the others." She looks pissed just remembering it.

"Anyway, you don't have to worry he'll do anything else to you now. And it was Sean who helped me figure out how to keep you safe until I could get back to Jewel. To you. I've…really missed you, Rigel."

The look in her eyes twists at my heart, making me feel something I have absolutely no business feeling. "I, uh… Thanks? I wish I could say the same, but—"

"But you can't miss someone you don't even remember knowing."

She sounds sad again, making me want to comfort her. But I don't dare.

Instead, I check my cell phone for the time and jump up. “Wow, we’ve been here longer than I realized. I should get home and you probably should too, huh?”

“Oh. I guess so.” She stands more slowly, looking like she wants to say more. But I’m afraid it might be something I’d be better off not hearing.

“Hey, thanks for filling me in about that guy last night and…and everything else. And don’t worry, I won’t say anything to Sean about his dad, since it sounds like he feels bad enough about it already.”

I also don’t plan to tell Sean about this hour in the arboretum. In fact, I don’t plan to tell anybody. Because much as I want to remember everything, what I want even more is to spend more time with M. And that’s dangerous on a whole different level.

20

Minimum approach distance

THE arboretum looks a lot different covered with snow. I look around at the gardens, buried under a blanket of white. The gravel walks have been shoveled or swept, so they're walkable, barely. I'm alone, but keep looking eagerly toward the arched entrance, waiting…

I feel her even before I hear her—my M! A moment later she rushes into the arboretum, her taekwondo bag swinging at her side. Even sweaty and flushed, she looks like heaven. As soon as we're out of sight from the street, her duffel hits the ground with a thud and we're in each other's arms, kissing like there's no tomorrow. It's been way too long!

Strength and well-being flow into me from her touch and I know she feels the exact same thing. I slide my hands inside her coat, rub them up and down her back, pull her closer. She runs her fingers through my hair, doing her part to mesh us into one.

"Mmm. I will never get tired of this," I whisper against her mouth when we come up for air. "I've missed you so much, M."

She answers silently, since we're already kissing again, that this is the only thing that really makes her feel right. Whole.

I totally agree, even if I can't form whole sentences in my head right now. She pulls my body so tight against hers I feel like I might explode. I let my hands drift lower and she doesn't stop me. If only—

A loud voice right by my ear shatters the mood. I lurch away from M, drawing back my fist to deck the intruder…then groggily realize it's my alarm clock, with some obnoxious car commercial on the radio. I smack the off button so hard the whole clock flies off my nightstand and crashes to the floor. Serves it right.

My pulse is still pounding. Not only from the shock of being jerked awake. The after-effects of my dream—the best one I've ever had—are still surging through me. I lie there for a minute, reliving the bits I remember, savoring them. Then I remember why that's a bad idea.

It takes every bit of my willpower to shove the lingering images—and feelings—out of my head. After a few deep breaths, I jump up and head to the bathroom for a much colder shower than I normally take.

When I get off my bus, I catch myself craning my neck to see if M's is here yet. It is, and it's already empty. Just as well. Not that I can exactly avoid her, since we have practically all the same classes.

As I approach first period, it's like her *brath* reaches out to drag me forward, making me speed up. Which is ridiculous. I square my shoulders and slow back down. Still, the instant I'm through the door, I can't seem to keep my eyes from turning her way.

Unfortunately, she looks every bit as hot as she did in my dream. Hotter, even, since she's wearing a tank top and shorts instead of the jeans and heavy coat from the dream. No, I will *not* think about how she felt under that coat. It was just a dream!

Wasn't it?

I'm busy lambasting myself for totally inappropriate thoughts when she turns her head and smiles at me. I smile back, but stiffly. And suddenly feel like I could use another cold shower.

I sit down in my seat with a thump, vowing not to look her way again. A vow I can't keep for five minutes, much less the whole class. Every time I let my focus drift from Pre-Cal stuff, scenes from that dream assail me again. Get me all worked up again.

When the bell rings, I scoop up my books and rush off to Spanish, where I won't have to deal with this torture.

Determined to scrub that dream—and especially the feelings associated with it—from my mind once and for all, I make a point of talking to Trina before class starts.

"So, how was the party after the game Friday night?"

She shoots a flirty glance my way. "Not nearly as good as it would have been if you'd come. It was like the guest of honor wasn't even there! We toasted you a lot."

"Yeah, well, my folks thought I should be home in case the cops had questions about that lunatic on the sidelines, the one Mr. Cormac hauled off."

"And did they?"

"Nah. Guess they got all they needed from Mr. Cormac." From what M said, I doubted the police had been told at all. "Wish I'd come to the party instead."

Trina gives me a limpid look from those big blue eyes and I try—I really try—to feel attracted to her. She's pretty. And well-built. Most guys seem to consider her way hotter than M. Which I totally don't get. M is so much more—

I yank my thoughts away from M and back to Trina. *Why* is it so hard?

"I'll, uh, try to come to the next one," I half promise even though my folks won't like it. They know full well there's drinking at those parties. I must have stupidly told them that last year. They claim alcohol would screw up my brain even more.

I've quit mentioning my random memory flashes to them, they're so jumpy about the idea of me remembering things I shouldn't. And obviously, since I never mentioned the arboretum at all, I couldn't tell them it seemed familiar. It looked so different in my dream…

And I'm right back where I started, obsessing again.

In Chemistry, I pay extra close attention to today's lab. But all the lab partners are talking to each other, reading instructions aloud. And every time M says something to Molly, on the other side of the room, her voice thrums through me more intensely than ever.

"Rigel! I said Sodium Chloride, not Calcium Chloride!" Trina snaps. "Here, let me do that or you're going to screw up the grade for both of us. Where is your head today, anyway?"

Back in that snowy arboretum. Again.

Lit class is even worse. With M sitting just three feet from me, Ms. Raymond might as well be speaking Mandarin Chinese. To keep from totally losing my cool, I force myself to make a mental list of all the reasons I can *not* let that insane dream make me do something stupid. Like ask M out.

Reason One: she's the freaking Sovereign. The supreme ruler of at least a quarter million people. And I'm basically nobody, no matter what kind of "special connection" she claims we have. Had. Last year.

Reason Two: according to Martian law or tradition or whatever, she's supposed to end up with Sean. So asking her out would be like asking out somebody else's fiancée. Whether they're technically dating right now or not.

Reason Three: even if *she's* not on board with the whole Sean-being-her-Royal-Consort thing, Sean obviously is. Last week I told him flat out I was no poacher, and I meant it.

Reason Four: according to M herself, one reason my memory got erased was because of the relationship she and I used to have.

Reason Five: my parents are obviously worried, even scared, about what could happen if I get too tight with M. They're not stupid, so they probably have a good reason for that.

Reason Six: anything I want as badly as I want M right now can't *possibly* be good for me.

I spend the rest of class going over and over my list, determined to commit it to memory for easy reference in case I get too tempted to do or say something I shouldn't. It helps a little.

But not much.

When everyone heads to lunch, I hang back so I can be sure not to be anywhere near M in the cafeteria line. After she goes to her usual table, I go to mine—and sit with my back to her.

"Hey, Rigel, no relapses over the weekend?" Matt Mullins asks, peering into my face. "You looked like you were gonna hurl before that fourth quarter turnaround. Food poisoning or something?"

I shrug. "Yeah, I figure it was something I ate. Or maybe some twenty-four-hour bug. Just glad I got over it in time to do my job last quarter."

"Weren't we all," agrees Jimmy Franklin. "Don't scare us like that again, man."

I have a sudden, irrational urge to tell Franklin to shut up or even punch him in the face. But I realize in time it has nothing to do with what he just said. It's because of those memory flashes of him dancing with M—which never bothered me that much before. Didn't M say those flashes were fake anyway?

No, just that they were "safe" memories those so-called patriots stuck on top of more dangerous ones. Like any about M and me together. Reason Five.

"I'll do my best," I finally say. "Anyway, I feel fine today." Not true, exactly. In fact, I'm kind of a mess. But hopefully not in a way that'll affect how I play football.

In Government, I feel awkward and uncomfortable around Sean and M. Reasons Two and Three keep running through my head, especially when M asks to borrow a pen from me and brushes my hand when she takes it. I manage not to flinch from the way-too-delicious jolt I get. But just barely. Knowing she did it on purpose doesn't help.

For the last fifteen minutes of class, we're supposed to talk to our partners about our projects. That gives me an excuse to move farther away from M, though talking with Sean feels weird now.

"You okay today?" he asks when I space out again and don't answer whatever he just asked. Proving I suck at hiding my feelings.

"Yeah. Just a little…scattered. Sorry." I absolutely can't be thinking about M like that right now! Or ever. But especially now. "What did you ask?"

"Just whether you want to come over and work on this at my house some night this week. My mum and dad want to thank you for what you, um, did Friday night. I do, too. That guy was seriously bad news. If you hadn't been there—"

I shrug. "Just glad I saw him in time to run interference until Mr. Cormac got there."

"Hey, don't downplay it. That was really quick thinking and follow-through. So, you think you can come by sometime?"

The muscles in my neck tense up and I shift in my seat, hoping I don't look as uncomfortable as I feel. Not only is Sean treating me like some kind of hero when I'm actively lusting after his girl, but now that I know what his father did to me, there's no way I want to go to his house.

"I'll, um, check with my folks. Anyway, what do you think? Should we go with one of the Articles or maybe how the Constitution got ratified?"

To my relief he switches to the topic of our project for the rest of class—a much less dangerous subject. I'm starting to relax around him when M comes up from behind me and touches my arm.

"Here's your pen back, Rigel. Thanks."

I practically have to climb back inside my skin before I can answer in a normal voice. "Sure. No problem."

She smiles and goes back to her seat while I'm still resonating from that unexpected touch. Again I feel the surge of strength she somehow gives me. It would be great if I could use that strength to *resist* her. Somehow, I don't think it works that way.

In Weight Training, I spend the whole time doing circuits on the machines—stuff I don't need a spotter for. I need to come up with a good excuse before Sean mentions coming to his house again. Even if his folks really do just want to thank me for playing hero, I don't want to go. Because I absolutely don't feel like any kind of hero right now.

I'm half tempted to ditch last period. The last thing I need is alone time with M, if only because I *want* it so bad. But I didn't plan ahead, so I go anyway—and Ms. Raymond comes to my rescue.

"Our first issue goes live Wednesday morning," she announces right at the start, "so today and tomorrow will be a little crazy. Fair warning to those of you who are new on staff this year. Here's a list of everyone's assigned tasks. It's going to take complete focus by each of you if you don't want to stay late either or both days."

She tacks the list up on the bulletin board and I'm relieved to see I'm doing formatting while M will be proofing—from a printout, so not at the computer.

Angela is obviously in her element. She immediately takes charge, barking orders like a general. She sends the proofers to the table in the middle of the room, me to the desktop computer and the photo and layout people to the long table along the wall.

"And get it right the first time," she cautions. "I remember once or twice last year we were here till ten o'clock the night before deadline because somebody was careless. The good part is, once this issue goes live we can relax for a day or two. So you'll have time later this week to catch up on anything you have to let slide while we're scrambling to meet deadline."

I get right to work since missing football practice isn't an option, grateful for both the distraction and the reprieve from dangerous one-on-one time with M. By tomorrow, I'm sure I'll have mostly forgotten that dream and be able to act like a normal person around her.

Even though I don't *remember* dreaming about M again when I wake up Tuesday morning, I need another cold shower. At least I'm not haunted by details…except the ones from yesterday's dream. And my own imagination.

At school, I'm every bit as obsessed with M as before, no matter how I try to talk myself out of it. Last night I put my Six Reasons in writing, but it doesn't seem to have done a lot of good. Just like yesterday, I'm hyper-aware of her every time she's within sight or earshot—which is a lot.

Twice in Lit I fight the urge to reach across the aisle and touch her arm on the pretext of asking a question about theme. The second time, I convince myself I really *need* to ask her, but realize just in time it's safer to ask the teacher or even Trina. After which I realize the answer is in the book.

At lunch I sit with my back to her again, but that doesn't keep me from picking her voice out of the babble, even from thirty feet away. I keep losing the thread of the football discussion at my table, I'm so focused on what M is saying at hers.

"Are you serious?" she's asking Molly. "Trina actually *told* Penny she's not pretty enough to be a cheerleader? To her face?"

"Yeah. I could tell Penny didn't really want to try out, but apparently she promised her mom, who was a cheerleader here back in the day. It probably took her forever just to work up the nerve to talk to Trina about it."

"I'll bet. And now she's sitting all by herself over there. See you in a bit."

I can't help it, I turn my head slightly so I can watch M out of the corner of my eye. She's going to talk to a little stringy-haired girl with bad acne sitting alone near the wall. Nodding absently at whatever Jaworski is saying about last Friday's game between Elwood and Frankton, I listen harder.

"Hey, Penny! I'm Marsha Truitt, but you can call me M. Do you mind if I sit here?"

I can't hear what the other girl says, but M might as well be right next to me. "I wanted to tell you how brave I think you are, trying out for cheerleading as a freshman! I never, ever would have had the guts to do that."

Again something inaudible from Penny. Then, "No, it wasn't stupid at all! But cheerleading is like Trina's own little queendom and you've probably figured out by now she's not somebody you want to spend a lot of time around. Trust me, she's said way worse to lots of people. You were just her most recent victim. Everyone knows how mean she is, even her so-called friends. Anyway, there are lots of other extracurriculars here at Jewel, most of them *way* more fun than cheerleading."

She goes on to list some clubs and activities and even invites the girl to check out her taekwondo school. She sits with Penny the whole rest of lunch, makes a point of introducing her to a few other kids nearby, then says she's welcome to sit at M's table tomorrow if she wants.

Watching M ahead of me in the hall on our way to Government, I'm conscious of a new respect that has nothing to do with her being Sovereign. She totally had nothing to gain by being nice to that *Duchas*, but she did it anyway. Because she knows what it's like to be an outcast? Hard to believe, though that's what she told Molly.

It's bad enough I'm already more attracted to M than I've ever been or can ever imagine being to any girl. That she's beautiful and smart and sexy and we have this weird touch thing between us. Now I find out she's genuinely nice, too.

I'm doomed.

21

Soft reset

BY Lit class Wednesday, I can't fight it anymore.

"Hey, M?" I whisper ten minutes into class. "Do you have an extra sheet of paper?"

She looks surprised—she has to have noticed I've been avoiding her—but also pleased. "Sure." A second later she hands me a couple sheets of paper and I don't even try to avoid brushing her fingers when I take it.

That tiny touch feels so good I shudder—inside, anyway. "Thanks."

Her lips quirk up, making her even cuter. "No problem." I know she's talking about the touch as well as the paper—and that she noticed the little shudder I tried to hide. "Really."

The look she gives me with that "really" reminds me she claimed to get the same jolt—the same boost—from touching me that I get from her. Which means I'm being selfish if I *don't* let her touch me, now that I think about it.

Sounds good in my head, anyway.

That afternoon, Sean specifically asks if I'll spot him on the bench press. I'd rather not, but don't have an excuse not to. Sure enough, he wants to talk.

"Hey, wish I'd known you were going to say something to M about your, uh, memory thing happening on purpose."

Oops. "Sorry, man. It kind of…slipped out. Was she pissed?"

"Mainly that I didn't tell *her* I told you. Took her off guard when you mentioned it, I guess."

"Yeah, well, I can't keep track of who's keeping what secrets from who anymore. There's so much stuff my folks aren't telling me, and you—" I break off, but he obviously knows what I was about to say.

"Never said my dad was one of the people involved in what happened to you. M said she told you. No wonder you've been, y'know…"

I lift a shoulder and start putting weights on the bar for him. "Not so keen to come to your house? Or talk about it?"

He nods unhappily. "I don't blame you. In your place, I'd want to avoid my dad, too. He was way out of line. But…he gets that now. Really."

Yeah, M claimed the same thing. Still doesn't mean I want to spend time with Sean's dad anytime soon.

A couple of guys come over to take turns with us on the bench so we switch to safer topics for the rest of class. But that doesn't stop me thinking.

What could have happened on Mars that has to be kept so secret? Since finding out Mr. O'Gara wanted my memory erased, I've been tempted to mention it to my parents. I have to wonder if maybe they already know. Since they think the guy's such a hero, that could explain why they don't want me to get my memory back.

Which I absolutely need to do. All these secrets are starting to feel like land mines that could destroy more than me if I stumble across one because I don't know any better.

The atmosphere in Publications is totally different today. Instead of the frantic chaos of yesterday afternoon, everyone's relaxed and relieved. Especially Ms. Raymond.

"I'm really proud of how you all pulled together these past few days," she tells us once we're all there. "I'm not saying this issue couldn't be better, but it's not bad. Next week we'll put together our quarterly parent newsletter and start talking about yearbook layout, but today and tomorrow you can take it easy. If anyone needs a pass for the media center, let me know.

Five of the staff of eight immediately start asking for passes. Ms. Raymond leaves, too, saying something about a call. Angela stays in the room but retreats to a corner with her laptop, ear buds in, to work on some class project or other. Leaving M and me effectively alone.

At first I open my Government book, thinking I should attempt an outline for the project Sean and I are doing. But with M just a few feet away—also with a book open—I can't concentrate. Plus it's a perfect chance to get a few more questions answered.

"So, um, any more news about that guy who went after you Friday night?" I keep my voice low enough that Angela wouldn't be able to hear even without her ear buds.

M glances up from her book so quickly I doubt she was really reading it. "Not yet. I think they're planning to do the, ah, procedure this weekend. Apparently the equipment they have in Montana isn't as sophisticated as what they have on…" She tilts her head skyward. "So it needs some modification."

I want to ask how that works, how they can pull memories out of somebody's head and actually *see* them. Instead, I shock myself by blurting out the question that's been driving me nuts.

"What exactly *is* the deal with you and Sean? Can you tell me?"

Now that they're out, those words I never intended to utter hang in the air between us. I hold my breath, since her answer could whittle my Six Reasons down to four. Or etch all six in stone.

Though she's clearly startled, she doesn't hesitate. "We're friends. And that's all we'll ever be, no matter what Nuathan tradition says. Everyone there is coming here over the next few decades anyway, so lots of traditions are going to have to change. That's definitely one of them."

I try to control the exultation expanding in my chest, afraid to hope *that* much. Because I still have Reasons One, Four, Five and Six to consider. And Three?

"I'm not sure Sean feels the same way you do about the 'friend' thing." Might as well get that out in the open, too.

She frowns. "That's on him. Because I've been completely upfront with him about my feelings from the very start."

"But…didn't you two date most of last year? After he got here, I mean?"

"Only for show. Because the Council insisted it was so important, I agreed to go along with it so they'd…um, for political reasons. But even they knew it wasn't real. So did Sean."

It wasn't just for show as far as Sean was concerned, though. I've seen how he looks at M, how he talks about her. But if it's really true she's been upfront with him all along…?

"The, uh, guys said—"

"I know. Everyone at school *thinks* we were a couple. That was the point. We even convinced Bri and Deb. But Sean knows better. So does Molly. If you don't want to ask him, ask her."

Her incredible eyes are pleading with me, willing me to believe. And I want to. So much. *Too* much.

"Why weren't you willing to go with him for real? I mean, he's a great guy and all, and—"

"Haven't you figured that out yet, Rigel?" Her perfect mouth twists into a wistful half-smile. "Because of you."

I swallow, hard. It's what I was hoping, dying to hear, but I can't seem to make myself *believe* it. Because I don't *remember* it. Except in that dream…

"You said the arboretum was a…a special place of ours. Did we ever go there in the winter?"

"We did! It was winter the very last time we were there before leaving for Ireland. Did you have one of your flashes about it?"

"Not a flash, exactly. A dream."

"Really?" She leans toward me eagerly. "What did you dream? Was I in it?"

"I, uh, don't remember exactly." Even if it *was* a real memory, no way can I bring myself to tell her the details. "Just that it was the same place but with snow."

She raises an eyebrow like she can tell I'm fudging. "Still, it's great that you remember even that much. And on Saturday you did say the arboretum seemed familiar. Have you had that feeling about any other place? Or person?"

I shake my head. "Not yet. Not even my room at home. Well, except… You didn't happen to give me a crystal hanging thing for my birthday last year, did you?"

"Rigel!" Her green eyes sparkle with excitement. "I did! You *are* starting to remember!"

"Not really. I just thought, since I hung it right over my bed, that maybe it was, I dunno, important to me."

Though she looks slightly disappointed, she's still smiling. "I think maybe it was. Then, anyway." She stares at me thoughtfully for several seconds. "You know, there *is* one other place that was just as special to us as the arboretum, maybe even more so."

"Yeah?" If visiting the arboretum jogged loose real memories in the form of dreams, would another "special" place unlock more? "Where? Can you show me? Or at least tell me?"

"It's not far—from the school, I mean. But…" She bites her lip, then glances up at the clock on the wall. The period is more than half over. "I don't think there's time now, unless you can skip football practice?"

"It wouldn't be fair to the rest of the team. Coach makes

everybody do laps if just one person's a couple minutes late. How about tomorrow? Maybe at lunch, or we could ask Ms. Raymond for a pass? Say we're going to the media center?" I'm definitely willing to risk getting into trouble myself for a chance to finally remember something concrete.

"Tomorrow, then." She grins at me and my heart speeds up. "It's a date."

I can barely concentrate over the next twenty-four hours. Football practice, homework that night, classes the next day—they're all a blur, I'm so keyed up at the idea of a "date" with M.

Not a real date, I keep telling myself. I don't dare think of it as a real date. She probably just wants to show me a classroom or some other corner of the school we sometimes went. There might even be other people there. Which would definitely be safer.

But the way she smiles at me in our classes together makes me think safety might be overrated.

Still, I can't completely ignore Reasons One, Four and Five for why we can't be together. Reason Six I'm less sure about. Hard to argue M can't be good for me when touching her or even being near her makes me stronger, faster, healthier. But she *is* the Sovereign. And my folks *are* worried about something.

After Weight Training—where I again avoid Sean by sticking to the machines—I change in record time and hurry to last period. M greets me at the door with a big smile.

"Come on. I suggested our story idea to Ms. Raymond and she gave me passes so we can go research whether the school has enough handicapped parking and other accommodations for disabled people."

Since the teacher's watching, I play along. "Oh. Good. I, uh, looked up the guidelines online last night."

I accompany M out of the room and down the hall, waiting till we're around the first corner to whisper, "So where are we really going?"

"You'll see." She slants a smiling glance up at me and my heart starts to race. Maybe because we're walking so quickly.

She leads me through the school and out the doors on the side opposite the football field, then into the parking lot—where there are six handicapped spots.

"Should I, uh, snap a pic of the spots with my phone or something? Just to make it look good?"

"She'll send Jeremy out for proper pictures if we run the story. Which we probably won't, unless Jewel really does fall short of the standards."

Still, just in case anyone's looking out a window or something, I take a couple shots of the spaces and signs. M's already crossing the lot, heading straight for the cornfield that borders it. I catch up just as she reaches the first row of towering stalks.

"Wait, we're going in there? Into the corn?"

Instead of answering, she heads between the stalks and holds out a hand to me. "You're not afraid, are you?"

Afraid, no. Nervous, yes. But she's practically daring me, so I take her hand—and suddenly I'm not even nervous any more. Just excited. "Lead on."

She does. For more than five minutes we make our way through the tall green stalks. I wonder how she can possibly find her way when we can't see more than six feet in front of us. I only realize she was worried about that herself when she breathes a sigh of relief. "Oh, good! I was right."

We step out of the corn into a little clearing that's completely screened from all sides. In the middle of the clearing is a huge gray rock surrounded by scrub grass and a scattering of wildflowers. That sense of *déjà vu* hits me again, even stronger than in the arboretum.

M turns to me, eyes wide and hopeful. But anxious. "Well?"

Slowly, I look around, trying to decipher all the conflicting emotions surging through me. "That rock. Did we…ever sit on it? Together?" It isn't a memory, exactly. More a certainty. I know the answer before she nods.

"Lots of times. The first time, when you first showed me this clearing, we sat there while you explained all about our bond and why some people wouldn't approve."

"*I* told *you*?" It sounded so backward.

"I'd only just learned, well, everything. From you and your parents. Then there was this whole interview and test thing at your house, with Scientists and some of the *Echtran* Council, to prove who I was once and for all. It was the next day that you brought me here."

She gives me a wistful smile, like it's a good memory. I wish I could share it with her.

"It must have been weird, having so much stuff thrown at you, stuff that had to be really hard to believe. You must have thought I was crazy when I told you—what did I tell you, exactly?"

Now she grins. "That you were a Martian. And yeah, I thought you were crazy. Or that Trina had put you up to playing a really mean prank on me, which was even worse. I'm not sure I *totally* believed you until your parents backed up your story, a couple of days later."

I shake my head. "Hard to imagine what that must have been like for you."

"Probably no worse than what you're going through now. Everybody knowing you, knowing more about you than you do. That has to be, well, awful."

"Awkward, anyway. Especially the first few days." I glance over at the big rock. "You want to sit down?"

M sucks in a little breath, then nods. We take the few steps to the rock, *almost* brushing hands, then sit down. Close, but not quite touching. Her *brath* seems to surround me, flow through me. I wonder if mine does the same to her.

"So, tell me more about the first time we ever came here. Sat here."

Her cheeks get two or three shades pinker. "Well, um, like I said, you told me about some Martian political stuff and why you'd kind of kept your distance from me the evening before, at your house, with the Council and all there."

I keep watching her, waiting for more, and she goes even redder.

"And we, um, kissed."

My mouth goes suddenly dry. "We did?"

She nods. "Kind of a lot. It was our first real, er, makeout session."

Then my dream… No, I still don't quite have the guts to tell her about it. Instead, I ask, "I don't suppose we were ever in a, uh, runaway car together? That crashed or nearly crashed?"

Her eyes get big. "Yes! Last fall, after a football game. One of Faxon's people sabotaged my uncle's car. We kept going faster and faster and he couldn't stop—until you thought to use our, uh, electrical thing to short out the ignition. Just in time. You remembered that?"

"I dreamed it. It seemed too bizarre to be a real memory, but now

—" Now I know it was. Which means that arboretum dream must have been real, too. Which means…

M leans in closer, drops her voice lower, even though we're completely alone. "What else have you dreamed, Rigel? Will you tell me now?"

"I dreamed…this." Even though I know there are way more than Six Reasons I shouldn't, I lean in, too, until my lips touch hers.

That first time M touched me was intense but it was nothing compared to this. It's like every cell in my body is expanding, exploding, shooting off fireworks. I have a sensation of falling. Automatically, my arms go around M for support—and her arms come around me, like she's falling, too.

Our kiss deepens, just like my dream. And now it's *not* a dream I'm remembering. I'm remembering exactly this, kissing M here, on this rock, in the cornfield. Kissing her in the arboretum. Kissing her before a football game. *After* a football game. In a car that doesn't belong to either of us. And in a posh little living room that I somehow know is on a space ship.

Other memories surface, faster and faster and faster. The first day of school last year, when I met M and figured out who she was. Freaking out the next day, when we touched for the first time. This cornfield again, facing off against a whole bunch of Faxon's forces, then M and me electrocuting that scary hovering sphere. And the whole time I'm kissing M and M's kissing me and the world is becoming a better and better place.

Finally, she pulls back far enough that I can see the wonder on her face. "I…I think I'm getting your thoughts, Rigel, seeing what you're seeing. You're remembering! Aren't you?"

"Yes!" I'm exultant now. Euphoric. "I remember you, I remember this, I remember everything! Most of all…I remember how much I love you, M."

III

M

22

Parallel connection

I stared at Rigel, feeling like my heart might explode from happiness. "Everything? You really remember *everything?*"

Grinning, he nodded. "I think so. It's like all the blanks just...filled in. First you. Us. Then everything else, in a big rush. Let's see..." His arms still around me, he furrowed his gorgeous brow. "I remember Ireland, the *Quintessence*, getting to Mars, then my grandmother dragging me away. Getting sick from being apart, a bunch of tests, then that serum that helped. It helped you, too, right? On the news the next day, on that panel debate, you looked way better, even without Sean sitting next to you."

I bit my lip. "I'm so sorry about that, Rigel. If I hadn't agreed to let them do that memory extraction, none of this—"

He squeezed my shoulders with the arm he had around me. It felt wonderful. "Hey, I never blamed you for that. I saw how they trapped you on the air. You had no choice. And it must have worked, since you got Acclaimed two days later. In the nick of time to stop the Grentl from pulling the plug on Nuath. That was the most important thing then, remember?"

"I know. But when I found out they'd kept you in that Mind Healing facility all that time against your will..."

"So you got my message? I figured you didn't, that it hadn't worked, since—"

"Since I didn't get you out of there?" Tears pricked my eyes. "That *was* my fault, Rigel! If I'd just checked my omni sooner, gotten your message in time... But I didn't, not until you were already gone, after they'd already erased your memory."

Rigel frowned, but not like he was mad. "Huh? Why—?"

"It was that other message! The one you didn't really send but I thought you had." Now he looked even more confused, so I blundered on. "It was the day after I got Acclaimed. I ordered your grandmother to bring you to the Palace—I didn't know you were still at that facility—and then I got a video message from you, only it wasn't really you. I mean, they faked it. But it looked so real..."

"What did it say?"

"That…that you'd decided to have the last year erased from your memory and go back to Earth, without me, for the good of Nuath and because you couldn't handle seeing me with Sean. That you didn't want me to come after you. I mean, it was your face *and* your voice saying those things. But I should never have believed you'd really leave me like that, have me erased from your life, on purpose."

I swallowed. Even knowing it was never real, the memory of that awful video still had the power to make my heart ache.

Rigel obviously sensed my pain. "Hey." He gave me another squeeze. "It was probably a *way* better fake than that picture Trina had on her phone last spring. Which I believed even though you told me you hadn't done anything. You forgave me anyway, remember? That video must be why Devyn and Gordon asked me all those questions—so they could use my voice and face. Convince you it was all my idea. That must have been awful for you."

"I…kind of fell apart," I admitted. "Believe it or not, it was Sean who helped me pull myself together in time to stop the Grentl. He's also the one who figured out that message was fake." I didn't mention *when* Sean figured it out. He and Rigel were getting along so well now, I didn't want to undermine that.

"I guess I'm glad he was there, then. But I hate that they used *me* to hurt you like that. So it was Mr. O, along with Devyn and Gordon who decided to wipe my memory in the first place?"

I nodded. "Nels Murdoch, too. And…your grandmother."

His jaw clenched for a moment, then he deliberately relaxed it. "Well, I have it back now. All except the part between getting shoved back into that memory contraption and waking up in Ireland, not knowing what the hell happened. What did, exactly?"

It took all my self control not to throw myself at him again instead of answering, I was so relieved he wasn't mad at me. "A lot, but… Oh, Rigel! You're back! You're really back! You can't imagine how much I missed you. In some ways, it was even worse after I finally made it back to Jewel. Because you weren't quite *you*."

"I wasn't. But I am now, M. The same guy who loves you more than life."

And then we were kissing again and I was happier than I'd been since last fall, since before the O'Garas showed up in Jewel and my life got so complicated.

Unfortunately, my life was *still* complicated and we couldn't stay hidden in the cornfield, kissing, forever, much as I wished we could. After several more ecstatic minutes, I regretfully pulled away from Rigel again, my fingers twined through his.

"I guess I should at least *start* bringing you up to speed, huh? Though it'll take hours to tell you everything."

"I'd rather do this." He wore that crooked smile I loved so much. Had missed so much. "But yeah, I guess you should. Like, how *did* you manage to stop the Grentl? I take it you got to that device of theirs and used it?"

"I had help, mainly from Eric Eagan, remember him?"

Rigel nodded.

"He was literally on his deathbed but insisted on coming to the Palace to show me what to do." I went on to describe how Eric led me to the device and showed me how to use it. Then I told Rigel about the device itself, how it bombarded me with images and sucked my own memories out of me.

"So it was totally bizarre, but it worked. They didn't cut the power. Except then the Grentl activated the device again to say they were coming, which kind of panicked Mr. O and the others, especially Nels." I'd still been too devastated about Rigel leaving me to panic, but I didn't add that.

"The Grentl said they were coming? To Nuath? So did they?"

"No. A few days later, I sent them a report, an update on the colony that my grandfather helped me put together, since it had been almost fifty years since the last one. And then they said they didn't need to come after all."

"Wait. Your *grandfather*? You mean—?"

I shook my head. "Sorry, I'm not explaining very well, but there's just so much. There's this Archive and it has the stored memories and personalities and everything of previous Sovereigns, including my grandfather, Leontine. So even though Faxon really did murder him, he was still able to help me a lot. I know this probably all sounds crazy."

"A little," he admitted. "So what happens if the Grentl send another message, while you're here on Earth? There's not another launch window for like, two years."

"Oh! It turns out the device is portable, so I brought it with me. According to Sovereign Aerleas—and Shim confirmed it—the quantum entanglement technology they use has nothing to do with the physical location of the device. I'm keeping it at the O'Garas' house, since there's no place in mine I can be sure my aunt won't go snooping. My Scepter, too—that's what activates the Archives."

By now Rigel was looking slightly dazed. "Wow, I guess you weren't kidding when you said it would take hours to catch me up on everything. But you'll have time to explain it all properly later. Um, won't you?"

"Absolutely. Now that you have your memory back, we'll talk every chance we get. We can have lunch together, and even in class…" I stopped talking and sent silently, *We can talk like this. Can you hear me?*

A smile spread across his face. *I can! Believe it or not, I dreamed this, too, a few days ago. But it seemed too crazy to be real.*

I kept trying and trying in class, but you never—

Guess kissing you brought this and *my memory back. Shame we didn't try it sooner.*

Hey, I was more than willing! I thought, half-indignantly.

I know. I'm sorry I acted the way I did these past couple weeks. Forgive me?

Wasn't your fault. You couldn't remember. But now…let's just start fresh, okay?

Sounds good to me.

And then we were kissing again. Even though I knew our path ahead wouldn't be completely smooth, at the moment I couldn't help but believe we'd somehow get our happy ending after all.

Long before either of us were ready to stop, Rigel's cell phone vibrated. He pulled it out of his pocket and glanced at it. "Football practice. Guess it's a good thing I thought to set this, but I *so* don't want to leave you now, M. I don't suppose you can come watch, at least?"

"Sure I can. I told my aunt I'd be staying after again for newspaper staff. Just in case." I grinned. My "just in case" had turned out so much better than I'd dared hope!

"Excellent! We'd better head, then." He stood and held out his hand.

Walking back through the cornfield, fingers intertwined, I felt like I was walking on air—until Rigel asked a question that brought me back to Earth.

"So, what do you think? Do we just announce to everyone that my memory's back? Or will that be dangerous, like my dad implied?"

I hadn't considered that. "There *was* that guy who tried to attack me at the game. If somebody put him up to it, they obviously want me out of the way. Which I guess could put you in danger if they know we're together again."

"Hey, I'm not worried about *me* being in danger. But if being with me could make you a target again—"

"It's not like last fall, with Faxon's followers. Even most of the anti-Royals don't want me *dead.* They just don't like the idea of a Sovereign. Which is what makes that attack so weird. Probably just an isolated crazy." I shrugged. "Anyway, I'm not letting them, or anybody, keep us apart. Not now. We just have to figure the best way to, um, break the news to everyone."

"Like my folks?"

Startled, I glanced up at him. "You really think they won't be happy?"

"They might be happy for me, but they're also worried. Maybe even scared. Dad specifically warned me there were things it would be safer I didn't remember and that if I did, I should stay quiet about it. The Grentl, obviously, though he didn't know that. But the way he talked, I almost wondered if somebody had threatened them or something."

I recalled how the Stuarts had reacted at Rigel's first football game when I suggested I come to their house to spend time with Rigel in case it could help jog his memory. They *had* acted almost afraid, though at the time I assumed it was because of the Healers' warnings. If someone had actually threatened them, I needed to find out who. Maybe whoever was behind that attack?

"Well, people will definitely know something's up when I show up at practice with you. Especially like this." I squeezed his hand. "Not just the team, but the cheerleaders…" Which included Molly, I belatedly realized. "It'll be all over school tomorrow that we're back together."

"So we just wait for the news—about us, at least—to make the rounds and see what happens? I can always pretend I didn't get *all* my memory back, just pieces. It's the Grentl stuff that's most dangerous, right?"

Frowning, I shrugged. "It shouldn't be. I've thought all along that everyone—all Martians, I mean—deserve to know the truth. Especially now that the Grentl have backed off, so people would be less likely to panic. I haven't been able to convince the Council, though, or even Shim—though I think he was starting to come around by the time I left."

"It *is* a pretty scary concept," Rigel admitted. "But I get why you'd be sick to death of secrets by now."

"Totally. Which is one reason I don't want to keep *us* a secret. I absolutely don't want to go through that again! But…maybe we shouldn't let on you have your *whole* memory back until we know if there's a real threat out there?"

"Sounds good. Especially that first part." He let go of my hand long enough to put his arms around me for one last kiss before we reached the parking lot.

After that we had to walk faster, out of the cornfield and through the nearly-deserted school to the stands, where we finally had to part so he could go change. Sure enough, our clasped hands received a few startled glances along the way but we didn't stop or try to explain. Rigel had to hurry, plus we still hadn't figured out *exactly* what to tell people.

Sitting in the bleachers, well away from a handful of giggling girls at the other end, I was vividly reminded of the first time Rigel invited me to practice last fall—when I'd still been one of the biggest losers in the school. Not that I was hugely popular now, but at least I was no longer a social outcast, thanks to Rigel. And Sean.

Oops. What was I going to tell Sean?

I'd rather do it myself than have him find out through the grapevine—or even from Molly. Now that my initial euphoria over Rigel's recovery was fading, I had to face the fact that there were plenty of people, both on Earth and back on Mars, who wouldn't be happy with the news about Rigel's restored memory, and especially about us being a couple again.

We'd have to find out all we could, talk it over, then decide what our next steps should be. *We.* I nearly laughed out loud, I was so delighted it was *we* again, instead of just me! It was like a huge weight of responsibility had lifted from my shoulders—because now I had Rigel to share it with me.

You will, won't you? I thought at him as he emerged onto the field in his uniform, even though I knew he was way too far away to hear me.

Will what? he startled me by thinking back.

Help me with all the stupid Sovereign stuff I still have to do, I sent back. *And how cool is this, that you can hear me from all the way over there?*

Definitely cool! But…try not to distract me too *much during practice, okay? Don't want to have to try explaining why to Coach.* His affectionate amusement came through along with his words—from nearly a hundred yards away! I'd never been able to sense his emotions from more than a few *feet* away before.

I was fighting the temptation to keep "talking" to Rigel when the cheerleading squad ran out onto the track in their skimpy practice outfits. They'd barely started doing jumping jacks—which I suspected were as much to show off for the boys as to warm up—when Trina spotted me in the stands.

At her outraged expression, Molly turned to follow her gaze and stopped exercising to stare at me. "What are you doing here?" she mouthed at me.

Since there was no way to tell her right now, I just shrugged and mouthed back, "Tell you later."

Though she still looked worried, she gave a little nod and started jumping again.

I tried to do a little homework over the next hour, but watching Rigel and worrying about what I'd say to Molly after practice kept me from concentrating. Also, I couldn't resist testing our new long-distance telepathy a *few* more times, when Rigel was waiting his turn for some drill or other. It worked every single time.

Let's try while I'm in the locker room, see if I can still hear you from there, he suggested when practice ended and the team loped off the field.

I waited a couple of minutes after he disappeared into the school, then sent, *Well? Can you?*

I can! This is awesome. Wonder what our limit is now?

Maybe we can test it when we're on our buses?

Good plan. I'll be out in a couple minutes.

Just then, Molly broke away from the cheerleaders, who'd also finished, to climb up the stands to me.

"So, what gives?" She looked worried as well as curious. "Rigel's been staring at you in class all week, but every time you've tried talking to him, he's backed off. Have you decided to go stalker on him now?"

I laughed. Too happy to keep the news to myself any longer, I burst out, "Oh, Molly, he remembers! He remembers me, us, everything!"

Molly's gray eyes got huge. "Everything?"

"Well…" I remembered belatedly we'd decided to hold back on some things for now. "Everything about *us*, anyway. And our bond. Isn't it wonderful?"

Her smile was as cautious as it was happy. "It is. I guess. I mean, I'm really happy for you. For you both. It's just that Sean—"

"I know. Can you…not tell him yet? I'd really rather tell him myself. I can come over to your house this evening, and—"

"Come on, Molly," came Amber's shout from the track. "Do you want a ride or not?"

"Oops. Should I tell her I'll take the bus, so we can talk more? Or ask if you can ride with us?"

I shook my head. "No, you go on. I want to see Rigel again before we have to get on our buses. We'll talk more tonight, okay?"

Still looking dubious, Molly nodded and ran down to join the waiting cheerleaders.

By the time I finished stuffing my books back into my backpack Rigel had reappeared, so I ran down to join him on the track.

"Well, Molly knows now, but I asked her to let me tell Sean."

Though he threw an arm around my shoulders (even sweaty, he smelled wonderful) he frowned. "Yeah, he'll be— Sorry, this is kind of weird. I remember everything from last year, how Sean and I were always snarking at each other and all. But I also remember how he's been this year. It's…like we really are friends now."

"I always hoped you could be, eventually," I reminded him. "Though I wish it hadn't taken something like this to make it happen. I really hope our news won't screw that up."

"Me too. It's been cool having a guy I can talk to about, you know, Martian stuff. But whatever happens, the tradeoff is worth it." He squeezed my shoulders.

Much as I hated to hurt Sean more than I already had, I couldn't disagree.

When we got to the late buses, we shared one last kiss before separating—in full view of everyone who happened to be watching. Yep, it would definitely be all over the school tomorrow. Which meant I *had* to tell Sean tonight.

23

Attenuation

LINGERING with Rigel as long as I could made me last onto my bus, too late to snag a window seat. Even craning my neck, I couldn't see him now.

Will you tell your parents tonight? I sent as my bus pulled away, hoping he could still hear me.

I guess I'd better. His response was every bit as clear as when he was on the football field. *Especially since we haven't exactly tried to hide that we're back together.*

Just then, the girl in the seat next to me, a sophomore I didn't really know, said, "Wow, so you and Rigel are back together again, huh? How did that happen? I heard he's got, like, total amnesia?"

"Not total," I qualified. Out of the corner of my eye, I saw every head within earshot turn my way. "Just the last year or so. And he's starting to remember *some* things. Like, um, me."

"Awww." The girl—I was pretty sure her name was Hannah—smiled mistily. "I remember how cute you guys were last fall. But then you started going with Sean O'Gara, so I figured—"

"Yeah, I know. But Sean and I aren't together anymore, so he's cool with it." I hoped that would be true, when I told him tonight. "Guess I never really quite got over Rigel."

Another girl leaned across the aisle. "I sure never would have, if *I'd* ever gone out with him. Is he as good as he looks?" She waggled her eyebrows suggestively.

Rather than answer a question like that, I just smiled, then tugged a book out of my backpack so I could pretend to read and ignore her and all the others, determined not to give out any more information before I had a chance to talk to Sean.

Five minutes later, Rigel's bus, just ahead of mine, turned right while mine continued straight toward town.

See you tomorrow.

Can't wait. I could sense the smile in his mental voice. *We're going to test our new range now, right?*

Right. I think we're already farther apart than we were during practice.

A moment later we passed the intersection with another county road so I reported exactly where I was to Rigel.

And I'm just passing Donner's market. Corn's fifteen cents an ear. I should tell my mom.

We kept describing the things we were passing. It did get harder and harder to "hear" each other, but I was more than halfway home —as was Rigel—before we couldn't converse at all. The last thing I caught from him was a faint, *Nearly three miles.*

Aunt Theresa was just pulling into the driveway when I reached the house.

"I see you stayed late after all," she said by way of greeting as I followed her into the house. "You'd best get started on your homework. I'll call you down when it's time to set the table."

Aunt Theresa had mostly reverted to her old, strict self after acting *almost* happy to see me the night I got back. Relieved, anyway. More than once, she'd explained that the only reason she hadn't come to visit me in the hospital in Ireland was because Mrs. O kept insisting it was completely unnecessary. Which made me think she must have felt at least a *little* bit guilty about it.

Now, two weeks later, it was almost like I'd never been gone. At least I didn't have to make dinner tonight.

Back in my room, I was struck again by how tiny it seemed after three whole months in my humongous apartment in the Royal Palace. While I had no real desire to go back to Nuath, sometimes I couldn't help missing the luxury.

Thinking about Mars reminded me I needed to let Shim know about today's miracle. Quietly locking my door, I went to my nightstand and removed my omni from the old glasses case where I'd hidden it, then pulled up the holo-screen.

"Message to Regent Shim Stuart, Nuath, highest security setting." Keeping my voice low, I told Shim about Rigel getting his memory back and how we'd re-bonded (though I was vague on the whole kissing part of the equation). "This time we don't plan to keep our relationship a secret, at least at school," I concluded. "I'll leave it up to you how much to say at your end."

Once my omni was safely hidden again and I was settled at my desk with homework, I couldn't resist trying to mentally reach Rigel again. *Can you hear me? Even a little?* I sent as hard as I possibly could, focusing in the general direction of his house, well out of town.

After a few seconds I *almost* thought I felt something back. Not words, more like a vague sense of Rigel's mental presence. It made me smile, even if I'd totally imagined it.

I made sure to do the dinner dishes before asking Aunt Theresa if I could go over to the O'Garas' house. "Molly and I were hoping to work a little on our Government project," I explained.

Though I dreaded this visit so much I almost hoped she'd say no, she immediately agreed, just like the past two Saturday nights, when I'd needed to go there to meet with the *Echtran* Council (half of them holographic projections from other parts of the country).

Molly had invited me for a sleepover that first time, since Mrs. O had told her the meeting might go late. Sure enough, there'd been enough to discuss—and argue about—to keep them all there past midnight. The next morning, I'd managed to spend a few minutes alone with my Scepter while Molly showered.

"Make sure you're home by nine-thirty, since it's a school night," was her only condition. My curfew was a whole half-hour later than last year.

I steeled myself as I knocked, anxious to tell Sean about Rigel and me as gently as possible, but the moment he opened the door it was obvious he'd already heard.

"Hey. Molly told me you might be by. Come to share your good news?" He gave me a forced smile, trying to hide the hurt and betrayal I sensed from him.

I winced. "I asked Molly not to—"

"Don't blame Molly," he snapped, hurt shifting to anger. "She didn't say anything. But since you apparently didn't even try to play it cool, it's all over the internet."

Crap. I hadn't even thought of that, since I barely spent any time online myself, not having a computer or even a cell phone of my own.

Before I could say another word, he turned away. I followed him into their little living room, the mirror image of ours, and Mr. and Mrs. O'Gara jumped to their feet. The curiosity I sensed from them was understandable, since I hadn't exactly paid the O'Garas any social visits since getting back to Jewel.

"Excellency." Mr. O made a perfunctory bow. I hated when he did that, but knew he was still determined to get back into my good graces. "To what do we owe the honor?" His curiosity was tinged with wariness.

I kept my expression pleasant as I inclined my head in return. "I came to share the good news that Rigel has started recovering some of his memories, contrary to what the Healers predicted."

"Without any treatment?" Mrs. O frowned, clearly skeptical—and slightly alarmed. "It was my understanding—"

"Their own research shows treatment doesn't make much difference," I reminded her. "Some people back on Mars recovered their memories without it and for a few, the treatments actually made things worse."

All four O'Garas flinched at my inadvertent reference to Elana but rather than apologize, I forged on. "Anyway, the Healers don't have any experience at all with anyone *graell* bonded, like Rigel and I are."

"Were," Sean corrected me. "That serum you got—"

"Relieved our worst symptoms from being separated. And yeah, when I first got to Jewel, I thought maybe it *had* undone our bond. But…it didn't."

For Sean's sake, I tried not to *look* as happy as I felt about that, but his eyes still pinched at the edges. "You're sure that isn't just wishful thinking? I know how much you—"

"Yes. I'm sure. Since I got back, Rigel and I have both felt the same pull as when we first met last fall. It got to where neither of us could ignore it and now, as of today, our bond seems as strong as ever. And it's healing Rigel's memory." It would be cruel to tell Sean that *kissing* was what completed our re-bonding, but I added, "He remembers me now, remembers *us*. And…we're back together."

Sean gave a terse nod and looked away, his pain slightly tempered by resignation. But Mrs. O leaned forward, frowning.

"Excellency, this is most unwise. Remember, it was your relationship with Rigel Stuart that very nearly prevented your Acclamation. Clearly, the Council had good reason to insist—"

"The Council can't *insist* I do anything now," I reminded her sharply. "Nor am I bound by any promises I made to them last year, after they betrayed my trust so completely by *agreeing* to Rigel's memory wipe."

I sent an accusing glare at Mr. O, who averted his eyes.

"I played by their stupid rules, pretending to break up with Rigel. I stopped the Grentl from destroying Nuath. And look what happened anyway! If it wasn't for our bond, Rigel would probably have lost that year of his life permanently, and for what? For being a political *inconvenience*? You know as well as I do that nothing in Nuathan law *or* tradition sanctioned what was done to him. Rigel and I are together now and I have no intention of pretending otherwise, ever again."

There was a short, strained silence, then Mr. O'Gara spoke up. "What, exactly, has Rigel remembered so far, Excellency? Even you must admit there are certain things it would be, ah, safer he not recall."

I wasn't about to admit any such thing. "No matter what he eventually remembers, Rigel is no security risk. Unlike, say, Gordon Nolan. I don't suppose anyone has managed to track him down yet? He was supposedly living in Dun Cloch, but when I was there last month, no one seemed to know where he was or when he'd be back."

Mrs. O shook her head. "I called my brother as you requested, Excellency, as he and Gordon used to be friends. But all Allister could tell me was that Gordon had gone to visit family out west somewhere."

Maybe that's all Allister *would* tell her, but I was willing to bet he *could* tell a lot more, if he chose. When I'd met with him briefly in Montana, he'd given off all kinds of negative, deceptive vibes. I was sure if Mrs. O spoke with him in person, her ability would immediately tell her he was lying. But this wasn't the time to fling accusations I couldn't prove.

"My point is that Rigel is no more of a threat now, to me or anyone, than he was last year. Even before he remembered our bond, he kept that anti-Royal goon from snapping my neck Friday night. You know Cormac couldn't have gotten there in time."

None of them could dispute that, though I could tell they wanted to.

"I'll, ah, need to inform the Council about this," Mrs. O finally said.

"That's fine. They can tell everyone that Rigel has been reinstated as my Bodyguard or they can just tell the truth that we're *graell* bonded and fated to be together. But neither you nor they are going to tell me

I can't be with Rigel. Not anymore."

Though disapproval still came off her in waves, she managed a deferential nod. "As you wish, Excellency."

I knew this wouldn't be the end of it, though. At this Saturday's Council meeting they'd probably all join forces to "reason" with me. Not that any possible argument would change my mind.

"Speaking of the Council, was Kyna able to convince Nara to come back, as I suggested?"

Mrs. O seemed relieved at the change of topic. "She was. Which means we now need add only one Council member."

"I'm glad to hear that." Though I wished Nuathan law would let me dissolve the Council completely, I'd always liked Nara—easily the Council member most sympathetic to me. "Has Kyna suggested another Scientist or other *fine* representative to serve?"

"Not yet, though she may have a report Saturday." Mrs. O hesitated, then added, "Though, as Malcolm pointed out, the law does not specifically preclude five Royal members. If not Devyn Kane, then perhaps—"

"No." A four-person majority was already bad enough. "I've asked Shim for recommendations, too. You all were saying last weekend that our biggest need right now, with all these new settlements, is a more robust *Echtran* communication system, since MARSTAR was only designed for important bulletins. Maybe someone else from Informatics, like Shim, would be a good choice."

Which suddenly gave me an idea—but one I probably shouldn't mention until I'd had time to think it through. "We can talk more about this during Saturday's meeting. Anyway, I told my aunt that Molly and I were going to work on our Government project tonight, so we should probably do at least a little of that."

"Oh. Um, sure." Molly got up, glancing uncertainly at her parents. "Here, or in my room?"

Mr. and Mrs. O'Gara stood as well. "We'll clear out so you two can work. And yes, Excellency, we'll talk again on Saturday. I look forward to it." She sketched a little half-bow that her husband echoed more deeply and they both left the room.

Sean didn't. He sat on the corner of the couch, brooding a little and reading—or pretending to read—his own Government book. So even though I had the impression Molly wanted to talk more about my news, we stuck strictly to schoolwork for the next half hour. When we reached a good stopping point, I stood.

"Guess I'll head back. I still have a little other homework to do." That wasn't true, but I did want to check my omni to see if Shim had responded to my message.

Now Sean finally got up, too. "So that's it? You just wanted to give my folks a heads-up that you and Rigel are getting back together?" His jaw jutted out, his lips pressed together in a tight line—the way I did mine when I was trying to keep them from quivering.

"And you. I…knew you'd find out soon but I really did want you to hear it from me first."

He shrugged, but I could still feel his hurt.

"Walk me home?" I suggested on impulse, even though I knew Cormac would be out there somewhere, watching and waiting.

Sean blinked at me, frowning, then nodded. "Yeah, sure."

I said good night to Molly and he and I headed outside and down the street together. When we were nearly to my house, I blurted out, "I'm sorry, Sean. I know this isn't easy for you. Even though you've been doing all you could to, um, help."

Sean shrugged again, not looking at me—or touching me. "It's what I promised to do. Looks like it worked even better than either of us expected. And quicker. Guess I didn't—"

"I know. I'm not sure I expected it either, though I was probably hoping for it a lot more than you were. No! That's not an accusation," I added quickly, at his look. "If anything, it makes everything you've done that much more…noble. You were determined to do the right thing, even knowing it wasn't what you'd have chosen. I wanted to thank you. Again."

He lifted a shoulder, his mouth twisting into something that was half grimace, half smile. "Guess being a hero isn't all it's cracked up to be, huh?"

"No. In fact, it kind of sucks. But…it can pay off in the end. It has for me, anyway. And for Rigel. It will for you, too, Sean."

"Yeah. Maybe someday." He gave a mirthless laugh. "Meanwhile I'll try, really try, to be happy for you. For both of you."

The pain I felt from him made me want to cry but I forced a smile instead. "Thanks, Sean. Goodnight."

24

Ambient interference

MOLLY usually got a ride to school with one of the other cheerleaders these days, or with Sean and one of his basketball buddies who had a car. But this morning she was waiting at the bus stop, her expression serious.

"Hey, what's up?"

She gave a little shrug. "Things are a little…tense at home after last night. Mum's pretty upset and Sean…" She trailed off with another shrug.

"I'm sorry. But I've been honest with him about Rigel all along, you know that."

"I know. It's just…awkward. Because I really am happy for you, even if I feel bad for Sean and my parents keep arguing about it."

"Thanks, Molly. They'll get used to the idea, you'll see. Even if it takes a while."

A couple of other kids reached our corner then, so we switched to talking about homework. At least until Bri and Deb got on the bus at their stop a few minutes later.

"Is it true?" were Bri's first words, spoken loudly enough for half the bus to hear. "You and Rigel are back together? Katie mentioned it online last night, then Sara called to say Jenna saw you two *kissing* right outside the late buses! Tell us *everything!*"

She and Deb plopped into the seat across the aisle from Molly and me, excitedly waiting for me to spill.

"Um, yeah, it's true." Shim's reply last night had suggested Rigel and I be careful but he hadn't asked me to keep it secret, like I'd worried he might. "We talked yesterday and, well, he suddenly started remembering stuff. Including me." I couldn't suppress my grin, it was still so unbelievably wonderful.

They both squealed. "This'll show Trina." Deb was grinning, too. "I was worried she might really convince him— No chance of that now!"

"I don't think there ever was." Bri snorted. "They sit by me in French and it's pretty obvious he's figured out what she really is. But this is *awesome* news, M! Really awesome!"

Deb nodded enthusiastically, but then she sobered a little, looking past me at Molly. "Is Sean okay with it?"

"Mostly." Molly lifted a shoulder. "It's not like he and M were still together. Maybe don't talk to him about it right away, though?"

"No, of course not." Deb's blue eyes were wide with sympathy. "And we'll be extra nice to him, won't we, Bri?"

While they plotted how to take Sean's mind off any lingering hurt he might be feeling, I took the opportunity to reach out for Rigel with my mind.

I'm here, he responded immediately. *Just got off the bus. I'll wait for you out front.*

The O'Garas all know now. About us, I mean. Did you tell your folks?

He didn't answer, which made me worry he hadn't. Then we reached the school and I saw the gaggle of girls surrounding him, which totally explained his lack of response. As soon as I was off the bus, some of them converged on me as well, chattering away.

"Rigel says he's getting his memory back!" "Are you two really back together?" "What about Sean? And Trina?"

I let Bri and Deb do most of the answering, I was in such a hurry to get to Rigel.

"I missed you, too," he murmured as we twined hands and greeted each other with a kiss. Which had to be quick and discreet, since Cormac—Mr. Cormac to everybody else—was looking our way. Not that he'd dare reprimand *me*, but anyone else would at least get a throat-clearing.

Just like it always used to, Rigel's touch infused me with strength, energy and happiness. Especially happiness. I smiled up at him. "This fall is going to be even better than last fall—because this time we won't be waiting for the other shoe to drop."

"Yeah. But boy, when that one fell, it fell hard." He grimaced, remembering everything we'd gone through, being forced to hide our feelings.

"Hey, there are only two shoes to a pair, right? Cormac will find out if we still have any enemies out there and take care of them, and then it'll be smooth sailing."

Even if it's not, together we can handle anything, he sent silently.

We can. I feel that way whenever I'm with you.

We were besieged by more questions as we headed into the school but when the warning bell sounded, the crowd around us finally dissipated. Hand in hand, we walked to our first class.

So, did you tell your folks last night? I asked again as we reached the door.

Yeah, I did. They said they were happy, but I could tell they're worried.

The O'Garas didn't even pretend, but that's tough. Well, Molly really is happy for us and Sean's doing his best, but—

Yeah. I could tell that bothered Rigel nearly as much as it bothered me.

Though we had to pay *some* attention in our classes, we took advantage of our enhanced telepathic ability to talk off and on all morning, even from opposite ends of the school.

Little by little, I caught Rigel up on everything that had happened over the summer: my appearances all over Nuath to talk up emigration, how Shim was already winning people over as Regent and getting more competent people to stand for elections, my trip to Earth on the *Scintilla*, the very last ship of the launch window.

Then I told him about how I'd had to go around making speeches and official visits once I got back, first in Bailerealta, then Dun Cloch and three other settlements scattered around the U.S.—one in Maine and two in the Rockies. Others were forming in New Zealand, Australia and Scotland, which I was also supposed to visit eventually, if we could figure out how to arrange it without making my aunt and uncle suspicious.

I can't believe they're not suspicious already. Mrs. O must really have your aunt bamboozled, huh?

Yeah, Aunt Theresa pretty much believes anything she says. That was sometimes a problem last year, but it can be pretty handy.

As long as she doesn't convince her to forbid you to see me again. That would suck.

She wouldn't dare. I don't think. But I should probably order her not to, to be safe. I was way more comfortable giving orders to grownups these days than I used to be.

At lunch, Rigel and I both had the idea—at the same time—to go to the courtyard. I loved that we were so in tune again. We each bought a sandwich, then headed outside, ignoring the heads that turned our way, since that had been happening all day.

It was hot in the enclosed courtyard compared to the cornfield yesterday, but it was worth it for a chance to be truly alone for half an hour.

"Not as invisible, though." Rigel glanced at the glass doors into the school, where we could see people walking past in the hall. "Hope we can go back there—or someplace else really private—soon."

"Me too." As soon as we had our sandwiches unwrapped, I again threaded my fingers through his. "It's strange, but…do your senses seem even sharper when we're together?"

He nodded. "I was just going to mention I can hear people's conversations from inside the school. It's kind of distracting. I didn't notice it in class earlier, even when we were sitting just a few feet apart. Did you?"

Taking a bite of my sandwich, I shook my head. "Maybe we have to be touching?"

"Let's test it."

Rigel released my hand and scooted an inch or two away so we weren't touching at all—and sure enough, the voices beyond the doors were now muted.

"I can still hear them if I concentrate," I told him, "but not like they're right here."

"Ditto." He frowned. "We need to figure out how to block this unless we need to use it. Because I sure don't want to *not* touch you just to avoid sensory overload."

Touching you is sensory overload all by itself, I couldn't resist sending. *Let's eat, then experiment.*

Rigel grinned and stuffed half a sandwich into his mouth with a mostly-mental chuckle.

Eager to test this interesting new "power," we scarfed down our lunches, then grabbed hands again. Instantly, the volume of voices around us rose—not just from the other side of the glass doors, but from behind the brick walls of the courtyard, too.

"Can you block it out at all?" I asked, squinting as I tried.

He shook his head. "Not yet. Let me try something."

Because we were so in sync, I realized he was attempting to zero in on just one conversation. I did the same, picking a different one—Mr. Morrison giving Bobby Jeeter detention. The more I focused, the more I was able to isolate just those voices. The others were still there, but they weren't as overwhelming.

After about five minutes, we unclasped our hands. I immediately missed Rigel's touch but the muting of the voices was a relief.

"This could come in handy." Rigel regarded me thoughtfully. "Especially if we get better at controlling it."

I shrugged. Since I doubted there were any serious threats looming that would make it necessary, I was way more interested in finding a way to block it out so Rigel and I could hold hands…and stuff… without being bombarded. "We should head to class. The warning bell will ring any minute."

Pausing to throw our trash in the can by the doors, we went back inside—only to be confronted by Cormac.

"Miss Truitt, Mr. Stuart, will you come with me, please?"

Over his shoulder, I saw Trina smirking. She'd obviously tattled on us—not that eating lunch in the courtyard was strictly against any school rules. If I'd focused on *that* conversation, I'd know exactly what she'd told him.

Without a word, we followed Cormac to his office. He closed the door then turned to us, his frown now a worried one.

"Excellency, it is not my place to criticize or instruct you, but it is my place to keep you safe. Am I correct in assuming you two have resumed your prior relationship?"

I nodded. "As of yesterday afternoon. Rigel has his memory back, Cormac!" His eyebrows went up. "Because of our bond," I clarified.

"You think this will make her less safe, sir?" Rigel asked before Cormac could respond.

"If your memory has in fact returned, you surely recall what happened in Nuath when evidence of that relationship became public. There is still likely to be widespread opposition among our people. While most will be content to express their displeasure verbally, some may not. With so many Nuathans now on Earth, it is conceivable that some, perhaps many, will feel betrayed by this news, once it spreads beyond the school—as it surely will, if no effort is made to prevent that."

It was the longest speech I could ever remember hearing from Cormac.

"They might not like it, but why should that make them

dangerous?" I asked.

"In my experience, people can react…unpleasantly when their cherished ideals are overthrown or their heroes tarnished. Faxon used that unfortunate aspect of human nature to his advantage on multiple occasions to undermine support for the Sovereign and the Royal *fine*. If you insist on spending time together, it would be safest not to do so publicly."

I sensed worry from Rigel now, but I refused to share it. "No. We tried hiding our relationship to keep me safe when Faxon's people were actively trying to hunt me down and kill me. But our bond turned out to be the very thing that kept them from succeeding. We're not staying apart again because of some hypothetical threat that will probably never even materialize. Besides, with Rigel's memory back, I now have two Bodyguards, so I should be twice as safe."

"Very well, Excellency." Cormac bowed. "It was my duty to warn you, just as it will now be my duty to keep an even more vigilant watch."

"I'll be vigilant too, sir." Rigel sounded determined now rather than worried. "I'll do everything in my power to keep her safe."

"I appreciate the assistance," Cormac said gravely. "However, your safety could be at issue as well."

Rigel lifted his chin. "Do you let fear for your own safety keep you from protecting her?"

"Point taken." Cormac bowed slightly in Rigel's directly—which surprised me nearly as much as it did Rigel. "Ah, there's the bell. You two had best get to your next class."

For the rest of the day, Rigel and I tested our extra-enhanced senses whenever we got the chance. By sixth period, when I was in Economics and Rigel was in Weight Training, we'd figured out that even when we weren't together, our hearing was still more acute than it had been as recently as this morning. I wasn't bombarded by sounds now, but if I focused I could hear conversations in the next room.

Same here, Rigel told me when I shared my discovery. *Maybe you should let Mr. Cormac know. He might not worry so much.*

It'll only help if somebody actually talks about anything they're plotting, I pointed out. *It's not like we can read minds—except for each other's.*

But that gave me an idea.

Staring with mock attention at the teacher's budget calculations on the board, I concentrated on picking up emotions. First from the teacher—she was tired and bored—then from a student or two on the far side of the room. And the more I honed in, the more I was able to sense.

Gary very much had the hots for Amber, sitting in front of him. I wondered if his girlfriend, Heather, knew about that? Meanwhile, Amber was pissed about something, though I had no idea what.

I pushed farther, into the next room, where I could hear Bri's dad, Mr. Morrison, droning about computer keyboarding. When I brought my newly-strengthened emotion-sensing ability to bear, I could tell he was hiding eagerness and a bit of anxiety—probably about tonight's football game, since he was the defensive coach.

For the rest of the class, I probed the emotions of everyone I could "recognize" (from whispered conversations) in the next room. It got easier and easier. Just before the bell, I tried picking up sounds, then emotions from two rooms away, but that didn't work nearly as well. Would it, if I were touching Rigel?

Let's find out, he said as soon as I told him about my most recent experiment, on the way to last period.

Unfortunately, the newsroom wasn't so laid-back today. Angela, apparently unable to function without stress, announced she was assigning everyone online articles to fill the gap between official monthly newspaper blogs. Not only was there no chance of running off to the cornfield again, Rigel and I didn't even have a chance to touch each other, since she sent him to the computer to do some design updates on the website while I was stuck at the long table searching for story ideas in hard copy issues of a couple bigger schools' newspapers.

Picking up on my frustration, Rigel tried to soothe me. *Don't worry. After class we'll get a chance. Maybe we can meet at the arboretum again tomorrow? Safer than ticking off Angela while she's in dragon-editor mode.*

She and Ms. Raymond had both been clear, on the very first day of school, that if anyone had any personal issues—good or bad—with any other staff member, we were to keep it strictly out of the newsroom. So I impatiently waited until Rigel and I were out in the hallway after the final bell to grab his hand, for the first time since lunch. He felt wonderful.

So do you. He smiled down at me. *But the noise level…*

I know. Let's try focusing farther away, like out by the buses.

Walking slowly, hand in hand, we both directed our insanely-enhanced hearing toward the side parking lot. It took a few minutes, but soon I was able to pick out Bri's voice, talking to Deb.

"—with us at the game tonight? Is she getting a ride with the O'Garas again, do you know?"

Crap. She was talking about *me.* Super uncomfortable at the idea of eavesdropping, I shifted my focus to the left, to another group of students I couldn't see. A boy—Will?—stammered slightly as he asked someone if they wanted to go out after the game. Belatedly remembering to use my emotion-sensing ability, I picked up Will's intense nervousness, as well as that of the boy—boy?—he was talking to.

Huh. I never knew Will was gay, I commented to Rigel.

Really? After having him as your partner in Science all last year? But this is cool. Holding your hand, I can sense the same emotions you do. That's new. Wonder if it's your ability or our bond that's gotten so much stronger?

I think it's our bond making *my ability stronger. I can't pick up emotions from nearly this far away when we're not touching. I tried in Econ.*

Walking faster, since the buses would be leaving soon, we continued to test and analyze this interesting new power—which also helped to quiet the cacophony of voices around us to a bearable level. As soon as we stopped focusing, though, the volume crept back up.

Still, it's good we can turn it down when we concentrate. Maybe we'll get to where we can do it automatically.

Hope so.

Outside the school, Rigel kissed me—way too briefly—then we had to hurry to our separate buses.

"I was wondering if you were going to make it," Bri greeted me. Luckily, Molly had saved me a seat. "So, is Rigel taking you to the game tonight, or what?"

"Oh. Um…" *What do you think?* I quickly sent to him as the bus pulled away.

Didn't think to ask my folks. But if you get a ride there, we can definitely take you home after.

"He's giving me a ride home after." I hoped my hesitation hadn't been too noticeable. "He, uh, has to be there really early."

"Mom's letting me borrow the car tonight, so I can pick you up," Deb offered eagerly. "You really should sign up for the next Driver's Ed class they offer, since you missed it last spring.

I shrugged. "I can't see Aunt Theresa ever letting me drive her car and it's not like I can afford my own. But yeah, I probably should."

Again, Rigel and I kept mentally touching base as we headed home, whenever gaps in conversations on our buses allowed it. His emotions came through even more clearly than yesterday, and we were able to keep contact a little longer. Either we were getting better with practice, or our bond was still getting stronger. Which was totally fine with me.

25

Synchronous compensator

UNLIKE most of last week's game, Rigel was throwing the ball like a pro tonight. As usual, Bri couldn't stop gushing about it.

"That last series of downs, the whole team was playing better than last year. *Way* better than last week. When Rigel's on his game, he brings up the level for all of them. Look, even our defense is playing better. We're on fire tonight!"

Watching Rigel in his tight-fitting uniform certainly set *me* on fire. I couldn't help remembering the start of last year's football season, ogling Rigel from the stands and agonizing over whether or not he'd talk to me after the game. Shoot, I'd even done that this year, before he got his memory back.

Tonight, thank goodness, I didn't need to agonize—though I was doing just as much ogling.

At halftime, when the team sprinted off to the locker room, Bri and Deb went for snacks from the concession stand and I headed up three rows to talk with Rigel's parents again. When they saw me approaching, they looked every bit as wary as they had when I'd approached them two weeks ago.

"Um, hi," I said, weirdly more nervous now than I'd been then. Because Rigel and I were back together? "I guess Rigel told you what happened yesterday?"

"He did." Dr. Stuart's wariness edged into actual anxiety. "We're, ah, very happy for him. For you both."

I sat down next to her. "No, I don't think you are." In fact, I was positive. "Last year, even last spring, you both seemed okay with us being together, even when we had to hide it. What's different now?"

"Quite a lot." Mr. Stuart's anxiety didn't quite match his wife's, but it was still noticeable. "Your position, for one thing."

"We…don't want Rigel hurt. Again." Dr. Stuart's hazel eyes, so much like Rigel's, were wide and pleading.

"Neither do I! That's the very *last* thing I want. I thought you both understood that by now?"

They exchanged a glance. "Of course we do." Rigel's mother was still palpably uncomfortable. "But try to see it from our perspective, Ex—er, M. Over the past year, he *has* been hurt—physically, emotionally and mentally."

"Because of me." I guess they had a point.

"Not that we hold you responsible for any of those incidents," Mr. Stuart quickly assured me. "You have our total allegiance, as always."

I couldn't excuse my part so quickly, though. I *was* the one who'd convinced Rigel to run away last December, nearly getting him killed. And if I hadn't *pounced* on him our first night on the *Quintessence* in full view of those stupid cameras, then told him about the Grentl, he never would have had his memory erased. Maybe they were right. Rigel probably *would* be safer if I—

Forget it, came Rigel's thought from the locker room. *You said yourself we're not letting anyone keep us apart from now on. Right?*

I didn't know you were listening! But you're right, I did. I turned my attention back to his parents.

"I can't promise there won't still be…challenges. But I'm in a better position now to keep Rigel safe, to keep all of you safe, than I was before."

Dr. Stuart shared another glance with her husband, then turned to pin me with her direct gaze. "What about Sean O'Gara?"

"We're friends. That's all we've ever been and it's all we'll ever be. He knows that. So do his parents. They're not totally happy about it, but…" I shrugged.

Mr. Stuart was still frowning. "Surely, the greater good demands—"

"No. *Tradition* demands. But lots of traditions are going to be changing now. Including that one."

"Rigel said we might be giving you a ride home after the game?" Dr. Stuart managed a tentative smile.

I nodded. "If that's okay?"

"Of course! I was simply going to suggest that might be a better opportunity to, ah, discuss this further."

The stands around us were filling back up now that halftime was nearly over, making our sub-whispered conversation more conspicuous.

"Good idea. See you after." With a parting smile, I headed down to join Bri and Deb for the second half.

* * *

With the whole team playing so much better than last week, Jewel ended up beating Elm Grove by three touchdowns and a field goal—24 points. Bri, of course, was ecstatic, along with all the rest of our fans.

"Are you sure you can't come to the after-party?" she pleaded as we joined the throng surging toward the field to congratulate the team. "You can call your aunt, tell her you're spending the night at Deb's house, like I told my mom and dad. Which we really will, after the party!"

I shook my head, trying to look regretful. "I don't have my toothbrush or pajamas or anything. Besides, Rigel and his folks are giving me a ride home. He hasn't said anything about going, so he's probably not." *Right?* I sent quickly to Rigel.

Nope. I'd way rather be with you.

"Maybe next game?" I suggested. "If we plan ahead?"

Deb nodded. "You totally should, M. These parties are super fun, and you've never been to one."

I almost made a comment about how she and Bri should be careful but stopped myself in time. "Yeah, one of these times I need to find out what I'm missing. Have fun, but not *too* much fun." I added a wink so they'd think I was kidding. "You can tell me about it Monday."

After that, it took me several minutes to work my way through the crowd surrounding Rigel so he could greet me with a hug and a kiss I wished could have lasted longer.

Maybe tomorrow? he suggested as he released me. *Arboretum again?*

Absolutely!

When his parents came up I took a step back, since they weren't comfortable with us as a couple yet. I hoped I could change that during the car ride home. Meanwhile, I shared their glow of pride at all the praise people were heaping on Rigel. He really was perfection itself, both on and off the football field.

Another ten minutes passed before Rigel could diplomatically excuse himself to go shower. As I walked to the parking lot with his parents, I wondered if they were also reminded of the first time they'd driven me home from a football game last year—before I had any clue who I was, or even that there were Martians living on Earth (or Mars, for that matter).

Apparently so, judging by Dr. Stuart's first words once we were away from the crowd. "A lot certainly has happened in a year, hasn't it?"

"I was just thinking that." My sigh was *mostly* happy. "I've…missed you guys."

Her smile was sympathetic. "I suppose you've had rather a lonely time of it lately. Though I'm sure the O'Garas have done their best to —"

"Sean and Molly have been great. But their parents, well, we don't exactly see eye to eye these days. Especially after what happened to Rigel—what they *allowed* to happen."

Mr. Stuart seemed uncomfortable with my criticism. "I'm sure they felt they had good reason—"

"BS!" I snapped. "Sorry, that was rude. But I don't buy it. I didn't then and I don't now. *Nothing* justified what they did. I hope they haven't tried to convince you any of this was ever Rigel's fault, because it wasn't."

They exchanged a long, speaking glance—literally, since they also had the ability to communicate telepathically with each other. Though maybe not at the range Rigel and I could these days.

"Lili O'Gara never said in so many words that Rigel was guilty of anything, no," his father finally admitted. "But she made it clear he had, ah, learned things or perhaps been somewhere he shouldn't have. That he could have been a threat to Nuathan security. Also that it would be best for all concerned if he not regain certain memories."

"Has he?" Dr. Stuart asked me point blank. "He didn't tell us exactly what he has remembered so far."

Even though Rigel and I had agreed it might be safest to fudge on that, I couldn't lie to his mother's face. "He remembers everything—but I haven't told the Council or the O'Garas that. Just that he's remembered me and our bond, and that we're not planning to hide our relationship anymore."

At the spike of alarm I felt from both of them, I rushed on. "I promise, I won't let anyone do anything to Rigel, no matter what they learn or suspect about what he's remembered. Why are you so afraid they might? Has the Council, or someone else, actually threatened you?"

After a long, tense silence, Mr. Stuart nodded. "An anonymous message was left in Ariel's briefcase at the hospital. It reiterated what Lili told us, but in much stronger terms—that it would be dangerous for Rigel to remember too much or…to be seen with you, Excellency. I'm sorry. We should have told you at once, but we assumed it was sent or sanctioned by the Council."

Rigel came running up to us just then, after what had to have been the fastest shower on record. Despite my anger over what his dad had just told me, the delicious, clean-Rigel scent of him nearly made me lightheaded.

"What was that?" he asked, reaching out to lace his fingers through mine. "An anonymous message? How come you never told me?"

"Let's get in the car," his mother suggested, since a few stragglers were still passing us. "Then we can talk."

Rigel and I got in back—his body felt amazing, touching mine from knee to shoulder.

"Somebody actually threatened you?" he repeated as soon as the doors were shut. Though we'd both wondered, it was disturbing to have it confirmed.

"The threat was directed more toward you," Dr. Stuart told him. "At the time, you hadn't yet recalled anything about the past year, so there seemed no point in telling you about it. It would have required explanations it seemed safer not to make."

My jaw jutted out, I was so pissed. "I can't believe anyone on the Council would stoop that low, though maybe I shouldn't be surprised."

I'd definitely get the truth out of them at tomorrow night's meeting. Meanwhile… "Speaking of the Council, now that Shim is off it, there's something I wanted to ask you, Mr. Stuart."

"I, ah, don't know that I'll be qualified to answer any of your questions, Excellency. My father never discussed confidential Council business with me, to include his reasons for resigning. He simply said he believed he could be of more use on Mars than on Earth."

That was a surprise. I'd figured Shim would have told them the whole truth by now. "Actually, he resigned in protest. Because the Council voted to go along with erasing Rigel's memory—in complete violation of Nuathan law, by the way."

Despite the shock I felt from both of Rigel's parents I forged on, since we only had another few minutes of privacy. "Nara resigned, too. Kyna convinced her to come back, but the Council still needs one more non-Royal member. Will you be that member, Mr. Stuart?"

"Me?" His surprise was so extreme, I was impressed when the car didn't swerve even an inch. "Surely there are many people far more suitable—"

"Not in my opinion. The remaining Council members have made a few suggestions—all of them Royals. But our greatest need right now is for a secure communication network way bigger than MARSTAR—more like an *Echtran* internet. Who could be better than you to create something like that?"

Still, he shook his head. "I'd be more than happy to design such a network without the honor of a Council position. In fact, I've already mapped out a blueprint of sorts for something along those lines, as it seemed obvious it would become necessary with so many Nuathans relocating to Earth. And if the rest of the Council believe another Royal would be a better choice, perhaps—"

"No. It's bad enough they already have a majority on the Council. I'm not letting them make it five to two. Especially when one of their suggestions was Devyn Kane, who conspired against Rigel and me back on Mars. To be honest, at this point I don't much trust Royals, period—even if I am one. Other than Faxon, every single person who's threatened, bullied, or betrayed me has been a Royal. It's like they don't think normal rules should apply to them."

"My father occasionally expressed a similar opinion," Mr. Stuart admitted after a pause, his startled resistance fading. "Power does tend to corrupt. Though we *Echtrans* like to think of ourselves as morally and ethically superior to the *Duchas,* we are still very much human."

"Then you'll do it? Take Shim's place on the Council?"

Cornfields gave way to the outskirts of downtown before he answered. "If it is your wish, Excellency—and if the rest of the Council will agree—I am willing to serve."

"Thank you!" I saw no point in telling him I didn't plan to give the Council the *option* of disagreeing. "There's a Council meeting at the O'Garas' house tomorrow night at eight o'clock. How about you come around eight-thirty, unless I call and tell you otherwise?"

"Very well." I still sensed a certain amount of nervous uncertainty, but also determination, along with grateful pride. I had no doubt he'd turn out to be an excellent Council member.

When we pulled into my driveway, I thanked Mr. Stuart again for his willingness to serve, as well as for the ride home. Then Rigel walked me to the door, hand in hand. It felt *so* good to be together like this again!

"So, arboretum tomorrow, right? One o'clock?" he murmured as we mounted the steps to my wide front porch.

"Yep." I glanced at the sky, where clouds now obscured the stars. "Rain or shine."

At the door, he turned to face me. "Can't wait. G'night, M."

He leaned in and I eagerly turned my face up for his kiss. Last fall, winter and spring, every kiss had seemed better than the one before, and that hadn't changed. Only awareness that his parents were watching kept me from completely melting into him. I halfway hoped it *would* rain tomorrow, so we could have the arboretum to ourselves.

Kissing Rigel totally blocked out his parents' conversation in the car, which was good since they thought it was private. Luckily, we were still able to hear Aunt Theresa's footsteps in time to break apart before she opened the door.

"I thought I heard a car." She raised an eyebrow, looking from Rigel to me. I was probably a little flushed from that kiss. "Didn't you ride to the game with your friend Debra?"

I nodded. "The Stuarts offered me a ride back."

The look she now turned on Rigel was both suspicious and curious. "I see. I'd have thought they had enough on their hands, what with… Well. You'd best come inside, Marsha. It's late. Good night, young man. Thank your parents for us, if Marsha hasn't already done so."

"She has, but I'll tell them you said thanks too, Mrs. Truitt," he said politely. "Good night."

As he headed back down the steps he sent, *Don't let her rag on you, okay? Remember, you're the Sovereign now, even if she doesn't know it!*

I was still smiling at that as I accompanied Aunt Theresa into the house—which she unfortunately noticed.

"You seem quite pleased with yourself tonight, missy. Don't tell me you're dating that quarterback again? I heard he had complete amnesia after that accident last summer. Indeed, I'm surprised he can function at all."

Remembering Rigel's last thought to me, I squared my shoulders. "I'm sure Uncle Louie can tell you how well he's functioning on the football field—we won again tonight. Anyway, he only lost the last year of his memory and now he has most of it back. And yes, we're dating again, as of yesterday."

My aunt hmphed. "Well…don't let him talk you into any more midnight trysts. I trust you both learned your lesson about *that* sort of thing."

That "midnight tryst" in the arboretum last year had been just as much my idea as Rigel's, but I forced myself to nod. "Don't worry, Aunt Theresa. We're both more responsible now than when we were sophomores."

Besides, there was no reason to think anything else was going to happen that would force us to sneak around like that. No reason at all.

26

Superconductivity

I got my wish—when I left taekwondo the next day, it was beginning to drizzle. Pulling up the hood on my lightweight raincoat, I headed for the arboretum with a spring in my step, my gear bag swinging at my side.

Rigel and I reached the entrance at the same time, him with a poncho enveloping him and his bike, reminding me of one of our walks last year. He obviously remembered too—or picked up on my thought—because he held up an umbrella with a grin. "It's not a force field, but it gets the job done."

Laughing, I held out my free hand and he took it in his. Together we walked along the deserted gravel path to "our" bench, just out of sight of the arboretum entrance. I reveled in the delicious tingling sensation that went through me at his touch.

"I wished for this, you know." I tilted my face up to the falling mist. "And it worked—we have the place to ourselves."

Rigel took off his poncho, shook it, then spread it over the wet seat of the bench. "Excellent. Does that mean you can control the weather now?"

"What?" Oh, he was teasing. "Not yet. Maybe we should work on that next."

"No, what I think we should do next is this." Pulling me down onto the bench beside him, he lowered his lips to mine and for the next ten minutes I wouldn't have noticed if it had started blizzarding.

One hand still caressing my face, Rigel pulled back an inch or two. "No voices while we're kissing, have you noticed?"

I nodded. "I noticed last night, on my front porch. That means we can learn to control it, don't you think? So we only hear what we really want to?"

"I'd rather control it like this." And he was kissing me again.

Finally, with a happy sigh, I leaned back to look up at him, my arms still around his neck. "We really should practice other ways to shut out the voices, since we can't do this *all* the time. Much as I wish we could."

"I guess you're right." He released me to drape an arm over the back of the bench, holding the umbrella over both of us since the drizzle had picked back up. "And it would be great if we could figure out how to use your emotion-sensing thing to get fair warning in case whoever threatened my parents tries anything."

"Did they tell you any more about that anonymous note?"

He shook his head. "They mostly talked about the idea of Dad being on the Council. Even I didn't see that one coming. How come you didn't mention it?"

"I first got the idea when I was talking to the O'Garas Thursday, then last night it just kind of…blurted out. But I really do think he'll be perfect, what with his background and all. Plus, I trust him."

Rigel gave me that crooked smile I adored. "You made a good case. And I sure don't disagree with you about Royals in general. Not counting you, of course."

I gave the hand grazing my shoulder a quick squeeze of thanks. "Yeah, even if it wasn't a member of the Council who planted that note, I'll bet it was either a Royal or someone acting on the orders of one. I plan to find out—though I already have my suspicions."

"Yeah? Who?"

"The two with the biggest axes to grind against both of us are Allister and Gordon. It wouldn't surprise me a bit to find out they're in cahoots."

"But Gordon's still on Mars, isn't he?"

I blinked at him in surprise. "Oh, I guess you wouldn't know. No, he came back to Earth on the same ship you did, supposedly to supervise what you'd be told when they woke you up. But now no one seems to know where he is—though I'm pretty sure Allister's lying about that."

Rigel looked thoughtful, though I also sensed anger—and worry. "Do you think they sent that crazy dude after you last week, told him to say he was an anti-Royalist?"

"It definitely fits their style. Allister always got others to do his dirty work and Gordon seems the type who'd be happy to oblige—at least if he can do it without getting caught. There's nothing I wouldn't put past those two."

Turning to face me more fully, Rigel propped the umbrella over us and took both my hands in his. "Let's see if we can pick up anything in range, maybe find out if Gordon's right here in Jewel."

Our extra-sensitive hearing hadn't been a distraction since arriving, probably because the arboretum was a good three blocks from the nearest houses or businesses. Once we really *listened,* though, it was apparent we'd been controlling that ability without even realizing it.

The birds were suddenly a lot louder, as were the cars going past on the street outside. Soon, I could pick up voices, too—voices that *had* to be farther away than any we'd heard yesterday at school. Sharpening my focus, I again found I could ignore the extraneous noises to hone in on specific conversations.

Anything that sounds or feels like Gordon? Rigel sent silently.

Not yet. I listened harder, trying to push my hearing to its limits while also reaching out with my emotion-sensing ability. It wasn't easy. If I didn't limit my focus to one or two people at a time, it got confusing and uncomfortable. As I kept at it, though, it slowly got easier.

Ah! That was definitely Belinda, the bookstore owner, gossiping with old Mrs. Batten about somebody's cheating husband. They were both enjoying themselves immensely. A bit farther away, I picked up a woman complaining about the drugstore being out of her color hair dye. She seemed way too upset about it.

A few minutes later, I heard Mrs. Crabtree, my across-the-street neighbor, on the phone with someone. Maybe her daughter? Someone she was happy to be talking to, anyway. Did that mean I could—?

Sure enough, I was able to push my focus just enough farther to hear Aunt Theresa and Uncle Louie. They were arguing—again—about a couple of his buddies Aunt Theresa considered bad influences. Both of them felt resigned, almost bored, with the same argument they'd had so many times before.

Rigel and I stared at each other, then unclasped our hands. "Wow," he said. "That was…amazing. And totally weird."

"No kidding. And I felt like we could have kept going, reaching farther and farther away, didn't you?"

"I did. But…it's kind of exhausting—especially for you. Let's try just holding hands and *not* picking up anything. Recharge each other."

I was all in favor of that. Scooting closer to him, I took his hand again and snuggled against his shoulder. He felt even more wonderful than usual, his strength and vitality flowing into me, replenishing the energy I'd just spent on our experiment. I was careful to focus only on Rigel now—his thoughts, his feelings. It worked. *It's working for you, too, right?*

He nodded, smiling down at me. "See? I knew we could do it. Though I still like this way better." His hazel eyes darkening, he lowered his mouth to mine and soon I was so revitalized I felt like I could fly.

When the sun came out and other people started wandering into the arboretum, we finally, regretfully, decided it was time to head home. I'd told Aunt Theresa I was staying after at taekwondo for some make-up training but I didn't want to risk her calling the do-jang to check on me.

Still holding hands, we walked through through the archway to Diamond Street.

"Your bike is soaked."

Rigel shrugged. "No biggie. This hour with you was totally worth a wet seat."

Notice how we're still not hearing more than we want to?

Yep, he replied. *But we should try one last time, make sure no baddies are nearby.*

Standing next to his bike, hand in hand, we reached out again. This time it only took me a couple of minutes to find Aunt Theresa again after sifting through the wash of emotions between here and there. Some were happy, some were sad or upset, but none seemed to be plotting nefarious deeds. Aunt Theresa, on the other hand, was getting distinctly impatient—probably because I was going to be late starting my Saturday chores.

"Yep, definitely time to go," I said, releasing Rigel's hand. "Did you pick that up, too?"

"Yeah. Is that how it always feels when you…" *sense other people's emotions?* he finished silently as an older couple walked past us into the arboretum.

"Only if I focus."

"Focus any time you see a stranger then, okay? Promise?"

"I will. Promise." Going up on my toes, I gave him a last, quick kiss, then turned toward home.

I'll bet our telepathy range will be better than ever now, he sent as he passed me on his bike with a wave and a smile.

He was right. We kept thinking to each other the whole time I was walking and he was biking. I got home a few minutes before he did, still able to hear him. After apologizing to Aunt Theresa for being gone longer than I'd expected and getting started on the bathroom, I reached out to Rigel again. *Can you still hear me?*

I can! And…I'm home! Just got here. This is beyond awesome.

Totally! Should we tell your parents?

We discussed that and other things the whole time I was scrubbing out the tub and toilet, then off and on for the rest of the day, when we didn't need to pay attention to anyone else. Rigel was right. It *was* beyond awesome.

At ten minutes till eight, I headed to the O'Garas' house, again with my overnight bag since tonight's meeting would probably go even later than the first one.

"Mind you're a good guest," Aunt Theresa cautioned, like she always did. "Pick up after yourself, offer to help around the house and don't forget to say thank you."

"I know. I will. G'night, Aunt Theresa. G'night, Uncle Louie."

"Nearly everyone is already here, Excellency," Mrs. O'Gara greeted me when I arrived. "Quinn has taken Sean and Molly to a movie." The last two meetings, they'd been home and Mr. O had sat in, though he hadn't participated.

"Better than them being stuck in their rooms, since we have so much to talk about tonight."

"We do indeed."

I knew she meant my "ill-advised" decision to get back together with Rigel, but suspected the Council would disapprove of some other items on my agenda every bit as much. Shaking off the subservient attitude I had to assume around Aunt Theresa, I lifted my chin and preceded Mrs. O into the living room.

The two other local members of the Council, Breann and Malcolm, rose and bowed at my entrance. So did Kyna's and Nara's projected holograms—incredibly solid-looking, but without *brath* or emotions I could sense, since they were actually in Washington, D.C. They were still bowing, right fists over their hearts, when Connor's hologram beamed in from Denver.

Once he'd bowed, I sat down and the others followed my example. (I always assumed the holographic ones were on actual chairs elsewhere, though it looked remarkably like they were sitting on ones here in the living room).

"As you all know, we have a lot of business to cover tonight," I began before anyone else could speak. "First, Nara, I want to personally thank you for returning to the Council. It means a lot to me—as did your resignation and the reason for it."

Though the Royals all shifted uncomfortably, little Nara smiled and bobbed her head. "It is my great honor, Excellency. My allegiance is yours. Always."

"This still leaves us a member short." I looked around at the others, most of whose expressions were guarded, as were the emotions of those physically present. "So you'll be happy to know I've found someone both suitable and willing to serve by taking his father's place on this Council."

"What? You wish to appoint Van Stuart?" Connor exclaimed, frowning.

"I already have. Which is completely within my authority," I reminded them all as their surprise became tinged with disapproval. "Just last week you stressed the need for a decent communication system to connect the new *Echtran* settlements popping up around the world. You were worried because we have so few qualified Informatics Scientists on Earth, and because that person would need such a high level of security clearance. Appointing Van Stuart to this Council solves all those problems at once."

I held my breath, waiting, while my words sank in. One by one, heads started to nod, though some with obvious reluctance. Kyna was the first to speak.

"Yes, Excellency, I agree that Van will be a valuable addition. Through Shim, I've come to know him fairly well over the years and his loyalty and ethics are above reproach. As the person who originally designed the current MARSTAR system, his skills will serve us well in creating a more robust communication network to accommodate Earth's growing *Echtran* population."

Nara nodded enthusiastically, as though she were only just restraining herself from clapping. "Indeed! Van is the next best thing to Shim himself, now that Shim's serving in an even more important capacity in Nuath."

"I can't deny that this would resolve a few of our current problems, Excellency." Breann smiled thinly, then glanced around at the other Royals. "Do you not think so?"

"I suppose there is something to be said for maintaining a balance on the Council, as you so strenuously pointed out last week, Excellency," Malcolm admitted.

When Mrs. O and Connor finally murmured their grudging agreement, I breathed a quiet sigh of relief. "Great! I've invited Mr. Stuart to join us here shortly, so he can be brought up to speed on everything. Meanwhile, we can move on to other matters."

"Such as this news of you resuming a relationship with Rigel Stuart?" Malcolm said before I could continue. "We may have agreed to his father's appointment, but I thought surely you understood that pursuing even a fleeting teen romance with a non-Royal could have a detrimental effect on—"

"Yes, I'm well aware that most of you consider it politically *inconvenient* for Rigel and me to be together, just as you found it politically *convenient* to turn a blind eye to Nuathan law and agree to his memory being erased. Luckily, that memory erasure turned out to be temporary."

"What?" Kyna spoke sharply. "Are you saying that Rigel Stuart's memory is returning already? How is that possible?"

Second only to Shim in both age and bearing, Kyna had always intimidated me a little, but now I looked her directly in the eye. "It was possible because of our *graell* bond, something all of you have done your best to ignore from the start. When Rigel and I are together, when we touch, we have always had a healing effect on each other. In this case, it healed his memory."

Kyna still frowned. "While I did not sanction his memory erasure, Excellency, I was disappointed to learn you had informed Rigel of the Grentl's existence despite your sworn word. It was that breach which persuaded my Royal colleagues to disregard Nuathan law on this matter."

The Royals all began to murmur and nod, so I continued quickly. "I did try my best to keep the Grentl a secret from Rigel, since you forced me to promise. But he knew I was hiding something and, as my Bodyguard, I felt he needed to know. So once we were on our way to Mars, I finally told him, knowing he'd never, ever tell anyone else. Which he didn't."

"Excellency, are you implying that you now intend to share *all* official business, classified or not, with Rigel Stuart?" Connor was visibly indignant, as were the other Royals.

I debated with myself for a moment, then nodded. "I don't have much choice. One aspect of our bond is a mental link—sharing thoughts with each other. That made it incredibly hard to keep such a big secret from Rigel for three whole months. I never want to have to do that again."

"Really?" Nara squeaked excitedly. "You actually have the legendary telepathic link? Can you—?"

"Not now, Nara," Kyna snapped, then turned back to me. "We appreciate you sharing this with us, Excellency, but you can't deny it's a definite security risk. If Rigel Stuart should actually remember *everything*—"

"He does. Everything." Abruptly, I decided I was done fudging. "Just as if his memory had never been erased." The Royals acted so shocked, I decided to attempt a test. "Obviously, that's news you didn't want to hear. Is that why you threatened his parents? So they wouldn't help him get his memory back?"

As I voiced that accusation, I focused, hard, on the emotions of the Council members in the room with me and the expressions of the holographic ones. I didn't detect any guilt, though. Just surprise and confusion.

"Threatened?" Breann echoed, frowning. "The Stuarts have been threatened? By whom?"

"That's what I want to know," I replied. "An anonymous note was left for Dr. Stuart at the hospital where she works, saying it would be *dangerous* for Rigel to remember too much, or to spend too much time with me. Exactly what some of you have been saying."

Malcolm gave a little huff. "Dangerous, yes, in the sense of a security breach, but we certainly never implied we would take any sort of physical action against the Stuart family. I would hope something so cowardly as an anonymous note would be beneath any of us, no matter our views."

"I wanted to believe that, too, and I'm glad to have it confirmed.

But *somebody* left that note. Maybe Gordon Nolan? He was in on the original plot to erase Rigel's memory and now he seems to have gone into hiding. I'd like Allister Adair questioned about that by someone who'll know for sure whether he's telling the truth." I looked at Mrs. O'Gara.

"If…if that's your wish, Excellency, though I told you I've spoken with my brother and—"

"But not in person. I did, just a few weeks ago, and he was awfully evasive when I asked him about Gordon. It's also possible whoever left that note had something to do with the man who attacked me last week. Maybe even the attack in Ireland last spring, before I left for Mars. You never did figure out who was behind that."

"Indeed," Kyna said decisively. "Whoever is responsible must be found and stopped before he can again threaten the Sovereign or anyone else. Allister has proven himself capable of duplicity in the past, as has Gordon Nolan, in that matter of the hacked security feed aboard the *Quintessence*, an act of near-treason that could have resulted in Nuath's destruction, had it delayed the Sovereign's Acclamation any longer."

Though she clearly wasn't happy about it, Mrs. O nodded. "Very well. I'll fly to Dun Cloch tomorrow and do my best to persuade Allister to reveal Gordon's whereabouts—if he actually knows. I'll message you with whatever I discover."

I thanked her and prepared to move on to the next item, but Malcolm wasn't ready to let the matter of Rigel and me go yet.

"Excellency, surely you don't mean to make your relationship with young Stuart public, with no regard for how that might affect our people's trust in your judgment? What of our traditions? What of your destined Consort?"

"Tradition isn't the same thing as destiny," I told him. "Sean knows Rigel and I are bonded and that we're together again. If *he's* okay with it, why should anyone else care?"

Malcolm turned to Mrs. O. "Is this true? Your son is willing to step aside in favor of this non-Royal upstart?"

"He, ah, does seem surprisingly resigned to the idea." Mrs. O was radiating *way* more resentment than I'd sensed from Sean about it. "While I believe the old traditions have value, the rest of my family appears not to agree." She sounded bitter and I suddenly realized *this* must be why she wanted them all out of the house tonight.

"I don't like it," Malcolm persisted. "You are still young, Excellency, but—"

"You're not required to like it," I said bluntly. "All I require is that you cooperate to keep Rigel and the Stuarts safe from any other disgruntled *Echtrans* who may not be above threats or attacks."

He frowned but didn't dare argue any further, which was my goal.

Mrs. O was still working to subdue her mother-outrage on Sean's behalf when the doorbell rang. She jumped to her feet.

"That will be Van, I presume? You were quite right, Excellency, to anticipate this meeting going late. Informing him of everything he will need to know as a Council member will take quite some time."

27

Capacitance overload

THREE hours later, Mr. Stuart was finally able to assure us he had a reasonable grasp of all of the issues. The news about the Grentl's existence had thrown him for a loop, but he'd overcome his initial shock more quickly than, say, Nels Murdoch had. What would take longer for him to get over, I suspected, was the full story of how Rigel's memory came to be erased. I could sense his disappointment in people he'd formerly regarded as heroes.

I could also sense his gratitude when I insisted (over Council protest) that he was free to share everything he'd learned with his wife. I didn't mention the Stuarts' telepathic link, since that wasn't my secret to share, instead stressing the unfairness of Dr. Stuart being the only one in their family not in the know.

Once he was up to speed, Mr. Stuart outlined his preliminary ideas for a more extensive and secure communications network and how it might be implemented. Finally, I took care of the last item on my agenda by appointing Kyna as new head of the Council. Not only was she now the oldest member but, more importantly, she'd demonstrated both loyalty and wisdom by voting against what was done to Rigel, but refusing to leave the Council to be run entirely by Royals.

Well before we adjourned, Molly, Sean and their dad returned from the movies. Though Mr. O was clearly surprised to see Mr. Stuart here, he merely bowed respectfully as he passed the living room and followed his children into the kitchen.

When Kyna officially closed the meeting, it was past midnight. As everyone stood to say their goodbyes, Nara motioned me closer to her holographic image.

"Excellency, I would very much like to speak with you further about your *graell* bond, if that would not be too presumptuous?"

Remembering her earlier excitement, I smiled, though I was a little wary. "What do you want to know?"

"Well, you see, the *graell* has never been properly studied, which is why most of our people consider it a myth. If you and Rigel would consent to have a small team of Scientists independently verify and quantify the various aspects of your bond, it would be a valuable addition to our body of knowledge. And once our people are convinced the phenomenon really does exist, it should help overcome any, ah, resistance to the idea of you pairing with Rigel rather than Sean." Eyes bright, she clasped her hands in front of her as she waited for my answer.

My first impulse was to refuse. The last time *Echtran* Scientists "studied" our bond, it was just so they could devise an antidote to it. Still, I had to admit her reasoning was sound. Having the *graell* properly studied and the results publicly shared probably *would* go a long way toward getting people to accept us as a couple. Which would substantially cut any risks to Rigel from outraged *Echtrans*.

"Maybe you're right, Nara. I'll need to discuss it with Rigel, but you can message me with the details and we'll see what can be arranged. Um, discreetly arranged."

"Of course! I'll speak with a Mind Healer friend of mine and a few Scientists who have studied genetic affinities and let you know how they'd like to proceed. I know they'll be as eager as I am to learn more about the *graell.* Thank you, Excellency!" Bowing deeply to me, she vanished, the last to leave.

Molly was already asleep by the time I got upstairs, so once I was in bed I took advantage of our wonderfully increased telepathic range to reach out to Rigel.

Are you still awake?

Yep! Dad just got home, so I waited up, hoping you'd let me know how it went.

I told Rigel all about the Council meeting and also mentioned Nara's request to have our bond studied. After I shared her reasoning, Rigel agreed it made sense, especially if swaying people's opinions would make me safer. I was more concerned with *his* safety, but knew that wouldn't carry as much weight with him.

When I got home the next day, I messaged Nara that Rigel and I were willing to answer questions and let her researchers perform a few tests. Within minutes, she responded to ask if the testing might take place that very evening. *Way* sooner than I'd expected!

Though Nara's eagerness was unnerving, I figured if we were going to do this at all, it might as well be soon, so we could start turning public opinion (well, Martian opinion) in our favor as soon as possible. After touching base with Rigel again, I reluctantly agreed.

Maybe it was silly, but because of what happened after the tests done on Rigel and me at the O'Garas' last year, I suggested meeting at the Stuarts' house this time, instead. Both Rigel's parents and Nara were fine with that and within the hour, Dr. Stuart called Aunt Theresa to invite me to dinner.

"You're not having second thoughts, are you, Excellency?" Dr. Stuart pulled her car to a stop in front of the big, yellow farm house, once so familiar to me.

"No, I think we're doing the right thing." In fact, I was having an irresistible flashback to a similar scene almost exactly a year ago, when Dr. Stuart had driven me to their house for what turned out to be practically a trial, to determine if I really was the Princess. We'd used the coming-to-dinner excuse on Aunt Theresa that time, too.

Tonight shouldn't be nearly as nerve-wracking, I told myself. I was really, truly the Sovereign now, and *this* examination was completely voluntary—and wouldn't involve any scary blood tests with antique equipment. Still, the memory sent a tiny shiver down my spine.

"I hope you're right." I could tell she was anxious, too—probably also remembering that evening, plus the much worse one at the O'Garas' a couple months later, when Allister ordered Healers to concoct an antidote to my bond with Rigel so we could be permanently separated.

"It'll be fine." The reassurance was as much for myself as for her. "Allister isn't calling the shots this time, I am."

She nodded, her gorgeous auburn hair glinting in the late-afternoon sun as we approached the front door. "Of course."

Together we walked into the Stuarts' big, cozy living room. I glanced involuntarily at the chair I'd sat in last year for my "inquisition" before registering the other people present: Mr. Stuart, Rigel (also a little nervous), Healer Fiona, who'd helped develop that "antidote," and two men I didn't recognize.

Because I sent a quick *Don't you dare!* Rigel was the only one who didn't bow at my entrance. Instead, he just inclined his head slightly, trying to hide his sudden grin.

"Hello, everyone," I said. "Thank you for coming. And please, let's not stand on ceremony tonight. I prefer to keep things informal whenever possible."

One of the unfamiliar men stepped forward. "Thank *you,* Excellency, for agreeing to have your, ah, unusual situation studied. I'm Blair Hagan, head of genetics research at the World Health Organization. Shim Stuart was a colleague of mine before leaving for Nuath. This is Mind Healer and NASA psychologist Donnan Caith, and I believe you have already met Healer Fiona?"

"Nice to see you again, Fiona. You're a friend of Dr. Stuart's, aren't you?"

"I am, Excellency. She suggested I be present, as I've already done some research into the genetic affinity you share with her son. I'd… like to take this opportunity to apologize for the use to which my initial research was put. It was never my intention—"

"I know. You were following Allister's orders. I don't hold you responsible. Now, how did you all want to, um, proceed? Nara seemed especially interested in Rigel's and my telepathic link?"

Donnan nodded eagerly. "That ability has been quite rare among our people, though occasionally something of the sort has been known to develop over time between paired couples."

"I've heard that." I managed not to glance at Dr. and Mr. Stuart, since I didn't think it was generally known what they could do. "Our link developed a lot faster, within a month or so of our bond forming. Which, by the way, wasn't intentional—or avoidable."

"So I understand. If you're amenable, we'd like to begin by taking the two of you into separate rooms to answer a few questions, after which we'll conduct empirical tests of your telepathic ability. These will be tabulated for our records and included in our final report. If you, Excellency, will go with Fiona, and Rigel, if you'll come with me?"

Rigel shot me a quick, concerned look. *You sure?*

Should be okay. I don't sense anything but curiosity from any of them.

I followed Fiona into the kitchen, while Rigel and Donnan went upstairs, leaving the Stuarts with Blair in the living room.

"Now, Excellency." Fiona sat across from me at the big kitchen table where I'd spent so many happy hours last fall. "I have about two dozen questions to go through, then we'll attempt a few pre-arranged tests, shall we?"

"Go ahead."

For the next ten minutes I answered various questions about how our *graell* bond had formed, at what point we'd been able to sense emotions and then thoughts from each other, as well as the unpleasant physical symptoms we'd experienced every time we'd been separated since then. Some of the questions were simple, some more complex. She recorded all of my answers on her omni, which seemed to have lots of special Healer apps installed.

When I'd answered the last question, she made a note of the time. "Now for the empirical tests. The distance between you and Rigel may well prove too great for communication. If that's the case, I'll have Donnan bring him back downstairs. As long as you can't actually see each other, the tests will be valid."

"I, um, think we'll be fine."

She looked dubious, but pulled up a different holo-screen, again noting the time. "Very well. See if you can send the sentence displayed to Rigel's mind."

What numbers are you being shown? I read off the screen.

Rigel immediately reeled off a series of eight numbers, which I repeated out loud to Fiona.

Then, from Rigel, *What colors, in order, are you being shown?*

Fiona's screen now displayed eight color blocks, one at a time. *Red. Purple. Brown. Yellow. Blue. Green. Orange. Purple again.*

They progressed to more and more complicated questions, which Rigel and I had to take turns relaying to each other, then answering. Finally, Fiona deactivated her screen and smiled.

"That concludes this portion of the test, Excellency. Thank you for your patience. Shall we rejoin the others?"

We reached the living room just as Rigel and Donnan did. Donnan synched his device with Fiona's to tabulate their results, then looked up in surprise. "This is remarkable. Not a single error on either side."

Rigel took my hand and we exchanged a smile. *We* weren't surprised. "Is that it?" I asked.

"Not quite." Blair came forward. "I'd like to take a few genetic readings as well, to compare with the data Fiona gathered last year. If you'd each be willing to provide me with a hair follicle?"

Just like we'd done that day at the O'Garas,' we both plucked strands of hair from our heads and handed them over so he could feed them into his tricorder-thingy. As he watched the display, his eyebrows rose.

"Interesting. The genetic affinity you shared then is much more marked now. Have you noticed a commensurate increase in your joint abilities?"

"Um—" I exchanged a glance with Rigel. "We can communicate over greater distances than before." We'd already agreed not to reveal just *how* great a distance. Keeping a few secrets seemed wise after all we'd been through over the past year. Rigel had also urged me not to mention my emotion-sensing ability, insisting it would be less valuable if everyone knew about it.

"I understand the two of you are also able to generate an electrical charge? Shim told me that you disabled an Ossian Sphere last fall when Faxon's adherents attempted to use one."

Rigel frowned. "We, uh, haven't tested that since getting back together. We only ever used it to defend ourselves."

"Then there were other instances than the one involving the Ossian Sphere?"

I tightened my grip on Rigel's hand. "A few. The very first time it happened, Rigel was defending me from a bully and we, er, accidentally shocked him."

"Was he injured?" Fiona looked genuinely concerned.

"I don't think so." Rigel shrugged. "Just stunned him for couple seconds. He thought I'd hit him. But he didn't hassle M again after that."

"I imagine not," Blair said drily. "Very well, let's see if we can get a read on that particular ability. Excellency, if you'll step over here?" He set a small gray box on an end table and punched up a holo-display.

Letting go of Rigel's hand, I walked over to the box. "Um, it only seems to work when we're touching."

"I understand. But I'd like to get individual readings from each of you first. Now, if you'll please use your right forefinger to touch this spot here? Slowly, as it may register before you actually make contact."

Nodding, I extended my right hand toward the dime-sized red circle he'd indicated. I was maybe an inch away from it when a spark skipped from my finger to the dot, giving me an all-too-familiar static shock.

Blair examined the screen's readout. "Hm. Rather impressive,

Excellency. The average *Duchas* produces somewhere on the order of fifty to one hundred millijoules of electricity with a static touch, whereas the average *Echtran's* touch tends to be roughly two to three times that, for physiological reasons I won't go into right now. However, you registered nearly one joule just now—three to five times normal for an *Echtran*."

"Huh. No wonder I've always tended to fry electronics."

"Yes, I imagine that might be rather inconvenient at times. Rigel, if you'll do the same?"

Rigel's result was about half of mine, but still more than twice "normal" for a Martian.

"And now, if you two will link hands and try with one of your free hands?"

We did. Oddly, we actually produced *less* power than either of us had done alone. Blair seemed at least as surprised as Rigel and I were. After staring thoughtfully at the readout for a moment, he turned to us. "You say you've only used this…power for defensive purposes in the past?"

We both nodded. "When we were really upset or scared," I added. "Maybe that makes a difference?"

"Perhaps. It also seems that when you are not stressed, together you are able to control your static output more easily than either of you can do alone. Fascinating." He tapped a finger thoughtfully against his nose, then shrugged. "I have no wish to upset or frighten either of you, of course. But perhaps if you could, ah, *pretend* to be upset for a moment, just as a test?"

Let's try, Rigel thought to me. *I'd like to find out just what we can do.*

Okay. How about we imagine something bad that really happened, like…that moment when they caught us, after we ran away. Remember? In our panic, we'd knocked out three of our captors, using our electrical ability.

Got it.

We both concentrated for a second or two, then, trying to pretend the measurement device was an enemy, we unleashed a blinding spark. The gray box flew off the end table, bounced off the wall behind it and hit the floor.

"Oops." I looked apologetically at Blair and the others, who were all staring at us with varying degrees of shock. "Did we break it?"

Blair gave himself a little shake, then went over to retrieve the device. "No, it appears to be intact. Let's see if I can bring up a measurement for what you just generated."

He brought up the holo-screen again and tapped through three or four different displays. After blinking several times, he turned to face the rest of us. "Assuming this multimeter is still functioning properly, it indicates that the Sovereign and Rigel have just produced 1.21 *giga*joules of electricity—as much as a small lightning strike!"

"Impossible!" Mr. Stuart exclaimed. "That sort of discharge could kill a person instantly, which they've certainly never done."

The surprise with which everyone had been regarding us was now tinged with fear. It was Dr. Stuart who found her voice first.

"Then I'd say we can assume that their telepathic ability is not the only thing that has strengthened since they were reunited. Do try not to make any more lightning bolts in the house, you two. And now, why don't we all have dinner?"

Her words lightened everyone's mood, much to my relief. I was freaked out enough by what Rigel and I had done without having people actually *afraid* of me. Us.

28

Bandwidth expansion

RIGEL came along when his mother drove me home after dinner. She seemed thoroughly impressed by the strength of our bond and admitted that even after eighty years together (a length of time that still boggled me), she and her husband still had to be in the same room to communicate in full sentences.

Because of the way Dr. Stuart had helped me shield my thoughts from Rigel last spring when our telepathic ability had become awkward, I was tempted to tell her what our real range was now…but didn't.

Once I was in my bedroom for the night, I checked my omni and discovered a voice message from Mrs. O'Gara, who was now in Montana.

"Excellency, I'm sorry to say it seems you were right to suspect my brother of being less than truthful." Even on minimum volume, Mrs. O's voice sounded strained. "Once I impressed upon him the seriousness of abetting a traitor, he admitted that he believes Gordon to be somewhere in the general vicinity of Jewel. He also volunteered his opinion that Gordon was likely behind the anonymous note Ariel Stuart received.

"I must apologize for my earlier skepticism, Excellency. Tomorrow I will speak with Allister again before returning to Jewel and should I receive any more useful information from him, I will of course let you know at once. Meanwhile, I recommend you share what I've learned with your Bodyguard and perhaps the Stuarts, so that they can be alert for anything else Gordon may attempt."

I sent Mrs. O a quick message thanking her, then reached out mentally for Rigel. *Are you still up?*

Yeah. It's kind of hard to wind down after what happened tonight, you know?

No kidding. Anyway, I just listened to a message from Mrs. O and it sounds like we were right about Gordon. Allister admitted he's hiding out somewhere in Indiana and he probably left that note for your mom. I'll bet he also sicced that anti-Royal dude on me, though Mrs. O didn't mention that. So he may be the only person we need to worry about.

She couldn't tell you exactly *where he is?* Even from five miles away, I sensed Rigel's frustration. *We need to know that to stop him. Maybe we should do what we did in the arboretum again, see if we can reach farther out, find him.*

I'm kind of scared to try that in school or even in town, after what happened tonight. What if we do sense a threat and…lose control?

Good point. Maybe the cornfield? Where else can we be really alone?

The cornfield should be safe enough. I hope.

Hope so, too, he thought back. *It's scary to think what we might do if we were* really *upset.*

I couldn't disagree. Though neither of us said so, we both suspected that what we'd produced for that test was only a fraction of what we were actually capable of. Which was a terrifying thought.

Before going to sleep, I messaged Cormac to relay Mrs. O's information about Gordon—something Rigel had insisted I do right away. Cormac messaged back almost instantly that he'd be using every surveillance method at his disposal to detect Gordon if he got anywhere near me.

Rigel was relieved to hear that when I told him the next morning, but he still wanted to get to the cornfield—today, if possible—to see if we could pinpoint exactly where Gordon was. Then Cormac could nab him and our only problems would be political ones. And once last night's *graell* research was released to Martians everywhere, surely any lingering *Echtran* resistance to us as a couple would die down.

In Lit class, Rigel silently suggested I try "scanning" for particular emotions, especially negative or hostile ones. *If you get used to what they feel like, maybe you can sort of sensitize yourself, make it easier to spot Gordon—or any other enemies—if they get close.*

I gave it a try, lightly "touching" each person in the room with my emotion-sensing ability. It was even easier today than it had been Friday in Econ—so easy I was surprised I hadn't noticed everyone's emotions *without* trying. Just as well, though. That would be worse than the voices had been, before Rigel and I figured out how to control them.

What I sensed now was about what I'd have expected. At least half of the students were bored, while the rest ranged from anxious to hungry to lustful to sleepy. Not surprisingly, the most negative emotion I picked up was from Trina, on Rigel's other side. Glancing over, I saw her texting on her phone under her desk, a mean little smile playing across her face. I wondered who she was tormenting this time.

Trina, I decided, could be my baseline for identifying enemies. Rigel sent back a silent chuckle at that, then started outlining a lunchtime plan to goad her into even more hostility toward me. It wasn't nice, but it *would* give me an idea of what a truly dangerous enemy might "feel" like.

When we got to the cafeteria twenty minutes later, we put Rigel's plan into effect by getting into the lunch line right behind Trina.

"I can't believe Bryce Farmer actually called you," Rigel said to me, just loudly enough for Trina to overhear but not so loudly it would seem like he wanted her to. "I didn't think you two knew each other that well."

"We didn't, really," I replied at the same volume. "Though he did flirt with me a few times before we left for Ireland last spring. Still, to think he'd invite me, of all people, to the Homecoming dance? I figured he'd take some college girl, if he came at all."

Bryce had been Jewel's quarterback before Rigel got here last year, and he and Trina had dated off and on until Bryce graduated and went off to Purdue. He'd also been a bully, which was ironically what led to me figuring out something seriously weird was going on between Rigel and me when we accidentally shocked him senseless.

"You told him no, though, right?" Rigel had clearly noticed Trina's head twitch at the word "Homecoming," like I had.

"Well, duh. I'm with you now, Rigel, you know that."

Though she was pretending not to hear us, Trina couldn't quite suppress an indignant little snort. I quickly focused on her emotions, then flinched, they were so nasty. If she thought she could do it without getting caught, it was clear she'd gladly strangle me right here in the lunch line.

Yep, good baseline, I thought to Rigel, brushing his hand with mine so he could sense what I was sensing.

Even as his eyes widened at the intensity of Trina's hate, I disconnected myself from her, feeling slightly soiled by that contact. I was *definitely* glad I needed to concentrate to use that particular ability!

Doesn't that mean an enemy could sneak up on you, though? If you don't know to focus? Rigel asked worriedly.

Not sure. I'll play with it some more while we eat, I promised him, even though I shouldn't be at any risk with Cormac on the alert.

We made a point of sitting off in a corner by ourselves for my experiment. Bri grinned after us, but the look Sean sent our way bothered me a little—sad but resigned, exactly what I felt from him when I focused. Not that I knew what to do about it.

Once seated, I very cautiously "opened" my senses to the lunchroom, not aiming in any particular direction, just trying to pick up anything similar to what I'd sensed from Trina a moment ago. At first it didn't work at all. I got such an overwhelming jumble of conflicting emotions from all directions, I had to quickly shut down.

Rigel shifted his left arm to rest against my right. I wondered if it was because of Sean, knowing what I'd sensed from him, that he didn't hold my hand.

Try again, Rigel urged.

I did. This time the emotions were both more intense and more identifiable—but even more overwhelming. I hastily backed off again, then tried to barely, barely open myself to the feelings around me. It took several tries, but by the end of the lunch period I'd found a sort of "sweet spot" that allowed me to search the room for specific emotions without being painfully bombarded.

Trina's were still the most negative in the whole cafeteria. Over at the cheerleaders' table, she was indignantly telling Amber and Donna what she'd overheard me saying in the lunch line and wondering if she should call Bryce to find out if it was true.

This is good, Rigel insisted as we headed to class afterward. *I'll feel better if you learn to do that even when we're not touching, but that was a great start.*

If I can't, we'll just have to touch a whole lot more often, won't we?

He grinned down at me. *All for the sake of the Sovereign's safety, of course. Think the Council will vote in favor of that?*

During our next two classes, we mentally rehearsed article pitches for Ms. Raymond that would guarantee passes to get us out of Newspaper. If that didn't work, I'd ask Cormac to summon us to his office tomorrow, so we could go out to the cornfield then, instead.

But when we got to last period, our preparation turned out to be totally unnecessary.

"Tomorrow we'll get cracking on that parent newsletter but today Angela and I have a video conference with Center North's newspaper editors, so the rest of you get another day's reprieve," Ms. Raymond told the staff. "You can use the room as a study hall or I can give you passes for the media center—whichever you prefer."

Though I was almost disappointed not to be able to hit her with my great idea, I was still first in line for a pass, with Rigel right behind me. I could always use that idea the next time we wanted to escape—which might be as soon as tomorrow, if we didn't locate Gordon this afternoon.

"I gave Cormac a heads-up we'd be doing this," I murmured to Rigel as we led the small exodus out of the newsroom. "So no worries about getting in trouble if anyone sees us leaving."

It was a beautiful afternoon with just a hint of fall in the air as we crossed the parking lot and headed into the cornfield, hand in hand. The trip to the clearing seemed faster this time, partly because I was more confident of the direction but mainly because I was really *with* Rigel now, unlike last time.

Though we were both eager to find out how much farther we'd be able to push our combined senses, we couldn't *not* kiss, once we reached "our" rock. Rigel gathered me into his arms and I responded eagerly. After a blissful couple of minutes, though, it was time to get down to business.

"Okay," Rigel said, firmly taking my hand in his, one arm still around my waist. "Ready?"

I nodded, then focused. As we'd agreed, I first attempted to pinpoint Trina inside the school based solely on the hostile (to me) emotions she nearly always broadcast. It was harder than I expected.

Trina should be in Government this period, on the left-hand side of the school, but it took me several minutes to zero in on her. Once I listened in, I realized that was because she was flirting with Nathan Rice instead of plotting any new nastiness. Even so, I was able to detect the residual meanness she apparently always had simmering. Sort of a muted version of the "bad guy vibe" I felt from certain *Echtrans.*

That's good, though, Rigel thought encouragingly. *You always got that vibe off Gordon, right? So you probably* will *be able to sense him if he's in Jewel.*

Carefully recalling exactly what I'd felt off Gordon the last time I'd seen him, I started scanning, extending my senses in all directions, pushing them farther and farther. For a while, there was nothing—not surprising, since we really were in the middle of nowhere—but then I felt a faint ping near downtown Jewel. Not Gordon, just a regular angry *Duchas,* but still encouraging.

By the time I'd been at it for ten minutes, though, I was getting tired and frustrated.

Rigel instantly noticed. "Let's take a break, okay? We don't have to spend *all* our alone time on this project."

He turned me to face him, his smile irresistible. I leaned into his kiss and for the next minute or so, nothing else mattered. My stress and frustration drained away as I absorbed a wonderful healing dose of Rigel-ness. All too soon, he pulled away, though with obvious reluctance.

"We really do need to try some more." He gripped both of my hands this time. "Let's see if we can reach past Jewel."

Taking a deep breath, I concentrated again, drawing strength from Rigel's touch to help me extend my emotion-detector farther than I'd ever attempted. First in one direction, then another, I pushed my senses ever outward, searching for Gordon's distinctive bad-guy vibe. Then, incredibly, I found it!

Rigel and I locked gazes, eyes wide. Even after that scary bolt of lightning we'd produced last night, neither of us had really believed we were capable of *this.* I concentrated harder, trying to pinpoint both direction and distance.

"He's in…Elwood, I think, two towns away—that's nearly thirty miles! How can that be possible?"

"No clue, but it's awesome! Now you just need to let Cormac know."

I nodded. "He should have him in custody by tonight."

Rigel hugged me to him, his relief palpable. He'd been more worried than I had, for his parents' sake as well as mine. After a brief, blissful silence, again drawing strength from each other, he checked the time on his cell phone. "Still more than twenty minutes before I have to head to practice. Wonder what our actual limit is?"

"Want to try to find out?" Now that we'd found Gordon, I felt giddy and playful, looking forward to wonderful, worry-free times ahead.

We indulged in another long kiss, partly in case it had made a difference before, but mostly because it was our favorite thing to do. Then Rigel grasped both my hands and we started reaching out again, eager to see how far we could go.

I was easily able to locate Gordon again—definitely Elwood, or very close to it. On the theory he might have henchmen, I psychically probed the area a mile or so around his location but didn't detect any other Martian vibes, negative or otherwise. Maybe it was easier to identify someone I actually knew. But who else's vibes would I recognize at a distance?

How about Allister? Rigel suggested.

All the way in Montana? I laughed at his absurdity, then gave a little shrug. What was the risk in trying?

Chicago, for one thing, I discovered. The amount of concentrated negativity in a city that size made me recoil, even though none of it was identifiably *Echtran.* Hurriedly pushing my senses farther west, I scanned for Dun Cloch, way up in northern Montana. Soon I began to feel the strain again, but Rigel pulled me closer, releasing one of my hands so he could spread his palm along my cheek and jaw, a more intimate touch.

It helped. In fact, sensing where we were "going" got so much easier I could almost *see* where my mind was traveling. Not visual details, but a distinct sense of areas where people were concentrated —or not. Cities and towns versus nearly-empty—swaths of countryside. Thinking I might possibly be getting close to Dun Cloch, I tried harder to filter for *Echtran* emotion-vibes, since there had to be lots of them there.

Weirdly, I somehow knew when we passed south of it, sensing it was now northeast of my scan instead of west. With Rigel's help, I adjusted my mental trajectory slightly, and there it was—an unmistakeable concentration of Martians. A few seconds later…yes! I felt Allister's vibe—distinctly unpleasant, though not quite "bad guy." Blown away by what we'd done, I was about to exclaim aloud when I sensed another vibe near Allister that was downright nasty—even worse than Gordon's.

With a shudder, I shut down my probing, feeling ten times more soiled by that contact than by Trina at lunch. "Ew! Who *was* that?"

"Lennox, would be my guess. The guy who nearly killed me, remember? Pure evil." Rigel sounded as disgusted as I was. "At least we know he and Allister are both still safely under house arrest up there in Montana."

I nodded. "But how amazing was that? We didn't imagine it, did we? We really picked up emotions, vibes, from as far away as Montana?"

"Yeah, we really did. And…I still don't think that was your limit, M." Rigel was regarding me with something like awe.

"*Our* limit," I corrected him. "No way I can do this without you. It's like the electricity we can only generate when we're touching. Like…synergy. Should we let the Scientists study this ability, too? I mean, who knows what good we might be able to accomplish? We could, I don't know, fight crime or something!"

I could feel excitement bubbling up in Rigel, too. "Okay, let's try again—even farther away."

"Farther than Montana? Where?"

"How about Ireland? Bailerealta?" His eyes were alight with the thrill of our latest discovery. "They still haven't caught those guys who attacked you near the cliffs, right?"

"They weren't *Echtran,* remember? Plus the very idea of reaching Ireland is crazy. But…so was Montana, I guess. Oh, what the heck. Let's try. Bailerealta ought to feel a lot like Dun Cloch."

Grinning, Rigel gathered me into an embrace, his bare arms against mine, his cheek nestled against my cheek, maximizing our physical contact. "Maybe this will help," he murmured, his lips just an inch from mine. Almost but not quite close enough to kiss…

"M, you're not focusing."

"Sorry." With an effort, I yanked my attention away from how Rigel felt, how he smelled…and cast outward again with my mind.

This time I pushed eastward, trying not to be distracted by towns and cities along the way. When I sensed we were getting close to New York City, though, I balked, remembering how icky Chicago had felt. New York would be even worse.

Maybe try going up and over?

Nodding, I did what he suggested, shifting my focus straight up from where it was now, just north of Philadelphia. I wasn't sure how high I needed to go, since up was a direction I hadn't tried. To be safe,

I pushed good and hard. I had no references to guide me, since there were no emotions or vibes way up in the air…

Except, suddenly, there were. Strong ones. *Familiar* ones!

With a gasp, I stumbled to my feet, abruptly breaking contact with Rigel and with the presence my mind had touched. Rigel stood too, his eyes wide and confused as he reached out to take my hands again.

"What was that? It felt so weird! So…big. Terrorists? On a plane or something?"

I shook my head, my heart pounding so hard I could barely think. "No. Not a plane. I…I think we went higher than that, way higher than I meant to."

"Then what? The Space Station? Some *Echtran* astronaut?" he asked doubtfully. "Except I've never felt anything like that before."

"I have. And no, what we just sensed wasn't *Echtran.* Or *Duchas.* It…it wasn't human at all." I swallowed, forcing myself to continue. "Rigel, I think…I'm almost sure…it was the Grentl. They're here!"

29

Stress multiplier

RIGEL stared at me, not yet comprehending but clearly sensing my horror. Then his face paled and that same horror reflected back from him.

"The Grentl? Here? Right…right above Earth? Are you sure?"

Swallowing, I nodded. "I've communicated with them enough times now to know what their…their consciousness feels like and I can't think of any other reason I'd have felt it just now. They must have a ship in orbit or something."

"No way. No *way!* Ireland would have been a long shot. But sensing something in *orbit?* Besides, if there's a ship out there, NASA or somebody would have spotted it."

Despite his insistent denial, the more I thought about what I'd felt, the more certain I became. "Even if they have, they probably wouldn't put it on the news," I pointed out. "And the Grentl are so advanced they might even have cloaking technology or something. Rigel, suppose it *is* true and nobody knows except us? What do we do?"

He frowned, then pulled his cell phone out of his pocket. "My dad's on the *Echtran* Council now. He knows about the Grentl. I'll—Oh, *crap!* I'm late for practice. And you're going to miss your bus!"

Mundane dangers momentarily crowded out galactic ones, sending us racing back toward the school, our faces and arms whapped by yellowing corn leaves as we ran. Powered by adrenaline, we reached the parking lot in record time—but not before the last bus was pulling away.

"Guess you're coming to practice with me again." Rigel attempted a laugh but it came out shaky and breathless. He was covered with corn detritus. I probably looked like a scarecrow, too.

"No, I…I'll find Cormac. I need to tell him where Gordon is anyway. Maybe he can give me a ride. But go ahead and call your dad. Tell him what we sensed and ask him to tell Kyna. She might have some way to confirm it."

Rigel nodded, looking a little sheepish. "Why don't I come with you? Football's nowhere near as important as—"

"No, get to practice. Otherwise you'll have to explain why you didn't show up, and that could lead to questions we probably shouldn't answer." Unless the Grentl had come here to destroy us all, in which case everyone finding out the truth hardly mattered.

He still hesitated, clearly not wanting to leave my side at a time like this. "Are you sure?"

"I'm sure. We'll stay in touch…" *like this. I'll let you know right away if I need your help. I promise.*

"You'd better. Okay. I'll call Dad and figure out something to tell Coach for why I'm late." He grabbed me for a quick, hard kiss, then loped off around the side of the school, his phone already at his ear.

I watched him go, then headed into the school, to Cormac's Vice Principal office…only to discover he wasn't there. Biting my lip, I realized he'd have followed my bus home, like he always did after school, since I hadn't told him I wouldn't be on it.

I went back outside, wondering if I could bum a ride with someone else, someone with a car. Glancing around the parking lot, I spotted Sean, just getting into a pickup truck with Pete Griffin, a basketball buddy of his.

"Sean! Wait!" I yelled on panic-driven impulse.

Sean and Pete stopped and turned. "M? What's up?" Sean asked, clearly startled.

"Would…would you guys mind giving me a ride home? I, uh, missed my bus."

Pete looked me up and down. "Get lost in a corn maze or something?" he asked with a snicker.

Oops. I'd forgotten I was still covered with corn litter. "Yeah, something like that." I started brushing myself off. "Anyway, can I have a ride? I live right around the corner from Sean, so it shouldn't be out of your way or anything."

Sean must have picked up on the anxiety I was trying to hide, because he gave me a long, penetrating look, then nodded. "You don't mind giving her a lift, do you, Pete?"

His friend shrugged, though he still looked curious. "No problem. Climb in."

Three in the front seat of the pickup was a little tight, forcing me to sit closer to Sean than I'd have preferred, but I wasn't about to complain. Sean continued to regard me curiously as Pete pulled out of the lot, but I gave him a quick head shake in answer to his unspoken question. Taking the hint, he started talking basketball with Pete, like I wasn't even in the truck. Which was fine with me. It gave me time to think.

And to realize that even if Kyna and her NASA colleagues couldn't verify that the Grentl were really here, maybe I could, with their device. I might even be able to find out their intentions. It was definitely worth a try.

When Pete dropped me in front of my house, Sean got out, too. "What's up?" he asked as soon as Pete pulled away. "I can tell you're upset. You and Rigel have a fight or something?"

"No, nothing like that. It's…" I hesitated, not wanting to panic him until I was absolutely sure. "I think I've discovered something important and I need to get word to the Council, so they can figure out what to do if I'm right. Your mom's still out of town, right?"

He nodded, positively radiating curiosity. "She gets home this evening. Can't you just tell me—?"

"I need to run up and use my omni, but then I'll come over to your house and fill you in, okay?"

"Um, okay. See you soon, then."

Aunt Theresa wasn't home yet, so I ran straight up to my bedroom and opened a channel to Kyna. As head of the Council as well as a NASA astrophysicist, she was the obvious person to talk to first. I was mentally composing a rational-sounding voicemail when Kyna surprised me by answering.

"Excellency?" She sounded wary. "I apologize for the delay in picking up but I thought it best to move to a private room before speaking with you."

"Sorry to call you at work like this. I figured you probably wouldn't even have your omni there."

"Most Council members have omnis designed to look like normal cell phones."

Huh. I definitely needed one of those!

"I assume you are calling with the same unlikely news I just received from Van Stuart?" Kyna continued. "He received some garbled message from his son about the Grentl, but—"

"Yes. I think they're here, in orbit, or at least very close. I…sensed them."

There was a pause before she responded. "You sensed them. How?"

I decided this was no time for secrets. "We, um, didn't mention it to those Scientists last night, but Rigel and I have discovered that together we can…sense things at a distance. Emotions, mostly. We were experimenting, trying to locate Gordon—which we did, by the way! But then, well, it's kind of a long story. Has anybody at NASA noticed a strange ship in orbit or anything?"

"No, nothing. I made certain of that after receiving Van's message."

"Is there some way you can, I don't know, look closer? I mean, maybe our regular Earth technology can't see them."

"There are *Echtran* instruments that would likely detect even a cloaked ship, but I don't have direct access to them. I can contact those who do."

"That would be great." I hesitated. "Kyna, I…I know this whole thing must be really hard to believe, but I'm asking you to give me the benefit of the doubt, at least until someone can verify for sure if there's a Grentl ship out there."

"You are my Sovereign. Donnan showed me the preliminary results of last night's testing, and they are…remarkable. Indeed, Excellency, I feel I owe you and apology for my earlier skepticism about the *graell.* According to the data I saw, your bond with Rigel Stuart is far more powerful and far-reaching than I ever guessed. As a Scientist, I am embarrassed to think I may have allowed prejudice or preconceptions to cloud my judgment on the matter."

"Thank you, Kyna." I was as gratified as I was surprised by her words. "I'm going over to the O'Garas' now. It's possible I can find out more using the Grentl communication device."

"Has it activated?"

"It must not have before school this morning, or Molly would have told me. She checks it every day for me. But even if it hasn't, I'm going to try using it."

"Do be careful, Excellency. And bring your omni. I'll contact you should we discover anything at this end and you can notify me about whatever you learn from the device. Then we can plan from there."

I agreed and we broke the connection. I was relieved she hadn't simply assumed I was crazy—which is what I probably would have done in her place. Tucking my omni in my pocket, I headed over to the O'Garas' house.

On my way there, I reached out to Rigel with my mind, since he was probably getting worried by now. *Can you talk for a minute?*

Just a sec. Then, after about five seconds, *Okay. What did you find out?*

Nothing yet, but Kyna's going to look into it and now I'm on my way to the O'Garas' to see if I can make the Grentl device work. Wish me luck!

Oh, wow, good luck, M! I'll be there as soon as I can, okay?

The very thought of having Rigel at my side made me a lot less nervous. *That would be great. Maybe let your dad know what's going on?*

Will do.

Sean was pacing his front porch and as soon as he saw me, he came striding out to greet me. "So, can you tell me now what's going on?" Curiosity—and worry—came off him in waves.

"Okay. This will sound crazy, but try not to freak out. Sean, I think the Grentl are here—in orbit around Earth, or close. I told Kyna and she and some other *Echtrans* at NASA are going to check it out."

Sean rocked back on his heels, staring down at me in mingled shock and doubt. "Here? How can they be? And how would you know, even if they were?" He glanced up at the clear, sunny sky above us.

"I just… It's a long story and I don't know any details yet. I need to get up to Molly's room, though, to their device."

He paled slightly. "You don't plan to…to *use* it, do you? Dad's gone to pick Mum up at the airport, so it's just me here. What if—"

"At the very least, I need to see if they're trying to contact *me*."

"Yeah, okay. I guess that makes sense. C'mon."

I followed him into the house and upstairs to Molly's closet, where we'd hidden the Grentl device, along with my Scepter. Unfortunately—or fortunately?—the device looked the same as always, sitting inertly on a box of books that had never been unpacked. Whatever the Grentl were doing, they hadn't tried to warn me about it.

Sean peered at it over the top of my head. "Good. It's not glowing or anything. That means you can wait, right? At least till Mum and Dad get back? Or maybe for the NASA folks to find out if there really is anything out there?"

I bit my lip, hesitating, trying to remember *exactly* what I'd sensed in the cornfield with Rigel. It had only been for a second or two, then I'd panicked and closed down. What if I was wrong? What if I'd imagined it?

Deep down, though, I was sure I hadn't. The Grentl hadn't even been on my radar (so to speak) when I'd been blindsided by touching their consciousness.

The last time I'd used the device, to send that report, I'd been able to pick up images and impressions from them. One of those images, I suddenly remembered, had been of a blue marble that looked like Earth. Had they been planning to come here even then? And if so… was it my fault?

"I'd better go ahead and do this now." It's not like the O'Garas, or even Kyna or Shim knew any more about the Grentl or their device than I did. "They may not answer, but I might learn something."

"Or piss them off." He sounded worried again.

"I'll try not to." My decision made, I took a step forward—Molly's closet was no bigger than my own—and poised my hands over the prongs sticking up from the device. *Okay, I'm doing this,* I thought to Rigel as well as myself. *One, two, three!*

I grabbed both projections simultaneously. Like the last time, back on Mars, nothing happened right away. Rather than wait for them to realize I was there, I immediately started probing with my mind, drawing on the extra practice I'd had with Rigel since re-bonding.

It was noticeably easier now. In fact, after only a few seconds I started "seeing" things from the Grentl's viewpoint. That same blue marble was there, huge now, but between me—or, rather, the Grentl—and the Earth-marble, I also saw a nearer, smaller white one. Earth's moon. The Grentl were on the other side of the moon!

Even as I registered that, the projections in my hands started to warm. The Grentl had noticed me using the device, which meant they were getting ready to suck out everything I'd experienced, everything I knew. I felt their familiar mental presence touch my mind and braced myself, determined to resist if I could.

To my amazement, it worked. Though I could tell they were *trying* to pull memories out of my head, I was somehow able to block them. It wasn't easy, though. In fact, it was taking every ounce of mental energy I could summon to keep them out. Slowly, their collective consciousness began to overpower mine. I started to shake, then sweat. Gasping, not knowing what else to do, I threw myself backwards, releasing the device and the Grentl's inexorable pressure on my mind.

Sean caught me before I could hit the floor. "What happened? Did they…zap you?"

I took a few deep breaths, then shook my head. "No. I let go on my own. Before they could— But they're *definitely* here! They're on the far side of the moon. I need to let Kyna know, they probably won't look that far away. Then I need to—"

"You need to come downstairs and have a cup of tea." Sean gave me a gentle shake to stop my panicked babbling. "Calm down, take time to think, before you do anything else."

He was right. I needed time to untangle the images I'd picked up. Last time, it had taken a while before they'd sorted themselves out—before I'd recognized that blue marble as Earth, for example. Maybe if I waited, more things would come clear.

"Okay. I guess that did take a lot out of me."

Sean led me unresistingly back downstairs, to the O'Garas' warm, cozy kitchen, where he busied himself making a pot of tea. Even though it was still in the mid-seventies outside, I was shivering slightly from my experience—or maybe the accumulated experiences of the day. When he handed me my cup, I wrapped my hands around it before lifting it to my lips.

After a few fortifying sips, my brain started working again. "I need to call Kyna. And Cormac. Before we sensed the Grentl, Rigel and I found Gordon. He's in Elwood. Cormac can—"

"Elwood? Gordon? What do you mean, you and Rigel *sensed* it?" Sean stared at me in utter confusion.

Of course. Sean still had no idea of what Rigel and I could do, wouldn't even have heard about last night's tests yet. "Oh. Yeah. We, um, can talk telepathically. Because of the *graell.* We've been able to do it all along, but now it's way stronger. In fact—" I focused for a moment— "he should be here any second. Amber's giving him a ride, along with Molly."

Even as I spoke, a car door slammed out front and a moment later the front door opened. Sean's eyebrows rose into his hairline as Rigel burst into the kitchen, followed closely by Molly.

"What happened? Are you okay?" Rigel demanded. "I tried to

listen in, but I couldn't tell what was going on. Did the Grentl—?"

"I'm fine. I'll fill you in right after I call Kyna. Did you tell your dad?"

Rigel nodded. "He says it's good that Kyna's on it. That if anyone can find out—"

"Wait." Sean put up a hand, looking wildly from me to Rigel and back. "You can do the telepathy thing to talk to your parents, too? Can you, like, hear *everybody's* thoughts?"

"No, just M's." Now Rigel looked confused. "I guess you told him?" I nodded.

"Then how did you talk to your dad just now?" Sean demanded.

"Um." Rigel pulled his cell phone out of his pocket and held it up. "With this."

There was a long moment of silence, then all four of us started laughing. It had a slightly hysterical edge, though. Because we all knew the situation wasn't funny at all.

30

Independent verification

WHILE Molly made another pot of tea, I went into the living room to let Kyna know what I'd learned from the device, then called Cormac and told him about Gordon. When I joined the others in the kitchen, Rigel was filling Sean and Molly in on our newly enhanced abilities.

"But you still don't know what your real limits are?" Molly asked, eyes wide. I was relieved to feel more curiosity than fear from her. Sean was mildly outraged at having been kept in the dark all this time —though also avidly curious.

"Not yet." I glanced at Rigel, then back to the others. "I mean, we only re-bonded or whatever four days ago." We'd both been careful not to mention the kissing part. "And we only found out today that we could sense things farther away than the Jewel town limits."

Sean gave a mirthless little laugh. "Like, other side of the *moon* farther away! Sorry, but that still seems impossible."

I couldn't disagree. In fact, until Kyna's team independently verified my discovery, I wasn't sure I'd fully believe it myself. But what if the Grentl really were here to destroy Earth? With our relatively limited resources—even counting Nuathan technology—would there be anything we could do to stop them? I had a horrible feeling that, once again, the fate of the world might rest squarely on my shoulders. Only this time it was the fate of *this* world, the one I'd grown up on, with billions more lives at stake.

Rigel put his hand over mine. *Don't borrow trouble, M. We don't actually know their intentions are hostile. Maybe they're only here to observe.* But I could tell he didn't believe that any more than I did.

"I should head back," I said, standing. "Aunt Theresa will be home by now and I didn't think to leave a note."

The others didn't argue. Until we knew more, we still had to pretend, at least to the *Duchas*, that everything was normal. Rigel called his dad to come get him and I went home to help Aunt Theresa with dinner.

Twice while I was in the kitchen with her, my omni vibrated in my pocket and I ran upstairs—first claiming I needed the bathroom and the second time that I wanted to change into my slippers.

The first call was from Cormac, saying he'd already caught Gordon Nolan in Elwood and had him in custody—though by now he was the least of our worries.

The second was a message from Kyna that she'd called an emergency Council meeting that evening to discuss the situation and our options.

I'd just put the noodles on to boil when Molly called to ask my aunt if I could come to her house and work on our project over—and after—dinner. When she relayed Molly's request, I tried not to sound *too* eager.

"I should probably go. This project will be half our grade this quarter."

Aunt Theresa quirked an eyebrow. "It sounds as though you've put things off till the last minute. Probably spending too much time with that quarterback."

Shrugging, I tried to look contrite. "Maybe a little. I'll try to make sure I don't fall behind in my schoolwork again, though."

"See you don't. Go on, then. I'll finish getting dinner. And try not to be too late."

That was exceptionally accommodating for Aunt Theresa but I didn't argue, just grabbed my backpack and headed out.

As though determined to prolong everyone's suspense as long as possible, Kyna was the very last one to join the Council meeting.

"I was waiting for a late report from Ennis Gill, who is monitoring our *Echtran* orbital sensors this evening," she explained when she finally shimmered into focus, "but she has unable to find anything definitive. If a ship is indeed using Earth's moon as a shield, our technology may not be able to separate its signature from Luna's natural one. Ennis has contacted Nuathan astronomers for assistance, as they have a better angle from which to view the far side of Earth's moon, but it will undoubtedly take time for them to redirect their own orbital telescopes."

"Thank you, Kyna." I tried to ignore the raised eyebrows of the Royals on the Council, all of whom clearly suspected I'd just imagined sensing the Grentl. If it hadn't been for my session with the device this afternoon, I probably would, too.

Kyna nodded deferentially to me, then turned to the others. "Malcolm, you indicated earlier that you had other business you wished to discuss tonight?"

He stood. "Indeed. By now, I trust everyone has seen the raw data from the tests performed last night on the nature of the purported *graell* bond between the Sovereign and Rigel Stuart?"

Everyone nodded. Some now looked wary and I even detected traces of fear from the Council members physically present.

"As they appear to have developed a joint ability to create extremely dangerous static discharges, I feel this Council should discuss the ramifications of that discovery. In particular, we must find a way to control this ability in order to ensure the safety of both the *Echtran* and *Duchas* populations."

"Agreed," Connor said. "Until they can reliably prevent such an occurrence, it's clear that those two should keep their distance from each other." There were murmurs of agreement.

I jumped to my feet. "What? No! Rigel and I have always been able to do what we did last night, it's just stronger now. But we've never done it unless we were directly threatened. It doesn't just happen randomly."

"And yet last night you were able to produce enough electricity to kill when simply requested to do so. No threat was present at your home, was there?" Connor asked Mr. Stuart, who reluctantly shook his head.

I glared at Connor. "Of course there wasn't. But we had to *imagine* one before we could create that energy bolt. The first time Blair asked us to, nothing happened. *Because* we weren't threatened. Or didn't you read that part of the report?"

He shifted his gaze away from mine. "That isn't the point, Excellency. The risks—"

"Are practically nonexistent," I insisted, despite how unnerved Rigel and I had both been last night. "If anything, this ability makes Rigel a better Bodyguard for me than anyone else could possibly be—though Cormac has been great."

They all started arguing, talking over each other, some insisting it was still too risky while others agreed I made a good point. Finally Kyna took charge again.

"I believe this discussion should be tabled until more research can be done. At the very least, we need to allow Blair and his colleagues to finish tabulating the data and determine whether further tests might be necessary."

"Yes, please!" Nara exclaimed. "I'm the one who requested this research be done in the first place and the Scientists involved were very happy to have the chance. I refuse to have the Sovereign *punished* for agreeing!"

The Royals still looked dubious. "Even so, I'm not certain—" Breann began, when Kyna held up a hand.

"Excuse me. I'm receiving another call from Ennis. I'll return in a moment." Her image blinked out.

We all sat around uncomfortably, the room still fraught with tension. A mixture of indignation and fear emanated from Breann, Malcolm and Mrs. O'Gara, while Mr. Stuart felt defensive and embarrassed. Though I couldn't read their emotions, Connor clearly shared the other Royals' feelings, while Nara was still visibly distressed.

Suddenly, Kyna was back.

"I've just received word that a Nuathan telescope has indeed discovered a ship on the far side of the moon. Its sophisticated cloaking technology, more advanced than our own, made detection extremely difficult, despite the fact that it is nearly a mile in diameter. Excellency, it appears you were correct. The Grentl are here. And there's more."

"More?" Mrs. O'Gara's voice shook slightly.

Kyna nodded grimly. "The Grentl ship has begun launching dozens, perhaps hundreds of smaller objects. It was the release of those objects that allowed the Nuathan orbital telescope to pinpoint the exact location of the, ah, mother ship. I believe it is safe to say we have an emergency situation on our hands."

31

Reverse polarity

TERROR, mine and everyone else's, crowded out every other emotion in the room, terror so palpable I found it hard to breathe.

We were right, I sent frantically to Rigel, five miles away. *The Grentl are definitely here—with an enormous ship!*

I should be with you, he sent back. *I can tell you're scared…*

I was. I was terrified. But I was still the first one to find my voice.

"Let's…let's not panic, not yet. Not before I figure out why they're here, what they plan to do. I should use the device again—that's how I found out they were behind the moon. Maybe if I get Rigel to strengthen me first…"

"No, Excellency, it's too dangerous," Kyna declared. "Remember what that device did to Faxon? We can't afford to lose you at a time like this."

"What am I good for, if not this?" I demanded. "It's why I needed to get Acclaimed so quickly, remember? Because I'm the only one who can talk to the Grentl."

Mr. Stuart spoke up for the first time since the meeting began. "You've been good for far more than that, Excellency. Your very existence was instrumental in Faxon's overthrow, and your Acclamation has gone a long way toward restoring stability to the Nuathan government and confidence in its people. Since then, you have done great good by convincing our people to begin emigrating to Earth."

"All true," Breann agreed. "Pray do not sell yourself short, Excellency. I agree with Kyna that we should not allow you to put yourself at risk. Quinn O'Gara reported that your earlier sessions with the device were at the very least traumatic."

Irritation now warred with my fear. "It can be exhausting, yes, but they've never injured me in any way. How else are we going to figure out what they're up to? Just…wait until they do something?"

Nobody seemed to like that option much, either. Much fearful muttering ensued before Kyna again put a stop to it.

"What exactly do you suggest, Excellency?"

"Let me use the device again, with Rigel right beside me. Only… Molly's closet is kind of small. I should probably do this someplace safer anyway, just, you know, in case."

Kyna nodded thoughtfully. "A good point. Apart from concerns for your safety should the Grentl, ah, retaliate via their device, those nearby might conceivably be at risk as well, not to mention the danger of discovery by the *Duchas*. The O'Garas' house is in a rather densely populated area of Jewel, as I recall."

"How about Rigel's house? Um, if that would be okay, I mean?" I turned belatedly to Mr. Stuart.

"Ariel and I would be honored," he said. Then, to the rest of the Council, "We have no neighbors within half a mile to notice or be endangered by anything the Grentl might do via their device. Which, of course, I very much hope they won't, for the Sovereign's sake."

"For all our sakes," Kyna said dryly. "Very well, unless anyone has a better suggestion?" She looked around at the frightened Council members, who all either shrugged or shook their heads. "Any further delay at this point seems unwise. I recommend the device be moved immediately, after which we will reconvene at the Stuarts' house so that the Sovereign can attempt communication."

With my help. Rigel was now monitoring every word through me.

Just having you there with me will be a help, I assured him. His presence, his touch, was bound to enhance anything I did.

Aunt Theresa wasn't expecting me home before nine-thirty, which gave us more than two hours. Mr. O'Gara offered to pick up a few pizzas along the way, since nobody had eaten dinner yet, while Mr. Stuart and Malcolm packed the Grentl device into an innocuous-looking box and carried it out to the Stuarts' SUV.

Half an hour later the Council—physical and holographic—stood in a big circle around the device, which now crouched on the Stuarts' coffee table. That circle also included Mr. O and Dr. Stuart. Sean and Molly were here as well. They'd begged to come along, with the stakes this high, and everyone on the Council had been too distracted to forbid it.

"I do wish I were there in person." Kyna stared at the device in fascination. "It's far smaller than I imagined."

"I thought the same thing, the first time I saw it. So, um, I guess I should do this, huh?" Having all these people watching would make this weird. Weirder than usual, that is.

Rigel wrapped an arm around my shoulders. "How can I help?"

I circled his waist with my own arm, pulling him closer. "The way you always do." I took several deep breaths, concentrating on soaking up all the strength and confidence from Rigel's touch that I could.

"Not while you're touching the device, though, right?" Sean frowned, worried and slightly jealous. "Remember what Eric Eagan said?"

Nodding, I let go of Rigel and moved out from under his arm. "Good point. Okay, you should all probably keep your distance. Just in case."

Everyone but Rigel and the holograms took a step backward and I took one forward. Positioning my hands above the copper projections, I braced myself and took hold. Again, nothing happened, and again, I didn't wait for it to. I needed to get all the information I could while I was still strengthened by Rigel's touch—preferably before the Grentl noticed me.

Unfortunately, they were much quicker on the uptake this time. I'd barely brought the moon and Earth into mental focus again when the prongs warmed in my hands and I felt them probing at me. Again I resisted, but either they were trying harder or I wasn't nearly as strong as I'd hoped. In less than a minute I felt myself sweating and shaking. I was either going to have to give in and let them do their brain-sucking thing or let go—which would be the same as giving up.

As my resistance weakened, I felt them pulling out memories of what I'd done on Nuath since the last time I'd "talked" to them: Shim's appointment as Regent, my going from town to town talking up emigration…

Suddenly, the series of images stopped—and I simultaneously became aware of Rigel's hand on my forearm.

Together. We'll do this together, he thought firmly to me. Too startled—and relieved—to argue, I nodded and tightened my grip on the prongs.

Now, with Rigel's help, I had no trouble at all resisting the Grentl's pull at my mind. Scrunching my face in concentration, I pushed outward again, determined to probe them instead. The Earth and moon snapped back into focus, then I found myself *inside* the Grentl ship, inside the Grentl's very thoughts. In a blindingly fast kaleidoscope of images, concepts and emotions, I absorbed their entire appalling plan, along with the reason for it. The moment I was sure I had it all, I jerked my hands away from the copper prongs, breaking the connection and collapsing into Rigel's waiting arms.

"Are you okay? You did it!" he murmured into my ear, his cheek pressed against mine.

Still shaking, overwhelmed by the experience, I nodded. "*We* did it. But… Oh, Rigel!"

His arms tightened around me as we shared our mutual horror at the enormity of what we'd just learned. For a long moment we clung to each other, drawing what comfort we could. Then, slowly, I became aware of everyone in the room watching us.

"Oh. Um."

I felt myself reddening as we broke apart, but Rigel kept a firm grip on one of my hands as he led me to the couch, where he could sit beside me while I faced the others. "You'd…better tell them," he said.

"You learned something?" Kyna's image leaned forward eagerly. "You were actually communicating all that time?"

"How long?" I glanced curiously at Rigel, who shrugged, then at Sean.

"About twenty minutes this time."

I wasn't too surprised after my previous experiences with the Grentl, but Rigel was. *I'll explain about that later,* I promised. Then, to Kyna, "I learned…everything. What they plan to do, how they plan to do it, and…why."

"They actually *told* you all that?" Connor sounded disbelieving.

"Not exactly by choice," Rigel said. "Right, M?"

"Right. I explained in my reports how the Grentl get information from us, by extracting memories through the device. They started to do that again just now but when Rigel touched me I was not only able to resist, I managed to reverse it—do to them what they've always done to me. I got memories, intentions, thoughts, everything."

"And?" Kyna demanded impatiently.

"It's still sort of unpacking itself in my brain, but it's…not good." I leaned back against the cushions. Rigel's hand in mine was helping a lot but I still felt drained—and scared.

Rigel took up the explanation. "Once it started, it was sort of like…receiving a zipped computer file. It might take her a while to, um, unzip all the details."

Kyna was clearly trying to rein in her frustration. "Can you tell us what you *do* know, Excellency? What do they intend to do with those smaller craft they're launching? While you were, ah, communing with the Grentl, Ennis received another message from Nuath. Those craft now definitely number in the hundreds."

"Seven hundred and twenty, to be exact." The number popped into my mind, one of many details that were starting to come clear. "And they're not craft, exactly, not with pilots. They're satellites. Over the next four days, they'll take up evenly-spaced positions all around the Earth. Then, once they're in place, the Grentl plan to…to zap us all back to the Stone Age. It will be like a Carrington Event on steroids."

"A what?" Connor exclaimed. "I'm afraid I don't understand, Excellency."

I'd assumed even Royals would know about an astrophysical phenomenon like that, but apparently not. "Basically, a huge EMP. Electromagnetic pulse," I clarified when he still looked confused. Really? This guy was on the *Echtran* Council? I'd learned this stuff in eighth grade—though not, technically, in school.

"Surely you learned about this in elementary astrophysics, Connor?" Kyna also wore a rather condescending expression.

"Elementary astrophysics was a long time ago," he mumbled.

"It occurred late in Sovereign Aerleas' reign, Earth year 1859," Kyna explained. "The Carrington Event was a series of solar flares of such magnitude that the rudimentary distance communications of the time were disabled. Some telegraph operators received severe shocks. Nuath, fortunately, was far enough beneath the surface of Mars to escape the worst effects. And, luckily for Earth, they were not yet reliant on electronics, satellites or electrical power grids. Now, however…"

"It would be devastating," Mr. Stuart finished for her. Then, to me, "And you say this will be even worse?"

I nodded. "The Grentl plan to wipe out all our technology—everything we've developed since they transplanted that Irish village to Mars for their experiments nearly three thousand years ago."

"But…why?" Mrs. O'Gara, her face still pale, clung to her husband's hand for support.

Though I wasn't sure I understood it all myself yet, I did my best to explain. "Apparently, ever since Faxon used the device last year, the Grentl have been concerned that their, ah, experiment—that's how they think of the colony, Nuath—had become unstable and potentially dangerous. They really were planning to destroy Nuath, but when I sent my report and they saw how soon the power there was going to run out, they decided that wasn't necessary. Not only was Faxon gone, but Nuath wouldn't last much longer anyway. To them, fifty years is like nothing."

Rapt faces nodded and Kyna motioned me to go on.

"Anyway, between what they got from Faxon and then me, the Grentl found out there've been regular comings and goings between Earth and Mars for the past few centuries and that worried them enough to take a good look at Earth for the first time since kidnapping the original colonists. And they, um, didn't like what they saw. They've decided humans are a violent, greedy and power-hungry species that will eventually become a threat to the whole Galaxy if we're not stopped. Since they feel partly responsible—I guess because Nuathans helped to spark the Renaissance and all—they seem to think it's their duty to stop us. This is how they plan to do it."

Mr. Stuart nodded slowly. "Ingenious. And probably effective. An evenly dispersed EMP of sufficient magnitude would render virtually all modern technology useless, destroying electrical transformers, communication satellites and most electronics. It would take months or even years to get the electrical grids up and running again. We'd have nothing to use as a jump-start, so to speak. By then, chaos and anarchy would likely spread across the globe, finishing what the Grentl began. Economic systems would collapse and communication would be all but impossible. We might indeed revert to the savages of the Stone Age."

"But…the people!" Nara gasped. "Think. Such a catastrophe would kill millions, perhaps billions. If not immediately, then within a month or two."

"I've read predictions that another solar storm similar to the Carrington Event could result in the eventual deaths of up to a fifth of the Earth's population." Dr. Stuart sounded as though she were holding back tears. "This sounds even worse."

"There must be a way to stop them!" Malcolm sounded panicky.

"Excellency, can't you…talk them out of it? Like you did on Nuath?"

I bit my lip to keep it from trembling. "I can try, but I doubt it. Even on Nuath, I didn't really talk them out of anything. First I just…answered their call, which got them to stop the power outages. Then sending them that report on the colony's status showed them Nuath would eventually fall apart on its own, without their help."

Looking around at all the frightened faces, I shrugged helplessly. "Maybe if I could persuade them we—humans—aren't really a threat they'd back off. But honestly? All the stuff they've learned about us is pretty much true. Given enough time, we really might become a scourge on the Galaxy."

32

Phase discrimination

"THAT may be true of the *Duchas*," Connor exclaimed indignantly. "But certainly not of *Echtrans*. If they no longer mean any harm to Nuath, maybe they'll let us all go back there before they…" He trailed off at the scandalized expressions of some of the others.

"Connor, I'm surprised at you," Kyna said severely. "Even if it were possible, do you really believe our best course would be to leave billions of *Duchas* at the mercy of the Grentl while we save ourselves? Is this an example of how comparatively 'enlightened' *Echtrans* are? No, we need another solution. We must either convince the Grentl that humans are not a threat—which I agree is likely to be impossible, given Earth's history—or develop a defense against what they intend. Quickly. Thanks to the Sovereign, we at least have the advantage of four days' warning. We must use those days to good effect."

"But won't the Grentl realize that?" Breann asked fearfully. "Suppose they change their plans because the Sovereign has learned of them?"

"I really don't think they will," I said. "They don't consider humans—even *Echtrans*—to be any kind of threat, not yet. It's what we might become in a century or two that they're worried about. Their technology is way, way beyond ours, and they seem to have planned everything down to the smallest detail."

"And you know *all* of those details?" Malcolm sounded skeptical but also hopeful.

My fear, which had spiked again at hearing the potential death toll, receded a tiny bit. "Things are still sort of unraveling in my brain, but yes, I think I do—or I will. I'm pretty sure I got all their specs, everything, even if I don't understand most of them. I can give it all to our Scientists. Maybe it will help."

"Which Scientists?" Mr. O was paler than normal, too. "For nearly three centuries, the secret of the Grentl has been kept from all but a select few. Now, however—"

Kyna nodded. "A good point. Once those satellites disperse, every *Echtran* with an enhanced telescope as well as some *Duchas* astronomers will likely notice them. Some sort of explanation will have to be given, one that will not induce global panic. That would be devastating in itself, even if we can somehow prevent what the Grentl plan."

"I've thought all along that keeping the Grentl secret—from Martians, at least—was a bad idea," I reminded them. "It's led to an awful lot of trouble for me, anyway. If you want to prepare some kind of statement to send out to *Echtrans* and Nuathans, I'm willing to deliver it."

Dr. Stuart suddenly stood. "It's nearly eight-thirty. While we continue to discuss our options, I recommend we all eat something. Molly, will you help me warm up those pizzas?"

A few minutes later Molly and Dr. Stuart returned with half a dozen pizzas, a pitcher of lemonade and a pot of coffee for those physically present, while the others winked out briefly to grab something to eat for themselves before we continued our discussion. The pizza was good, but no one except Rigel and Sean seemed to have much appetite. I sure didn't. Not when the world might end before the weekend.

"What I want to know—" Malcolm waved an uneaten slice of pizza in the air— "is what we're going to tell the *Duchas* world leaders. Once their scientists notice those satellites, they'll assume they were launched by some other nation. That could begin yet another war, if we don't tell them *something*."

Breann set down her coffee cup. "Do you think we'll be able to stop them from doing something foolish even if we do explain everything? If they actually *know* the Grentl's intentions are hostile, what's to stop military leaders from firing missiles or even nuclear weapons at the satellites?"

"But isn't that exactly what they *should* do?" Connor looked anxiously around at the rest of us. "If the *Duchas* military powers all join forces, maybe they can shoot down the satellites before they release the EMP."

"We simply don't know enough yet," Kyna told him. "Nor am I hopeful that even news such as this will convince nations worldwide to join forces. Certainly not in time to do any good. I agree, however, that most of the top world leaders should be apprised of the situation. It's as well we've already established relations with them.

Again, with your help, Excellency."

One of the things I'd done during my first month back on Earth was speak with a handful of heads of state or foreign ministers from the more developed countries, including the U.S. Secretary of State. It had been beyond weird, all those important men and women treating me like a dignitary from some foreign kingdom.

At least they weren't learning about Martians for the very first time. Several decades ago, Shim had persuaded the *Echtran* Council to approach certain *Duchas* leaders to cautiously educate them about the existence of Nuath and *Echtrans,* since even then he'd foreseen the need for large-scale emigration. Since then, the knowledge had been kept on a strict need-to-know basis, with incoming leaders only briefed after they took office. Shim's foresight would save us time now. I hoped.

"Meanwhile, we should get as many *Echtran* and Nuathan Scientists as possible working on the problem," Mr. Stuart said. "Surely it would be useful to have a few options on hand before we spring the situation on any *Duchas* leaders?"

"Assuming any can be found." Kyna didn't sound hopeful. "But yes, I'd like the Council's agreement to lay the matter before as many qualified Martian Scientists as possible, in hopes that collectively they might be able to produce those options."

I could tell none of the Royals liked the idea, but they were too frightened by the alternative to argue against it. Finally, Breann said, "I suppose we must trust Kyna, Shim and Van to identify the most appropriate Scientists for the task."

Mr. Stuart nodded. "I'll message my father tonight."

"I'll start immediately, as well," Kyna said. "Excellency, expect to hear from me within the next day or so to arrange for you to share everything you've learned with the Scientists we select."

"Um, sure. Like I said, I'll help any way I can." Rigel squeezed my hand, giving me a much-needed boost of confidence.

Mrs. O'Gara cleared her throat. I thought it was because Rigel and I were still holding hands until she said, "It's past nine o'clock. Unless we intend to inform the Sovereign's *Duchas* guardians of the situation tonight, we should get her home. Surely anything else she must do can wait until tomorrow?"

"Certainly." Kyna again looked around at those assembled. "We'll adjourn for now, but everyone should feel free to contact me with any ideas or suggestions you might have on how we should proceed. Excellency, your very good health." Fist over heart, her image bowed to me, then disappeared.

Nara and Connor did likewise, and then Mrs. O'Gara was ushering me toward the front door. "We haven't much time if we want to avoid questions from your aunt, dear."

"Okay. Just a sec." Still clinging to Rigel's hand, I stood up and gave him a kiss—a quick one, since everyone was watching. *I'll let you know anything else I figure out or hear,* I promised him.

Deal. And ditto. We'll beat this, M. Together we can handle anything, remember?

I could tell he was every bit as scared as I was, despite his bracing words, but I smiled. *You're right. We proved it again tonight and we'll keep proving it.*

Reluctantly, we loosed hands and I accompanied the O'Garas out to their van. Meanwhile, details I'd obtained from the Grentl continued to surface into conscious knowledge I'd be able to share with the Scientists. I just hoped it would be enough.

No further word came before I left for school the next morning, so I did something I'd been cautioned not to—I stuck my omni in my jeans pocket so I could check it occasionally during the day. Surely, the stakes justified the minuscule risk of having it discovered? It's not like any *Duchas* would know what it was, anyway.

On the bus I noticed a few curious looks aimed my way, but it wasn't until Bri and Deb got on at their stop that I found out why.

"Is it true?" Bri asked in an excited whisper, plunking into the seat behind me and Molly. "Did you really ride home with Sean yesterday? Did you and Rigel have a fight?"

Deb's eyes were also wide and worried. Really?

I laughed. "No, of course not! I missed my bus, that's all. I saw Pete Griffin and Sean getting ready to leave, so I asked if they could give me a ride."

Deb looked relieved, but Bri said, "Okay, but I *also* heard Rigel got a ride with Amber after practice…"

"To my house," Molly said matter-of-factly. "He and M hung out with Sean and me for a while, then they both went home. Why is this a big deal?" Though Molly was every bit as keyed up as I was over the whole Grentl thing, she was doing an awesome job of hiding it.

Bri shrugged, seeming almost disappointed. "Guess it's not."

I almost made a crack about her needing to look somewhere else for the juicy gossip she craved but I didn't need Bri mad at me on top of everything else.

The kiss Rigel gave me out in front of the school a few minutes later went a long way to silence any remaining rumors about us fighting. High school, I realized, was a lot like Nuath, with everyone eagerly pouncing on scandal after scandal, manufacturing them if there were no real ones. And while they were all busy following this or that bit of so-called "news," nobody ever had a clue about the real dangers out there.

All of which made school that day surreal. While the Grentl inexorably deployed their deadly satellites around our planet, everybody went to class like any other day, worrying about trivial things like tests and who was going out with whose ex. When Bri asked me at lunch if she could nominate me for Homecoming Court, I looked at her like she was crazy.

"What are you talking about?"

"Homecoming, dummy. It's this weekend, remember? Rigel's a no-brainer, like last year. As his girlfriend, you've got a shot at knocking Trina off the Court. Deb and I can get the signatures and run your campaign. Molly will help, too, won't you?"

Molly did a very slight double-take, then grinned. "Oh, yeah, of course! You'd be great, M."

"You two sure seem preoccupied today," Deb observed, looking from Molly to me. "Is anything wrong?"

"It's that Government project," Molly instantly replied. "We're kind of behind the curve on it. I think we might have been a little too ambitious with our topic."

She went on about all the research we still had to do, leaving me free to continue my intermittent—and worried—silent conversation with Rigel about the Grentl issue. Not that either of us had any new ideas…but how were we supposed to think about anything *else* right now?

More than ever, I wished I didn't have to go to such great lengths to hide the truth. Rigel, Sean and Molly could at least let down their guard at home, while I always had to be super vigilant to avoid rousing Aunt Theresa's always-ready suspicions. It wasn't fair.

So it was a relief when Molly called my house right after school, asking me to come over. Again using our Government project as my excuse, I wrote a note to Aunt Theresa and headed to the O'Garas', where Molly greeted me with a slightly strained smile.

"What's up?" I sensed discomfort from her, but not the fear I'd more than half expected.

Instead of answering, she led me straight up to her room. "Sean's not home yet, and I thought it might be better to show you this when he's not around," she said, plunking down in her desk chair while I perched on the edge of her bed.

Glancing around, I noticed that the houseplants she'd reclaimed from Heather after our return were already starting to droop. Not that I'd ever mention it, since her brown thumb was a serious sore spot for Molly.

Quickly, I averted my gaze from the plants. "What did you want to show me?"

In answer, she turned to her laptop, clicked to a website and typed in a long, complicated password. "This." She handed me the laptop.

On the screen was the front page of the *Echtran Enquirer*, a secret online newspaper of sorts, though both Sean and Molly had told me it was often more like a weekly tabloid than real news. This week's headline read: *"Sovereign Emileia Rekindles Forbidden Romance."*

Groaning, I started to read.

According to an exclusive interview granted by Gordon Nolan, who traveled with the Sovereign to Nuath last spring and back to Earth with Rigel Stuart a month later, the two teens have recently resumed the relationship both previously swore they had ended.

The article went on to detail how Rigel and I had spent every available moment together since my return to Jewel—which totally wasn't true—and how our flouting of tradition had the potential to undermine both Nuathans' and *Echtrans'* confidence in the new government. It included comments like, *Sources close to him say Sean O'Gara is taking her defection rather badly,* and *Rigel Stuart's parents pleaded with him not to pursue this ill-advised romance.* Gordon claimed to be deep in Rigel's confidence, saying he'd done his best to point out how important it was that Rigel and I stay away from each other, for the good of the Martian race.

The article concluded, *No one seems to know how Rigel Stuart's memory came to be restored. Gordon speculates that it was never erased at all, that his supposed amnesia was simply a ruse to play on the Sovereign's sympathies. Our sympathies, of course, are with Sean, who is again a victim of the Sovereign's poor judgment in dallying with a non-Royal. We must hope this story will ultimately have a happy ending for all of us, unlikely though that now seems.*

"Ugh!" I exclaimed, pushing away from the desk. "That awful woman. Gwendolyn Gannett seemed so nice when she interviewed Rigel and me last fall, and then Sean and me last spring."

Molly nodded sympathetically. "Because she wanted the story. But I don't think Gwendolyn cares who gets hurt if she thinks it'll make a good headline. Mum says she's already applied to be a reporter for the new *official* news outlet Mr. Stuart is putting together."

I snorted. "I'll have to tell him what a terrible reporter she is. Most of this crap isn't even true!"

"I know. But she'll claim she just reported what Gordon told her—which she probably did, though with her usual snarky little asides."

Molly was right that I should be way madder at Gordon, who'd obviously used Gwendolyn to get back at Rigel and me. He'd been shipped off to Montana last night, but it looked like he'd managed to wreak some havoc before Cormac nabbed him.

"How many people really read this thing, anyway?"

"Um…kind of a lot. I mean, most people know it's sensationalistic and all, but other than MARSTAR or messages from friends, it's been about the only way to get Martian news here on Earth."

"Great. Just great. Like I needed this on top of everything else."

"I know. But hey, in the good news department, Bri and Deb got enough signatures by the end of today to put your name on the Homecoming ballot."

A sour laugh escaped me. "Oh, sure, the popularity contest I *don't* care about winning. Maybe I should have taken those two to Mars with me to help me get Acclaimed last spring."

Molly giggled. "Can you just imagine their faces if we told them the whole truth about you?"

Thinking about that lightened my mood. Slightly. "So, is there any other news I should know about? Has your mom heard anything from Kyna or the Council?"

"Not that she's mentioned to me."

After that we really did do some work on our Government project, since I hadn't been lying about us being behind on it. Tomorrow the class was taking a half-day field trip to the State House in Indianapolis and we were supposed to have questions on our topic written up for legislators or their aides to answer.

As soon as I headed home I filled Rigel in on that stupid *Echtran Enquirer* article.

I know. Dad showed me when I got home from practice. It won't be like Nuath, though. You're already Acclaimed so the worst they can do is call us bad names, right? Anyway, we have more important things to worry about now.

He was right, but the idea of people blaming Rigel—again—still upset me more than I wanted to admit, especially to him. One more thing for me to fix, assuming we survived the Grentl attack Friday night.

I checked my omni again when I got home and found a long message from Shim that had just come in. Most of it was about the Grentl issue, updating me on which Nuathan and *Echtran* Scientists he and Kyna believed might help us come up with a solution. He seemed confident they'd be able to do so, making me wish I could talk to him in person to gauge how he *really* felt. Kyna would be contacting me shortly, he said, to arrange for me to share the details of what I'd learned from the device with those Scientists.

At the end of the message, he added that the news about Rigel and me being back together had reached Nuath and was creating a bit of a sensation, now that the networks had picked it up.

"If nothing else, this should serve as a useful distraction while our Scientists determine our most effective counter to the Grentl's plans. But please don't let it distract you from what needs to be done, Excellency."

The message ended and I glared at my omni as though it were at fault. What was *with* these supposedly-advanced Martians and their ridiculous addiction to gossip? Maybe once the news about the Grentl broke—which both Shim and Kyna seemed sure it would—*that* would finally shift their focus to something a little less trivial.

33

Influence quantity

AT the sound of the doorbell, I shook my thoughts free of stupid Nuathan gossip and stuck my omni back in my pocket before leaving my room. When I came downstairs a minute later, it turned out to be Molly at the door.

"Hey, M! I was just asking your aunt if you can *please* come help with the junior class Homecoming float this evening. Three of the people I had lined up just bailed on me, so we really need you. They'll call out for pizzas, so at least she'll get dinner out of it," she explained to Aunt Theresa.

My aunt smiled at Molly, then raised an eyebrow at me. "I hope this means you two finished that project you were working on this afternoon?"

"We did," I lied. "Can I go help?"

"I suppose so." Aunt Theresa seemed to have as hard a time saying no to Molly as she did to her mother.

As we headed to the curb, where Mrs. O'Gara waited in their minivan, I turned to Molly apologetically. "It's great to get out of the house again, but I'm really not sure I should go. I'm expecting to hear from Kyna any time now, asking me—"

"I know. To give the Scientists all your info. This is your excuse. Kyna's already at the Stuarts' house—she flew in from D.C. this afternoon and is staying there—so I guess she'll be one of the Scientists asking you things. And Mum says the Council will convene there afterward, too."

I blinked at her. "Oh! Um, okay, then. Let's go."

Ten minutes later, Mrs. O dropped me off at Rigel's house. "Are you really going to go work on the float?" I asked Molly as I got out.

"Yeah. All the cheerleaders have to. Trina's heading up the junior class float, and you know how she is." Molly made a face. "She'll probably keep us at it till midnight. Hope you really do beat her out for Homecoming Court."

The second I rang the Stuarts' doorbell, Rigel opened the door and pulled me into a welcome kiss that lasted until approaching footsteps made us break apart. Combing my fingers hastily through my hair, I turned to greet his parents—and Kyna—with a slightly embarrassed smile.

"Hi! I, uh, made it. So, how are we doing this?"

"The others are conferencing in," Kyna responded with only the faintest answering smile. "It's as well you could come so quickly, Excellency, as we have rather a large number of questions we're hoping you can answer."

Following her to Mr. Stuart's office, I stifled a sigh and heard Rigel mentally echo it. No more alone time.

On the big flat-screen monitor on the wall of the office, two men and a woman were already conversing with each other. Not quite as futuristic as the holograms the Council used, but still pretty cool. At my entrance they all bowed to me, then introduced themselves as Kathleen, a NASA xenobiologist, Patrick, a NASA astrophysicist like Kyna, and Arthur, a NASA aerospace engineer.

Three chairs were positioned in front of the monitor. I moved to the middle one. "Wow, is there anyone who works at NASA who isn't *Echtran*?" I was only half joking.

"We are rather disproportionately represented," Kyna admitted, taking the right-hand chair. "Though we still comprise barely five percent of the staff. Shall we get started?"

I nodded and sat down, not sure what to expect. Rigel took the chair on my left, at which point all the Scientists, Kyna included, proceeded to pepper me with questions.

"The Grentl satellites—you said there are seven hundred twenty of them?—at what height will they take up their ultimate positions?"

"Are they manually controlled by beings on the mother ship, or are they on an automatic sequence?"

"Do they have any sort of armor or shielding? What sort?"

And on and on and on. The Scientists seemed both surprised and gratified by the level of detail I was able to provide. So was I. Apparently I really had absorbed everything the Grentl themselves knew, judging by the way I was able to quickly respond to every single question the Scientists threw at me. Except one.

"Are you *certain* they have not, or will not, deviate from their original plan?"

"Like I said before, I really don't think they will, but no. I guess without contacting them again I can't be absolutely positive. Do you…want me to do that?" I cringed inwardly, though Rigel silently assured me he'd help again.

"Not yet," Kyna said. "If we are able to come up with anything that looks like a viable defense, however, we may ask you to do so closer to the scheduled time of their attack, as a miscalculation of even minutes might be extremely important."

"So…is that it for now?" I'd been answering questions for almost two hours and felt a little like I had after doing back-to-back press conferences in Nuath.

"Unless there is anything else of importance you can recall?"

"I don't think so. But then, I didn't realize I knew half that stuff until you asked me," I admitted.

"The rest of the Council will be arriving shortly," Kyna said then. "If we should come up with more questions later, I'll let you know."

Rigel took my hand. "C'mon, M, you need a break before that meeting starts—and something to eat."

I brightened immediately, both at his touch and the thought of food. "Sounds good to me."

He led me to the kitchen, where both of his parents waited. Almost immediately, I noticed a slight tension from both of them.

"Is, um, something wrong?" I asked uncertainly.

After a second or two of awkward silence, Mr. Stuart blurted out, "I, ah, don't suppose you've read the latest *Enquirer*?"

"Molly showed it to me this afternoon," I admitted, suddenly understanding what I'd sensed. "And I'm really sorry. I had no idea Gordon would be able to get in touch with that reporter. Most of what he told her wasn't even true."

Dr. Stuart quickly said, "You have nothing to apologize for, Excellency. But this is likely to make things a bit…difficult, especially for Rigel."

"Has someone actually hassled you guys already?" I asked indignantly.

"Only a few nasty emails," she assured me. "Nothing threatening. Of course, this is an extremely minor matter compared to the, ah, other one. We just thought you should be aware, in case it should escalate."

When Kyna joined us a moment later, I figured it was a good idea to let her know about that stupid article, too, as well as those emails Dr. Stuart had just mentioned.

Rather to my surprise, she just waved a hand dismissively. "Consider the source. I always expected Gordon Nolan to do something underhanded. I'm relieved it turned out to be so relatively innocuous. Unless name calling progresses to physical threats, I recommend you keep your focus on the more pressing matter of the Grentl for now. We'll deal with any personal or political fallout from malicious gossip later, if necessary."

In other words, if it still mattered by next week.

Realizing she was right, I turned my attention to the two slices of leftover pizza Dr. Stuart had just set in front of me.

"I'm still not certain telling *all* of our people is the best course." Malcolm frowned worriedly at Kyna. "You've said yourself, many times, how crucially important it is that we keep them from learning about the Grentl's existence and their continued ties to Nuath. If it would have caused panic before, why should you think it won't now?"

Kyna had begun the meeting with an overview of what she and the other Scientists had learned and the very preliminary conclusions they'd drawn. Now she reiterated the most pertinent one.

"Don't you understand? Within a day or two, our people will realize something is out there anyway. Personally, I would far rather tell them the truth than placate them with some elaborate lie that will make them less inclined to take necessary precautions. Once they are made to understand the nature of the threat, I believe our people can be trusted to take appropriate action to safeguard themselves and perhaps the *Duchas* around them, as well."

"Kyna is right." Mr. Stuart spoke more forcefully than he'd yet done at a Council meeting. "Already I'm picking up chatter between three or four of the most extensive Earth-based telescope arrays, which means we also need to bring a few *Duchas* space programs into the loop on this, along with the heads of state already discussed."

Connor looked anxiously from one to the other. "But there's still a chance a solution will be found, isn't there?"

"We've already begun running simulations," Kyna assured him, though I could tell she considered a solution unlikely. "Meanwhile, it's essential that nations, cities and individuals around the globe do whatever is possible in advance to minimize the potential devastation. With enough cooperation, we may be able to keep casualties far lower than they would otherwise be."

Mr. Stuart nodded. "If critical systems can be taken offline and power grids shut down before the EMP, that would decrease our recovery time substantially. But convincing so many municipalities, even whole countries, to take such drastic steps will require a higher degree of candor than we have been in the habit of practicing."

"Are you suggesting we inform the *Duchas* at large about our existence?" Breann was clearly aghast. "We'd risk having our people put in containment camps…or worse."

"No, no," Kyna quickly replied. "The common folk are by no means ready for such information. Our hope is to convince those leaders who already know about us to spread word of a fictitious impending solar storm so appropriate measures can be taken for the safety of their people. And ours."

Though it was obvious the Royals still had reservations, none voiced further objections.

"That's settled, then," Kyna said with grim satisfaction. "Our next order of business is to decide which details will be shared, both in the announcement to our own people—which I recommend the Sovereign read aloud—and with the *Duchas* heads of state."

By the end of the meeting, we'd hammered out a draft statement for me to read, as well as a few crucial bullet points I'd need to share with the various heads of state via video-conferencing.

"Are you sure Kyna wouldn't be a better person to talk to them?" I squirmed at the thought of looking stupid in front of the most important people on the planet. "I mean, I'm just sixteen. What if they don't take me seriously?"

Kyna smiled understandingly—which made her look surprisingly attractive for her age. "I will introduce you, and will be on hand, Excellency, but you are our Sovereign and the spokesperson for our people. Trust me, the recommendations will have more weight coming from you."

Then, to all of us, "Clearly, this needs to take place as quickly as possible. I doubt we'll be able to arrange any video calls with leaders before midday tomorrow, but we shouldn't delay longer than that. Excellency, can you arrange to be here at that time?"

"Well, I have school, and tomorrow's that Government field trip…"

Mrs. O spoke up. "If we can somehow arrange for the Sovereign to appear to leave with the group while actually remaining behind, she would have all of tomorrow afternoon to devote to these calls and to record the statement she's agreed to make to our people."

"We'll arrange it." Kyna didn't say how, but I had no doubt she'd manage it.

The meeting adjourned a few minutes later. When Rigel kissed me good night, he did his best to calm my worries—about everything.

Let's just focus on making sure we're still here and functioning come Saturday…and enjoy every minute we have together between now and then.

I promised to do my best on both fronts.

During the drive back, I still sensed lingering resentment from Mrs. O'Gara underneath the worry we all shared. I wanted to say something, try again to explain, but I didn't think it would do any good. While she might claim to understand, I wasn't sure she'd ever forgive me for what I'd done to her son.

Even if it wasn't exactly my fault, I couldn't really blame her.

Then she surprised me by saying, "Excellency, Sean requested that if the meeting adjourned in time, I bring you by our house briefly before you go home. Would you mind terribly?"

"Uh, no, I guess not. Why?"

"He said he'd like to talk to you, but that it shouldn't take long."

Great. I already had all that ridiculous Homecoming stuff and a stupid gossip column to worry about on top of the Grentl. I *so* didn't need Sean trying one more time to talk me out of being with Rigel. But I might as well get it over with.

"Sure, that'll be fine."

Like yesterday after school, Sean was already waiting on the porch. When his mother and I joined him there, he said, "You go on in, Mum. I'll talk to M out here."

"Very well." If anything, the resentment I felt from her increased. As she went inside and closed the door, I braced myself.

"Your mom said you wanted to talk to me?"

Sean nodded, his expression unreadable, his feelings a jumble of sadness, determination and…relief? "I do. Can we sit down?" He indicated the porch swing.

Still trying to decipher what I was sensing, I cautiously sat next to him. "What?"

"I think Mum knows what I'm going to say and she doesn't agree. So I wanted to do it out here. M, I get it. I finally do get it."

"Get it?" Now I was even more confused. "Get what?"

"You and Rigel. Your bond and…and everything. I saw what happened last night—how you were starting to lose it, using the Grentl device, and how that changed when he touched you. It was… amazing. For almost a year I've been fighting it, trying to convince myself it was just a crush or some temporary genetic anomaly, but I…I know now it's not. What you two have is real. And important. And I don't want to get in the way of it. Not anymore."

"Sean, I—" I began, but he shook his head.

"No. Don't apologize. Not again, not now. I'm the one who needs to say I'm sorry, for doubting you all this time—or trying to, even when I knew, deep down, your bond with Rigel was real. Sure, I had Nuathan tradition on my side, but that doesn't excuse how I acted—to either of you. I just wanted you to know I'm taking myself out of it."

Now I was alarmed. "Out of it? What do you mean?"

"Nothing drastic." He managed a twisted smile. "I'm not leaving Jewel or anything, not yet. Probably not before I graduate, unless we all—" He broke off, but I knew what he'd been about to say.

"The Scientists are doing all they can and we're going to get as many people as possible, all over the world, to take precautions, just in case." I tried to sound more reassuring than I felt.

He nodded. "If anyone can stop them, you can. With Rigel. I just meant that I plan to back off, try to move on. Maybe ask other girls out, not that there are any other *Echtran* girls in Jewel right now. But…I don't want you worrying about me anymore. I know you have been, and the last thing I want is to be a distraction right now."

I swallowed, trying to dislodge the sudden lump in my throat. "Thank you, Sean. I've always liked you, you know. It's just—"

"I know. It's not the same. It can't ever be the same. Like I said, I get it now." He stood, making the swing rock. "I'll go get Mum to drive you home, since your aunt will expect that."

"Okay. You're…you're a really good person, Sean. Don't ever let anyone tell you otherwise."

"Hey, if my Sovereign says so, it must be true. G'night, M." His parting smile was sad, but there was also strength behind it, and that strength reassured me. He was going to be okay, even if it took a while.

34

Disconnection

AT school the next day, the candidates for Homecoming Court were included in the morning announcements and campaigning began in earnest.

"C'mon, M," Bri chided me at lunch. "Deb and I are working our butts off trying to get you elected to Homecoming Court and you act like you don't even care!"

I wrenched my thoughts away from the intimidating prospect of talking to a bunch of world leaders this afternoon. Homecoming Court was such a minor matter compared to everything else going on this week, I really *couldn't* bring myself to care. But I couldn't tell Bri that.

"Sorry. I'll do more tomorrow—if only to keep Trina off that float with Rigel."

"Exactly! The main point is to make sure *she* doesn't get it this year." Bri's serious expression suggested a life-or-death issue. "If we can even split her vote so Rosa Garcia wins, I'll be happy."

"Yeah, me, too." Rosa was captain of the girls' volleyball team and both popular and pretty. And way nicer than Trina.

You might as well humor them, Rigel thought to me. *It gives them something harmless to focus on and they're having fun.* He didn't add that they might only have two more days left for fun, but I knew he was thinking it. Just like I was.

So I reluctantly let Bri and Deb drag me around the cafeteria while they talked me up as the best choice to represent the junior class. At least I looked my best, since with Molly's guidance I'd worn an outfit appropriate for both school and my on-camera appearances later. She'd even done my makeup in the bathroom before classes started.

"It's too bad you have that dentist appointment today, right when both Government classes are going to Indianapolis," Deb said worriedly when we returned to our table. "You know Trina will use the whole bus ride to schmooze people into voting for her."

Bri made a rude sound. "We can out-schmooze Trina any day. You'll help, won't you, Rigel? And Molly, get Sean on board, too. He's probably going to be elected Homecoming King so his support will count double!"

I'd told Rigel about my conversation with Sean last night, and he was as relieved as I was that Sean finally seemed willing to move on. Maybe even more relieved.

Bri and Deb strategized how to use this afternoon's four-hour field trip to my advantage while I went back to mentally phrasing what I'd say to people like the U.S. Secretary of State and the Chancellor of Germany.

When the bell rang, Rigel and Molly hung back for a moment as the rest of the Government students headed to the waiting bus.

"You going to be okay?" Rigel asked. "If you want, I can—"

"No, it's fine. Kyna will be there, and your dad. Besides, we don't have an excuse for you to miss the trip." I turned to Molly then. "I feel really bad making you do all the work on this Government project. I'm totally not pulling my weight."

Molly grinned at me. "It's no biggie. Really. How about we divide up the work this way: I'll finish the project and you save the world. Deal?"

I couldn't help but laugh, despite the looming threat. "Deal."

The two of them hurried off then to catch the bus to Indy while I went to the front office, where Kyna and Cormac had already cleared me for my fictitious dental appointment. I signed myself out, then met Kyna at the curb so she could drive me to Rigel's house. Before pulling away, she handed me a tablet.

"Van Stuart and I finalized the statement you'll be recording for broadcast via MARSTAR and the Nuathan networks. You can personalize it if you wish, but it's fairly straightforward, worded with an eye to minimizing panic."

I scanned the text. The statement was brief but stilted. As we drove, I edited it slightly, hoping a more casual delivery might make it a little less scary. When we reached the Stuarts' house, I handed the tablet back to Kyna for approval.

"Ah, yes. That does sound more like you. Well done. Let's get this out of the way first, before this afternoon's video conference."

Mr. Stuart was waiting for us inside. "Everything is still set up for you in my office." The main emotion I sensed from him was determination, with just a touch of nervousness. Way less nervousness than I was feeling myself.

Wishing Molly were here to give me a final once-over, I carefully brushed my hair and touched up my lip gloss. Then Kyna positioned me in front of the big screen, where Mr. Stuart had uploaded my edited statement so I could read while looking at the camera.

"Ready?" he asked. I nodded. He turned on the camera and I started talking.

"Hello, everyone. What I have to tell you may sound like a history lesson at first, but please bear with me." I tried to smile pleasantly—not nervously. My tiny image in the lower corner of the screen helped. "As most of you know, Nuath was originally created well over two thousand years ago when an alien race transplanted the inhabitants of a small Irish village to a prepared habitat under the surface of Mars.

"Most of Nuath's earliest history has been lost in the mists of time, but we know that our alien abductors remained for less than a thousand years before inexplicably disappearing. They left a lot of their technology behind, though, and over the centuries Nuathans put most of it to good use. For example, by adapting alien technology for space travel, nearly six hundred years ago, we discovered that our nearest neighbor, Earth, was our species' home of origin.

"But while we figured out many ways to use their technology, we never did figure out who those early aliens were—until now. I have recently been contacted by those aliens—they call themselves the Grentl—and have learned that they are worried about what humans, particularly Earth humans, are evolving into. They feel partly responsible for what they consider some wrong turns by our race, and now plan to undo as much of our modern progress as possible.

"By now, some of you may have heard about the satellites taking up positions around the Earth. The Grentl plan to use them to generate a massive electromagnetic pulse with the intention of disrupting all Earth communications and technology. This is expected to occur this coming Saturday at 12:47am Eastern time on Earth, or 5:47am Nuathan time. While Nuath itself should not be directly affected by this pulse, Earth is likely to experience a complete loss of power and possibly much worse.

"The *Echtran* Council and our most qualified Scientists recommend that everyone living on Earth shut down and disconnect *all* electronics before midnight Friday night. This includes car and other batteries and anything else that could be affected by an EMP. If you can, please urge your *Duchas* neighbors to do the same. A story is already being sent to *Duchas* media worldwide, warning of unusual sunspot activity and encouraging them to take exactly these precautions.

"If enough of us do this, we may weather the Grentl's assault with minimal damage or casualties. I'm sure you have a lot of questions. You can direct them to Regent Shim Stuart on Nuath and to Kyna Nuallan of the *Echtran* Council on Earth. Above all, please don't panic. We are a resilient people and I have every confidence that we'll all come through this challenge stronger than ever. Thank you, and God bless you all."

Mr. Stuart switched off the camera, then played back the recording. Kyna watched it carefully, then nodded her approval.

"I believe that will do quite well. Excellency?"

Though I always hated how my recorded voice sounded, I was amazed I hadn't stumbled over any of the words—and also amazed by how *not* nervous I looked on the screen, since I totally was inside. Practice had obviously made me lots better at hiding it than I used to be.

"I doubt I could do it any better if I tried again."

"Then I'll convert it into the proper formats for broadcast at whatever time the Council should decide," Mr. Stuart said. "When is the video conference supposed to start?"

Kyna checked the time. "Germany's and Ireland's Ministers of Foreign Affairs and the American Secretary of State all agreed to call in at one-thirty. I'm hoping that Japan's and Australia's Ministers and the Minister of External Affairs from India will be able to join us as well, though they didn't firmly commit. Needless to say, these are extremely busy people and I was unwilling to give enough details to their assistants to adequately convey the urgency of this meeting. Quite honestly, I'm surprised even this many agreed on such short notice."

Mr. Stuart nodded. "Excellency, if you'd like to take a break, I can get everything set up before the calls come in."

"Oh, okay, thanks."

I hurried off to the bathroom, trying to quell nerves that were so ramped up now, I was afraid I just might puke. I managed not to, but it was close. When I emerged, Dr. Stuart was waiting with a cup of peppermint tea.

"I seem to recall Rigel saying this is one of your favorites?"

I cupped my hands around the warm mug with a grateful smile. "Thank you so much. This is exactly what I need." Sipping slowly, I headed back to Mr. Stuart's office for the ordeal ahead.

The video conference lasted a full two hours and left me nearly as drained as using the Grentl device. India's Minister hadn't shown up, but all the others had—and they'd been nearly as unwilling to accept such incredible news from a teenaged girl as I'd predicted. Even after Kyna had them confirm with their own astronomers the existence of numerous unexplained satellites, they were clearly skeptical.

"Do you realize what it would do to our economy to shut down the entire nation's power grids for even an hour or two?" the U.S. Secretary of State demanded at one point.

Kyna assured them that *Echtran* Scientists would continue trying to find other solutions but made it clear she considered that unlikely. She and I both stressed repeatedly that taking our recommended precautions would be *far* preferable to the alternative, but by the time we disconnected, only Ireland and Australia were willing to admit that the potential risk justified such extreme measures.

After they'd all signed off, I pushed myself away from the enormous computer screen with a frustrated sigh. "Wow, and I thought the Royals on the *Echtran* Council were stubborn."

"It *is* an awful lot for them to take in all at once," Mr. Stuart pointed out. "We knew this might not work, but we were ethically obliged to at least try. You did as well as you possibly could have, Excellency."

"Not well enough, obviously." I looked pleadingly at Kyna. "Do you think there's *any* chance our Scientists will come up with a defense we can use in time?"

The emotions I sensed from her answered my question, though she tried to smile reassuringly. "There's always a chance, of course. If nothing else, we'll be able to shut down quite a few power grids whether those in charge agree or not, and blame it on that fictitious solar storm. I have people working on that already, in fact. And as more and more astronomers verify the existence of the satellites, those skeptics may yet come around."

I tried to be comforted but knew that, at best, only a tiny fraction of the world could be protected if the Grentl carried out their plan.

"I should use the device again. Try one more time to talk them out of what they're doing."

The look Kyna gave me was almost pitying. "Do you really believe that will help, Excellency?"

"No." Once everything absorbed from the Grentl had finally clarified in my mind, I'd become more positive than ever that it wouldn't. "But…what else can I do?"

"If we are unable to come up with anything by tomorrow night, perhaps you can make another attempt at communication," Kyna finally conceded. "You and your bond mate, I should say, as his assistance seemed to make such a difference."

It was actually a relief to get back to my house and such mundane chores as homework and laundry after such a nerve-wracking, high-stakes afternoon. Bri called with an update on how many people she, Deb and Molly had talked into voting for me for Junior Class Princess. Frivolous as it was, I played along, welcoming the temporary diversion from far more life-and-death matters.

But when Aunt Theresa got home an hour or so later, things took an even more absurd turn.

"I ran into Melinda Andrews in town just now, and she tells me *you* have been nominated for this year's Homecoming Court?" she greeted me, eyebrows nudging her graying hairline.

Her astonished skepticism didn't even hurt my feelings, I was so used to it. "Um, yes. Bri and Deb filled out the petition for me and got all the signatures. I know I probably don't—"

"Marsha, this is *wonderful*! Homecoming Court is a great honor. Melinda and I agreed that we need to do all we can to make sure you win, as it could be a nice addition to your college resumes next year. I thought perhaps cookies that you can hand out to your classmates tomorrow? Now, which do you think your little friends would like best—my cranberry walnut oatmeal cookies or classic chocolate chip?"

Too startled to answer, I just stared at her. "Um—"

"Let's make a few dozen of each, shall we? Here, I have an extra apron you can wear. I'll phone Louie at work and ask him to pick up a pizza on his way home so we don't have to worry about dinner."

I could never remember Aunt Theresa being this pleased with me —and for something I'd had virtually nothing to do with! We spent the evening baking cookies together while she chatted about how much more I would enjoy school, now that I was finally becoming more popular. Unreal as it seemed, I was grateful I'd at least have this one happy memory of Aunt Theresa to file away for whatever future lay ahead.

As I was getting ready for bed, I received a message on my omni from Shim. My statement had already been broadcast all over Nuath and he reported that while at least half of the population was in frightened denial, many were offering their help to the Scientists already working on the problem. He also mentioned that after receiving the results of our *graell* tests from Kyna, he had gone on the air himself to share an edited version of the researchers' conclusions.

"While this Grentl news has already done much to turn people's minds from the topic of your potential out-of-*fine* pairing, I'm hopeful that providing them with scientific evidence of your bond may prevent it again becoming an issue, should the Grentl attack be somehow averted."

Any humor I might have found in the first part of that sentence was wiped out by the last. Clearly, Shim didn't think it any more likely we'd find a way to stop the Grentl than Kyna did. Still, on the off chance we could, Martian opposition to Rigel and me as a couple would again be the biggest problem facing us, so it was good Shim had a plan for that.

Though I felt beyond foolish carrying my huge box of cookies onto the bus the next morning, Aunt Theresa turned out to be right. Even before we got to school, Bri and Deb seized the opportunity to hand some out to the few other juniors on our bus.

"Cookies were a great idea, M," Bri told me as we headed into the building. "Yesterday I didn't think you were really into the whole campaigning thing."

I shrugged. "Actually, the cookies were Aunt Theresa's idea. Deb's mom told her I was nominated and she went nuts. Got totally excited about it. It was weird."

"Didn't we tell you Homecoming Court was a big deal?" Deb grinned at Bri, who grinned back. "Go stash these in your locker for now and we'll hand out the rest over lunch.

Rigel had been hanging back, but joined me as I turned toward my locker. "You might as well have fun with it," he murmured. "Who knows if—"

"Yeah." But I knew. We both knew.

35

Potential transformer

THE news that her cookies were a hit put Aunt Theresa in such a great mood that evening, she didn't even question me when I said I might be later than usual getting home from Molly's tonight. We would supposedly be putting a few finishing touches on our Government project.

"Your grades are even more important than Homecoming Court, so be sure to do your best."

I nodded, hoping Molly really had been able to finish that project like she'd promised, since I'd been way too busy to help.

"I'll leave the front porch light on. Call if you'll be much past ten so I don't worry."

The whole O'Gara family was already waiting in their minivan when I arrived.

"Kyna messaged that we'll be at the Stuarts' house again," Mrs. O explained. "We'd best hurry, since it's likely to be rather a long meeting."

Like when we'd reconvened here Monday night for me to use the device, Kyna allowed Rigel and his mom, as well as Molly, Sean and Mr. O to join us. I was glad, since I could already tell from the emotions of those physically present that no one had good news to report. Having Rigel in the room would help keep my courage up.

"My colleagues have spent nearly all day running simulations," Kyna told us right at the outset. "Unfortunately, assuming the specifications given us by the Sovereign are correct, no weapon we might create in time is likely to have the least effect on the Grentl satellites."

"What about weapons that already exist?" Connor asked anxiously. "*Duchas* weapons? I heard something in the news today about missile tests and wondered—"

Kyna nodded, but grimly. "Yes, those so-called tests were attempts by the American military to destroy Grentl satellites. Israel made a similar attempt, though it was not publicized. All, unfortunately, were ineffective. Even had one worked, there would be no way to destroy all seven hundred and twenty of those satellites, distributed as they are. In addition, an experimental anti-satellite laser weapon was fired at two satellites. It was no more successful than the missiles. More countries do seem to be taking the threat seriously now, at least, which increases the likelihood that they will implement our recommended precautions."

"By tomorrow night?" Mr. Stuart was clearly skeptical. "I've seen the news stories relaying the astrophysicists' predictions of an intense solar storm, but it's no small matter to shut down power grids worldwide, not to mention grounding all flights."

"Precisely," Kyna agreed. "Due to the inevitable bureaucracy involved, I consider it extremely unlikely that more than a small fraction of the planet will be protected in time."

Which, I knew, would ultimately mean billions of deaths. "Then you need to let Rigel and me try again with the device. It sounds like it's our only hope at this point."

Kyna sighed heavily. "Despite the potential danger to you, Excellency, I am inclined to agree. If you can in any way dissuade the Grentl…"

"Even if we can't," Rigel volunteered from the corner, "maybe we'll be able to find some chink in their armor. Some vulnerability we didn't pick up on last time. Definitely worth a shot."

"It is. We should do it tonight. Now." Though I cringed at the prospect, I'd just as soon get it over with.

"That's the primary reason we're meeting here instead of at the O'Garas' house," Kyna admitted. "I realized earlier today it would likely come to this. I'm sorry, Excellency."

At her signal, Mr. Stuart and Malcolm left the room and returned a few moments later with the device, which they again set carefully on the living room table.

"Right, then. Let's do this." Rigel's voice sounded surprisingly firm and confident compared to the wildly fluctuating emotions I sensed from him…and shared.

His dad frowned worriedly. "You're sure about this?"

We both nodded.

Kyna, Breann, Malcolm, the Stuarts and the O'Garas arranged themselves around us in a circle. The holograms of Nara and Connor stood slightly closer, since they weren't at any real risk if the Grentl zapped us.

"Together from the start this time?" Rigel suggested, moving with me to the device.

"Right." I hoped desperately they wouldn't suddenly decide to hurt Rigel for bending their Sovereign-only rule.

This time he put a hand on my shoulder, skin on skin, before I even touched the thing. Absorbing one more fortifying dose of strength from him, I reached out and grabbed the copper projections.

One heartbeat, two, and then the prongs warmed in my hands, even faster than last time. They already knew I…we…were here. I felt them pulling at my mind almost immediately. Before shutting them out, I tried sending a thought.

Please, spare our planet! We are no threat to you. Billions of lives are at stake.

Would they answer? Again I counted heartbeats—three, four—and then, *"RISK TO GALAXY TOO GREAT. EXPERIMENT UNSUCCESSFUL."*

What would count as success? I pleaded. *Can you give us another chance?*

This time they didn't answer, just tried to suck memories and experiences out of me again. Not knowing what else to do, after another second or two of resisting, I let them. As the images flashed past at lightning speed, I was aware of them accessing some of Rigel's memories as well, no doubt because our minds were so closely linked with him actually touching me. I felt him flinch once or twice and knew he was experiencing the same thing I was—the replaying of particularly upsetting recent memories.

From him, they pulled his experience in the Mind Healing facility on Nuath, to include what it felt like to have his memory erased, then his awakening in Ireland and his increasing confusion at school between what he'd been told and the memories trying to surface. From me, they pulled the heartbreak I'd felt when Rigel hadn't recognized me and even actively avoided me. Then, from both of us, the memory of our incredible kiss in the cornfield when we'd re-bonded and Rigel's memories had come flooding back.

Finally, they were done. I waited, but they still didn't say anything. Frustrated, drawing on every bit of Rigel's mental strength as well as my own, I again tried probing *their* minds, determined to find out whether they were at all reconsidering their plan.

They weren't.

Their timetable for the EMP was exactly the same as before, following all the same steps I'd extracted from them last week. Tears of defeat were starting to prickle behind my eyelids when I caught Rigel's careful thought, sent only to me: *Look for a weakness.*

Nodding, I screwed up my face and pushed harder, trying to sense even the tiniest trace of uncertainty or fear from their collective consciousness. Nothing. Except…

There! A quick flash, an image of Rigel and me holding hands, focusing on the night sky. Then, before I could figure out exactly what it was we were doing, it was gone. The copper projections cooled and I could feel the Grentls' minds retreating, closing themselves off from me. I was about to try again when I felt Rigel tugging on my arm and realized I was shaking and sweating again, nearly spent.

Relief warred with disappointment as I let him pull me away from the device, releasing my hold on the prongs. *You stopped me! Maybe if—*

You were about to hurt yourself, M. Besides, I think maybe we got what we needed.

Turning away from the device, I blinked up at him. *We did?*

That last image. I think maybe we *are their vulnerability. You and me. Somehow.*

I stared at him as understanding dawned. *I think you're right! I was trying, hard, to sense any doubts or reservations from them and that's what popped up. Then they shut us out as fast as they could.*

In sudden excitement, I swung around to face the others so quickly, Rigel had to steady me on my feet. "It's us! We think it might be us!"

At their confused expressions, I realized Rigel's and my exchange just now had been silent. My voice shook slightly as I attempted to explain.

"The Grentl—they pulled out everything about our bond. How we can talk to each other, the electricity thing, and…how we feel about each other. Then I did everything I could to find some weakness of theirs we might be able to use and saw…" That image came back into my mind, clearer this time.

Rigel picked up the explanation. "She saw—we saw—us. Together. Doing something—we're not sure what, exactly—to fend off the Grentl. Can you somehow add the data from Sunday's *graell* tests to your simulations? See if there's something *we* might be able to do to stop them?"

Kyna and Mr. Stuart exchanged perplexed looks, then Kyna gave a little shrug. "We have nothing else to try at this point. I'll get our Scientists on it immediately and let you know if they turn up anything at all promising. Let's all pray they do."

"Look at Trina, that big copycat!" Bri hissed to Deb, Molly and me at lunch Friday. Following her gaze, I saw Trina walking up and down the rows of tables, a big, beribboned basket over her arm, handing out what looked like plastic-wrapped muffins.

Deb jumped up and ran to one of the tables Trina had already hit, then came back a minute later. "Candace's Gourmet Muffins. With stickers on each one saying 'Trina Squires for Junior Princess' and little tags on ribbons inviting everyone to a party at her house after the game tonight. Those must have cost her a fortune!"

Matt Mullins, passing our table just then, overheard. "If so, she didn't get her money's worth. You want the rest of mine?" He dropped a half-eaten muffin on Deb's tray. "Your cookies were way better, M. You've got nothing to worry about." With a wink, he continued toward the tray drop.

I had to laugh. "Like the vote will hinge on who hands out the best goodies?"

"It could," Bri said seriously. "Last year Tiffany gave out doughnuts with sprinkles, and she made Homecoming Queen. Rosa just passed out chocolate kisses, though, so no threat there."

I just rolled my eyes. "Look, if I get it, great, but I'm not going to cry if I don't and I don't want you guys to, either. Okay?" Homecoming Court might barely be on my radar just now, but I didn't want my friends feeling bad if I lost.

"At least we're making Trina work for it." Deb sounded philosophical.

Bri nodded. "Still, I'd give almost anything for you to win, M, if only for the look on her face when it's announced. I'm going to have my phone ready this afternoon to snap a picture of that!"

Ten minutes into seventh period, everyone was dismissed to attend the big Homecoming spirit assembly in the school gym. Rigel and I walked hand in hand, oblivious to the excited buzz of voices around us. The votes would all be collected and tallied at the start of the assembly, but with the Grentl attack looming tonight, neither of us had attention to spare for anything else.

Wouldn't your dad have called if the Scientists found something? I asked Rigel for at least the fourth time today.

Maybe not. He was way more patient with me than I deserved. *He'll definitely let me know as soon as I get home, though. You sure you don't want to come straight to my house after the pep rally?*

I'd better not. If I'm going to have to stay out super late tonight—if they figure out something we can do—I'll need to butter up Aunt Theresa all I can first.

Everyone was putting their voting slips into a big, decorated box outside the doors as they entered the gym, which was festooned with black and gold streamers and paper cutouts of diamonds and jaguars. Once inside, Rigel had to join the rest of the football team so I went to sit with Bri and Deb in the bleachers. The cheerleaders were already in action, waving their black and gold pompoms and leading cheers at the tops of their lungs.

"TWO, FOUR, SIX, EIGHT! WHO DO WE APPRECIATE? JAGUARS! JAGUARS! GOOOO, JAGUARS!"

"C'mon, M, you're not getting into the spirit," Bri chided me. "Look! They're about to introduce the team—you have to yell for Rigel!"

Doing my best to shake off my sense of impending doom, I plastered a smile on my face and screamed along with everyone else as our team jogged to the middle of the gym so the coach could announce all their names—like everybody didn't already know. He saved Rigel for last, as our star quarterback, and everyone in the gym jumped to their feet and redoubled the volume until the air throbbed.

After half a dozen more cheers, the players filed out and Principal Johannsen walked to the middle of the gym floor, taking the microphone from Coach Glazier.

"As you all know, this year marks Jewel High School's seventy-second year, our twelfth in this building. Since its founding, our school has produced several notable graduates."

She went on to list a handful of athletes, several war heroes, an artist and a musician that had achieved relative fame, then launched into more trivia about the history of the school. I tuned her out and went back to obsessing over what was likely to happen tonight until Bri gave me a hard nudge.

"—the moment you've all been waiting for," the principal was saying. "It gives me great pleasure to announce this year's Homecoming Court! Our Freshman Prince is Toby Mullins and the Princess is Andrea Perkins." The two fourteen-year-olds made their way down from the bleachers, where they were draped with black and gold sashes.

"Ooh, Matt's little brother," Deb whispered excitedly, pointing at Toby.

The Sophomore Prince and Princess were Jared Gross and Ginny Farmer, and then it was our turn. Even though I'd been telling myself all week I didn't care about silly Homecoming Court when the fate of the world was hanging in the balance, I caught myself holding my breath.

"Our Junior Prince this year is again Rigel Stuart," Ms. Johannsen announced, to no one's surprise. And this year's Junior Princess is… Marsha Truitt."

Deb let out a squeal, while Bri exclaimed triumphantly, "You did it! And…I got it! What an *awesome* picture of Trina's expression."

I barely glanced at her phone because I had to climb down the bleachers to join Rigel in the middle of the gym to receive my own sash.

Junior Princess! Rigel thought to me as I crossed the floor, walking right past Trina's still-outraged face. *Not quite as big a deal as Sovereign of a whole race of people, but still pretty cool.*

And without nearly as many strings attached. I grinned as I took my place next to him. *Wish all the Sovereign ever had to do was ride on floats and wave at the crowd.*

As Principal Johannsen announced Homecoming King and Queen —Sean, of course, and Missy Gillespie—I couldn't help thinking how my status at school had changed nearly as much as it had on Mars. Until last year, I'd been one of the least popular dweebs in school. And look at me now!

Catching my thought, Rigel took my hand. *How can anyone not look at you? You're pretty much perfect. Maybe now you'll believe me?*

I smiled up at him. *Nah, it was Aunt Theresa's cookies that got me elected. Still cool, though!*

We all had to stand there in our sashes while Jeremy took pictures for the website and yearbook, then everyone in the stands was allowed to come down and congratulate us. Bri, Deb and Molly were practically jumping up and down with excitement at my win, while Trina glared daggers my way. I very carefully did *not* read her emotions.

A few minutes later the bell rang and everyone started streaming toward their lockers and the buses. I wanted to ask Molly if she'd heard anything from her mom but I couldn't, with Bri and Deb right there. At times like this it would be convenient to have that telepathy thing with people other than Rigel…though definitely not worth the hassle of guarding my thoughts from everybody.

After stopping by our lockers for books we might never need again after tonight, we headed outside. Rigel, Sean and I were standing around by the buses, still being congratulated, when we saw Mr. Stuart waving at us from the parking lot. Quickly excusing ourselves, all four of us hurried over to him.

"What? Does this mean there's news?" I asked breathlessly.

"Apparently so. I'm to bring you home immediately so you can be briefed. Molly and Sean can come, too."

We all piled into the SUV, bursting with excitement and questions.

"I don't know any of the details yet," Mr. Stuart told us when we let him get a word in. "Just that the Scientists have come up with something based on what you suggested last night. Let's all hope it's a solution."

36

Flash hazard

RIGEL and I jumped out of the car as soon as it stopped in the driveway and raced into his house, with everyone else on our heels, eager to hear how we could stop the Grentl from blasting Earth back to the Stone Age. The full Council was waiting in the living room. So was Arthur, the NASA aerospace engineer who'd participated in Tuesday afternoon's video conference about the Grentl plan specifics.

At everyone's somber expressions, my eagerness turned to disappointment. "You didn't find a solution after all?"

"In fact, we may have." Kyna looked as serious as I'd ever seen her, which was saying something.

Rigel's confusion mirrored my own. "But…that's *good* news, right? You really found some way M, er, the Sovereign and I can stop the Grentl?"

"Perhaps," Arthur replied. "After trying various simulations all night and most of this morning we finally found one that could possibly work. In theory, at least. We were forced to extrapolate from your test results to predict the power you might produce under a true threat situation. However, to be certain, we really should measure your potential output again, see if it can be increased at all."

"Okay, fine," I said impatiently. "Let's do that."

Nodding, Arthur motioned us to follow him into the dining room, where another multimeter sat in the middle of the table. It was similar to the one from our *graell* tests Sunday night, but about three times larger.

"This meter is capable of measuring far greater voltages than the one previously used. Hopefully without sustaining damage." He gave us a dry smile, though I could tell he wasn't joking.

"So you want us to create a bigger bolt than before?" I asked.

"I'd like you to try. Even if you can't, this device should be able to measure your full electrical potential, though crudely."

Swallowing, I linked hands with Rigel like before. *Let's imagine we really are fighting off the Grentl. That ought to create the biggest spark yet.*

No kidding.

We waited while Arthur adjusted some settings on his meter and then stepped back, motioning everyone else who'd crowded into the room to move away as well. "All right. Stand just a bit closer, so we can capture as much charge as possible without losing it to the surrounding air. And…go." He took one more big step back.

Okay. They're coming, and we're the Earth's last line of defense, Rigel thought to me. *Ready?*

I forced myself to focus on the mental image of attacking Grentl satellites instead of the feel of Rigel's hand in mine. *Ready.*

The bolt we unleashed forced us both backward half a step as it arced between us and the silver contraption on the table. It definitely *looked* stronger than last time, though I wasn't sure by how much. Strong enough to leave a big scorch mark on Dr. Stuart's nice maple dining table.

"Oops," I said, just like Sunday night when we'd sent the little multimeter flying. "Sorry, Dr. Stuart!"

It was only then I became aware of the breathless amazement in the room. Some fear emanated from a Royal or two, but Arthur mostly registered excitement.

"Well?" Kyna said, as Arthur hurried forward to check the meter.

"6.7 gigajoules." Arthur was visibly impressed. "Very nearly enough. If being under a true threat allows them to manage just a bit more—and if they are able to maintain the burst for approximately twice as long—there is indeed a chance."

"A chance to do what?" I demanded.

"To turn the Grentl's EMP back upon itself, essentially short-circuiting it and destroying the satellites in a chain reaction. But the risk—"

He and Kyna exchanged glances.

"A worse risk than what the Grentl plan to do?" I asked disbelievingly. "What, could we blow up the planet or something?"

"No, Excellency." A deep crease formed between Kyna's eyebrows. "The risk wouldn't be to the planet, but to you and Rigel."

I let out a breath, hope bubbling back up. "We're just two people. If the Grentl let off that EMP, you said billions could die. This should be a no-brainer."

Rigel took my hand in a firm grip. "What would we need to do? And what exactly is the risk?"

"Arthur, would you like to explain?" Kyna's voice was tight, distressed. "You headed up the simulations."

He nodded. "Our simulations so far had indicated that a series of positron emitters would be our best hope. Unfortunately, we only have three and they are far too small to have the sort of effect on the satellites that would be necessary."

"Cool!" Sean exclaimed. "I didn't know *Echtrans* had created a positron emitter. Why wasn't that ever mentioned in—?"

Mrs. O shot him a stern glance and he subsided. "Oh, sorry, never mind. Go on."

"We could think of no way to amplify an emitter's output sufficiently to achieve the desired result until Kyna suggested incorporating the data from Sunday's test of your electrical, ah, ability. Even that seemed doubtful, as nearly eight gigajoules are needed to have a chance of disrupting the EMP. What you have just produced is close enough to give me hope that you may indeed be able to do what is needed. However—" He paused to glance at Kyna— "there is no question that the attempt would put the two of you at extreme risk."

"Risk of what?" Rigel persisted. "Exactly?"

Arthur hesitated, looking from me to Rigel and back. "Death by electrocution. Or, more precisely, by vaporization."

Okay, that didn't sound fun, but… "Would that be if we succeed or if we *don't* succeed?"

"Possibly either. Eight gigajoules of electricity can vaporize organic matter instantly. That energy would be doubled as it rebounds from the just-forming EMP field, even if your timing is precise enough to abort it before it reaches Earth. The positron emitter will almost certainly be destroyed and, quite honestly, I don't see how anyone in its immediate vicinity could survive the resultant explosion."

I could feel my palm sweating in Rigel's. *We have to try,* I thought to him. *I don't see how we have any choice.*

Rigel nodded. "If it's the best hope we have, we're in. Just tell us what to do."

The various Council members' expressions ranged from relieved to awed to—in Nara's case—tearful. She started to say something, but Kyna stopped her with a raised hand and motioned for Arthur to continue.

"First, we need to find a place that is relatively isolated from other humans, where we can set up the positron emitter in advance. Somewhere you can reach by shortly after midnight tonight. I strongly recommend no one else be within a quarter mile, to reduce the chance of additional casualties. And the timing must be precise. The burst must happen just as the EMP is released. Too early, and the stream will dissipate before having the desired effect. Too late, and the EMP will be impossible to stop."

He went on to detail the precise sequence of events necessary, going over them until he was confident we would be able to do this on our own without hands-on guidance.

"But where can we do this?" Connor asked. "Where, within an easy distance of Jewel, can we be certain there will be no one else within a quarter mile?"

Together, Rigel and I said, "The cornfield."

At everyone's confused looks, Rigel elaborated. "The same place we fought off Faxon's forces last year. There's a clearing between a quarter and a third of a mile from the school. At that time of night, nobody should be anywhere around. If you can put the emitter in the clearing for us ahead of time, we should be able to pull this off. If we succeed, then…" He swallowed. "Someone can come back afterward to see if we, um, made it."

Mr. Stuart volunteered that he remembered where the clearing was and offered to drive us to the edge of the cornfield around midnight. I had no idea how I'd get away without Aunt Theresa noticing, but that was the least of my worries right now.

Finally, everyone seemed satisfied that all the details had been worked out as thoroughly as possible on such short notice. Fervently wishing us luck, the holographic Council members winked out and Breann and Malcolm left. It was four-thirty, according to the clock on the Stuarts' mantel.

"Aunt Theresa will be home any minute, so I'd better get back. Maybe she'll be happy enough about me making Homecoming Court that she won't ask too many questions if I'm extra late."

Molly suddenly launched herself at me for a bear hug. "You really are my hero, M! And don't worry, we've got the *perfect* excuse. As Junior Princess you're *required* to come to the party after tonight's game. Tell her my mum will pick us both up and then you'll spend the night at my house."

"Required?" I asked skeptically.

"She won't know any differently, will she?"

I had to smile. "I guess not. Okay, that's what I'll tell her. If she doesn't buy it, though, I'm making you come up with something else. You're way better at that sort of thing than I am."

Molly laughed. "It'll work. Actually, if we can stop by my house first, I'll come with you. I was going to ask to come over anyway, so I can dress you for tonight. I totally get to play Handmaid again, since tonight you get to be Royal in front of everyone—and I know just the outfit!"

Sure enough, Aunt Theresa was over the moon about me making Homecoming Court. So much so, she didn't even raise an eyebrow when Molly showed her the dress she was "lending" me—a gorgeous purple, sleeveless, chiffon-like confection that was actually one of mine she'd brought along from Nuath and had been keeping at home in her closet.

"That's very generous of you, Molly. I hope Marsha has expressed proper gratitude for everything you and your family have done for her."

Molly nodded vigorously. "She has—lots of times! Oh, did she tell you about the party after the game tonight? The football team and cheerleaders and the whole Homecoming Court are expected to be there, for pictures and things. My mother offered to drive us and pick us up, and M can sleep over at my house after, if that's okay?"

"Of course." My aunt wore that rare, genuine smile that always creeped me out a little. "I'll be sure to thank your mother when I see her at the game tonight."

With that, Molly hauled me upstairs to my bedroom to play dress-up on me—something she claimed to have missed terribly since leaving Mars.

Looking at my reflection an hour later, after she'd put the finishing touches to my hair and makeup, it was obvious that a couple months without practice hadn't made her lose her touch.

"Wow, Molly, you've outdone yourself. Thanks!"

Her reflection grinned at mine. "Least I could do for someone about to risk her life to save the world." Though I could sense her intense anxiety, she hid it impressively well.

"And hey, if the worst happens, at least I'll go out in style," I answered in the same spirit.

"Exactly. Oops, I need to run! Amber's picking me up in less than half an hour and I have to change into my cheerleading outfit. See you at the game!" With a convincingly cheery wave, she grabbed my packed overnight bag and raced off down the stairs, leaving me to follow more slowly.

Uncle Louie had come home from the dealership early—Homecoming was a big deal for the whole town of Jewel—and Aunt Theresa was just putting dinner on the table.

"My! Don't you look nice," she exclaimed, surprise slightly undercutting the compliment.

Uncle Louie was less reserved. "Theresa tells me we have a princess in our midst, and boy, don't you just look it! Make sure you wave at us from that float tonight, you hear? Want to show you off to everybody."

I promised, flattered and embarrassed by more praise than I could ever remember receiving from either of them.

After dinner they drove me to the game, where I had to go sit with the rest of the Homecoming Court until the halftime parade. Since Rigel couldn't be with me, I felt awkward and out of place despite knowing I looked my absolute best. Even Sean treated me more formally than usual, though I wasn't sure if it was because of what would be happening later tonight or because his devastatingly gorgeous partner was monopolizing him so thoroughly. Which he didn't seem to mind at all.

Since we were right down front, we had a great view of both the game and the cheerleaders—which meant there was no missing the venomous glances Trina kept shooting my way. For the first time, I felt a prickle of discomfort about going to that party at her house, even for half an hour.

Halftime was wonderful, though. Since there wasn't time for him to change, Rigel rode on the float in his football uniform—though not his helmet—and held my hand the whole way around the track.

"You look amazing tonight, M, you know that, right? I'm the luckiest guy in the world."

I shoved him gently with my shoulder, not minding his dirt and sweat a bit. "I'm the one sitting here with the star quarterback who's in the process of winning yet another big game."

It was like we'd made a pact *not* to talk about what we'd be doing later on, even silently. As we waved to the Homecoming crowd in the stands with our free hands, we kept our banter light and mostly about the game. Only once did Rigel hint, obliquely, at what loomed tonight.

"Coach has yelled at me twice now for being distracted. I'll have to do better next half," he commented as we finally finished our slow circuit of the stadium.

Swallowing, I made myself say, "Gee, maybe I shouldn't have let Molly make me look so good after all."

In answer, he wrapped an arm around my shoulders and hugged me to him. "Maybe not. I'll just have to do my best not to stare at you too much. See you after, M." He gave me a quick kiss, then jumped off the float to go join the team, now gathering on the sidelines for the second half.

Even though Rigel wasn't playing *quite* up to his usual standard, our team still beat Elwood 31-20. I was one of the first to congratulate Rigel, since I was practically sitting on the field, then I had to run and find Aunt Theresa and Uncle Louie before they left.

"You looked very pretty up on that float." My aunt was all smiles, though I suspected some of that was for the benefit of her friends standing nearby. She was obviously enjoying the heck out of lording it over them with my status tonight. "I hope you didn't let that quarterback smudge Molly's dress."

"Oh." I glanced down at myself, partly to hide my temptation to laugh. "Um, I don't think so. Anyway, I wanted to say goodbye to you and Uncle Louie before you went home."

Seized by a sudden premonition that this might be the last time I'd ever see them, I pulled them both into a hug. They looked surprised but hugged me back.

"I'll, uh, see you guys in the morning." I awkwardly released them. "Don't forget to unplug the computer before you go to bed tonight, plus all that other stuff they recommended in the paper."

Turning away before my unexpectedly-threatening tears could escape, I hurried off to find the O'Garas.

"There you are!" Molly greeted me. "Where's Rigel?"

I forced a smile. "Probably still changing. I wanted to say goodbye to my aunt and uncle. In case…you know."

For a split-second, Molly's fear showed on her face, then she hid it again. "It's going to be fine. I just know it is. Won't it?" She looked to her parents for confirmation.

But I could tell they were worried, too, despite their smiles. "I have great faith in our Scientists," Mr. O'Gara said with more firmness than his emotions reflected. "And in the Sovereign and Rigel, as well. They've demonstrated repeatedly what a powerful force their bond can be." The look he sent me held yet another apology for all he'd done to the two of us last spring.

Mutely, I accepted it. "Right. And we've beaten the odds before," I reminded them all, as well as myself. "Like last year, against Faxon's people."

Mrs. O, at least, seemed to take comfort from that. "Indeed you have, dear, and I have confidence you'll do so again. Now, where is Sean? We should be going."

"Oh, he said he was getting a ride with Missy," Molly volunteered. "Sorry, I should have told you. I think he might be just the tiniest bit smitten." She giggled, then sent me an apologetic look. "Oops, sorry, M, I didn't mean—"

"No, I think that's great," I said quickly—and meant it. Sean had clearly been serious Tuesday night about trying to move on, and that was all to the good. "But…do we really have to go to this party? I wouldn't put it past Trina to poison my punch or something."

After all her nasty looks, I was positive she'd do *something* to get back at me for taking "her" spot on the Court.

"It will look odd if you don't at least put in an appearance," Mrs. O said. "Or so Sean and Molly tell me. You needn't stay long."

Rigel came jogging up then, looking gorgeous—and slightly anxious. "Sorry. Had a hard time getting away from everybody."

"Here's the man of the hour." Mr. O's heartiness was only slightly forced. "Let's go, then, shall we?"

37

Field current

"*No,* Gary, I don't want to do a shot," I insisted for the third time, looking around for Rigel. There he was, on the far side of Trina's big, opulent living room, surrounded by cheerleaders—as usual.

Do you need me to punch him? he thought to me.

No, it's fine. I turned my back on Gary. Thankfully, he didn't persist.

This was the first time I'd ever been inside Trina's house, and it was even more ritzy than I'd expected. Her parents obviously loved to flaunt their money. When envy momentarily threatened, I reminded myself that my Royal apartments in Nuath made this place look like a hovel by comparison.

Glancing again at the clock above the seventy-inch flat-screen TV, I was disappointed to see only five minutes had passed since I'd last checked. Mr. Stuart wouldn't be here to pick us up for at least another fifteen minutes. The noise was starting to get to me, and seeing so many kids from school drinking made me feel a little squicky. I wondered where Trina's parents were.

I needed to escape…and maybe center myself a little. *I'm going out front for a minute,* I sent to Rigel.

You okay?

Yeah. Just need some fresh air.

This was his first time at one of the after-parties and he was clearly enjoying himself. I didn't want to be a wet blanket—especially considering what we'd be attempting less than an hour from now. Grabbing my wrap, I let myself out the front door and went to the edge of the porch. Maybe I'd just wait out here till Rigel's dad arrived.

Looking up at the stars, breathing in the cool night air, I started to feel better. Calmer. Everything would be fine. Rigel was right. Together, we could handle anything.

Taking slow, measured breaths, I'd nearly managed to empty worry from my mind when I heard the front door open behind me. I turned with a smile, expecting Rigel, but it was Trina.

"You know, Marsha, you've got some nerve coming here, to my *house,* after everything you've done to me. Breaking my nose last spring wasn't enough, huh? You had to ruin Homecoming for me, too?"

I let out a disgusted breath, my hard-won calm evaporating. "Seriously, Trina? If we totaled up all the mean stuff you've done to me over the years compared to those two things—neither of which were my fault—you'd come out way, way ahead. Why can't you just let it go?"

"Obviously *you* haven't, or you wouldn't have gone to so much trouble to keep me off the Court."

"What, like it's your *birthright* to be one of the princesses?" I couldn't help laughing, since I was the one with the birthright…and it had been nothing but trouble. "Trust me, being a princess isn't always all it's cracked up to be."

"Then step down and let me be Junior Princess."

I laughed again, even though it was obvious she wasn't kidding. "If I *was* going to step aside, it would be for Rosa, not you. At least she's nice to me. I can't remember you ever doing anything nice for anybody without expecting something in return. You know, I almost feel sorry for you."

"Sorry? For me? Are you kidding? When I live in this—" she gestured at the house behind her— "and have all these friends? You —what do you live in? And if it weren't for Rigel, you wouldn't have any friends at all except those two losers you always hung with."

"And yet here you are, out here with me instead of inside with all your so-called friends. Maybe you—" I broke off as Mr. Stuart's SUV pulled up in front of the house. A spike of adrenaline went through me. It was time.

Your dad's here, I thought to Rigel.

"Never mind." I'd lost track of whatever I'd been about to say to Trina. Nothing important. "My ride's here." I turned toward the porch steps, knowing Rigel would catch up in a minute.

"No. What were you about to say?" she demanded, grabbing my arm and yanking me backward so hard I almost fell. "You weren't actually trying to imply I consider you *important*, were you?"

I pushed her away from me and this time she was the one who stumbled. "I couldn't care less what you think of me, Trina." Which was absolutely true. Right now, her pettiness was the least of my worries.

"Yeah? Well maybe you should. Where'd you get that dress, anyway? Shoplift it? Maybe I'll just—" She made a grab for the fabric at my shoulder but I sidestepped her.

"Stop it, Trina. I'd have thought you'd learned your lesson by now."

"*My* lesson? You're the one who needs to be taught a lesson, Marsha. This is for what you did to my nose!" Her eyes were mean little slits as she launched herself at me with the obvious intent of pushing me over the porch railing.

Before I could react, Rigel was suddenly right there on the porch with us, pinning Trina's arms behind her. "Leave M alone, Trina." I'd never heard his voice sound so…hard. "We're leaving anyway."

"What—? How—?" He released her, and she swung around to glare at him. "You're not going anywhere after assaulting me like that," she spat.

"Assaulting you?" Rigel let out a laugh. "Stopping you from shoving M counts as an assault?"

Mr. Stuart stepped onto the porch just then. "Is there a problem?"

Completely ignoring Trina, Rigel said, "Hey, Dad. Ready to go?" I could feel his tension spiking now, too.

"Oh, no you don't!" Trina declared hotly. "You're not going anywhere. Your son just attacked me, Mr. Stuart, and I intend to press charges. You all wait right here while I go call the cops." She turned back toward the house.

"Charges?" Mr. Stuart was clearly startled—and alarmed. "I'm afraid we don't have time—"

Trina had her hand on the doorknob when I said, "You really want the cops here, with all the underage drinking going on in your house?"

She froze, then whirled to glance nervously from me to Mr. Stuart. "You can't prove that! Besides—"

Just then, Cormac appeared behind Mr. Stuart. "Is there a problem, Miss Squires? Perhaps we should go inside so you can tell me what happened."

Trina's mouth opened and closed a couple of times, as her brain finally re-engaged. "Um, no, Mr. Cormac, no problem," she said sweetly. "There's no need for you to come in at all. But thank you."

Without another word, she scuttled back into the house and shut the door.

"Let's go." Mr. Stuart was giving off high levels of stress, too. "We're cutting things a little bit closer now than I'd hoped."

Arthur and Kyna were waiting for us in the school parking lot when we arrived.

"I'd rather hoped to go over everything with you one last time," Arthur said anxiously, "but I'm not sure… I thought you'd be here a bit sooner."

"We had a slight delay." Mr. Stuart was doing a much better job than Arthur of hiding his nervousness. "Is everything in place?"

Kyna nodded. "We've anchored the positron emitter's base to the rock in the clearing, as it needs to be perfectly stationary while emitting. It has already been activated, though of course its range is too limited to affect the satellites on its own. This chronometer is calibrated for the exact moment you two need to release the burst of energy that will amplify the emitter. It will beep ten seconds beforehand, then count down. Try to sustain your burst for a full second, if possible. Longer would be even better."

She handed the tiny chronometer to Rigel, who pocketed it.

"The rest of us should move as far away as possible before that happens," Arthur cautioned. "Even if all goes well, there will almost certainly be an explosion when the feedback hits the emitter. And if the burst is mistimed, or if my calculations were off by the merest fraction—"

"They were checked multiple times by multiple people," Kyna reminded him, her voice impressively calm. "And I have every confidence you will do exactly as you were coached," she said to us. "Good luck."

She shook Rigel's hand, then bowed to me, but I extended my hand as well. "Thank you, Kyna. For…for everything."

Clearly startled by the gesture, she gingerly took my hand, then gripped it firmly. "In your short time as Sovereign, you have proven yourself an exceptional leader, Excellency. I wish I could adequately express the respect and admiration I have for you."

I was too touched for words. From Kyna, that was high praise indeed.

Mr. Stuart wrapped Rigel in a fierce hug. "Good luck, son."

"Thanks, Dad. Tell mom…tell her I love her, okay?"

His father nodded, blinking rapidly. "All right, everyone, let's go."

Kyna and Arthur got into their car but when Mr. Stuart headed to his, Cormac didn't follow. "I prefer to remain here, sir."

"But the risk—"

"Is irrelevant, except as it pertains to the Sovereign." There was no compromise in Cormac's tone. "My place is here, as near her as I can be without interfering. Once the moment is past, if I am able, I will find her and notify you of her status."

Since there was clearly no time to argue, Mr. Stuart gave a quick nod and shook Cormac's hand. "Very well. I hope to hear from you shortly." With that, he got into his car and followed Kyna and Arthur out of the parking lot.

"Cormac, are you sure…?"

"Yes, Sovereign. Go. You have barely fifteen minutes now."

He was right. Hands linked, Rigel and I plunged into the cornfield.

We'd never been in here at night before, and once we were out of range of the parking lot lights, it was incredibly dark. "What if we can't find it?" I asked in a worried whisper—not that there was anyone to hear.

"We will. Look. They left us a trail."

Sure enough, a phosphorescent glimmer wove through the corn stalks ahead of us. My confidence restored, I didn't protest when Rigel picked up the pace. My eyes quickly adjusted and I realized that between the myriad stars and the setting crescent moon, there was easily enough light to keep us from stumbling over fallen stalks or ruts in the ground. Sooner than I expected, we burst into the clearing.

There, perched on "our" rock and humming faintly, was the positron emitter—a metal tube about a foot and a half long, its cone-shaped end pointing at the sky. Just as Arthur had instructed us this afternoon, we moved to within four feet of it, positioning ourselves so that any bolt of electricity we produced would intersect the invisible stream of positrons on their way into space.

Rigel checked his cellphone. "12:41. Just over five minutes to go."

We stared at each other, the enormity of what we were about to attempt—and the likelihood that it would be the last thing we ever did—hitting both of us at once. I swallowed.

"Rigel, I…I'm so glad you're with me. If we don't—"

"Shh." He touched a finger on my lips. "We'll do this, and we'll be fine. And if I'm wrong, well, there's no one in the whole universe I'd rather spend my last moments with. I love you, M."

My heart was so full, I thought it might burst. "Oh, Rigel!" I flung myself into his arms and then we were kissing like there was no tomorrow. Which there might not be. For us, anyway.

For several moments we clung to each other, our emotions too intense for even mental words as we both mourned a future we might not get to spend together.

"I love you so much," I finally murmured against his lips, determined to tell him one more time before it was too late. "More than I—"

I was interrupted by the beeping of the chronometer in his pocket.

My heart leapt into my throat. Instinctively, we tightened our embrace for an instant, then turned to face the emitter, hands still linked. We both swept our free arms upward until they were nearly touching above us, aiming at a point a few feet over the emitter.

This is it! Let's save the world, Rigel thought to me with all the confidence he could project.

Right. I tried to match his certainty. *It's us against the Grentl. Biggest bolt ever.*

He nodded. The chronometer counted down, beep by beep. "Okay. Two, one, NOW!"

A sizzling blue-white bolt erupted from our outstretched hands to race toward the night sky. Fueled by pure adrenalin, we held the burst for nearly two full seconds—much longer than we ever had before. From the point where it intercepted the positron beam, a glittering trail arced up, up, to an unseen destination more than two thousand miles away. Hearts pounding in unison, we stared breathlessly after that sparkling path.

"Do you think—" I started to say, when, at the edge of sight, there was a flash, like a distant supernova. As we watched, it expanded from a brilliant point into a breathtaking rainbow of liquid light pouring out and down, filling the sky from horizon to horizon. It was beautiful…and terrifying.

Rigel tightened his grip on my hand with a surge of triumph just as the cascade of colors reached us. Abruptly, the positron emitter stopped humming…then exploded, the blast of energy knocking us off our feet.

Rigel's hand was torn from mine. Terror that he'd been injured, or worse, was my very last sensation as everything went black.

I opened my eyes to see the night sky still above me, the spectacular wash of color fading. Then I became aware of the comforting sensation of being carried in a strong pair of arms. Turning my head slightly, relief abruptly became terror again when I realized it was Cormac, not Rigel, who held me.

"Rigel! Cormac, where's Rigel? Is he—?"

"Likely he was merely stunned, as you were, Excellency," came Cormac's steady reply. "Once I have you safely away, I will return for him to make certain."

"No!" I struggled against Cormac's encircling arms. "Put me down. Go back now! I need to know if he's okay!"

For the first time I could remember, Cormac failed to instantly obey my order. Instead, he continued on for several more seconds, until we were out of the cornfield. There, he laid me gently on the grass at the edge of the parking lot.

"I promised to notify the Council members as to your status as soon as possible, Excellency, if you will recall?"

"Fine. Call them on your way back to get Rigel."

He frowned, clearly reluctant to leave me. "If that is truly your wish, my Sovereign."

"It is." I was nearly crying in my agony of suspense to know whether Rigel had survived that blast. "*Please*, Cormac!"

Pulling out his omni, he strode back into the cornfield. I could hear him speaking rapidly as he went, talking to Kyna, it sounded like. Only when I heard him say, "appears to have been successful," did I realize I hadn't even thought to ask if we'd saved the world.

Though I knew I should be glad, if I'd lost Rigel in the process I doubted I could ever be happy again. Luckily, before I had time to work myself into complete hysteria over that prospect, I distinctly heard two sets of footsteps approaching. Sure enough, a moment later they both emerged from the crackling corn stalks, Rigel walking shakily and with Cormac's support, but under his own power.

The sight of him, apparently unhurt, gave sudden strength to my legs. I propelled myself up and into his arms—only to land us both on the ground in a heap. Not that I cared. I wrapped my arms tightly around Rigel, tears of happy relief pouring down my cheeks.

"You're okay! You're okay!"

"So are you!" He hugged me back just as tightly. "I was never so scared as when I woke up and you were gone. I was afraid you'd been vaporized."

We were still kissing—Cormac standing stoically by and looking off into the distance—when two cars came screeching into the parking lot. Rigel and I reluctantly broke apart to see Kyna, Arthur and Rigel's dad racing toward us.

"Success!" Mr. Stuart shouted exultantly. "Thank God you're both all right!"

"The EMP never reached Earth," Arthur confirmed, "though that light show your intervention produced did cause a few scattered power outages. Nothing that can't be restored within a day or so, however."

Kyna positively beamed at us. "Sovereign, Rigel, the people of this planet, *Echtran* and *Duchas*, can never repay the debt they owe you for what you have done this night. It is no exaggeration to say that you have quite literally saved billions of lives."

Still clinging to each other, Rigel and I scrambled to our feet. "Are the Grentl leaving, then?"

"It is too soon to know, but from what you told us earlier, it's unlikely they have the resources here to make another attempt at this time. Let us hope they will not wish to."

The triumph I'd felt a moment ago faded slightly. "I, um, guess I should find out. Use the device again, I mean." A wave of exhaustion swept through me, amplified by the weariness I felt from Rigel.

"Not tonight, though, right?" he asked.

Kyna shook her head. "No. Not tonight. You two both need rest—extremely well-deserved rest."

"I'll take the Sovereign to the O'Garas' house on our way home," Mr. Stuart said. "I've already notified them. Needless to say, Rigel's mother is anxious to see him, as well."

After another effusion of gratitude from Kyna and Arthur, Rigel, Cormac and I got into Mr. Stuart's SUV. I was asleep, leaning against Rigel in the back seat, before we were out of the parking lot.

It was broad daylight when I opened my eyes again to find myself alone in Molly's bedroom. I had no memory of how I'd gotten there, but felt remarkably refreshed. I must have slept at least ten hours. When I made my way downstairs a few minutes later, I discovered it was nearly two in the afternoon—so more like thirteen hours.

"Kyna messaged me not to wake you, dear," Mrs. O'Gara explained. "Still, I'm glad you're up. Your aunt has called twice to ask when you might be coming home."

"Oh, wow. Yeah, I'd better get back. What am I going to tell her?"

Molly grinned at me. "Don't worry. Mum told her you were helping me shop for a Homecoming dress and we wouldn't be back till late this afternoon."

"Which should give you time to conduct certain necessary business at the Stuarts' house." Mrs. O was suddenly serious. "First, though, let's get some food into you. You must be famished."

I was, though the prospect of another session with the Grentl device kept me from eating as much as I might have otherwise.

Less than an hour later, we were all gathered again in the Stuarts' living room around that deceptively innocent-looking cube with its coppery projections. Rigel, I'd discovered, had slept every bit as long as I had—which was good, since I was going to need his help for this.

"Ready when you are," he said now, placing a hand on my shoulder like last time. Warmth and strength flowed into me, along with a welcome dose of courage.

"Right. Let's find out what they plan to do next." Trying not to broadcast my fear that it might be something even worse, I reached out and grabbed the prongs.

They warmed instantly in my hands, almost as though the Grentl had been expecting me. Before I could even try to block them, they quickly extracted the last forty-eight hours from both my mind and Rigel's. The moment they finished, I tried probing the Grentl's collective minds for some sense of their future plans.

I received impressions of curiosity and satisfaction, which puzzled me, since we'd foiled their attempt to EMP us back to pre-industrial times. Then I caught a distinct vision of the Grentl ship retreating, hurtling through the blackness of space to a planet I now recognized as their home world with its hovering clouds of energy-beings.

You're leaving?

"TEST RESULT INDICATES SIGNIFICANT POTENTIAL.

FURTHER STUDY NECESSARY."

More rapid-fire images assaulted me, too quickly to comprehend all at once, and then the projections cooled in my hands. They were gone.

I let go and took a step back, exchanging a puzzled glance with Rigel, who'd heard what I had and seen at least some of what I'd seen.

"Does that mean—?" he started to say when Kyna spoke.

"Excellency, I've just received word from Nuath that the Grentl ship appears to be moving off at extreme speed. They're leaving!"

Hardly daring to believe, I stared at her, those final impressions from the Grentl still unfolding in my brain. "I think… I think they're done with us for now. They said—" I tried to remember the exact words— "that the test result indicates we have significant potential."

"You mean this whole thing was just a test?" Malcolm seemed outraged. "They weren't really planning to release the EMP after all?"

I shook my head. "No, it was real. They released it. But…they *wanted* to see if we could stop them." The truth came clear to me even as I put it into words. "If we hadn't, they'd have considered it proof that humanity isn't capable of progressing past our inherent savagery."

"But you *were* able to stop them!" Little Nara looked both pleased and confused.

"Yes. Because of my bond with Rigel. Because of our love. *That's* the potential they see in our race, what they now plan to study for another millennium or two. Love."

38

Recombination

"ARE you nearly dressed?" Aunt Theresa called up the stairs. "Your friends will be here in half an hour."

"Almost," I called back, trying to get a look at the back of my dress in my little hand mirror. Molly had just finished fastening me into another of my less formal (but still way formal for a high school dance) Sovereign outfits, this one a rich green that exactly matched my eyes.

Sean's friend Pete was taking Molly to the dance and all six of us—me, Rigel, Molly, Pete, Sean and Missy—were going to dinner first at The Rib House, the closest thing Jewel had to a fancy restaurant. Last night I'd been way too distracted to properly appreciate my role as Junior Princess but tonight I planned to thoroughly enjoy myself—now that I no longer had the freaking fate of the world hanging over my head.

"Don't worry, you look great," Molly assured me. "How does the back of my hair look?"

"Fine." I couldn't help being amused by how excited she seemed about her first date with Pete, after all the disparaging remarks she'd made about *Duchas* boys. Or maybe she was just happy to be going to the dance and Pete was incidental. I had no intention of asking.

Deciding my silver barrette might look good with the dress, I dug into my nightstand for it. "Do you think this will go with—?" I started to ask when I noticed the message light on my omni blinking. "Oops, guess I should have checked this when I first got home."

The message was from Kyna and had come more than two hours ago. "Excellency, I must warn you that you will shortly have an extremely important visitor—the President of the United States."

"*What?*" I nearly shrieked.

The message continued, "He should arrive at your home at approximately five o'clock this evening. You may wish to prepare your relatives in some way beforehand."

According to my bedside clock, it was five o'clock now!

I stared at Molly. "The *President?* Here? Why… How… What will I tell Aunt Theresa?"

Hearing a car door outside, I flew to the window in time to see a black SUV with darkened windows pull up in front of my house. Two other, identical SUVs were already parked, one with a black-suited man standing next to it.

"Holy crap! I think he's here! How do I look? What should I *say?*"

Molly shrugged, looking nearly as stunned as I felt. "Guess you shouldn't keep him waiting, huh?"

That was enough to send me clattering down the stairs, hoping to somehow head off Aunt Theresa before she started asking questions I'd had no time to make up answers to.

She came out of the kitchen wiping her hands, clearly unaware of what was going on out front. "Marsha, I know this dance is an important one, but I'd still like you home at a decent hour tonight. You were out late last night, and I was quite worried when I heard about that explosion or whatever it was near your school."

I nodded jerkily, barely registering her words. "Um, Aunt Theresa, I should probably—" Before I could finish, the doorbell rang.

Unfortunately, Aunt Theresa was closer to the door than I was. She opened it, then took a half step back at the sight of two black-suited, sunglass-wearing Secret Service agents on the doorstep.

"What on Earth is going on?" she demanded. Then, rounding on me, "Marsha, what have you *done?*"

"I… Um…"

"Ma'am, we'll need to secure the area," one of the men said to my aunt.

When she just gaped, I tugged her away from the door. "Okay. Come on in," I told the agents.

They swept inside, one quickly surveying the entire first floor while the other went upstairs. After five minutes, during which Aunt Theresa kept shooting me accusing—but also frightened—glares, they reconvened in the front hall.

"What is this about?" my aunt demanded. "You have no right—"

"Building has been secured," said one of the Secret Service guys into his little earpiece as the other turned to Aunt Theresa.

"Ma'am, the President requests an audience with the Sovereign of Nuath."

"I have no idea what you're talking about! You have obviously come to the wrong house. What sovereign and what president?"

In answer, the front door opened again and, sure enough, the freaking *President* stepped through, flanked by two more Secret Service agents…and Kyna. I saw Aunt Theresa's jaw literally drop—and realized mine had done the same. As we both stood gaping, the President leaned over and whispered something to Kyna, who whispered back.

The President nodded, then clumsily placed his right fist over the middle of his chest and bowed…to *me.*

"Sovereign Emileia? Please allow me to express the gratitude of both my country and my planet for the heroic act you performed last night, in which you risked your own life in order to safeguard us all. I've been told that without your intervention, the resulting cataclysm would have cost many, many lives.

"Under normal circumstances, you would have been invited to the White House for public recognition of your heroism. However, as it is clearly inadvisable for the general public to learn the truth about your identity or last night's events, I was persuaded to suspend the usual protocols in order to come here instead, and with as little fanfare as possible." He flicked a glance at Kyna.

"Excellency, it is my very great honor to personally present you with the Presidential Medal of Freedom. Please accept this small token of our nation's thanks."

One of the Secret Service agents handed the President a small, wooden box, from which he took the medal—a shiny white star on a red and gold background. He held it up by its blue ribbon. "If I may?"

"Oh! Um, sure." I inclined my head slightly so he could put it around my neck, just like the awards outstanding students sometimes received before my taekwondo tests. Out of the corner of my eye, I could see Aunt Theresa staring at me in disbelief.

"I hope this will be the beginning of a long and mutually profitable relationship between your people and ours," the President said.

With an effort, I straightened my shoulders and forced myself into Sovereign mode—something I'd never expected to be necessary in front of my aunt.

"Thank you, Mr. President. I hope that, as well. I greatly appreciate your cooperation, and that of the Secretaries of State and Defense, during this recent crisis. May both our peoples build upon that cooperation going into the future."

The President bowed again and I inclined my head. Then he and his entourage all went back outside to the waiting SUVs, though Kyna remained behind, on our porch.

As the cars pulled away, my aunt finally found her voice—sort of. "What…what…?" She looked from me to the three retreating SUVs and back.

"Um, Aunt Theresa, there's some stuff I should probably tell you."

"Yes. Yes, I should think so. Or…perhaps I am simply dreaming all of this?"

Tempting as it was to let her believe that, I doubted it would work for long. "No, sorry. I'm afraid you're not. It…it all has to do with who my real parents were. It turns out they were pretty important people."

The look she turned on me was dazed. "Your real parents?"

Mrs. O'Gara came hurrying up the front walk just then. She and Kyna exchanged a few words on the porch, then they both turned to us where we stood in the doorway.

"Theresa, why don't we all go inside?" Mrs. O suggested gently. "This explanation may take some time."

Between them, Kyna and Mrs. O managed to convince Aunt Theresa that my whole fantastic story was true, though it was obvious, from the disjointed questions my aunt kept asking, that it would be days or even weeks before she really understood it all.

"Louie will never believe this," she said more than once, shaking her head and staring at me like I was a complete stranger to her.

"Um, maybe we shouldn't tell him? He's not exactly great at keeping secrets and this still needs to be mostly secret. Right?" I glanced questioningly at Kyna, who nodded.

"Yes, Mrs. Truitt, we would prefer all of this be known to as few people as possible. As Sovereign Emileia's guardians, you and your husband deserve to know the truth, but please don't let it go any further."

Aunt Theresa was looking dazed again. "Of…of course. If I do tell Louie, I'll make certain he understands that. Just think. The President of the United States, in our house!" she marveled again. "I should at least have offered him a plate of cookies…"

We had to hurry to the O'Garas' then, where Sean, Pete and Rigel were already waiting for Molly and me. On the way there, Molly told me she'd called her mother the second I'd run downstairs.

"Yes, and I came as quickly as I could," Mrs. O said. "I was fairly certain you would need a bit of assistance when it came to explaining everything to your aunt."

"Thanks. She never, ever would have believed me if you and Kyna hadn't been there to back me up." Then, to Kyna, "I didn't have the nerve to say so to the President, but shouldn't Rigel get a medal, too? He risked his life every bit as much as I did."

Kyna smiled. "Indeed he did. And yes. At my suggestion, the President called at the Stuarts' house before coming to yours. They had more warning than you apparently did, however. Did you not receive my message?"

"Not till about five seconds before the President arrived," I admitted. "It's all good now, though. I hope."

Turning the corner, we saw the three boys waiting on the O'Garas' porch and dropped the subject, since Pete had no idea of the truth.

"Ready to go?" Sean called out. "Missy's going to wonder why we're so late picking her up."

Grinning a little shyly at Pete, Molly shrugged. "Sorry, it's my fault. I kept changing my mind about which shoes to wear, didn't I, M?"

Rigel, meanwhile, came over and took my hand with an expression that nearly melted me on the spot. *You look even more amazing than you did last night,* he sent silently. *Have I mentioned how much I love you?*

Maybe, but I never get tired of hearing it. And ditto, on both counts. He was beyond drool-worthy in his subtly pin-striped black suit and crisp white shirt.

Dinner was fun, though it was a little frustrating not to be able to talk to Sean and Molly about the amazing events just past, what with Pete and Missy sitting right there.

At one point, when Sean leaned in close to offer Missy a bite of his dessert, I caught his eye and gave him smile and a little thumbs-up. He smiled back but lifted one shoulder slightly, as if to say, "Hey, I'm trying."

The Homecoming dance itself was nothing short of magical.

Now and then I did suffer a definite sense of *déjà vu*, like when I overheard Bri, Deb and their dates discussing last night's explosion in the cornfield.

"It's like a new tradition," Bri was saying with a laugh. "Something weird happened out there on Homecoming weekend last year, too, remember?"

But unlike last year, once the Homecoming Court was crowned, I danced the traditional slow dance with Rigel, instead of being forced to watch Trina mash herself against him while I danced awkwardly with Jimmy Franklin. Much, much better.

Happy? Rigel asked silently as we swayed to the music, though I'm sure he could sense my joyous contentment as strongly as I sensed his.

Happier than I've ever been in my life. It was true. The Grentl were no longer an issue and the story of what Rigel and I had accomplished together was already being broadcast all over the *Echtran* and Nuathan news. Surely that would do away with most of the remaining resistance to us as a couple. And now that Aunt Theresa knew the truth, life at home should get easier, too. Right this moment, my future looked beautifully bright and mostly trouble-free.

And even if it's not, Rigel sent, catching my thought, *we know now that together we really can handle anything.*

Absolutely. I love you, Rigel.

He lowered his lips to mine, sending so much love back to me that tears of happiness pricked my eyes. Over the past year, our love had proved powerful enough to withstand every test the universe had thrown at us, growing stronger in the process. I was confident now that it always would.

ABOUT THE AUTHOR

Brenda Hiatt is the New York Times bestselling author of twenty novels (so far), including traditional Regency romance, time travel romance, historical romance, humorous mystery and young adult science fiction. She is as excited about her STARSTRUCK series as she's ever been about any of her books. In order, those are *Starstruck, Starcrossed, Starbound* and *Starfall.* The series is now complete, though novellas or even a spin-off series have not been ruled out. In addition to writing, Brenda is passionate about embracing life to the fullest, to include scuba diving (she has over 60 dives to her credit), Taekwondo (where she is currently pursuing her 3rd degree black belt), hiking, traveling, and pursuing new experiences and skills.

If have you enjoyed reading *Starfall* or any of Brenda's books, she hopes you will consider leaving a review wherever you buy or talk about books. For the latest information about upcoming books in the STARSTRUCK series as well as Brenda's other books, please visit www.starstruckseries.com or www.brendahiatt.com, where you can subscribe to her newsletter and connect with her via email, Facebook, Twitter or Tumblr.